An Unsuitable House

Kayla Danoli

COPYRIGHT

Cataloguing-in-publication data
Creator: Danoli, Kayla, author

Cataloguing-in-Publication details are available from the National Library of Australia
www.trove.nla.gov.au

ISBN: 978-0-9953533-5-0 (paperback)
ISBN: 978-0-9953533-6-7 (eBook)

Cover design: T A Marshall, Marshall, Mackay QLD

CONTENTS

Granger Family Owners of Wellsprings v

Chapter 1 1

Chapter 2 10

Chapter 3 18

Chapter 4 29

Chapter 5 37

Chapter 6 47

Chapter 7 57

Chapter 8 69

Chapter 9 82

Chapter 10 93

Chapter 11 106

Chapter 12 117

Chapter 13 131

Chapter 14 144

Chapter 15 157

Chapter 16 169

Chapter 17 180

Chapter 18 193

Chapter 19 206

Chapter 20 218

Chapter 21 229

Chapter 22 241

Chapter 23 253

Also by the Author 258

About the Author 259

Granger Family Owners of Wellsprings

Thomas Granger married Lady Elizabeth Prendergast

William Prendergast Granger – second son of Thomas and Elizabeth, immigrated to Australia. Married Caroline Stanhope

Rupert Prendergast Granger – Eldest son of William and Caroline. Married Gwendolyn Cavendish

Wilfred Prendergast Granger – Eldest son of Rupert and Gwendolyn. Married Jessica Fitzmaurice

Thomas Prendergast Granger – second son of Wilfred and Jessica. Married Catherine Bonham-Stewart

Edwina Granger – Fourth child and youngest daughter of Wilfred and Jessica. Becomes known as Aunt Eddie

Esther Granger – Only child of Thomas and Catherine. Known as Essie. Was brought up by Aunt Eddie.

Anthea Granger – Only child of Esther Granger. Current owner of Wellsprings.

Chapter 1

At last, the big day has arrived. After today, I will no longer be a guest, but independent and in my own home. It has been a long ten days, but worth it. Although not unpleasant by any means, after the first couple of days the stress set in. Living in someone else's house, amongst someone else's things, and being mindful of not disrupting your host's life by your very presence had become a real consideration in spite of both our best efforts.

My host – or should that be hostess? – Suzanne (Zanne) Bennett is a bestselling author whose life is governed to some extent by deadlines. Although she claims there are no looming deadlines at the moment, I am aware of imposing on her writing time; intruding in her writing life. As I pack my things, my mind wanders back to my arrival in Charlotte Cove those ten days ago. Ten days that somehow now seem much longer. Today's schedule is tight, or at least the morning is.

I snapped my seatbelt on and felt my nerves start to tighten as I prepared to drive away from Tern Cottage. My morning's schedule flashes before my eyes: drive to *Wellsprings* and dump my things before heading to the Charlotte Cove General Store. I had not even a biscuit in the house, but had invited Zanne to lunch. No time to sit here pondering how it might all come together. Make a start, I told myself, or you won't be ready for Zanne.

The first part of the schedule went according to plan. I drove to the house and unloaded the car. With everything dumped in the room that would be my interim bedroom, I left sorting it out until later, when the stress had reduced. Then I was off to the store with a long list of supplies to buy.

While I had no preconceptions about what the store would be like, the place caused a moment of hesitation. The yellow painted walls were a shade darker than butter. None of the sparkle and shine of modern supermarkets here, and nor was there any space or energy wasted on setting up enticing displays of select products. Around the walls, above the shelving, faded posters advertised various products. A couple of the posters – and the products they advertised – I hadn't seen since my childhood. Nevertheless, although tired looking, the place was clean and products appeared arranged in a neat and logical way.

In some ways, shopping at the Charlotte Cove General Store was easier than in a large chain supermarket. There is only one brand of most things, thereby eliminating dickering about which brand to buy. With my trolley overflowing and doing my best to prevent the bread becoming squashed, I approached the tiny checkout. At least the bored-looking frump manning the cash register didn't give me the mandatory welcome and enquiry about how my day was going. She interspersed the sullen silence as she rang up the various products with curious – even suspicious – glances in my direction.

"That's quite a shop you've had today, Miss. Planning on staying long? We don't get many tourists coming here to Charlotte Cove, and none at this time of year. Well, I suppose they wouldn't come at any time of year would they? There's no accommodation for holidaymakers." The question in her voice remained unspoken. There was no doubt she viewed me as something of an interloper. I felt her tone almost contained a reprimand for being here.

My inclination was to ignore the question, but manners dictate I should respond, so I indulge the frump on the checkout with a smile while ferreting about in my mind for some safe response. It wouldn't do to get off on the wrong foot so soon with someone I'd be in regular contact with in the future. In the end, I came up with a response I thought safe enough. "I see, but the lack of holiday accommodation is not a problem for me. I'll be here for quite a while. I'm in the process of moving in… hence all the supplies."

"Most people around here shop regular like… maybe not every day, but regular. That way, they don't have such a trolley full." Okay, I can see there is quite a bit to learn about living at Charlotte Cove, and it appears I am learning the hard way: by getting it wrong. I failed in the first instance by coming to live here, and I've broken another rule by having such a trolley load of groceries. I didn't trust myself to respond, so another smile and a few nods would have to suffice.

As I made my unimaginative response, a sharp-featured elderly woman came from the rear of the shop and stood beside the checkout operator. She looked as though she had been sucking lemons all morning. Her mouth was screwed up in a tight moue of disapproval. When she spoke to the checkout operator, her voice echoed the sourness of her face. "Come now, Gloria. Don't be standing around gossiping all day. The customer wants to be on her way, and you have the biscuits stock to rotate."

"Sorry, Marion; I became interested when the young lady said she was moving in and would be living here in Charlotte Cove."

"Here… in the village? I wasn't aware there was any rental accommodation available." The elderly woman fixed me with a steely gaze that questioned the veracity of my statement and challenged me to correct it.

"Oh, I'm sorry. Let me correct any confusion I've caused. I'm not renting. I'm moving into my own place, *Wellsprings*."

"*Wellsprings*…? What's that?" prune-face asked.

"It's the big old house at the end of Gull Lane. You probably know the one I mean. It's along there at the far end of the village." I thought I detected a sharp intake of breath in unison by the ladies.

"The old Granger place…? Why in heaven's name are you moving in there? What possessed you to choose that house? Real Estate agents have a lot to answer for these days. It's almost unthinkable that any real estate agent who knew anything about that place would have talked someone into moving into it. I can see the need for all those cleaning products. The place has been unoccupied for years. It must be a mess." The two women exchanged a knowing look before the older one continued. "You're only new to Charlotte Cove, so let me give you some advice. If you know what's good for you, you won't hang around here – and you won't move into that house. Nobody in their right mind would stay there; let alone a young lady on her own. It's a most unsuitable house for a woman alone. Too many things have happened there. It must be cursed. How did you come to find out about the place being empty anyway?"

Gloria nodded enthusiastically as Marion said her piece before throwing in her own comment. "Bad things happen up there at that house. You'll not be safe there, you mark our words."

This was not going well, and the bounds of my 'polite behaviour' were being stretched to the limit. And I was aware time was slipping away. Time to bring this nonsense to an end I think, and be on my way home. "Look at the time! Oh, I just realised… How remiss of me. I should have introduced myself: I am Anthea Granger. I've been in Charlotte Cove for the best part of two weeks now. I haven't spent much time in the village and haven't had a chance to meet you as I've been busy getting the old Granger place, *Wellsprings*, ready to move into. Looks like I'll be seeing a lot more of you in the future though. Nice to have met you both, but I'd had better be off. I've still plenty to do."

There was something unsettling about the conversation. As I drove through the village, I decided it wasn't what they said. Precious little was said. No, it was what wasn't said. It was what was hinted that was unsettling. There is no time to worry about it now. After my extended visit to the local store, I had about an hour in which to produce something for Zanne for lunch.

Once the quiche was in the oven, I stashed the groceries in the pantry and set the table, tasks that required no concentration. These left my mind free to reflect on my decision to relocate to Charlotte Cove. Not a difficult decision, it was one made more than six months earlier. That my long-time best friend, Suzanne (Zanne) Bennett, had lived here for a while now, and I could stay with her until my house was ready, made the decision easier. I made a mental note to ask Zanne about her early days at Charlotte Cove.

A car door slammed. My reflective moment abandoned, I bounded to the front door to welcome Zanne. From the car, she waved a bottle of champagne at me. "…For a proper celebration of your having moved in; to christen the place, so to speak."

Lunch went well and conversation flowed freely, mostly about our times together in the past. As soon as an opportunity presented, I quizzed Zanne about her first days at Charlotte Cove.

"What was your reception like when you first moved here?"

"All right I think. Much as you might expect when you move to a new place, especially a small closed community like this one. Why do you ask?"

"Oh, nothing really; I just wondered what sort of welcome to town you received."

"Ah, I see. You've been to the store. I can imagine how that went."

"I don't know how to tell how it went. Perhaps 'a bit frosty' might describe it. There wasn't any actual welcome-to-our-village involved. Nor did they tell me to leave, well not exactly. I suppose 'unsettling' is the best word to describe it."

"Yeah, they can be a bit starchy, but the starch does soften with time. Mind you, you have to live here for at least a hundred years before you have any chance of being considered a local. At the store, you would have met Marion, the prim elderly owner, and her daughter-in-law, Gloria. Just so you know, Gloria and her husband, Marion's son, moved in with Marion when they married and both of them worked in the store. Then Gloria's husband legged it some years ago and is now 'whereabouts unknown'. Word is Gloria was left with nothing and nowhere else to go. She continued living in the house with Marion and working in the store. Marion makes Gloria's life a misery, but the poor woman has no way of breaking free."

"It's a sad story, but one that fits with my assessment of the situation this morning. While it's good to know all that, it was the comments they made about this house that unsettled me. There was nothing definite. It was more like inferences being given. Unless I'm misinterpreting those inferences, it sounded as though they were warning me off living here. They were suggesting it wasn't safe for me to be here… well, not alone anyway."

"What…? Not safe alone in Charlotte Cove…?

"No; more like it wasn't safe for me to be alone in this house. Although they didn't know where I was talking about when I said I was moving into *Wellsprings*, once I explained, they were quick to tell me the place was 'cursed'."

"Oh God, they actually said it was cursed?"

"Marion did. Gloria was content just to tell me 'bad things' happen here."

"W-e-l-l, there seems to be a wealth of myths … legend … rumour… whatever you want to call it, surrounding this house that flourish in the village. It was mentioned once. I remember making a mental note to follow up on it as I thought it might provide the inspiration for a story – fictional of course. I think it was old Frank who mentioned it in passing some time ago."

"What was his take on all this stuff? Did he say what it was about or how it all started?"

"Not really, we weren't discussing it as such. He mentioned it as part of another conversation and I didn't ask about it at the time. I was writing something else then, and didn't want to be distracted from the plot I was working on. I think it had something to do with a woman. Some sort of incident that happened at, or associated with your house. This might be a good time to go back and ask him about it though."

"I would appreciate that. Who is this Frank you are talking about? Is there a new man you haven't told me about in your life? You kept him well hidden while I was staying with you. I don't imagine being ignored for that long would have gone down too well with him."

"Chance would be a fine thing. Where would one find an eligible bloke in Charlotte Cove? That is, assuming one was interested in finding a bloke to start with. I'm not and, given my previous experience, I'm unlikely to be for some time to come."

"Okay, apologies; my comment was a bit tactless. But you still haven't told me about Frank."

"Frank Kane used to be a fisherman. Now well into his eighties and retired, he lives in a small cottage further along the coast past the wharf area. Hard to imagine though it is, Frank, like his parents before him, has spent his whole life in Charlotte Cove. He fishes along the beach most days and sometimes takes his dinghy out onto the bay to fish or put his crab pots in around near the point. I usually run into him when I take my kayak out for a paddle. If he's still around when I come back, we sit on the rocks and have a chat. Every so often, he accepts my invitation to come for coffee."

"Do you think you might invite Frank for coffee again sometime soon?"

"Yes, but you will not be invited to join us. He is solitary by nature. Not a true reclusive, but he wouldn't come if a stranger were present. If he turned up not knowing a stranger would be there, he wouldn't stay for coffee, and would refuse to discuss anything."

"Uh huh, I get the message. It's over to you to see what you can do… but please make it soon or the suspense will kill me."

"Zanne, that woman you mentioned has taken hold of me. I have to know more. I need to know what happened and who she was."

"…And whether there was any such woman, or anyone else associated with the house, who might have been involved in an 'incident'," Zanne added in an attempt to bring me back to earth.

"You're right; there might not be any truth or mystery in the story at all. Nevertheless, I want to know about my house, who built it, when it was built, and who has lived here over all those years. I suppose the first step is to get a copy of the title deed."

"Yeah, that's where I would start. The title deed will give you dates and names. Once you have those, you be able to do some family history research to establish who was who in this zoo and when. Then, I think it might be a case of searching the newspaper archives to find anything relating to anyone you've uncovered. This could turn into an interesting – even exciting – project."

"I think 'exciting' is the right word. It has me that way already, and I don't know anything yet. M-a-y-b-e this will turn into something right up your alley; something that becomes your next novel."

"I write crime fiction, not true crime. Anyway, there might not be a crime. You can't discount that possibility."

"You might be right, but if that is the case, couldn't you manufacture a crime to go with the mystery and intrigue that's already here?" Zanne's negative response suggested she wasn't keen on that idea. However, I thought I detected a hint of interest in delving into this mystery.

"I could just see it becoming a best seller and your house ending up featured on tourist advertising everywhere; *come and see the House of Horrors*. You could make a fortune from charging the long queues of tourists at your door, all of them wanting the thrill of being in that house." We both are joking, but I suspect we are only half joking and there is more than a hint of interest by both parties in such a writing project.

'Lunch' dragged on until late afternoon. During that time, we returned several times to speculate on what the 'bad things' that happened here might be. Perhaps it was the champagne, but the scenarios we conjured up became increasingly fanciful as the afternoon slipped away. Too late to start anything after Zanne left, I wandered aimlessly out to what I believed to be a conservatory added to one end of the house at some time after the house was built. No hint of its probable original glory remained. The area now was crammed with dead potted plants. Like the rest of the house, neglected and abandoned for so long since Aunt Eddie's death, the plants succumbed to the inevitable. Were they some sort of message… another warning perhaps?

I do hope Zanne and Frank have coffee soon, or the innuendo about this house will get the better of me. I scanned the area around me as I wandered back to the kitchen. My eyes came to a standstill on the rough timber partition that closed off this narrow front strip from the rest of the house. Positioned immediately behind the staircase leading to the upper floor, the barricade was incongruous with that staircase. Meant to impress, the sweeping stained timber staircase reminded me of something from the movie Gone with the Wind. Another similar partition installed near Aunt Eddie's bedroom also remained unpainted.

Why were these partitions in place, and when were they installed? I dredged my memories for any latent images of this ground floor of the house without the partitions, but found none. Had Aunt Eddie installed them at some time during the period when she lived here alone? If she did, I still don't understand why she would want to do that. It certainly didn't add anything to the look of the place but, for the moment, the tiny space available in this area at the front of the house suits me fine.

If I keep creating questions for myself about this place and its people, I'll drive myself balmy. It wouldn't be so bad if I thought we might soon find answers to some of them. My gut instinct tells me that will not be the case. In an effort to create a distraction for myself, I prepared dinner. But once dinner was over, there was the problem of what to do to fill in the rest of the evening. I tried unpacking a few more of my things. As that didn't require much concentration, I felt my mind trying to create more questions.

Although I took my book to bed with the intention of reading myself to sleep, I wasn't interested in the book and still wasn't sleepy when I turned the light off at almost midnight. I knew a restless night lay ahead.

Chapter 2

Since arriving in Charlotte Cove, I managed to refurbish and render liveable – by my standards – the kitchen, downstairs bathroom and one other small room that would be my bedroom for the time being. The few other areas on the ground floor not boarded-up and still accessible continued to cry out for attention, while the upper floor remained an ignored and unexplored territory. However, I was in need of an office, a room where I could set up my computer, and somewhere to leave anything I was working on. A smallish room at the front of the house was earmarked as an office. Its huge mullioned window overlooked the front yard. "Not much of a view at the moment," I told the universe. "That huge industrial rubbish skip parked in the front yard blocks just about everything else."

The fluorescent pink blob with *Sam's Skips* emblazoned along its sides in an equally fluorescent blue was an eyesore since the first day I started cleaning out the house. Full to overflowing now, it looked even worse. More importantly, until the owner of the firm saw fit to send someone to remove the existing skip and replace it with an empty one, work on clearing out the place was at a standstill. There was some suggestion the skip rotation might occur today. So, for something to do to fill in time until that happened, and in the hope she had some information, I rang Zanne.

"My skip is overflowing and I can't do much more, so I thought I'd talk to you and maybe organise for us to have coffee. I don't suppose you've had a chance to talk to Frank yet."

"Nothing to report about Frank; I haven't been to the beach for a few days, so I haven't seen him. If you're at a standstill, come to my place for coffee – say, ten o'clock?"

Coffee with Zanne and a visit to the general store had me back at the house not much before lunchtime. Frustration has set in. I am at an impasse on every front. With a sandwich for lunch and my feet up on one of the other chairs, I abandoned work for the day and settled down with a book I'd been trying to read since arriving at the Cove. That didn't go so well either. After a few pages, I realised I hadn't absorbed a word of what I'd read. My mind insisted on pondering other things. It went back to this morning's coffee with Zanne and the wide range of 'nothings' covered in our conversation. Then, it head back down memory lane.

I first met Zanne here in Charlotte Cove when we were both young children. Zanne is about a year older than I. She lived here, strangely enough in Tern Cottage, with her parents. Her father was something to do with the Department of Fisheries and was stationed here for a few years before being transferred elsewhere. My mother brought me to Charlotte Cove for weekends and holidays until I went off to university. We would stay here at Wellsprings with my mother's Aunt Edwina who owned the place. She lived here alone. Zanne and I became best friends, and spent our days together at either one or other of our houses, or at the beach.

At about the age of eight I experienced my first true heartbreaking moment. My mother had been busy and we hadn't visited Charlotte Cove during first term that year. But, when Easter arrived, we headed for the Cove with the intention of staying on for a few days after Easter. No more than a few minutes after we arrived, I was off down the street to Tern Cottage. When I arrived at Tern Cottage's gate, a strange woman and a teenage boy were getting into a car…a strange car, not the Bennett's car. The woman came to the gate to speak to me.

"You look a little lost, dear. Can I help you?"

"Where's Zanne? I've come to see my friend Zanne. Who are you? You're not Mrs Bennett."

"Oh, I see. I think the Bennetts used to live here some time ago. They moved away. We've been here for about two months now. I'm sorry about your friend. I don't know where they went, so I can't help you with that."

I cried all the way home and for most of the day, if I remember correctly. My ever-practical mother assured me this was all part of growing up, and that there would be many other such occasions as I went through life. It didn't help. Visits to Charlotte

Cove were never the same again. As I grew up, Zanne often came to mind. Funny little things would trigger memories of our time together. For a moment, I wallowed in the disappointment of that day.

After graduating from university, like so many others, I took my brand new IT degree to work in London. About eight months after I arrived there, at a work-related party celebrating some event I can't remember, I met Zanne again. Like me, she too moved to London after completing her degree. It was towards the end of the evening, when I was covertly trying to weave my way to the front door to escape, that that I caught a fleeting glimpse of a familiar face. I told myself I had imagined it. How could it be Zanne? The front door and escaping the party forgotten, I elbowed my way through the crowd in search of that face I'd seen.

Zanne was standing by herself next to a huge potted palm in a corner of the room. I saw her, elbowed the last couple of people out of the way, and rushed towards her. As I broke through the last of the crowd, I saw her expression change from startled to disbelief. Then we were hugging and laughing. Tears flowed freely. "Let's get out of here," Zanne said when we finally released one another. "We have s-o-o much catching up to do, let' go somewhere quiet and get on with it."

That rekindled our earlier friendship and it became stronger than ever. "Heartbreak again seemed inevitable when, a couple of years later, Zanne announced her engagement to the wealthy son of a stockbroker family," I told the empty kitchen. "To me, it seemed like her impending marriage would end our friendship again." I chuckled at the memory of Zanne's strenuous denial that a marriage would interfere with our friendship. How wrong could she be?

The marriage was a disaster from day one. Her husband continued his playboy ways and was a serial womaniser. Worse, Zanne almost became a prisoner in their home. It seemed to me, it was a rare occurrence for her to escape the confines of the house, while he appeared to spend most of his time out on the town with his mates – or a woman. At home, he was controlling, domineering, abusive and physically violent. Zanne had been an investigative journalist and loved to write. It was to writing she turned again, I think in order to maintain her sanity within that terrible marriage.

After five years of marriage, her husband's planned skiing holiday in the Swiss Alps with a few of his mates provided Zanne with the opportunity she needed. By then, she was well-established. Her first novel had soared to the top of the bestseller list, and her subsequent works kept her there while providing her with a very nice income. She had it all planned.

On the afternoon of the day her husband left for his skiing holiday, the removalists arrived and packed her belongings. Next morning, I went with her to Heathrow to see her off on her way to Australia. It was three or four weeks before I heard from her again. Her email told me she had sorted out her bank situation, and found a property she was thinking to buy. That evening after reading the email, I was elated that things had turned out well. The next morning, I didn't know how to feel. Police arrived and questioned me about Zanne's whereabouts. I wasn't about to tell them anything that might be detrimental to my friend, so I simply said I didn't know.

Perhaps they doubted me, as they then spent some time explaining their visit. "We need to contact Suzanne. An incident has occurred. She needs to know about it as it impacts heavily on her. We understand you are old friends and thought you might know where we could locate her."

"What sort of incident, and how might it impact on Zanne?" I didn't expect them to tell me, but I thought it worth a try. I was right, they weren't about to share details, but what they said made me rethink my position.

"The nature of the incident is something for Suzanne. She may choose to share the information with you later. All we can tell you is that, a couple of weeks ago a tragic incident occurred, and it is imperative we talk to Suzanne about it."

That word 'tragic' caught my attention big time. My mind was working at warp speed as it tried to picture what that might mean. After a few moments of deep thought, I asked a question I thought they might be able to answer. "This 'tragic incident', did it occur here in England or outside this country?"

"Er, well now, I think we are able to confirm that it occurred elsewhere." I felt a cold wave envelop me from head to toe and, for a moment, I thought my legs were going to collapse under me.

"It's true. I don't know where she is – exactly. All I can tell you is that she flew back to Australia the day after her husband left for a skiing holiday in the Swiss Alps. I had an email from her last night, the first contact since she left, but it didn't tell me where she is. All it said was that she had sorted out her finances and was considering purchasing a property."

As soon as the police left, I sweated over composing an email to Zanne. I really didn't know anything, but I think what the police told me indicated Zanne's husband had somehow been involved in some 'tragic incident'. For a few moments after I hit the SEND button, I debated the wisdom of my action. But the email had gone. It was now up to Zanne to decide what to do about it.

In the end, the outcome was good – as heartless as that may sound. Three men were killed by an avalanche while skiing in the Swiss Alps. Zanne's husband was one of them. The incident happened only a couple of days before the group of friends was due to return to London. For Zanne, the news created an emotional turmoil, a mixture of grief and relief. After all the legal and administrative paperwork was dealt with, she inherited a considerable fortune from her husband's estate. Although by then financially secure in her own right, the inheritance meant she was set for life, even if she never wrote another book.

By the time probate was granted and death duties were paid, Zanne had bought Tern Cottage and was settling into a new life at Charlotte Cove. About twelve months after she left England, I received an email from her telling me her husband's estate finally was settled and she at last felt able to get back to writing. The following day, an email from my mother shook me to the core.

When I opened the email and saw it was from Mum, I caught my breath. Mum and I spoke regularly by phone. She never emailed me unless there was detailed information that was better provided in writing. I was not waiting for anything from her. A quick scan of the message and I knew why she emailed instead of phoning me. She had been diagnosed with cancer. So far, it was manageable, but it was an aggressive form and she expected to deteriorate quickly unless the new drugs and management regime they were trialling achieved nothing short of a miracle.

There had only ever been the two of us. Mum trained as a doctor and then worked at major hospitals around Sydney for many years before buying into a medical centre in an outer Sydney suburb. She never married and would never discuss how she managed to get me. All she would say was that, as a GP, many of her patients were pregnant women. Never having experienced the same situation herself, she felt inadequate when dealing with such patients. She told me many times, "There is a difference between knowing about it from text books, and having experienced it firsthand."

She was at the end of her thirties when she had me, turned forty a couple of weeks later, and went straight back to work afterwards. I knew a succession of carers until my final High School years when she decided I was old enough and probably responsible enough to look after myself if she wasn't around at times. After that, I was off to university and living in student accommodation on campus. The news of her cancer rocked me. I began putting things in place so that I could return home as soon as I managed to convince her I needed to be there.

It was six months after that email, when I received the news that all treatments had ceased having any impact on her now rampant cancer. I flew home two days later and spent the next two months watching her slowly and painfully die.

A solicitor rang home sometime during that last horrible week when morphine, or whatever the drug was, eased Mum's pain by keeping her comatose. The solicitor said that he needed to speak to my mother, as she was the executor of Aunt Edwina's will. After explaining the situation, we arranged to meet the following day. I had forgotten about Aunt Eddie's death. She died about two years previously. Mum rang to tell me about it. Neither of us saw the need for me to return to Australia for the funeral.

My mother's last week is something of a blur. The solicitor arranged a meeting. That's when I discovered Mum inherited everything from her Aunt Edwina including, Wellsprings, several Sydney properties, some other investments and a small fortune in cash. Quite a bit of work was required before Aunt Eddie's estate could be wound up. The solicitor and I agreed it would take longer than the time my mother had left. Apart from anything else, the future of the Sydney properties required decisions.

In hindsight, Aunt Eddie's solicitor was a godsend. He and my mother were to be the executors of Aunt Eddie's estate. However, with my mother so ill, he dealt with everything himself. I think he had something of a sweet spot for the old girl. Aunt Eddie had been the firm's client since she was a young girl. The solicitor's father had looked after her interests until he retired, passing Aunt Eddie onto his son. For some reason, and I don't think it was merely a courtesy, he insisted on involving me where he could in the probate process. I suspect it was his way of dragging me away from the hospital for a break from my mother at that stage of her life.

As predicted, my mother died before settlement of all the issues associated with Aunt Eddie's estate, but not before the inheritance passed to my mother. At the end of a tumultuous week, my mother died and I was plunged into the world of executor of the will. Although less complicated than Aunt Eddie's, mum's estate also took some time to finalise. Six months later, all estate wrangling was complete and I found myself the sole beneficiary of my mother's estate, including that part of it which she inherited from Aunt Eddie. That included *Wellsprings.* It took a while, but the day finally arrived when I could leave all that behind me and relocate to Charlotte Cove.

Although I stayed with Zanne for almost two weeks, we hadn't spent much time together, usually only a little time each morning and again in the evenings. I spent all day every day making a small part of *Wellsprings* ready to move in. "…And I should be getting on with the task now instead of sitting here thinking about the past," I announced to no one in particular before taking myself off to the room that was to become my office.

None of the furniture I could see in the room resembled anything I would want in an office. The room's original use was lost in the passage of time. There was something about the accumulated junk in there that suggested the room had been out of service for a long time. I couldn't guess what its intended purpose was, as I didn't know the role this house played in the day-to-day life of the family.

Not only didn't I know about those previous owners and their lifestyles, but I also didn't know how they ran their households. For instance, there are acres of grounds surrounding the house. I doubt the 'lord of the manor' looked after them himself. Maybe he had a gardener or two. What other staff would a place such as this require, and what variations in staff numbers occurred over the decades? Such thoughts only served to remind me that I didn't know who, or how many might have lived in the house at any given time.

"Finding out about the stories associated with this place might be stalled for the moment, but what about who the various previous owners were? I mused aloud, "Who knows what mysteries might lurk in their past? Where does one start? At least Zanne has something akin to a black belt in such research..."

Good God, I've started to talk to myself. I had better find something worthwhile to occupy me before I lose the plot completely.

Chapter 3

At last! It had arrived. In reality, it took only three days for the copy of the property's title deed to arrive. Having decided finding out who had been associated with the place might be the first step in coming to terms with the myths about *Wellsprings,* I requested a copy of the title deed. "Thanks, Bill," I called as the mailman extracted the large envelope from his bag and attempt to stuff it into the mailbox at the end of my driveway. "I hope that's the one I've been waiting for." I was halfway down the driveway by the time I finished speaking. Bill flicked me a mock salute and rode off before I reached the letterbox.

He seemed to insert the envelope with a lot less effort than it took me to remove it without tearing it. By the time I was back in my kitchen, I had the envelope ripped open. "I'm almost not game to read this," I told the kitchen as I tipped the envelope's contents onto the table and flattened them out. "How ridiculous is that? It's only going to tell me who has owned this place. There can't be anything scary in that." Oh hell, I'm doing it again. I'm talking to an empty house.

Most of the first page was taken up with technical jargon spelling out the proper land description. After skipping over it to the bottom of the page, I started to turn the page, but stopped when I realised I needed to understand this stuff. I needed to understand what I had inherited and everything about it. In the hope of achieving that, I returned to the top, and this time read carefully to the end of the page. While I didn't comprehend all it said, what struck me was the size of the block the house sat on. It had been enormous when first purchased but, in more recent times, the government resumed some of the property to incorporate into a new national park that now surrounds the property on three sides.

The next few pages held the information I wanted. It listed the owners and transfers of ownership from the time of its original purchase through to now. My name was the last entry. A quick scan of the pages of names, dates, official stamps and handwritten annotations left me none of the wiser. I really didn't take in any of the details. Then common sense kicked in. I fetched a notebook and pencil and my car keys. Even such a quick flick through the pages told me Zanne needed to see this.

I sent gravel flying in all directions as I screeched to a halt at Zanne's gate. It took me a few moments to gather up the pages of the title deed which had fallen from the passenger's seat and spread themselves over the floor of my car. Then I yelled as I raced up the path, "Zanne, Zanne, you won't believe this unless you see it yourself. ...And yes please, I will have a coffee." Zanne was on her postage stamp sized patio with her mid-morning coffee.

"Right; now we both have coffee and are calm and collected again, what is it I'm not going to believe?" Zanne asked as she studied me across the top of her mug. "What's got you excited? Last time we spoke, you weren't too happy about being lumbered with some huge programming job, and were moaning about it getting in the way of the work you needed to do in the house. I don't believe any programming job could excite you to this extent, so what has?"

"If you stop talking, I'll tell you; show you." I opened the extra photocopy of the title deed and spread it out on the table in front of her. "The story of my house begins with Rupert Prendergast Granger about 130 years ago."

Zanne gave me a tell-me-more look coupled with a restrained reply. "Right... Rupert Granger... Should I know who he is?"

"Probably not, and nor do I – yet. But it is a start. Look at all this on the end of the document. It lists everyone who has owned the house, and every one of them was a Granger. I wonder if that means it has never been outside the family, just handed down through the generations within the one family."

"Hmm...," Zanne murmured as she ran her finger down the page. "Interesting names you've got here; be worth investigating why 'Prendergast' carried on down the line. You have to agree it was considerate of your mother not to have married and changed her name so the Granger name could continue on the deed."

"Thank you, Girlfriend. I was excited about what I learned from the title deed until I talked to you about it. Now I feel as though I didn't learn much at all. Who were these people? I assume they lurk somewhere in my family tree but, apart from the three owners before me, I don't know anything about them – or the name 'Prendergast'."

"So now you have some family history research to do to find out about them and what the connections are. I'll bring my laptop to your place tomorrow and we'll get stuck into the research together."

As I drove home, I pondered what I might do tonight to prepare for tomorrow's research. Tomorrow seemed a long time to have to wait to find out anything. With Zanne involved, tomorrow had the potential to become epic. I am pleased she is interested though. I'll be relying on her expertise and experience. When we were in London, she told me some of the amazing stuff she uncovered in the course of research for her crime fiction novels. I couldn't help but think that, to a crime fiction writer, the mystery we were about to investigate, especially if a crime were involved, might be the basis for a future novel.

We sat with our laptops set up on opposite sides of the kitchen table and connected via a hub to a printer at the end of the table. Researching the early owners' names proved quicker and easier than I imaged, no doubt thanks to Zanne's knowledge and experience. As we searched and found information, I copied out an impressive list of family history details on a few members of the Granger clan. "I didn't expect it to be so easy to identify so many people," I confessed to Zanne.

"This part of our research wasn't too difficult. Use of the Prendergast name down the line made it easier and confirms we have identified the right people. Once we get this lot sorted out …"

"Sorted out…? What do you mean?"

"We need them entered onto a chart – some sort of family tree if you like – so it's easier to see how they all fit together.

There may be other names we haven't gathered yet that might be required later on to verify other information we uncover." Zanne explained how to draw up a blank family tree chart.

"I can do that. It might take me a while though. Is there something else you want to go on with while I'm about it?"

"N-o-o; it's almost lunchtime. I don't think there is anything more to do today. We should reconvene here in the morning and start the day by studying the family tree you create. Besides, I have something I need to do. I'll head off now and I'll see you here again in the morning."

We left everything as it was on the kitchen table. Zanne didn't need her laptop. I made do with eating at the clear end of the table. It was at that end of the table that I settled down after a late lunch to work on the promised family tree chart. By almost four o'clock, I had entered every piece of information onto the chart and meticulously checked each entry.

After sitting inside researching all day, I needed a walk around the grounds to clear my head, which now buzzed with names and dates, and more questions than I can count. I decided research is both tantalising and frustrating. "I can't wait for tomorrow to come and hopefully provide answers to some of my questions," I told an ancient rose bush. "I suppose talking to you is a little better than talking to an empty house," I confided to the rose bush. "You are in serious need of pruning. That's something else I'm going to have to learn about, along with a whole lot of other gardening-type stuff."

Having decided there was nothing worth watching on TV after dinner last night, I tried reading my book. With concentration in short supply, I gave up on reading and opted for an early night.

My early night meant I was awake earlier than usual this morning. Not sure what time to expect Zanne today, I rushed about getting all the routine stuff out of the way in the hope that she would arrive early. That wasn't to be. It was a little after ten o'clock before I heard her car coming up the driveway. "Coffee, coffee…," she gasped as she came through the front door.

"Caffeine levels are low. I'm overdue for my morning dose."

"I was beginning to have withdrawal symptoms myself. I had just started the machine when I heard your car."

For a few moments there was silence as we sat taking in our caffeine fix. "I thought you might have come a bit earlier for coffee, so I laid everything out ready to start when you arrived. What are your ideas on what we should do today?"

"I would have been here earlier, but I needed to check on something before I came. It took longer than I expected. Although I thought it was unlikely, I did manage to catch up with Frank Kane yesterday. He is a wealth of knowledge about the Cove, and I ended up spending a couple of hours with him talking about all sorts of things relating to the history of this village. Last night, when I was typing up all my notes so that they would make sense to both of us today, I noticed a couple of them weren't clear, or raised some questions. Anyway, I decided to hang around the beach for a bit this morning in the hope Frank might come down to do some fishing. The upshot of all that was that I spent about an hour and a half watching Frank fish as I went over some of the things I needed clarified."

"Well, come on, don't sit there all morning drinking coffee and talking around it. What did you find out, and does that influence the research we might undertake today?

Zanne reached for the family tree chart I'd produced last night and studied it for a moment before answering. "This is a good visual representation of what we did yesterday. Now that I can see it all laid out clearly, I think more family history research is needed. There won't be much, just a few more names needed to clarify things before we go any further."

We agreed that I would search for the family history information Zanne thought we needed while she looked at some other records that might prove useful. A bit over an hour later, I stood up and stretched my back. "I think I covered everything you suggested. I've got a hell of a long list of names and dates and places, but I don't know if they're relevant or not. It's almost lunchtime. How about you look through the list of information I dug out this morning while I make lunch?"

As I brought the salad rolls to the table, Zanne moved our paperwork out of harm's way. "I think we found all the people we need –for now anyway. Straight after lunch, we should enter them on the chart, and then move on to finding out more about them. I'm thinking we should search the newspaper archives, but we will update the chart first, and then see if it suggests something different."

No time wasted on lunch. Afterwards, it didn't take me long to add the extra names to the family tree. Zanne checked the chart and announced, "Right, the newspaper archives are where we need to go next. The title deed gives us a starting date indicating when the property was acquired, so let's see if *Wellsprings'* purchase rated a mention in any newspapers around that time." She showed me how to access the National Library's *Trove* newspapers archive website. I noted she still had not shared whatever information Frank Kane gave her. So far, I resisted asking point-blank for her to tell me, but my control was running low. If I didn't get busy with something soon, I would end up demanding to know what Frank had said. Regardless, she would not be leaving this afternoon until she shared that with me.

It took me a while to figure how best to interrogate the database, but I soon found myself absorbed in the wealth of historical information it offered. So much so that I kept wandering off track as interesting comments in newspaper articles led me off on unrelated tangents. Zanne's yelp startled me. "Yes! That Prendergast name had me intrigued. I figured it would prove important to the story. I think I've nailed it."

"What… what? Come on; is the name significant to the story of this house or not?"

"What was Rupert's father's name?"

I reached across for the chart. "Uhmm… William Prendergast Granger."

"Okay, we need a bit more family history information. I think we need to go back another generation. See if you can find William's parents."

A couple of minutes later, I vented my frustration. "Aargh, how many William Grangers can there be? There are hundreds of them… b-u-t only one William Prendergast Granger."

He appeared almost at the bottom of a long list of William Grangers. I was becoming desperate by the time I found the right one. I had wondered how we were going to check all those Williams who had no recorded second name. I scribbled details of William's birth. Now armed with his parents' names, I searched and found an entry for their marriage. Those details were added to my note, which I pushed across to Zanne to read before I entered the new information onto the chart.

"I was right. This is the correct family." Whatever Zanne found had her excited. "I'll print this out so it's comfortable to read." For a minute or two there was silence as we read the print-out.

With everything cleared from my screen, I brought up Word and composed a precis of the information Zanne found. "Have a listen to this, Zanne, and tell me if I've missed any salient points." She nodded and I began reading my file note. "The whole story of this property starts with William Prendergast Granger, the second son of a well-to-do English family. William's father, Thomas Granger, was a small-time storekeeper before his marriage and the family's rapid rise to the ranks of the well-heeled upper class. Thomas Granger's sudden affluence subsequent to his marriage resulted from the injection of his wife Elizabeth Prendergast's inherited money and lands. As the second son of Thomas and Elizabeth Granger, William Prendergast Granger stood to inherit nothing, so he immigrated to Australia and, with some family money backing him, became a wealthy landowner and entrepreneur in his own right."

"Stop there for a moment. You might have more to add to your note. I've just found a bit more on Elizabeth Prendergast. Elizabeth was in fact *Lady* Elizabeth. She inherited because her two older brothers, her only siblings, and her mother predeceased her father," Zanne said as she précised whatever she had on her screen. Then, after a momentary pause, to consider what Zanne had uncovered, I sought clarification.

"Wasn't it strange for a woman to inherit anything substantial back in those days. So far, I've found where Thomas and Elizabeth's marriage produced two sons and three daughters. There might have been more, but I don't think they are of interest. As we already know, William was their second son. I understand what we discovered about William, Zanne, but he doesn't excite me too much. The story of this house starts with Rupert Prendergast Granger. Why did we research William? Shouldn't we be looking for information on Rupert?"

"Hmmm...," she mumbled and I knew she wasn't listening. "Hang on... I'm just trying to read something." As she spoke, I heard the printer whir into life and start spitting out pages.

When the pages stopped spilling out, I grabbed, sorted and stapled them before giving one set to Zanne. Another period of silence reigned as we digested their information. Zanne is a faster reader than I, or perhaps she already had read the article on the screen before printing it.

"This confirms what we previously established: that Rupert was William's eldest son," Zanne said, more to herself than to me. "It doesn't tell us what happened after William's arrival in New South Wales, but it seems he did all right for himself."

"Yeah, by the time this was written, he had one of the largest pastoral holdings in the region, owned several properties in Sydney and was involved in a number of business ventures. It's not hard to see why William was such a prominent figure in Sydney as well as locally. See if you can find anything more on William that might give us some clues about what Rupert was doing," I suggested.

Zanne was way ahead of me. The printer sprung into life again. She found another article and it caused a bit of an outburst. "I'd say he probably could afford to give his son birthday presents worthy of mention in the local newspaper."

I scanned the latest printout. "There's some information on the young Rupert. Poor kid...!"

"What...?" This time it was my outburst that startled Zanne.

My tone of voice as I gave Zanne my paraphrased version of the article reflected my indignation. "As a twelve year old, Rupert was sent to boarding school in England and, after completing his education there, began training as a doctor. He doesn't seem to have come home – back to Australia, I mean – in all that time. Then, his training was interrupted when he turned 21. On having attained his majority, Rupert, accompanied by a couple of other well-heeled lads of the same age, embarked on the then fashionable for upper crust youth, a twelve-month long 'grand tour of Europe' before he returned to London to complete his training. I don't think he returned home during that time."

"It looks like he didn't celebrate his twenty-first with family, and didn't collect his presents for a while afterwards," Zanne mused.

A quick check of papers in my family tree file confirmed in my mind that it was sometime later before he claimed his birthday presents. "No, this article confirms it. This suggests it was six years after his twenty-first birthday when he arrived home to receive his presents: a pastoral selection adjoining William's holding and a *significant parcel of land situated at Charlotte Cove.* Information on Rupert's return to Australia provides background to the article, which is from early the year after his return. It reports that, at the time of the article, a rough timber shack stood on the Charlotte Cove block. Rupert and a handful of his friends used it as a seaside weekender. The article goes on about copious quantities of rum being consumed on such weekends."

That brought me to the end of the printout. Zanne was staring off into the distance and appeared deep in thought. I interrupted. "Zanne, is there anything else we can find about Rupert? I think we need to know more before we move on from him." I watched her return to the here and now and begin tapping furiously on her keyboard. I went to make coffee while she searched, but her yelp brought me running back to the table.

"Bingo! I think I've found another gem. I'll print it out." …And what a gem it was. It reported the return to Australia of Rupert Granger and his new bride, the former Gwendolyn Cavendish. "There's no mention so far of his having practiced as a doctor when he first returned to Australia. It appears he settled into the life of the landed gentry on his pastoral holding.

"Yeah, there is a bit at the end of the article that makes mention of his training as a doctor having been interrupted again when he contracted a debilitating illness. It doesn't say what the illness was. He couldn't have been too ill though. While he supposedly was recuperating, he had time to woo and marry the lovely

Gwendolyn – and finish his medical training," Zanne replied.

"They got to know one another at some point during all those years Rupert spent in London and 'rekindled their friendship' – so the article claims – while he was recovering from his illness." I was talking to myself. Zanne was engrossed in scanning other articles and mumbled as she read.

"…A son … another son … a daughter…a second daughter… It doesn't look like he suffered any lingering after-effects from his illness. They had the reproductive process going well. This is interesting…" Zanne elbowed me in the ribs to get my attention as she read from her screen. "The old timber shack that was here originally was demolished to make way for a more permanent structure. Although construction was delayed due to shortages of materials during the War – that's World War I they're talking about – work on the new brick building was nearing completion in 1919." I heard the printer do its thing again as Zanne continued scanning newspaper articles. "Ah, here's the next report on the house. The family moved into their new permanent residence at Charlotte Cove shortly after the new house was completed."

I wanted to ask Zanne whether the article gave any details of the house or what staff was employed, but her phone rang as I was about to pose the questions. She moved away from the table to take the call. I couldn't hear what it was about, but it involved a lot of nodding on Zanne's part. She rushed back to the table at the end of the call. Her mood had changed.

"I have to go. That was my agent. There has been some talk about a producer wanting to do an interview for one of those arts and culture shows on TV, but it was all a bit vague. Turns out they do want to do the interview… now … in half an hour's time. I have to go home, change into something suitable for TV, try to tidy my hair and slather on make-up. From experience, I know what works well on TV, but if you saw me face-to-face when I was prepped for TV, you would think you had encountered Frankenstein's daughter. I also need to scribble a few notes so I'm ready for all the inane questions that are likely to be asked. These types of interviews all seem to adhere to a similar script."

"You don't seem too enthusiastic about the interview. Why do it… or at least, why agree to do it right now? They might have had the courtesy to give you more notice."

"Yeah, that would be nice but, if you don't do it when they are ready, it tends not to happen at all. Like they say, 'any publicity is good publicity'. My books are selling well, but I can't afford to sit on my hands or become complacent when it comes to marketing opportunities. Gotta rush; see you again in the morning."

With that, Zanne was out the door and climbing into her car. I stood stunned as she drove away. The table remained littered with research notes, chart, printouts and coffee mugs. I grumbled to the universe as I tidied the table. "I feel just a little put out at the moment. She's gone for the day. I know we've made good progress today, but she still hasn't told me what Frank Kane had to say about this place. If she doesn't share something with me tomorrow, I think I'll blow a fuse… or demand an introduction to Frank."

Chapter 4

After a poor night's sleep, I awoke with a foggy head this morning. In spite of my best efforts to come to terms with the fact that Zanne hadn't told me what Frank knew of the stories associated with my house, I remained miffed. It wasn't that I was ungrateful for the help Zanne gave me in discovering what we had about the family. It was more about being left out of my own story. What was clear to me in the cold light of a new day was that I needed to fix my attitude before Zanne arrived today, or risk losing a friend.

There would be no improvement in my attitude if I sat around stewing about the situation. "I need to do something, anything that gives me something else to think about," I told the universe. A quick scan of the family tree and my notes suggested more family history research was required. After all, whatever the stories about this place were, there was nothing to suggest they related to Rupert's era of ownership. For all I knew, they might have arisen from something that occurred quite recently, even as recently as during Aunt Eddie's time.

In the best tradition of family history research, I decided to work from what I knew towards what I didn't know… except I would be working forward towards today rather than backwards through previous generations as Zanne told me is the usual practice. I marched to the kitchen table, took a deep breath and said aloud, "Right, yesterday Zanne mentioned something about Rupert's children. Let's find out who they were." I booted up my computer and began searching the UK indexes where we found Rupert's marriage. When nothing turned up after more than half an hour, I stopped to consider where else I might find the information. That's when I realised the children were born in Australia, and that I should search local records rather than overseas indexes. A more seasoned researcher wouldn't have wasted so much time looking in the wrong place.

An index of the local birth registers provided the answers. The couple's first child, Wilfred Prendergast Granger, was born early his parent's marriage as was the usual case in those days. Although I managed to identify the births of five children, the first child's birth held my interest. Wilfred Prendergast Granger was born at the beginning of the second year of his parents' marriage. Rupert's next child and second son, Michael Prendergast Granger, arrived about 13 months later. A quick check of the title deed confirmed Wilfred as the second owner of the Charlotte Cove property. It showed Wilfred assumed ownership in 1924.

Regardless of having established Wilfred's place in the order of things, I didn't know much about him. Do I need to know more, or is it a case of my becoming addicted to family history research. Somehow, I convinced myself it was necessary to discover more about Wilfred. I turned from the index of births to the marriages index.

After deciding on a likely date range for Wilfred's marriage, it took no time to find the entry for the marriage of Wilfred Prendergast Granger and Jessica Fitzmaurice. Wilfred didn't waste any time. He was younger than I expected when he married. Okay, the marriage is nailed; now for the children. A return to the births index provided something of a surprise. Wilfred and Jessica's first child, Randolph Prendergast Granger, was born eleven months after their marriage. Can that be right? Maybe I missed the birth of a previous child. No, that can't be the case. There wouldn't have been time for another child before Randolph's birth.

Another check of the title deed confirmed the owner subsequent to Wilfred was Thomas Prendergast Granger. A return to the births index uncovered three more children born to the couple: a second son, Thomas, followed by two daughters, Clara and Edwina. Therein lies the mystery. According to the title deed, it was Thomas who was the next owner of *Granger Hall,* as the place became known at some point along the way. The inevitable question that arises then is: why wasn't Randolph the next owner?

I sat back to ponder the question for a few moments before perusing my latest additions to the family tree chart. My head was spinning. Although the chart was set out in the traditional way, it was hard to grasp the whole picture. The more names I added, the harder it became to comprehend. Time to give it a rest, I decided.

In a bid to quell the whirlpool of names and dates swirling around in my mind, I wandered aimlessly away from the table and through the kitchen to end up in the backyard. It's a few days since I ventured out here. Some of the gum trees bordering the yard have burst into blossom since I last saw them. I watched the light breeze tickle fluffy particles of blossom free from the pendulous bunches of flowers and waft them towards the house. Wandering around with mind in neutral does work. As I stood watching Nature doing her thing, from out of nowhere a new thought occurred to me. Rupert and his family occupied Granger Hall for only a short time before Wilfred assumed ownership. At that time, both Rupert and Gwendolyn still were quite young. What happened to allow Wilfred to take over the property?

A car came up the driveway, ending any further thought on the matter. I decided it might be a good idea to close the rear of the house to prevent ingress of the gum blossoms and avoid a major housecleaning job. Zanne called from the kitchen as I closed the last of the windows.

"I'm coming. I wasn't sure I'd see you today." Oh dear, that sounded a touch more sarcastic than I intended… or was I still feeling put out, and had intended it to sound that way? I gave myself a mental slap on the wrist as I flashed a wide smile of welcome.

"Got held up just as I was about to leave: my agent. He was checking on how the interview went yesterday. Is it about coffee time? I could do with one before we start work."

"Take a look at the family tree chart while I make the coffee. I've added a few more names, but still don't know much about anyone. I keep finding questions rather than answers."

"Hmm… yeah, I think that's often the case with family history research. You have been busy. Oh, this is interesting. As the elder son, how come Randolph didn't inherit the property?" Zanne was studying the title deed as I carried the coffee to the table.

"I've no idea but it would be good to know. By the way, how did you go with your mate, Frank Kane? Did he have any information about the stories associated with this place?" I had asked the questions before I realised. Never mind; might as well clear the air before we begin the day.

"Didn't I tell you what I found out? Must have gotten wrapped up in the research and forgot. He gave me a sketchy outline of the story as he knew it. I was hoping for more. He must have seen I was disappointed because he said he would go home and try to recall what he heard over the years. Yesterday morning, before I came here, I decided to try my luck and went to the beach in the hope Frank might be there. He was, and he told me a little more. I queried him about different bits of the story. Something didn't make sense. There were either big gaps in what he knew, or the whole thing was a figment of someone's imagination. There's nothing wrong with Frank's mind. He never had much interest in the story, and as such, I guessed he hadn't taken much notice of any of it."

"Well, I suppose anything is better than nothing. It would be a help to have something that leads us in the right direction, otherwise we could spend forever researching in the hope of finding something."

"Yes, but that's not the end of the story. Frank said his father, before he died, filled exercise books with notes on the history of the village. He wondered whether his father might have included something about this place. He is going to check those notebooks and will let me know if he finds anything. I didn't go via the beach this morning, so I didn't see him. I will make a point of keeping an eye out for him to remind about what he promised to do for me."

"Okay, sounds like a plan, but what has he told you so far?"

"I grant you all this sounds a bit naff, but it's what Frank could remember off the top of his head. It seems the locals decided many years ago that the place was cursed. 'Cursed' might not be the right word. 'Unlucky' or even 'evil' might be better descriptors. However, it all seems to stem from something to do with a woman who lived here."

"There were plenty of those over the years. Did Frank indicate when that occurred or what happened to her?"

"No, as I said, Frank admits he didn't pay attention to the stories. He suggested there might be more than one event that contributed to the stories. The one thing he did seem sure about was that those events weren't recent. When I questioned him about what 'recent' meant, he explained they hadn't occurred in his lifetime. Frank is now in his mid-eighties, so we're talking about events – if they did occur –clouded by the mists of time and the fallibility of memory."

"That's a start I suppose, and we are grateful for whatever we get. However, I admit to feeling disappointed. I'm pinning my hopes on his father's notebooks producing something more."

With coffees in hand, we took up our usual places at the table. I showed Zanne the family tree enlarged by my efforts this morning. She murmured approvingly as she scanned the chart and cross checked it with entries on the title deed. "You've done well. That's coming along nicely, but it would be handy to have more idea of what we are looking for."

"There are two things I've found somewhat intriguing. They relate to the two owners subsequent to Rupert. I might be reading something into nothing, but it's strange that ownership passed to Wilfred so soon after Rupert and his family moved into the house. The other thing that intrigues me is that it was Wilfred's second son, Thomas, who followed him as owner of the place and not Wilfred's first son, Randolph."

Zanne continued studying the chart. "I think there is at least one more generation to add to this chart before we've got everyone pegged. I see you found Aunt Edwina. What we don't know is where on this tree the Thomas Prendergast Granger, who follows Wilfred as owner, fits in."

"That Thomas might be my grandfather. It sounds strange I know, but I never knew my grandparents. I don't think my mother knew her parents either."

"You're right, it does sound strange. How can that be? We've known each other for a long time, but I don't think we've ever talked about our families, or at least our family histories."

"We haven't because I didn't have anything to contribute. This is the closest I've come to knowing anything about my immediate past family history. Even my mother never discussed her parents or grandparents with me."

"Okay, then let's press on with identifying at least one more generation. That should reveal where 'branches' are necessary to clarify the situation." Zanne checked her watch. "I guess that should take us through to lunchtime. I'll slip away after lunch to catch up with Frank."

"Will he be fishing at the beach so late in the day?"

"No, he'll be home by then. I'll visit him at home, but I'll go straight after lunch. He has a nap every afternoon, so I don't want to wake him or interfere with his nap."

Time disappeared after our late start. Adding the next generation's information to the tree took us to lunchtime. Once we identified who Thomas Granger married, we could search for his children. That sounded easy enough, but proved otherwise.

There were numerous marriages between Thomas Grangers and various women. The problem was which one was my Thomas Granger? "There's a whole lot who are just 'Thomas Granger' with no middle name. Only a few have middle names. None has Prendergast," I grumbled as my frustration level escalated. "Most of those marriages are around the same time. To make things more complicated, that means it's likely they were all having kids at the same time too."

"Pity the indexes don't give a bit more information. Even the place where the marriage occurred would be useful," Zanne suggested.

"Maybe not… if they were married where the bride lived, we still wouldn't be any better off."

"You stick with the marriages index to see if anything emerges. If Thomas was your grandfather, your mother's birth was too recent to appear in the index. I'll attack the newspapers to see if I can find anything useful."

I wasn't hopeful, but went along with Zanne's suggestion. There was nothing new to find there, so I started noting dates of each marriage and the brides' names. I was about three parts of the way through the list when Zanne's shout startled me.

"Found one! This one gives the father's name as Thomas Prendergast Granger." She scribbled out details from the article while the printer spat out a copy. "Hang about. I'm going to look back earlier to see if this is the first mention of the couple."

"You keep looking. I'm going to make a salad for lunch. We will need to have lunch soon or it will be too late for you to visit

Frank afterwards. By the way, what was the mother's name on that birth entry?"

"Mother's name was Catherine. It doesn't give her surname. Maybe now we have her given name we will be able to find her and Thomas in the marriages index."

"I think there was an entry like that. I'll have a look when I've finished making lunch."

As I made room on the table for lunch, I noticed the deep furrows creasing Zanne's brow. "I don't like the look of this. What's gone wrong?"

"What do you mean? Nothing that I know of has gone wrong. Why do you ask?"

"What are you frowning about?"

"Was I? That wasn't because anything had gone wrong. I was trying to come to grips with something, that's all." I motioned 'gimme' to Zanne and she continued. "All the generations we looked at so far produced multiple children. We haven't searched for every child for each couple, just enough of them to understand where the next owner of the house fitted into the order of things. From what I've seen, all of those couples were dedicated to populating the planet with numerous Granger offspring…until we come to Thomas. I've only found one child for him so far."

"I agree that does sound unusual for this Granger mob, but that doesn't make it wrong or impossible. It does give us something to think about though. However, lunch is ready, so let's eat. Our little grey cells probably need a break from this morning's hard slog."

Lunch was eaten without further mention of family history research. Conversation focused on how Zanne's interview went yesterday, the likely release of her next book, and what promotional events were scheduled for the near future. As we sat down to lunch early, it wasn't much after twelve o'clock when Zanne left. I was concerned that she would arrive in the middle of Frank's lunch and not receive the warmest of welcomes.

"It won't be a problem. I know he watches the midday news on TV before he thinks about eating lunch. I'll collect the chicken caesar salad I have in the fridge to take with me. It should sweeten the situation enough for me to ask questions while he has lunch, and allow me to press him about his father's notebooks."

Once again I found myself at a loose end. As I cleaned up after Zanne left, I knew I wouldn't be able to leave the research alone with yet another question begging for an answer. As Zanne pointed out, it was strange for Thomas and Catherine to have only one child. A quick check of the notes I made from the marriage index suggested the entry for a Thomas Granger and Catherine Bonham-Stewart might be the marriage I wanted. The Stewart part of Catherine's surname intrigued me. Hadn't I come across another hyphenated Stewart somewhere earlier in this research?

I dragged Zanne's notes across the table and read the date of the birth of Thomas and Catherine's daughter. A daughter…! That birth date looked familiar. I checked the family tree chart. "Yes…!" I shouted. That's why the birth date looked familiar. It was my mother's birth. I had found Esther Granger, known for most of her life to everyone who knew her as Essie. Yet another check of the title deed and some mental arithmetic confirmed Thomas was only in his mid-twenties when he assumed ownership of the house. It wasn't that I doubted Zanne's research ability, but I felt compelled to look at birth notices in the newspapers for other children born to the couple. After starting with Esther's birth and working forward, it didn't take long to realise Zanne's assessment of the situation was correct. There was only one child.

That exercise hadn't answered any questions. All it did was prove that Thomas didn't own the house for long before it passed to the next owner, his sister Edwina. Ah well, I suppose it gives me something to ponder while I'm trying to get to sleep tonight. But for now, I think I've done enough family history research for today. After tidying the kitchen table, I fetched the book I'd been trying to read, and went off to lose myself in another (literary) world for a few hours.

Chapter 5

I couldn't help myself. Before I knew what I was doing, I hit my speed dial for Zanne – and found myself flustered and embarrassed when she answered. "Sorry Zanne, I know I'm being a pain, but I wondered how it went with old Frank today. Did you get to speak to him about his father's notebooks?"

"Yes, well, sort of… As soon as he ate lunch, I swung the conversation around to your old house and his father's notebooks. Frank told me he found the box that held all the notebooks but it would take a while to find information on your house and its occupants. He showed me the box of books. There wasn't time for much more. By the time he ate lunch, it was time for his customary nap."

Even over the phone, she must have heard me sigh or heard something that alerted her to my disappointment. "It was disappointing, but he promised to get on with going through the notebooks straight after his nap. I left it with him to contact me as soon as he found something, or finished going through the books, whichever came first. I don't imagine I'll hear from him tonight and, given the speed of his past efforts, it's likely we won't hear anything for a day or two."

Disappointment is a terrible emotion. I suffered a major dose of it via that phone call. However, I agreed there wasn't much else we could do, and that we push on with other things tomorrow. Zanne even tried to convince me it might be good to give our minds a break from research for a day or two. "Maybe we would come up with some new ideas on how to progress our research."

While what she says makes sense, I know I won't be able to stay away from researching for a day or two. I don't know what I'll do, but I do know I'll be driven to get on with it somehow.

Later, expecting sleep to elude me for some time tonight, I propped myself up in bed with a notebook and pen and started a list. It developed into quite a long list covering the research undertaken so far and the places we've searched, followed by a substantial list of potential future research. If I'm honest, that second part of the list – the future research part – looks more like a list of questions to which I needed answers. Although after midnight when I turned off the light, it took quite a while for asleep to come.

I woke early this morning, but my late night endeavours left me woolly-headed and feeling decidedly grumpy. By the time breakfast was over, I had planned my day. So much for leaving research alone for a day or two; that wasn't going to happen. For me, the danger in that would be losing the thread of the story uncovered thus far. I retrieved my list from last night and revised my plan for today.

Family history research was not a priority at this time. I had more names on my 'tree' than I thought necessary. Were some of them relevant at all to the story? As I sat sipping my coffee, it became clear what was important now was finding out more about the people whose names appear on the title deed. More so than adding more names to the family tree. That realisation made planning my day straightforward. I would search newspaper archives for any mention of anything to do with anyone listed on the title deed.

Although I now knew how to use the newspaper archives, by mid-morning, new information was almost none. What I found amounted to the odd mention of a name in the 'social jottings' pages rather than anything of importance to my research. Nevertheless, after my morning coffee, I returned to the newspapers. At least, I will feel I did something, even if I find nothing. That was better than sitting around being frustrated and grumpy, or so I told myself.

It was lunchtime, but I wanted to finish searching the newspaper I had open on the screen before taking a break. That's when the 'Eureka' moment occurred. The name search indicated that somewhere in this edition of the *Sydney Morning Herald* was mention of something relating to Rupert Granger. My thorough search of the paper failed to find anything. In a final bid to find something on Rupert before closing it, I flicked back through the pages. The Granger name almost leapt off the page, although why it should do that now when it hadn't done so before was a mystery. A two-sentence paragraph emerged from its hiding place.

Tucked away in the 'Regional News' section, the article advised the local police investigation continued into the incident involving Gwendolyn, the wife of Mr Rupert Granger. It added that extra police had arrived to assist with the investigation. "What investigation… what incident?" I demanded of the universe. No response. What to do next…? Whatever the 'incident', it happened sometime prior to this edition of the newspaper. I changed the search criteria to 'Gwendolyn Granger' and sent it off to find earlier mentions of Gwendolyn for me.

No earlier reference appeared in the *Sydney Morning Herald.* Frustrated, I scanned back through the editions of the paper, only to discover a gap of a few months between copies available in the online archives. Maybe the local paper or one of the other regional newspapers might tell me what happened. I went to the site I knew provided online copies of early editions of this area's 'local' paper. I flicked through the edition dated immediately prior to that Sydney edition.

There it was. The same article as appeared in the metropolitan paper. This time it included comments about the police being no closer to solving the mystery, and all those involved frustrated by the lack of progress. Not much to go on, but enough to send me scanning back through earlier editions for details of when and what happened. To my frustration, I found there were gaps in the online editions of this paper as well. Where a run of a number of copies was missing, someone had inserted a notice advising that a fire in the newspaper office had destroyed the missing copies.

My stomach rumbled loudly, reminding me that lunchtime had long since passed me by. A break seemed a good idea. It would give me time to think about what to do next. It doesn't take long to make and eat a sandwich, not nearly enough time for inspiration to occur. I returned to where I left off and continued scanning back through earlier papers. The legacy of the fire was obvious. A few copies here and there punctuated a long run of missing copies. Some of the survivors existed only as partial pages darkened by smoke and with ragged singed edges.

After searching back over several weeks, I was about to give up. With no further information on the incident involving Gwendolyn Granger forthcoming, I announced to the universe, "Five minutes more and that's it. I'll give it away if nothing turns up by then."

Seven minutes later, I checked the time again. Okay, that's it. I'll give up when I finish this edition. I was about to flick to the last page when something my subconscious had noted made me stop. Back at the front page, I scanned every piece of text for the Granger name. It was at the top and halfway across page two. I read excerpts from the article aloud. "…Speculation over the disappearance of Mrs Gwendolyn Granger running rife in the community… police investigation stymied by lack of evidence… no clues emerge from exhaustive interviews."

"Ah hah, so Gwendolyn disappeared." I wondered whether 'vanished' might be a better word. Spurred on by this tantalising hint of what happened, I renewed my resolve to continue, and moved to the previous edition of the paper. Damn! The next paper was from late in the previous year. The editions from the first few months of 1920 were missing. I continued scanning earlier editions in the hope that Gwendolyn's disappearance occurred late in 1919. It wasn't to be. Admitting defeat, I logged off, shut down my computer, and took myself for a walk around *Wellsprings'* grounds.

Nothing registered with me as I wandered aimlessly around outside. Was anything in flower? Was there birdsong? Probably, but I didn't notice. My mind had gone into hyperdrive as it manufactured a range of possible scenarios to explain Gwendolyn's disappearance. There's only so long before one's built-in self-preservation mechanism kicks in. Mine seemed to take longer than usual. I can continue to wander around out here until dusk, but it won't change anything. It won't provide me with details of what happened. After about half an hour, I managed to persuade myself to go inside and find something productive to do for the remainder of the afternoon, preferably something that takes my mind off Gwendolyn. My hope now is that Zanne's mate, Frank, finds something significant in his father's notebooks.

With nothing more I could do towards unravelling the mystery of the disappearance of Rupert Granger's wife, Gwendolyn, I opted to get on with making *Wellsprings* more liveable. So much of what I had to do was mind-in-neutral activity, requiring the application of effort and elbow grease rather than thought and concentration. That freed my mind to explore and analyse the little we had uncovered about the house and its occupants.

My chosen place to expend some physical energy is the room I earmarked to become my office. I stood in the doorway surveying the task ahead of me. Where to start? Over the years, this room was a dumping place for any surplus small furniture, knickknacks, and strange things that might best be described as *objet d'art.* "Much of this stuff is going out," I told the room. "In fact, I think most of it can go." I set to work, picking up small items, like side tables and footstools, and walking them out to the skip. Larger items would require the trolley from the shed, and possibly others to help shift them. I wondered if there might be a market in the Charlotte Cove area for second-hand furniture. What was I thinking? The ludicrous nature of that thought made me giggle. It's likely every house in Charlotte Cove already has its own collection of such junk.

About half an hour of exertion later, it occurred to me that, in spite of all the research and all the names added to the family tree, I still don't know much about any of those people. If I start at the top of the list, what do I know about Rupert? More importantly perhaps, what were the lives of those people like? How did they run their households? That recalled similar thoughts I had early in our research. The same questions still prevailed. A place this size required a bevy of household staff, not to mention gardeners or other groundsmen.

By the time I removed most of the small pieces from the room, dusk had arrived and there was a satisfying pile in Sam's fluoro pink skip. Now it was time to assess of what remained. Not much interested me, with the exception of a large polished timber desk. Pushed against the wall in a far corner of the room, it looked as though shifting it required plenty of muscle. After close inspection, I decided it was a real 'find'. It would remain, but over near the big window. Then it was time to turn my attention to mundane matters such as food.

As I stood shovelling my stirfry in the wok, a rogue thought skittered through my mind: how many Granger wives have stood here doing just this? I was about to dismiss the thought, but it pounded for attention and I awarded it a few moments of contemplation. "None...," I yelped and smacked my forehead. "None... Not one of them ever stood here – and probably none of them ever cooked." That led me back to how much I don't know about the people who owned and lived in this house and who presumably were my ancestors.

What now is the kitchen area had been the kitchen as far back as I could remember. This is where Aunt Eddie cooked for herself, and where my mother took over the cooking when we were here for holidays. But this couldn't have been the *real* kitchen. You only have to look at this house to know it's about making a show and creating an image. It was to serve as a statement about the owners' place in society's rankings. Apart from anything else, its purpose was to announce to the world that those living here were upper crust or, at the very least, upwardly mobile. This would not have been the kitchen, and I think it highly unlikely that any owners' wives bothered themselves with the task of preparing food for the family.

In a house this size, and being so much about image, visitors never would come through the front door and straight into a kitchen. Somewhere hidden away from sight in this rambling pile of bricks and mortar must be the real kitchen where a real cook prepared meals. "When did it change? Why was this area turned into a kitchen and what event precipitated the change?" The empty house provided no answers. My temptation was to call Zanne, but I resisted... until after I had eaten, anyway.

"Please tell me if I'm interrupting something. I can call you at some other time." Zanne's reply eased my conscience.

"You're not. I was about to get up and make something for dinner, but I detect your need to talk to someone. Tell me what has happened."

"I don't know that anything has happened. I suppose I'm feeling a bit frustrated by everything. Random thoughts keep bugging me. While they're okay in themselves, they just keep reminding me about how much I don't know and how much I haven't learnt in spite of our research. Aarrgh… I'm not making any sense. Don't worry about it now. I'll try to be more articulate next time we meet. By the way, when might that be? Are you going to be tied up for the next few days?"

"I've been taking care of feedback from the editor on the final draft of my next novel. After I eat tonight, I'll check again that I've made all of the changes required. If that's the case, after I send it to my agent in the morning, I'll be free again. Well… that might be a bit of an exaggeration; perhaps by tomorrow afternoon. I'll let you know."

Our chat lasted a couple of minutes but left me feeling even more depressed. After giving myself a good talking to about my current state of mind, I took myself off to bed for an early night, but ended up reading my book till well after eleven o'clock. I should have kept reading. I seemed to spend the rest of the night more awake than asleep before abandoning any further attempt at sleep in favour of making an early start to the new day. The only problem with an early start is that it presents the problem of what to do to fill in the longer than usual day ahead of you.

While it wasn't a difficult decision, going back to do more in what will become my new office is not my favoured option for today. More research is what I want to do. My problem is, I don't know where to look for the information I want. I need Zanne's experience to point me in the right direction. If she isn't free to help today, I'm likely to be climbing the wall by this evening. I attacked the room with renewed vigour in the hope that maximum exertion might take my mind off what I really wanted to do.

When I stopped soon after nine o'clock for an earlier than usual coffee break, my new office looked spacious. A couple of largish cupboards still required a decision on their future. Apart from those, the office was ready for occupation. On my way to make coffee, I paused at the doorway to cast my eyes over the room again. I retained the desk, two long low cupboards and a small table. I'm not sure about one of those cupboards, but it can stay until I work out if I need it. The two large cupboards I didn't want. I managed to drag them out of the office. They are now parked outside the room. Their future is a decision for another time.

After coffee, I plan to move my filing cabinets into the office and load their contents again. That will leave only my computer work station to relocate and reassemble. As I sit sipping my coffee, I'm satisfied with my efforts this morning. However, that same problem still lurks: what to do after that. It was as I sat thinking about it that my spirits lifted.

A car door slammed followed by a most welcome voice. "Is it too early for coffee? If it is, may we dispense with tradition on this occasion?" Zanne had arrived. I managed to stop myself rushing to hug her.

This morning's coffee break stretched on for over an hour as I told Zanne of my extra research yesterday. "So, I've found it was Rupert Granger's wife, Gwendolyn, who disappeared. From the brief article I found, I estimate it happened early in 1920. However, as I couldn't find anything from the time of her disappearance, I can't be sure how long after the event the article was written."

"I know how frustrating it is when the copies of the newspapers are missing, but there are other ways around the problem. The local historical society has amassed an amazing collection. Their volunteers indexed copies of the local papers. It's worth a quick look there before anywhere else."

"But, if the papers were destroyed in the fire, how would the historical society be able to index them?"

"Some ancient local had a regular subscription to the paper. He never threw out anything, and those clearing out his house after his death found themselves faced with a hell of a job. That old adage about a silver lining applied. He bequeathed all the historical stuff he collected to the historical society. Come on; why are we wasting time yapping? Let's see what the historical society can tell us."

In no time, Zanne had her computer logged onto the society's index. She gave me a running commentary on what she did as she went along. "Okay; see, this is the index of articles in the local newspapers. Now, let's find the entries from the 1920 editions. Ah, here we go. I think there's somewhere to enter search criteria… Yes, here it is."

I watched Zanne type in 'Gwendolyn Granger'. It felt like ages before the search results appeared on the screen. I didn't count the entries but they continued onto a second screen. I was so focused on reading the computer screen, Zanne's voice seemed distant. What she said didn't register with me. "What? Uhmm… this is fascinating but where does it get us? Now we know there were lots of articles about the lady, but they are not much use if we don't know what they say." The printer whirred into life as I finished speaking. Zanne retrieved the printout.

"There is another database. We'll use this printout to cross reference entries. Our only problem now is whether they have digitised any of these articles yet."

Disappointment blighted my day again. While some of the articles were available, many were not. "Bugger…! How do we access the information in those other articles?" I shouted above the sound of the printer spitting out many sheets of paper.

"Don't get excited. We extracted quite a bit from the database. If nothing else, we've confirmed that Gwendolyn went missing around Easter in 1920. I've printed out all the articles from the database. The next thing we do is contact the society to ask for copies of the ones that weren't available online. It will cost a few dollars for the service and it might take a few days for them to arrive." Zanne explained that the society's volunteers would locate the articles requested, scan and email them to me. I gave her my credit card and left her to organise the copies while I perused the printouts.

"God, Zanne, we have to get everything we can on Gwendolyn's disappearance. From what's in these printouts, it's fascinating. It's the stuff of one of your mystery novels. Well, it seems like it is so far. We need to know more about it. Maybe she just wandered off and they eventually found her suffering from amnesia or something in some nursing home."

"I have a feeling it doesn't end like that."

"No, I don't think it does either. Such an ending doesn't explain why the property changed hands so soon after this happened."

Over lunch, we discussed other sources of information. Zanne was keen to search the police files held in the state archives. As she was due to go to Sydney for a few days the following week, I encouraged her to do what she could in whatever time she had available while there. I wasn't game to imagine the information such research might uncover. More disappointments were not what I wanted, and I knew that getting my hopes up was a good way of laying myself open to just that.

Lunch was so late, it was almost afternoon teatime when we adjourned to my new office. Zanne helped with putting the computer workstation together before carrying boxes from where I had dumped them. I loaded their contents into the cupboards and filing cabinets. Five o'clock found us both standing hands on hips admiring our handiwork. "This will be a great place to work," Zanne said. "It could do with a new coat of paint to lighten and brighten the room." She was right, but I wasn't about to let her comment ruin the moment.

After she spent so much time helping me, the least I could do was invite Zanne to stay for dinner. She declined. I was relieved. I had no idea what I might make. As she picked up her bag and headed for the door, she asked over her shoulder, "So, what's on the agenda for tomorrow? I don't know what time I'll be here or if I'll be here. It depends on whether my agent reads the manuscript I sent this morning and if there is more to do before it goes to the publisher."

Later, as I sipped a glass of wine before dinner, I realised I didn't know how I felt about today. We discovered quite a bit, but it made me want more. I knew tonight would be another restless night. My mind would be busy trying to make sense of everything we knew so far.

Chapter 6

You just know there's every chance it will be a good day when a pleasant surprise arrives first thing in the morning. That's why I can't wait to get started today. As I sat dawdling over breakfast, I booted up my computer to check emails before I moved the machine to its newly installed workstation in office.

The local historical society had come through to make my day. Nothing else that landed in my inbox overnight merited a look. Only the reams of scanned documents the society sent in response to Zanne's call yesterday mattered. For several minutes, the printer worked overtime. I wasn't turning off or moving anything until I had a hard copy of everything the historical society sent.

With the copies of the newspaper articles arranged chronologically, I pushed everything on the kitchen table out of the way. A couple of deep breaths to ready myself, and then armed with notebook and pen, I began a long, slow read of everything. The first article appeared in the edition of the local newspaper immediately after Easter 1920. It was brief, simply stating that the paper had received word of an incident that occurred at Charlotte Cove in the week prior to Easter: *It is believed the incident involved Mrs Gwendolyn Granger, the wife of Mr Rupert Granger. No further details of the incident are available at this time.*

Not what I hoped for, but it did confirm when Gwendolyn disappeared. It seems the reporter earned his wages. The next article appeared in the following edition. It appears the reported extracted a little more information from the police. I filled a page with scribbled key points from the article, then sat back to read my notes. Why have I developed a nervous feeling about this 'incident' and what I am about to uncover?

Another couple of deep breaths were required before facing whatever came next. I plunged in, adding more scribbled pages of notes before the jangling of my phone caught my attention.

Zanne. "What are we doing today… and is it too early for coffee?"

Brain dead from this morning's information overload, it took me a moment to realise it was almost ten o'clock. "It's never too early for coffee. How soon can you be here?"

"O-o-h, I detect a hint of something in that reply. Put the coffee on. I am on my way. See you in a couple of minutes." True to her word, I barely had the coffee machine doing its thing before her car roared up my driveway.

No time wasted settling at the table with our coffees, I soon was sharing what I knew about Gwendolyn's disappearance. "It's sad – tragic really – what happened to her. She was ill for some time. There was suggestion the family's move to live permanently at Charlotte Cove was because of Gwendolyn's ill health. Instead of improving, it seems she continued to deteriorate. I'm not sure what the problem was, but it sounds a bit like some form of dementia."

"She wasn't all that old, was she?" Zanne asked.

"No, I don't think so. According to my calculations, she would have been about fifty years old by then, and Rupert would have been about sixty-five."

"I don't suppose we can make judgements from this distance. It was a long time ago, and we don't know what life and conditions were like back then."

"N-o-o, that's true but, as I said, I'm guessing the problem was dementia. However, some other physical condition might have compounded the situation. What is clear, is her rapid deterioration. This house wasn't completed until 1919 and the family moved in straight away. By early the following year, she was an invalid."

"An invalid…?"

"So it seems. They had a nurse to look after the children. I imagine that she looked after the youngest children, as the older ones would be adults by then, or nearly so."

"I don't think you can make that judgement. The well-to-do lot always had someone to look after the kids. The wife's job was *to* produce the brood. Someone else had to bring them up."

"Okay, point taken. I don't know whether the nurse was with them before or after the move to Charlotte Cove, but it stands to reason that Rupert engaged her when the children were small and before they moved to the Cove."

"What makes you think Gwendolyn became an invalid soon after they moved here?"

"Uhmmm...," I flicked through my notes to ensure I had the facts straight before answering. "Here it is. One of the articles recounts how Gwendolyn's worsening condition necessitated the children's nurse becoming Gwendolyn's full-time carer. A 'nurse's assistant' was engaged to take over looking after the children. She still looked after the children when Gwendolyn disappeared."

"By then, the children wouldn't still be young ... not if Gwendolyn was aged 50 when she disappeared," Zanne suggest-ed

"I calculate the youngest ones were aged eight and six. There was a gap of a few years between them and child above them, who would have been about 13 or 14. In keeping with the family tradition, Rupert's two older sons went to boarding school in England when they were about twelve years old, just as their father had done. There was a gap of seven or eight years between the second son's birth and the next child, a girl. She died just before her tenth birthday." I checked if that clarified things for Zanne.

"Okay, I have the children sorted out now, thanks. The first two sons would be adults and the next child, the daughter, had died by the time Gwendolyn disappeared. Do I have that right?" I nodded, and she continued. "The girl who was 13 or 14 probably didn't need a nurse looking after her. She too might have been at boarding school somewhere by then... or even a *finishing school* somewhere. If we accept all that, there were only the youngest two children still at home for anyone to look after. Right, I'm just trying to get a picture of the household in my mind. What else do we know about Gwendolyn's illness and its progression?"

I consulted my précised information about Gwendolyn's illness and read it to Zanne. "It progressed to the point where she became bedridden, and spent most of her days in bed. When the weather was good, she would be wheeled outside to sit in the fresh air and take in a little sunshine. However, a later article quotes the nurse as saying that, in spite of Gwendolyn's poor health, there were occasional days when they noted slight improvement in her condition. Such improvement was short-lived, lasting no more than a day or two. Although the nurse didn't mention it, other townsfolk reported that, on some days after they wheeled Gwendolyn outside, neighbours observed her leave her chair and wander around the yard for brief periods. They claimed that on such occasions, as she stumbled about, she would shout and howl, and talk gibberish, although no one else was in the yard with her to whom she might be speaking."

"You were right when you said it was a sad story. It would be difficult for those around her to watch her deteriorate to such an extent. I wonder how those two young girls coped with what was happening to their mother. What was Rupert doing while all this was happening? Was he around, or was he off taking care of business elsewhere? He would not be the first husband to find some means of escape to avoid having to watch his wife's health spiral out of control."

"Hang on a minute. I have a couple of other notes in here somewhere that shed more light on the situation." It took me a moment to find them. "Okay, here's the information I picked out of other articles. They go back to the time of the building of this house. It seems that, at some time early in the 1900s, Rupert decided to build a more substantial place here at Charlotte Cove. His indecision about what he wanted made it impossible for builders to quote, or start construction. By the time he settled on a design, World War I had started and materials became scarce. This impacted construction of the house, and the associated delays resulted in completion of the basic part taking until late in 1919."

"Whoever the successful builder was – I won't say 'lucky' builder – he must have been thoroughly sick of Rupert by the time construction ended. I imagine that, if Rupert were so difficult to pin down on a design, he would be even worse when overseeing construction."

"You might be right about that. Anyway, he didn't waste any time moving his family into the new house. Gwendolyn already was ill. Rupert's thinking was that, by moving the family permanently to Charlotte Cove, Gwendolyn's health might benefit from exposure to the sea air. The family moved into the house at the beginning of 1920."

"Christ, Anthea, she had barely settled into the place before she disappeared. Those other articles tend to suggest her health continued to deteriorate rather than improve. I wonder what medical attention she received. Even at that time, there were no doctors in the village, and it doesn't sound as though it was an easy thing to transport Gwendolyn elsewhere for treatment. I can't understand, if she was so ill – so far gone – why they didn't admit her to a care facility; to a hospital or a sanatorium. That's what usually happened in such cases back then."

That's a good point Zanne raised, and I took a moment to consider it before commenting. "Perhaps it wasn't a good look in the upper echelons of society for people to see your wife in such condition. What I'm trying to say is, perhaps Rupert wanted to hide her condition, rather than have the public aware of it. He seems to be all about image, and I doubt Gwendolyn's condition would do much for his image at that time." Zanne nodded her agreement as I spoke.

"You might be right. That might also have figured in the move to Charlotte Cove; an isolated seaside village with a small closed community. We still don't know whether Rupert spent his time here at the house, or if he was dashing about taking care of his other interests."

"Well, I think I might have found something that sheds some light on that. It seems that, soon after the family took up permanent residence here, Rupert acquired a substantial parcel of land further along the beach. It's where the fishermen's wharves are now. As far as I can make out, a few boats based in this area were trying to eke out a living in the fishing industry. Rupert built that wharf complex and entered into contractual arrangements with the existing skippers. The way the complex operated opened the door for other boats to enter the industry and make Charlotte Cove their home port."

"If that's … what … was … happening," Zanne began slowly, "Then it is likely he based himself here during that period of Gwendolyn's illness. I can't imagine him running off to somewhere else while trying to establish his new venture. Maybe I should give him a mental apology for having misjudged him. I was sure he would have found something urgent requiring him to be at his pastoral property or in Sydney; anywhere but at home dealing with Gwendolyn's condition. Has the historical society provided all of the copies of the material we requested, or is there more to come?"

"I'm not sure what you requested. Quite a few came through last night, but I have a feeling we might be waiting for a few more." Right on cue, my computer pinged, announcing the arrival of another email. "More copies have arrived," I announced as I checked my inbox. For the next few minutes, we waited as the printer spat out the latest attachments.

"Oh, this is interesting," I squeaked as I took a quick glance at the first copy off the printer. "It records more comments from the neighbours about Gwendolyn's behaviour. The article hasn't reproduced well, but it's important. It claims that, on those good days when they took Gwendolyn outside, if nobody watched her, she would wander around talking to herself. It was…"

"Yes, we know that," Zanne said impatiently. "What was it about the article you thought was important?"

"As I was about to say when you interrupted, it was when Gwendolyn screamed and shouted about being held captive that people became alarmed, and suspected her mind was completely gone."

"Oh, I see what you mean. Was that down to her dementia?"

Before I could offer an opinion, another email arrived; another copy from the historical society. I sent it to the printer, but gave Zanne an overview of its content by reading from my screen. "I think it's about the day Gwendolyn went missing. Listen to this," I said, my excitement raising my voice a couple of octaves. "On that particular day, just before lunch, Rupert loaded onto a wagon, the nurse and her assistant, the children, and a large hamper, and drove to the beach. He left everyone at the beach, telling them he was going to the wharf complex to catch up on paperwork. He was to collect them at three o'clock to take them home."

"I can't see how this story is going to have a happy ending. Come on; get on with it. Let's get it over and done with."

"We already know it didn't have a happy ending. Nevertheless, here is what the rest of the article says. In the event, Rupert was late, and it was four o'clock before he returned to the beach. After they arrived home, everyone was busy. Children needed to bathe and get ready for bed. With the cook previously let go, the nurse had taken over meal preparation. They put Gwendolyn to bed before they left for their picnic at the beach. After they arrived home, nobody had a chance to check on her until the nurse took her a bowl of broth at about six o'clock. Gwendolyn was not in her bed and couldn't be found anywhere in the house or the yard."

"That's a long picnic. Even if he had picked them up on time, it was still a long time to be at the beach. Anyway, what about Gwendolyn's lunch, did they feed her before going off on their picnic, or was she supposed to go without lunch that day? That strikes me as odd."

I looked over at Zanne, expecting her to continue espousing her thoughts, but she didn't until I offered some encouragement. "What is odd? The whole thing is 'odd', if that's the word you want to use to describe it."

"Uhmm…I was thinking about the details provided in the article. If they put Gwendolyn to bed before leaving for the beach, and expected her still to be there in bed at six o'clock when they took her food that evening, how realistic was that? If the article has it right, they expected her to remain in bed for something like seven hours. How is that possible without the aid of something to keep her there?"

"What are you suggesting? Do you think they gave her something to knock her out? You think they drugged her?"

"How else would you make sure someone didn't get out of bed for seven hours?"

"Yeah, but she didn't stay in bed did she? Somehow, during those seven hours she managed to 'disappear'."

"Come on, Anthea. Did she disappear, or was she made to disappear? Did Rupert go to the wharf complex, and did he stay there the whole time? What about his lunch; did he take a cut lunch to work with him, or did he go home for lunch… or for something else he needed to do at home?"

While she spoke, Zanne had stacked together the printouts of all the articles we received from the historical society. "Without checking on my list, I think there still are some articles we haven't received yet. Maybe they'll arrive later today, or more likely they'll be in your inbox tomorrow morning … hopefully."

My stomach rumbled ominously. "Was that yours or mine?" Zanne asked.

"It could have been either or both. We've missed lunchtime by about two hours. I think the sound you heard were my ribs rubbing together. Shall we take a break?" I asked.

Lunch was a subdued affair. The chicken and salad rolls were delicious and quickly dispatched, but conversation was in short supply. We received so much information this morning, it was hard to take it all in and properly sequence it in my mind. The thought of Gwendolyn left in bed for seven hours without any attention upset me, and I became more so at the suggestion that drugs might have been involved. However, the doubt Zanne cast on Rupert's whereabouts during those seven hours rattled me.

No matter how hard I tried to convince myself that the lady probably got out of bed and wandered off by herself, I couldn't shake the possibility that her disappearance might be down to foul play. Of course, that was all speculation. We had nothing suggesting Rupert was anywhere but in his office at the wharf complex attending to paperwork. Nevertheless, try as I might, I couldn't help wondering, and I felt sure the police also might have wondered about it.

Revitalised by food, conversation again flowed freely. "I know we're still waiting for some copies from the historical society, but is there anywhere else we might search for information?" I asked Zanne as we cleaned up after lunch. "With all due respect to you and your journo colleagues of the day, newspapers only print what the public chooses to tell them, along with what little information they manage to extract from the police about their investigation. Is there any way to access the official case files, or whatever they're called, that might provide a fuller picture of what was going on?"

"It's possible. It depends on what happened to them and where they are now, but Gwendolyn's disappearance was sufficiently long ago for the case files to be in the police archives. Let's check the online indexes to see if we get lucky."

Zanne might be talking about some distant planet for all I understood. This was new territory about which I knew nothing. However, I tried looking both excited and intelligent while gesturing for her to get on with looking at whatever it was she thought was relevant. I watched as she pulled her laptop around in front of her and attacked the keyboard. After a few moments of mumbling to herself, I saw her face light up.

"I think we might be in luck. In the state archives' index of police files that cover the period in question, I found an entry that might refer to the police investigation into Gwendolyn's disappearance."

"Okay, that's great. So, what do we do about it? Do we ask them for copies as we did with the historical society?"

"No, it's not that simple with police files, or anything else in the archives. If we do it from here, we have to put in a formal request and then wait for them to tell us how many pages are involved and what it will cost to have them copied. The problem with that is, it takes time, can be expensive, and we could end up paying for a lot of useless rubbish."

"...And to think, for a moment, you had me excited. Okay, so it's not easy, but how do we go about getting a look at what's in those files and ordering copies of only what we want?"

"The most logical approach would be to go to the archives and have a look. That way we can print out what we want and ignore the rest of it. What's on your calendar for the next few days, anything that can't be ignored?"

"My hermit -like existence doesn't lead to a full calendar. The only thing that might happen is that programming job I mentioned previously might become a reality."

"Leave it with me until tomorrow. I'll give my agent a ring tonight. He wants me to run my eye over the final proofs of the cover of my new book. I should drive down to the city within the next day or two to take care of that. If you have nothing else happening, we could drive down together and schedule a day at the archives. I'll know a bit more after I speak to my agent this evening, but think about it in the meantime. It's a good time for me to give him a call now. I might go and I'll see you in the morning."

Prior to leaving London when my mother became ill, I negotiated to continue working for the IT firm on a contract basis from here in Australia. They send me a bit of work from time to time, which is about as much as I want. However, this Granger research is taking up all my time right now, not to mention all my headspace. I'd be perfectly happy if this potential contract didn't happen. From what they've told me so far, it sounds like a hefty job and not a particularly exciting one. If a trip to the archives were a possibility, anything from the IT firm would have to wait until afterwards.

In a bid to clear my head of the fog that built up during the day, I took myself outside for a wander around the yard. The cool edge to the breeze helped revive me enough to wonder how I might fill in the rest of the evening. As it turned out, it wasn't a problem. By the time I had dinner and a shower, I was ready for bed. I think my eyes closed the moment I hit the pillow. I don't remember anything after turning off the bedside light. This research lark is exhausting.

Chapter 7

In spite of a sound night's sleep, I struggled to get started this morning. For some reason, I had an almost overwhelming reluctance to face the pile of paper from yesterday's research. The prospect of visiting the state archives to search police files for anything to do with Gwendolyn's disappearance is creating mixed feelings. While I want to know what's in those files, we could waste considerable time and find nothing. That has me sitting here this morning, spinning my wheels instead of getting on with anything. I'm telling myself it's because I'm waiting to hear from Zanne but, if I'm honest, I think frustration at my research incompetence is the problem.

After dragging myself into my office, I wondered what to do next. I can't sit around waiting for Zanne to do it all for me. "Do something for God's sake, Anthea; make a start." The empty house made no suggestions so, as my computer booted up, I turned to the most recent printouts. Within seconds, what I had to do was obvious: go back to the newspaper archives for more on the investigation into Gwendolyn's disappearance.

Now that we had a definite date for her disappearance, and filled in the gaps created by the missing newspapers, I needed to follow the investigation as it progressed. I started with the major newspapers. From the most recent article I'd read previously, I moved forward. The printer worked overtime as I produced hard copies of anything relevant. After weeks of articles on the investigation, they stopped. I searched forward for some time, but it seemed the investigation had stalled. Perhaps it became a 'cold case'. Having decided that, I turned my attention to the 'local' regional papers.

While some of their content mirrored the major papers' reports, additional local 'flavour' provided real gems. The sequence of events following the discovery of Gwendolyn's disappearance made interesting reading. All those in the house assisted with a search of the grounds, which produced no sign of Gwendolyn.

Although it was becoming dark, the men of the village helped search the surrounding woods by lantern light.

I hadn't progressed too far with the regional newspaper archives when Zanne arrived. "Here are the printouts from this morning searches. I'm still working on the regional papers. You might read those printouts while I continue searching," I suggested.

"Yes, I could do that, but I'd much rather you told me what you've found. Have you come across anything exciting, anything we didn't know before?"

I gave her a potted version of the searching and interviewing that went on immediately after Gwendolyn was reported missing. Nothing in my overview was new or exciting, so Zanne turned her attention to reading the printouts. She had barely started when I interrupted her.

With still no sign of Gwendolyn next morning, Rupert notified the police. By mid-morning, an intensive full-scale search was underway. "Listen to this," I said. "In spite of all the men in the village at that time searching the woods and everywhere else by lantern light all night, Gwendolyn was never found. The police arrived next day to take over the search but had no success either. After a number of days, the police, convinced Gwendolyn had met with foul play, stepped up their questioning of Rupert and his neighbours."

"That's to be expected. What else could they do?"

I continued with paraphrasing articles. "With no trace of the woman in the immediate environs, they widened the search area. Although the search continued for several days, there was no sign of Gwendolyn. It appears that, while the search continued, some of the police concentrated on interviewing people. They interviewed just about everybody in Charlotte Cove. According to this article, consensus throughout the community was that Gwendolyn, after being ill for some time, had lost her mind, and was prone to wandering off when no one was around. The only shadow of doubt was caused by those statements by of the neighbours about hearing Gwendolyn calling for help because she was being held captive in the house."

"Yeah, we already knew some of that, although that bit about her being 'held captive' is interesting," Zanne said.

"Oh, listen to this. Here's the gist of it. The day after Gwendolyn disappeared, the nurse's young assistant was let go because, now that Gwendolyn was gone, the nurse would have ample time to manage the household and look after the children be herself, as the children at home were now quite self-sufficient."

"Rupert didn't waste any time did he? It's obvious he wasn't expecting Gwendolyn to reappear. What about the nurse; was she in on the whole thing as well? Otherwise, I can't imagine her being too happy about finding herself lumbered with having to do everything."

"Aah...this might be interesting," I said, and was aware of the excited edge to my voice. "This article claims the police again widened their search area to investigate all of the mineshafts in the area. What mineshafts and where are they? Was there mining in this area at some time? It doesn't look like mining country, and I haven't seen any evidence of it around here."

"Sorry, I wasn't listening. What are you on about?" I noticed Zanne had cranked up her computer and now focused intently on the screen. I tried again.

"This article talks about them searching the old mine shafts in the woods and talking to the hermit who lived there. What mineshafts...? There's nothing to mine in this area. This area's geology doesn't suggest it might be good for mining... and that hermit sounds intriguing." I had to stop myself wandering off on a tangent as the thought of trying to find out more about the hermit intruded.

"They did try mining here. My old mate, Frank, told me about it. Some bloke supposedly found gold back there in the hilly part of the woods. Hopefuls flooded into the place and sunk shafts everywhere. Of course, there was no gold. It was a ruse to lure miners away from where gold was found about thirty miles from here. Frank mentioned the old hermit too. Now, what did he say about him? I remember. He was a latecomer who arrived as most miners were packing up to abandon the place. The hermit stayed on, out there alone for some time before disappearing one day. It seems nobody knew much about him, or exactly when he left, and nobody made a fuss when he no longer was there."

"That hermit, was he from around here?"

"Not that I'm aware of, but that doesn't mean he wasn't. I don't know too much it. Mining only came up as part of a different conversation. If mining did occur around here, it wasn't too successful. I think we should ask Frank Kane about it. If it did happen, and if there were a hermit, he will have heard something about it."

Zanne didn't have to suggest asking Frank Kane for information. It already was in my notebook and imprinted on my mind as something to do at first opportunity.

"Are there any meetings with Frank planned for the immediate future? I'm wondering if I shouldn't go to the beach and wander around until I see some old bloke fishing off the beach."

"Why on earth would you do that, and then what would you do anyway?"

"I would go up and ask him if he were Frank Kane, introduce myself, and hopefully establish some sort of rapport with the bloke. Who knows, we might end up having coffee together. You'd be invited to join us of course."

"Very funny; as a matter of fact, I'm inviting you to lunch at my place tomorrow. Frank will be joining us at twelve o'clock. Do you think you'll be able to come?"

"What were you so engrossed in when I interrupted you to talk about mining?"

"It was an interview with a builder engaged to build the conservatory. I wouldn't say he was a fan of Rupert's. Work started on the conservatory, and the foundations were poured. The workers arrived to pour the slab for it the morning after Gwendolyn disappeared. When they became aware of what happened, they wanted to leave and not return to the site until things settled down." Zanne was paraphrasing from the newspaper article. "Rupert would have none of it. He insisted work continue on schedule, and that the floor be poured that day as planned. They poured the floor as instructed, but felt their presence on site inappropriate. As soon as they finished the pour, they left and did not return the next day."

"That doesn't make any sense. How could pouring the conservatory floor be so important on the morning after his wife went missing? Unless… Why was he so insistent it happen right then – that morning?" My mind sailed into murky waters and I didn't like where it was taking me. However, I had to admit that stage of the conservatory construction offered an ideal place to get rid of a body. "Does it say any more about the conservatory floor anywhere else? After those comments by the builder, the police must have questioned Rupert about it."

Zanne shook her head distractedly as she read something on her screen. "Hmm, it says the police questioned Rupert several times. It doesn't make specific mention of the conservatory, although I think you're right. They would have plenty of questions for him about it. The newspaper's assessment of the investigation generally was that Rupert was likely to be charged with Gwendolyn's murder." Zanne's voice increased in volume as she read the article. "How can they charge him with murder? They don't have a body or any evidence of foul play," she snorted indignantly.

We found more than I expected this morning. One day, I might research more about those previous owners, but for now, I had enough to come to terms with. As we ate a late lunch, we shared our assumptions about Gwendolyn's fate. Although Zanne wasn't so certain, to me, her fate seemed obvious. "As much as I hate the thought of it, I believe she is buried under the floor of my conservatory. Why else would Rupert be so insistent about pouring the floor that day? Perhaps he hadn't spent the afternoon at his office, not the whole time anyway."

Zanne argued that my assumption was based on supposition and coincidence, but no real evidence. In spite of refuting my argument, she didn't suggest any alternatives. Not long after lunch, Zanne left to deal with something to do with the release of her latest book.

I took care of a few domestic chores after she left, but I wanted to know more. There was more to the story of Gwendolyn's disappearance. I want to know everything about it…and my computer kept beckoning me back to it. I am weak. I caved in and went back to the newspaper archives – just to check if there was anything more about the conservatory ... or so I told myself. There wasn't. Somehow, I managed to shut my computer down, and contented myself for the remainder of the evening with sorting and filing the pile of printouts accumulated today.

This morning, I bounded out of bed with a renewed enthusiasm missing for much of this week. Sometime between climbing into bed and falling asleep last night, a few thoughts about additional research occurred to me. They had me eager to make a start. Zanne's movements today were unclear. However, having invited Frank Kane and me to lunch, I guessed she would be busy at home this morning and I wouldn't see her until lunchtime. I wasted no time completing my morning routine, before making a beeline for my office.

My first port of call again would be the newspaper archives. Last thing yesterday, we became so engrossed in discussing the few details we've uncovered, that it cut short our search. It took me a few moments to find it, but I managed to navigate through to the last article Zanne found that suggested the police had Rupert Granger targeted for the disappearance of his wife. The big question that came to me last night was what happened after that.

With fresh eyes and great care, I inched my way through the subsequent copies of the newspapers. I came across several short articles, no more than one or two brief paragraphs, that didn't tell me anything or progress my quest for information. The police still questioned people, some of whom were questioned previously. Rupert received special attention. It seems he was questioned several more times, and remained their prime suspect. The next article I found suggested an arrest was imminent, and the police intimated this might be as early as within the next day or two.

The newspaper didn't spoil the suspense in any way. Not surprisingly perhaps, the police hadn't divulged any names. Whom they planned to arrest remained a mystery until the newspaper from a couple of days later. While it didn't tell me the name of the person, it gave clear indication of the police's thinking on the matter.

I jumped; suddenly Zanne was peering over my shoulder. "What are you doing here? Shouldn't you be home preparing something wonderful for our lunch?"

"I've done that. That's why I was a bit late arriving. However, I will go home before lunchtime to make sure everything is ready. Let's have a coffee and, while we're about it, draw up a list of questions we want to put to Frank."

"If Frank thinks he's coming for a friendly meal, will being bombarded with questions upset him?"

"Not if we approach it correctly. It needs to be light and chatty until he feels comfortable around you. Then, we can start slipping in our questions."

The list of questions was short. If you don't know what there is to know, you don't know what to ask. In our case, the list comprised a couple of big general questions, but nothing else. I read the questions. "The list doesn't look too impressive at this stage, but I'm hoping that whatever Frank tells us might lead us to more detailed questions that take us to the heart of things."

As Zanne assured me there still was plenty of time before she needed to leave, we went back to my office and the newspaper archives. After progressing through only one or two editions of the paper, I let out a yelp that startled me as well as Zanne.

"What … What…? Come on; don't keep me in suspense after carrying on like that. Please make it something positive. I keep adding questions to our list. So far, everything we read produces more questions." She must have noticed my concern. "Oh, I don't mean more questions for Frank; questions whose answers won't come from anyone in the village. So, what have you found?"

"Okay, although there is no mention of finding a body, at about the time the police were preparing to charge Rupert, the family vanished."

"Not another vanishing act…?"

"After the police widened their inquiries, a farmer on the outskirts of the next town reported seeing a wagon carrying several people race past his farm at around midnight on the night Rupert supposedly absconded. Foxes were raiding the farmer's henhouse. On the night in question, he was out shooting the pests. It was quite dark when the wagon went past. Although he couldn't be sure who was on board, he did recognise the wagon as Rupert's."

"He got away with it…! The sly old bugger… And I suppose he took the nurse with him."

"It doesn't say anything about anyone other than Rupert, but I suspect that was the case. I'll try to find another article about Rupert's legging it to see if it provides more information. If he left the nurse and his daughters behind, I'm sure it would have made the papers." I didn't get a chance to do any further research. Zanne wanted to talk.

We spent some time discussing – maybe that should be 'speculating' – on where Rupert might have gone. Rupert's sons in England came up during our discussions. Had they been notified of their mother's disappearance? Were they hurrying home to Charlotte Cove when Rupert also vanished? A casual glance at the clock sent Zanne scurrying home.

After she left, I returned to the newspaper archives. I added several more printouts to the pile before checking the time again. It was a few minutes before twelve o'clock. I logged off and bolted for Zanne's place. About five minutes after I arrived, Frank wandered up from the beach. Zanne heard the gate squeak and went out to meet him while I took the tray loaded with glasses and a jug of iced tea out onto her patio.

It was pleasant outside. The sea breeze had come up and its briny scent competed with the aroma of the casserole in the oven. I hadn't felt hungry, but that casserole had my tastebuds' attention. I was sure my stomach would start rumbling at any moment. My presence didn't seem to faze Frank in any way. I think Zanne's assessment of him might be a bit off the mark. He seemed interested in me… Well, not in me as such, as in me is the new owner of *Wellsprings. I*t felt safe to ease into our question-and-answer time. I deliberately chose a not too specific question as a starter.

"Frank, although I came to Charlotte Cove often as I was growing up, I don't know much about the place, the community, or my house. Soon after I arrived this time, I heard of an incident that happened at the house. Since then, Zanne and I discovered that incident involved a Granger wife's disappearance in 1920. Over the years, have you heard anything that helps explain the reputation the house has acquired, or about the disappearance of Gwendolyn Granger?"

"I spoke to Zanne about the woman. It was before my time, but I remember my father mentioning it a couple of times while banging on about the history of the place. Now that I've given it more thought, there might have been more than one incident. I can't be sure, and I don't remember ever hearing exactly what happened, but there was something about two women. I think that's right, and that they both had something to do with your house."

I scratched a few words in my notebook and tried looking fascinated by what he said. Frank explained about his father's exercise books. "As he got on a bit, dad developed something of a fixation about recording the history of Charlotte Cove. It probably started because of questions I used to ask him about various people and things that supposedly happened here. He always said, when the old folk were gone, the history of the place would be gone too. There is no order to the stuff he wrote down. He just wrote something when he remembered it, or when I asked him a question that brought something to mind."

"Has he recorded much of the history?" I asked, in the hope that he would give me an estimation of how many books his father's scribblings entailed.

"Oh, miles of it; there are at least a couple of boxes full of those exercise books. All covered in dust, and looking a bit tatty now."

"What are you planning to do with those exercise books, Frank? There must be a wealth of information in them. If something happens to you or your cottage burns down, all that history will be lost anyway." What Zanne said sounded innocuous enough, but I couldn't help wonder whether, as a writer, there was another agenda behind it.

Frank turned to face me. He rubbed a hand across his stubbly chin. He appeared to be trying to summon some long buried memory. "Returning to your questions about the house, I knew

Edwina Granger reasonably well. She was a few years older than I, but we sort of belong to the same Charlotte Cove generation. She lived in that house alone for a long time, but seemed happy enough with the way things were. I heard some talk amongst the oldies a few times about her having a terrible time growing up. I don't know that I ever heard what those 'terrible times' were."

"Are you suggesting Edwina might have been connected in some way with those incidents involving the house?" I couldn't imagine Aunt Eddie being involved in anything scandalous. I liked the old lady and we got on well, but she was from a different era. She could be quite prim and severe when it suited her. Frank rushed in to dispel any concerns I might have.

"No, I don't think there was anything like that. Mind you, people around here did think her a bit strange; never marrying and living in the big old house all by herself. She often came down to the beach. If we ran into one another there, we parked ourselves on the rocks and chatted – sometimes for quite a while. Don't go reading anything into that. I never married either, so there was nothing more to it than two old single people chatting about nothing in particular."

I struggled to stifle a smile as an image of my rather 'proper' Aunt Eddie perched on a rock at the beach with Frank filled my mind. Zanne announced that lunch would be ready in a few minutes. I thought this an appropriate time to introduce my next question. "Frank, perhaps you can explain something. I read there were mineshafts somewhere in this area. Was there mining at Charlotte Cove at some time in the past?" Although Zanne answered this for me yesterday, I thought it a good way to lead into wider discussion of the subject.

"Oh aye, lass, you could say there was, but it happened a long time ago. However, I wouldn't say mining got going in this area, although I believe quite a few blokes rushed here to try their luck."

"I can't believe people thought there was anything to mine around here. From what I've seen of Charlotte Cove, nowhere looks as though it has mining potential. What were they chasing?"

"Gold…; it was gold of course. There hadn't been a decent gold rush for a while and, when word leaked out there'd been a find in this area, they flocked to the place. The whole thing was short lived though. But, in the short time the rush lasted, they managed to sink shafts all over the place. Someone 'salted' the place beforehand. Anyway, it didn't take them long to work out the truth, and they moved on. A few stragglers remained for a while, but they soon gave up and left too."

"What do you mean by 'salted'? Are you suggesting the miners were tricked?"

"That's about the size of it. Someone probably scattered a few flecks of gold around the place, and then let slip about the location of a new gold find. The only gold taken out of the area was the bit they used to salt the place to give credibility to the story of a new goldfield."

"I'm amazed people would be so gullible. Where was this supposed goldfield, and how far from the village were those mineshafts?"

"In behind your place… Oh, you can't see them from your place, unless maybe from an upstairs window. I think the trees in the scrub behind the house are too tall. Anyway, from your house, to get to this so-called minefield, you walk straight through the scrub. At first, it's quite thick but, after a while, it opens up onto stony, rubbly country leading up to the hill. That's the area where they dug all the shafts."

Zanne shook her head gently as Frank finished his story. "What's this hill you're talking about, Frank? I haven't seen any hills in this area. How far away was it? From your story, I thought this mining was fairly close to Anthea's house."

"Yeah, there's a hill in the back there, in that area I was telling you about. You probably can't see the hill either from Anthea's house." Frank chuckled before continuing. "When I say it's a 'hill', it might be a bit of an exaggeration. They refer to it as a hill, but it's really more like a bit of a lump on the countryside. Still, Tremaine's Bluff is considered a hill, and is probably the only thing that passes for a hill around here."

"Tremaine's Bluff, eh? Never heard of it. Just goes to show, you learn something new every day." With that, Zanne stood up and announced she was going to dish up lunch.

I was intrigued by Frank's story, and fascinated to think there was so much happened so close to my house that I might never have known about. "Have you ever been to that mine site to see those shafts?" The idea forming in the back of my mind was that a pleasant way to spend a Sunday afternoon might be to take a hike to the mineshafts.

"Oh yes, many times – when I was younger of course. Me and my mates from the village often went out there. We would sneak through the scrub beside your place. Go around the back, and then head straight through to where they used to mine. During school holidays and the like, we'd spend all day out there."

"What was out there for you to do all day? I had the impression mineshafts pockmarked the whole place. Was it safe to be there?"

"Your impression is probably spot-on. No, it probably wasn't safe to be out there. Our parents didn't think so anyway. They banned us from going out to the mine site. It didn't stop us though. Doing something we were not supposed to just added to the enjoyment. It wasn't like we got up to anything dangerous. We just sat around and talked, told yarns, had an illegal smoke or two, and generally just did what lads do when they get together. Of course, I haven't been out there for years, but I don't imagine it's changed much."

My questioning came to a halt when Zanne called us to the table. The casserole that had my mouth watering earlier didn't disappoint. After a lunch of casserole, fresh bread rolls, fruit and coffee, I felt like a carpet snake looking for somewhere to hibernate. It also was edging past Frank's normal time for an afternoon nap. As soon as I'd helped Zanne clear away, I drove Frank back to his cottage before heading home.

Frank has the right idea, I told myself as I opened the front door. Within ten minutes, I was revelling in the luxury of a short afternoon nap. It was great, but I woke up about an hour later with a thick head and feeling absolutely useless for the rest of the day.

Chapter 8

Despite the afternoon snooze yesterday and the sleep of the dead all night, I slept late this morning. Although awake, my eyelashes refused to untangle themselves so my eyes could open. In those languid minutes of being aware without being awake, my mind drifted back to the lazy day I spent yesterday. It revisited my discussions with Frank Kane. Then, like a blow from Thor's hammer a thought struck me. Now I was fully awake.

It occurred to me that, in all of my discussions with Frank, particularly those about mining in the area, I had forgotten to ask him about the hermit. That caused a wry smile; so much for not going off on any tangents, and not researching the hermit. Still, the hermit might be important. He was mentioned in articles about the investigation into Gwendolyn's disappearance. Maybe if I went to the beach, I might accidentally run into Frank and have opportunity to ask him about that hermit.

"For goodness sake, Anthea, get real," I chastised myself aloud. "You don't even know what time Frank goes to the beach to fish." There's no point lying here in bed talking to myself. It makes more sense to get up and do something practical.

The idea of going to the beach first thing this morning stuck with me while I made breakfast. Perhaps I should think about doing something, embarking on some sort of fitness regime. All this sitting in front of computers and shuffling paper around can't be doing me any good. I need to give that some hard thought, I told myself, but maybe leave it until after we are done with all this research.

Instead of getting too serious about anything fitness related, after breakfast I returned to my office and my computer. Check your emails first before you think about more research, I told myself. That presented the first problem of the day. There was an email from the IT firm that contracts me to work for them. They had mentioned the possibility of a contract for some work for an existing client. At the time, there was nothing definite, and their earlier email to me was to check that I would be available if the client decided to go ahead with the work. The client said yes, and the firm was checking I was still available.

An IT contract is not what I want this time. I am sufficiently well-off not to need to work, but I have no idea what it's going to cost to get this house to a liveable standard again. Besides, in the future, when my research is finished, I might be happy to have some occasional work. Best not to burn any bridges yet, I decided, and sent off a reply confirming my availability. I felt comfortable. There was usually a delay of a week or two before a brief arrived for me to start work on a job.

With no other emails demanding immediate attention, I logged out and headed for the National Library's *Trove* website. It took me a while to navigate to where I was when I last logged off this site. The site was slow to load, giving me time to think about what I wanted to find. The short answer is 'everything', but I don't think typing that into the search criteria will help. I settled for typing 'Gwendolyn Granger' into the search box and sent Trove off to do its thing. The web, my ISP, or whatever, was working at the rate of about a mile a month this morning.

I left it spinning its wheels and took myself for a wander out into the fresh morning air. Not knowing exactly what I wanted to search for today, I found it hard to focus. Procrastination came easily as I wandered around, noting what was in flower, and the general state of the plants in the yard. But that can only waste so much time no matter how dedicated to procrastination you might be. I forced myself to the back door, with the intention of going back to my office and settling down to some serious research.

If only life was that simple. Instead of going directly to my office, I detoured into the conservatory, and was wandering through it when the thought hit me. The builder's report of Rupert's insistence on pouring the conservatory floor on the morning after Gwendolyn's disappearance bobbed to the front of my mind. I felt cold all over. My pulse rate increased. As I raced back to the doorway, my breathing became shallow. By the time I left the room, I was hyperventilating. I stepped out through the doorway and stood in the hallway trying to control my breathing.

"Get a grip," I yelled at the universe. "What is wrong with you, Anthea?" But, I knew what was wrong with me. It was the thought that Gwendolyn's body might be buried somewhere beneath the floor of that conservatory. In spite of Zanne's scepticism, and common sense, I couldn't shake the thought that this might be where Rupert hid her. It was an ideal place. A place coincidentally available just when he needed it. Why else would he insist the floor be poured that day? A caring husband would be so concerned by the disappearance of his wife, he wouldn't give a damn about the conservatory.

What was I going to do about the conservatory? There didn't seem to be too many options. I could leave it in its current derelict state, close it up and never go in there again. That didn't seem like much of a solution but, short of jackhammering up the floor, I don't know how else I might overcome my conviction about what lies beneath it.

A sound made me jump. I spun around. I'm sure I cleared the floor by at least a metre before landing again with my pulse rate considerably elevated. "Are you all right? You look as white as a ghost." Zanne's concern was obvious.

"That's because you startled me."

"N-o-o, you looked like that when I arrived. That's why I rushed down to see what was wrong. Now, stop playing silly buggers and tell me what is wrong."

"I've told you, nothing is wrong. I was standing here thinking about what to do with the conservatory when you rushed up and startled me."

"S-o-o, what have you decided?"

"Eh…? Oh, I see. You arrived too soon. I haven't come up with any ideas yet."

"Of course you haven't….And you weren't standing out here because you were worried about what might be under the floor in there, were you? Come on; let's have a go at being realistic for a while. What research are we doing today?"

"I don't know that we're going to get much done at all. Everything is slow this morning. That's why I was wandering around. I gave it something to search for, but it took so long I decided to go for a walk." Zanne nodded her agreement but everything about her shrieked disbelief.

Back in my office, sometime during my absence, Trove had finished it search. There were quite a few hits, but the only article

I hadn't read already was the most recent one. I navigated to it, and took the dose of disappointment it delivered as best I could. It was short and tucked away on page four of an edition dated about three months after Gwendolyn's disappearance.

The article wasn't worthy of more prominence than it received. All it said was that Gwendolyn's disappearance remained unsolved. The investigation, now designated a cold case, would see no further action unless new evidence turned up. I printed it anyway and added it to the ever-growing pile of paper. As Zanne seemed preoccupied with her notes from yesterday's conversation with Frank, I decided to change the search criteria and send Trove off to hunt down other articles.

In response to my request for anything on Tremaine's Bluff, it came back with one hit from a metropolitan newspaper. The brief article in the 'Regional News' section reported a fossicker's find of gold at Tremaine's Bluff led to something of a gold rush as miners eager to try their luck flooded into the area. Not a particularly exciting article, but perhaps the other three hits from regional newspapers might have something more to offer. Between them, they told virtually the same story as Frank Kane gave us yesterday. They outlined how salting of Tremaine's Bluff successfully lured prospectors from the real goldfield some distance away. One article outlined how those who rushed to Tremaine's Bluff suffered disappointment, and in many cases, the prospect of financial ruin. Although, the final article reported the remaining stragglers from the gold rush preparing leave, it made no mention of the hermit.

Until coffee time, we both tried our luck searching on any criteria we thought remotely likely to produce information useful to our research. That proved a waste of time. My computer pinged, announcing the arrival of a new email. I thought I'd see who it was from before going to make coffee. I received a surprise.

It was from the historical society, and it roused my curiosity. We had all the scanned copies we asked for, but there was an attachment. I couldn't resist finding out what they'd sent. It seems that, while working on other stuff, the volunteers came across something they thought relevant to my research. Free of charge, they scanned the item and emailed it.

"Zanne, listen to this." On opening the attachment, I couldn't believe our luck. "The historical society sent this article. It begins with stuff we already know about the police interviewing Rupert several times. Then, it goes on to claim there now exists some doubt about whether Rupert spent that afternoon in his office at the wharf complex as he claimed. It talks about the police's increased liking for Rupert as instrumental in some way in Gwendolyn's disappearance. Then comes the interesting bit. It claims that *the house at Charlotte Cove now stands empty as Rupert, his children and a household staff member, have vanished.* It finishes with the comment that the police are waiting to complete their investigation of a last few possibilities in their search for bodies before taking their findings to the coroner."

"Yes…! Now we know who was on that wagon with Rupert the night he disappeared. It still leaves the question of where he went. Unless they went to some obscure place on the other side of the continent, they would be looking over their shoulders until someone recognised them and turned them in to the police."

"What about the Northern Territory, would that be a good place to try losing yourself?" I thought about the Territory and some of its more remote regions. "They might have to put up with harsh conditions. N-o-o, maybe not. The Northern Territory doesn't fit with my image of Rupert and his lifestyle."

"I suppose they could have gone overseas. I don't know where they would go or how they got out of the country, but it's a possibility. If I were writing a situation such as this in one of my novels, I'd have them heading overseas, not trying to hide out in Australia. I'm not sure how I'd have them leave the country, not if it was to sound believable."

At that point, another new email arrived. It was from the IT firm advising they would be forwarding the project details in a couple of days. Damn! I hadn't heard any more about Zanne's suggested a trip to the State archives. Maybe I should check the current situation so I can plan my life accordingly. That seems like a good conversation for over coffee.

Once we settled with our coffees, I asked about the trip to the archives. "Didn't I tell you about that? No, obviously not, or you wouldn't be asking about it. I thought I would spend an hour of so with my agent, and then we would spend the rest of the day at the archives. However, that's all changed. I still need to meet with my agent and publisher, but my agent arranged a couple of appearances at local bookstores around the same time. The bookstores are in smaller rural towns outside the city. Anyway, the upshot of all that is, what I planned as two nights and a day in the city, will now have me away from Charlotte Cove all week."

I groaned. "Sorry, I didn't mean to sound like that. I know you do have a life and these things are an important part of it. I was disappointed at the prospect of no research happening while you are away for the week. What's the schedule for all this?"

"Let's see; I'll spend Sunday night in the city, have meetings on Monday, cool my heels in the city for most of Tuesday, before driving to the first town for my appearances on Wednesday. I have appearances during the day and again in the evening, so I'll spend the night in that town and drive to the next place the following morning. The same arrangement applies for Thursday in the second town, and then I drive home on Friday. Anyway, aren't you going to be too busy with your IT project to worry about research while I'm away?"

"Yes, as it turns out, I'll have the project details by the end of the week. That gives us about three more days of research before you leave, but I suppose that depends on how busy you are beforehand."

"Not busy at all; it doesn't take long to throw some clothes in a bag and head out. It just occurred to me that, on Tuesday when I'm stuck in the city, I could spend the day at the State archives. They are on my way to that first town. If I leave the archives around four o'clock, I'll be checking into my motel for the night by a bit after five o'clock. I'll bring back whatever case files there are on Gwendolyn's disappearance."

"Good thinking; so what do we look at in the days before you leave?"

"I don't know. Is there anything more we can do in relation to Rupert and Gwendolyn's disappearances?"

"No, I don't think so; at least not until we see the case files. One thing is curious though. There's been no mention of the couple's sons in anything we've read so far. Did they know anything of what was happening here at home? Did they know about Gwendolyn, and that Rupert and the others also planned to disappear? Not being a parent myself, I don't pretend to know how such people think or behave. However, I have been a child and, if something like this happened to my parent, I would be on my way home in a blink."

"I see what you mean. Perhaps they did come home. The fact that we haven't found anything to confirm it doesn't mean it didn't happen. However, I have to admit, with Gwendolyn's and then Rupert's disappearances making it into the major newspapers, it would be hard for the sons to return without someone noticing. Okay, over the next few days, let's concentrate on… who was the next bloke to own this place?" Zanne grabbed the family history chart from the end of the table. "Ah yes, Wilfred; let's see what we can dig up on him."

Back in my office, I unrolled family tree chart on the table and anchored its corners with books to keep it flat. Once Zanne was at her computer, I refreshed our memories about Wilfred. "Wilfred Prendergast Granger, first child and eldest son of Rupert and Gwendolyn, born at the beginning of 1892, and exiled in England for a lot of years."

"I remember now. Did we find out what he studied after he finished his schooling? I don't know that it has any bearing, but I thought it might be interesting to know." I churned through my memory banks but found no recollection of Wilfred's chosen career.

"Okay, it doesn't matter. Let's see if we can find when he returned to Australia. It might be worth starting with the regional papers. He might have tried slipping back quietly after the notoriety attaching to his parents' disappearances."

"Do we assume he wasn't here when they disappeared? I'm just trying to work out from what date to start searching."

"Good question; let's assume he was still in England at that time. We start our search from the date Gwendolyn disappeared. We know ownership didn't pass to Wilfred until 1924; search from 1920 to 1924."

For the next half hour, we sat in silence with our eyes glued to our screens before a breakthrough occurred. "Bingo…!" Zanne's yelp made me jump. “I found something about him.” The printer came to life. “I’ll give you a copy of the article.”

The article announced the return to Australia of Wilfred Granger. After many years in England, Mr Granger, currently domiciled at the family’s pastoral property, *Whylara*, intended taking some time to determine the future direction for his life. Zanne and I must’ve reached the end of the article at about the same time. As I opened my mouth to make some derogatory comment, she snorted derisively.

“Do you mind, ‘to determine the future direction for his life’; what a crock. I’ll bet he wrote that for the reporter. He’s planning to enjoy a long bludge. That’s the life he has in mind.”

An article in a different paper dated a couple of days later was interesting. “This one says Mr Granger is unsure how long he will remain at *Whylara* as he is considering returning to his legal career. If this were to occur, it might necessitate moving to the city. So there; apologise to the man for misjudging him. He is not going to sit around and bludge. He is going to resurrect his legal career… in the city. Don’t people living in rural areas require solicitors?”

“I won’t honour that with a reply. Anyway, he didn’t say he was going to resume his career. He was going to think about it. I’ll bet you bludging wins out over going back to work.”

“How cynical you have become. However, we now know he arrived back in Australia in September 1920. There is no mention of him in connection with Charlotte Cove. I checked the date on the last article we have on Gwendolyn’s disappearance. By the time Wilfred returned, her disappearance was a cold file. He would be dependent on others to tell him about all that happened earlier in the year.”

“Strange that he went to *Whylara* on his return, rather than to Charlotte Cove. Does that suggest he knew there was no one here? I would think, if you were away from family for so long, you would rush to be with them again.” Zanne seemed deep in thought as she spoke. I waited, expecting further comment but, when she said nothing more, I move her along.

"I agree it's a bit strange, but let's see if we can find something more about Wilfred that sheds light on the man himself."

Zanne opted to stick with the newspapers archives while I searched family history indexes. I started with the marriage index. There were several Wilfred Grangers on the index. The difficulty was finding the right Wilfred Granger. A search from 1920 onward produced a shortish list of Wilfreds. "Argh… which is the Wilfred Granger I want when I don't know who he married?"

Zanne looked off into the distance for a moment before replying. "It is an assumption that he married in Australia. I know the newspapers don't say he returned with a wife, but he might have returned to England later to marry someone over there."

"Very helpful, thanks for the suggestion. How can there be so many Wilfred Grangers? I wouldn't have thought Wilfred was a common name and the Granger surname even less so."

"Who was the owner of *Wellsprings* after Wilfred? Maybe if you look for his birth, it will give you his mother's name."

Now why haven't I thought of that? Just when I thought I was getting good at this family history research stuff, Zanne points out how little I know. "Thank you for that. It would be Thomas that I'm looking for, but I don't have a likely birthdate. Never mind, as with the marriage, I'll search from 1920 onwards. O-o-h, hang on a minute."

"Eh…? What's up now?

"Any births would be after 1920 – presumably. The births won't be in the index." Zanne's eyebrows shot up in question at my statement. "Because of that one hundred years closure rule you told me about, the births are too recent for the index."

"A-a-h, that's true. Check the births notices in the newspapers."

It came as something of a surprise to find Thomas's birth notice in 1922. Now I had Thomas's birth date and also his mother's name, I now could look for a marriage between Wilfred Granger and Jessica Fitzmaurice. Back to the marriage index and entries for marriages of Wilfred Grangers. I began running the cursor down the list. Towards the end of it, an entry almost jumped off the screen at me. It was for Wilfred P Granger and Jessica Fitzmaurice, which occurred towards the end of 1920.

"God, he didn't waste any time," I exclaimed.

"Who … Wilfred … What's he done?" Zanne asked as she looked over the top of her screen.

"Yeah… I found his marriage; should have continued to the end of the list the first time. Identifying him was easy. Anyway, it was the date of his marriage that shocked me. Wilfred returned to Australia in September 1920, but here he is marrying Jessica Fitzmaurice in December of that year. I think it unlikely he knew her before he went to England. After all, he was only about twelve when they sent him to school there. As he doesn't appear to have returned home then until 1920, when did he meet, woo and propose to the lovely Jessica?"

"Yeah, he does seem to be a fast worker. There is another possibility I suppose. Maybe Jessica also spent time in England. Maybe their relationship began while they were both in England."

"That's a possibility. We don't know anything about Jessica, but she could be another one of the idle rich offspring, all of whom seem to head to England at some stage."

Now armed with a marriage date, Zanne went back to trawling the social columns of the major newspapers. A search on 'Jessica Fitzmaurice' didn't take long to find a hit in the *Sydney Morning Herald*.

"I see what you mean. He was a slick worker, or it was a well-established relationship. I have found an engagement notice for the happy couple in early November. Their marriage on Boxing Day merited several column inches in the social pages. Judging by the write up the marriage received, Jessica couldn't be anything but upper crust. The marriage was in the cathedral, she had no less than five bridesmaids and two junior attendants, and the reception was in a marquee overlooking Sydney Harbour. Jessica's father was Major Hugh Fitzmaurice, and those on the guest list worthy of mention include names I recognise as the Who's Who of Sydney at the time."

While the printer spat out copies of the articles, I busied myself with online ordering of a marriage certificate for Wilfred and Jessica, and a birth certificate for Thomas. If I hadn't learned anything else, I knew Zanne would expect me to look for other children of the marriage to ensure a sound understanding of the family group. I went back to the newspapers' birth notices. This time, armed with a bit more information regarding parents, I searched from 1920 to 1940. Within moments, I had a list of entries.

"Hang on a minute; this can't be right." I tore my eyes away from the screen to look at Zanne. In anticipation of some wild revelation, she looked back with her eyebrows raised almost to her hairline. I returned to my screen and spent a moment or two going over what I found.

"Argh, come on. You can't say things like that and then not tell me what can't be right. What have you found?"

I thought about how to explain it succinctly before replying. "From the title deed, we know Thomas was the next owner of this house after Wilfred. The strange thing about that is, Thomas wasn't Wilfred's eldest son. The couple's first son, Randolph Prendergast Granger, was born in 1921. Thomas, the second son, was born in December 1922. As the eldest son, why didn't Randolph inherit this place?"

Furrows creased Zanne's forehead as she pondered the matter. "I suppose there could be a few reasons why that occurred, but it is strange. Perhaps Randolph fell from favour with his father for some reason and found himself cut out of the will. An alternate situation might be that Wilfred split the inheritance between his two sons. Perhaps Thomas got this place, while Randolph got the pastoral property. Do we know what other children they had?

"It looks like they were all girls. Clara arrived in 1923 and Edwina – that's Aunt Eddie – was born in 1926. There was a stillbirth in 1929, before Bethany arrived 1934. That seems to be all there was."

"Who inherited this house after Thomas?"

"Oh, this is strange as well. After Thomas, Edwina inherits the place. She was his sister. Why did she inherit it?"

"Maybe have a look through the deaths index, see if some of them died somewhere along the line."

While I listened to Zanne, I added the children's names to the family tree. I looked at the generation above Wilfred and Jessica to check I added Rupert and Gwendolyn's children to the chart. That exercise only took a few moments.

The couple had a second son, Michael Prendergast Granger, who was born a couple of years after Wilfred, and then a daughter was born a couple of years later. There was a gap of quite a few years before two more daughters in quick succession followed. Okay, we know about the two youngest daughters. They were the ones who disappeared with their father and the nurse.

It was the second son, Michael, who caught my attention. What happened to Michael? Zanne's suggestion of splitting the property holdings between sons didn't happen in Rupert's day. Wilfred inherited the lot. It was the thought of the transfer of ownership of this house to Wilfred that raised another question. Such a transfer normally would follow the previous owner's death but, if they didn't know where Rupert was, how would they know he died? Something had to trigger an application for probate of Rupert's will, and therein lies another mystery, I suspect.

My family tree looked quite populated since adding a couple of generations' worth of kids. While the temptation was to look for births of Thomas's kids, I managed to restrain myself and stick to the task at hand. I brought up the deaths index and began searching for Wilfred's children, starting with Bethany. I don't know why I started with the last child. My decision was justified within moments.

Bethany only survived a few months. She was born and died in 1934. With only a stillbirth between those of Edwina and Bethany, I decided to move to the beginning of Wilfred's children and look for a death of Randolph. If Randolph died, it would explain how Thomas came to inherit this house. The search took only a few moments. Bugger, there was no death for Randolph.

Another late lunchtime intervened. I was happy to leave my office to do something physical by way of making lunch. It seems we were both 'researched-out' by the time it was ready.

"Do you think we might dine alfresco today?" Zanne asked.

"I can't think of anything better. Let's go and sit under that big ironbark tree. I think I'm coming down with a major dose of 'office fever' and need to be out in the open air for a while."

The afternoon sea breeze had arrived by the time we settled in the shade of the big old tree. For the first few minutes, conversation did not intrude. Although we attacked the food with gusto, it wasn't hunger that kept us quiet. It was the ambience; the sense of being at one with nature. With lunch dispatched in near-record time, neither of us felt inclined to hurry back to my office.

A gentle sea breeze, the birdsong, and the smell of the trees and plants mellowed us into an almost semi-comatose condition. When conversation made a return, it was spasmodic and inconsequential. A long, languid time ensued and, when I finally found the energy and inclination to check my watch, it was after four o'clock. That caused something of a flurry.

In less than ten minutes, Zanne collected her things and was on her way home to deal with various book-related issues, and I was shutting down my computer and tidying my office. For me at least, research was over for today.

Chapter 9

My first task this morning, I decided, was to go through everything we gathered yesterday, enter anything outstanding on the chart, file printouts appropriately, and be ready to dive into researching when Zanne arrived. I took the family tree chart and my file to study them at the kitchen table over breakfast.

After scrutinising the chart, I felt confident everything we knew about the Grangers was on the chart. It struck me that, although names on the tree had increased, we knew little about most of those people. Through our investigation of Gwendolyn's disappearance, I felt we learned quite a bit about that couple, but still didn't 'know' them. Maybe that's how this family history stuff works. You only ever get to know some basic facts about the people.

In the case of Wilfred and Jessica, I'd say we know nothing about them. I was reluctant to pursue more recent generations until I felt we had all there was to know about the previous generations. That helped me focus on what I would do today. I started a list of the information I wanted, and where I might look for it.

By the time Zanne arrived, the length and complexity of my list surprised me. We agreed Zanne would continue searching newspaper articles while I started with the births, deaths and marriages indexes. The atmosphere in the office seemed subdued today. Zanne didn't appear offside in any way, and I felt fine. Perhaps we both suffered research overload.

Before starting today's research, I decided on a cursory check of my inbox. The two certificates ordered yesterday for Wilfred and Jessica had arrived overnight. I printed them. There was an age difference of several years between the couple. Wilfred was born in 1892. From the marriage certificate, I calculated Jessica's birthdate as 1899. She was just twenty-one when they married.

As I transcribed information from the certificates onto the chart, something caught my eye. The couple's last child, Bethany, arrived in 1934. Jessica, about thirty-five at the time, was still a young woman in terms of childbearing age. Since they were prolific breeders throughout their fourteen-year marriage until then, it struck me as odd that no further children arrived in spite of Jessica's young age.

That sent me back to the newspaper births notices. Had I missed a child – some children – in yesterday's search? I was reasonably confident I hadn't, but was prepared to admit fallibility. I spared myself that embarrassment. No further births for the couple appeared. For the next minute or so, I sat staring into the distance in the hope that my limited knowledge of family history research might miraculously indicate what to do next.

Although it was slow, inspiration eventually arrived. One reason for no more children might be that something happened to Jessica. As I pondered what that might be, through the fog of my thinking, I Zanne murmured, "I might have something here."

She paused for a moment before enlightening me. "In the social pages, I found entries for when both Randolph and Thomas went to boarding school in England. The family must've been doing all right. It was at the height of the depression, but Wilfred could afford to send them overseas and pay what I imagine were expensive school fees."

I nodded and went to ask a question, but Zanne continued speaking. "I don't think the boys merited mention in the social columns because of their Granger surname. In both cases, the emphasis of the article is on the fact that they are the grandsons of *Sir* Hugh Fitzmaurice. It appears that, sometime between when Jessica married and Bethany was born, Major Hugh received his gong. I don't know about its impact, but I suspect his father-in-law receiving a knighthood might have been of some consequence to Wilfred. There's nothing I can put my finger on, but I feel that Wilfred had definite designs on entering the upper echelons of Sydney society. I will try to find when Hugh was knighted."

Zanne resumed attacking her keyboard. I'd forgotten the question I intended to ask. It took me a moment or two to reconnect with the train of thought. What might have happened to Jessica? I could mention it to Zanne, but I was loath to interrupt whatever she was doing. Okay, another reason there were no more children was if she died.

Back on the deaths index site, I thought about a possible death date for Jessica. Perhaps she died in childbirth with Bethany, or soon after. That gives me 1934 as a starting point. In the search criteria field, I typed in Jessica's name and an event date range from 1934 to 1944. That returned only one entry.

Jessica died midway through 1940. Only in her early forties, she was still a young woman. Without hesitation, I ordered Jessica's death certificate. I wanted to ask Zanne if there was anything in the newspapers about Jessica's death, but it could wait until we stopped for coffee.

My computer pinged, announcing the arrival of something new. Would they send the death certificate so quickly? No. It was unlikely to arrive before tomorrow. I opened my inbox. There was nothing exciting. Details of my new IT project had arrived. However, with Zanne away all next week, I might be able to knock over the project before she returned.

Over coffee, I mentioned finding Jessica Granger's death in the index, and my surprise she died so young. Zanne shrugged. "Could be due to anything," she commented. "Maybe it was some residual effect from all that reproduction, or she might have contracted some illness prevalent at the time. I don't know if there was anything virulent around then. I'm sure the papers will say something about her death, thanks to her connection to Sir Hugh."

Although talkative enough when needs be, Zanne seemed subdued; not her usual self. If she doesn't spark up by lunchtime, maybe I should ask about it. Perhaps talking about it might help. On the other hand, maybe she is resenting the demands of my Granger research. I need to find out if my research is the problem.

A few minutes after we returned to the office, I heard the printer come to life, and Zanne murmured, "I found Hugh's knighthood. It seems he is spending a lot of time in England." That left me wondering, but I consoled myself with the thought that I'd soon have the printout to read or myself. Definitely gotta find out at lunchtime what's bugging Zanne.

While Zanne continued what she was doing, I thought about what I might do. I'd given details of Jessica's death to Zanne, but she didn't seem interested. There's nothing like an occasional show of independence, and this might be just the time for it. I typed Jessica's name into the search box, sat back and waited. There weren't too many hits. The earliest had a 1939 date. It wasn't the correct date but, for some reason, it appealed to me. I navigated to the item in question and found it included in a series of entries in the 'shipping notes'. The few inches of column comprised a series of single sentences relating to passengers recently arrived on various ships. One of the entries advised that Jessica Granger, daughter of Sir Hugh Fitzmaurice, accompanied by her husband, Wilfred Granger, returned from England on the *Orcades* on the previous Friday.

Interesting but not helpful; I made a note of the article but didn't bother printing it. Stop mucking about, I told myself. Go to the entries for 1940. The first one I opened answered some questions. It was a death notice for Jessica Granger, daughter of Sir Hugh Fitzmaurice. In the social notes on the same page, I found a reference to Jessica's death. Although not offering much more, it was worth printing. Once again, Jessica was referred to as Sir Hugh's daughter, rather than as Wilfred's wife. This article claimed Jessica's death was sudden and occurred at home after an illness lasting more than two weeks.

I don't suppose it matters; dead is dead. But I was curious about the nature of her illness. What information is provided on a death certificate? Does it give cause of death or not? I was still debating whether or not the death certificate might provide that information, when Zanne cleared her throat to catch my attention. My stomach tightened when I looked over and saw the concern on her face. "What's up? Why are you looking like that?"

Zanne took a deep breath and seemed to have difficulty finding the necessary words. After a brief pause, she began. "If you remember, when we were talking to Frank before lunch the other day, we agreed the incident that led to this house's bad reputation was the disappearance of Gwendolyn. A bit later in the conversation, he returned to the subject of incidents at this house, and said he had of vague recollection that there might have been more than one. Although he couldn't remember details of another incident, he thought he remembered hearing talk of it in the village. One thing he thought he could remember was that it happened when he was young; around the time he became a teenager."

"Yes, I remember him saying that, and I remember he thought both of the incidents had something to do with women. We agreed that the first incident was Gwendolyn's disappearance. I thought the second one – if indeed there was a second incident – was based on muddled oldtimers' speculation about Gwendolyn's disappearance, and possibly that of Rupert and the nurse. Truth be told, I wasn't any more convinced about a second incident than Frank seemed to be. Now you have me concerned. What made you bring up that conversation?"

"You gave me the date of Jessica's death and made the comment that you were surprised by how young she was. As her paternal affiliation seems to count for so much with the major newspapers, I decided to check on what they had to say about her death. I'm sorry, Anthea, but I think we might have found that second incident."

"What…? Are you suggesting Jessica was the second incident; that she didn't die from natural causes?"

"I'm making a bad job of it, but I'm afraid that is what I'm trying to tell you. As well as the death notice, I found a number of hits from later in 1940. They intrigued me, so I worked through them."

"Yes, I saw the death notice, and it told me nothing other than she had been ill for a couple of weeks beforehand. What makes you think there's something untoward about her death?"

"We have more research to do. Jessica's death attracted quite a bit of attention locally, but also in Sydney because of her father. The articles indicate Jessica had been ill – they don't give details of the illness – but appeared to be on the mend at the time of her death. However, the illness left her weak and fatigued. As the story goes, on the night she died, she went to go downstairs to the kitchen for a glass of water but, due to her weakened state, fell down the stairs. Not much in the way of details, other than the fall was fatal and resulted in an extensive investigation into the accident. My reading between the lines gives me the impression that some doubted it was an accident."

"Do later articles provide more specific information? I mean, do they say that it was an accident and foul play was ruled out?

There would have been other people in the house at the time. I'm struggling to believe it could be anything but an accident. However, if it wasn't, how come she ended up dead at the bottom of the stairs? Do they suggest someone pushed her, or that she threw herself down the stairs?"

"Those possibilities were bandied about during the investigation, but they were disproved or dismissed. I suspect the articles were heavily edited so as not to provide much detail."

"I can imagine why that might happen. It wouldn't do to embarrass poor old Sir Hugh. You said there was an investigation. Are there more files we need to locate?"

I wasn't thinking straight. I couldn't comprehend everything. Is it possible another Granger wife, from the next generation, died in mysterious circumstances? Although, after Gwendolyn's disappearance, unless someone in this family dies of old age in their bed, their death might be considered suspicious. It was a good time to stop for lunch, and to regroup. While I made lunch, Zanne looked for Jessica's case files in the State Archives indexes.

When she joined me in the kitchen, she didn't have to say anything. I could tell her search hadn't gone well. She confirmed she was unable to identify any files that looked remotely associated with Jessica's case. That situation was beyond my comprehension. Zanne did her best to explain.

"Sometimes the files haven't been passed on to the archives yet and remain with the police or the coroner involved in the investigation. However, it might be that the files are at the archives, but are still within the closure period and not available to the public. Another reason the files aren't listed in the index might be because they haven't been indexed yet; are still to be processed by archives' staff. I'll ask about them when I'm at the archives next week."

"Sounds good; now what's bothering you?"

"Nothing is bothering me about it. I was explaining to you why I couldn't find the files in the index. I wasn't upset about not finding them."

"I'm not talking about the files. I'm talking about you. You are not yourself and it's worrying me."

"Yeah, you're right. I've been trying to work out how to say something. I…"

"It's all right, I know. Research into this house's history and my Granger mob is eating up your time. Time you should be spending writing. If your agent and your publisher aren't already unhappy about it, they soon will be. I appreciate all you have done, but I do feel guilty about it."

"Eh? Where did all that come from? Nobody is making me do this and, if you try stopping me, I'll quite happily go off and continue by myself. For your information, I run my life, not my agent or my publisher. Are we clear on that now?" I nodded and felt suitably chastised.

"Well, if that's not bothering you, what is? We've never had trouble speaking our minds before, so why are we dancing around one another now?"

"If you give me a chance, I'll explain. You might remember that soon after we started this research, we jokingly mentioned it being the basis of some future book. I told you I only write fiction, not non-fiction." She looked at me and raised her eyebrows in question.

"Yeah, I remember. I think we both were half joking at the time. Besides, at that stage, we didn't know what we might discover."

"Okay, well the question I have is, how would you feel about our research being turned into a book?" I opened my mouth to speak, but Zanne cut in before I could get a word out. "I know it is sensitive stuff. It's your heritage, your family history. If you agree to consider it, I wouldn't have to write it as non-fiction. I could try turning it into a fictitious story to camouflage the people and the house involved. There's still a shipload of research to do before we understand the whole story. Later, if you decide it's too sensitive to publish, even as a work of fiction, you only need to say so. You know I wouldn't do anything you didn't want."

"This is what has you so uptight; how to ask me about turning it into a book? Christ, do I look so savage that you are not game to ask me straight out? Like I said, we were only half joking about it becoming a book… well, I was anyway. Of course I want you to write it. At this stage, I think I would like to see it written as it really is, warts and all. If we find too many horrible incidents, I might have to rethink that."

The relief we felt was overwhelming, and we fell about laughing at how idiotic we were. Then Zanne became sober and her face was serious when she looked at me. "You know what I think? If I write what we already know as a work of fiction, no one would read it. My publisher wouldn't publish it. It would be considered too far-fetched even for fiction."

To celebrate our return to normal, we allowed ourselves a glass of white wine 'to remove the taste of lunch'. By the time we returned to my office, it was mid-afternoon and neither of us felt like work. As a result, the next hour or so was spent going over what we knew and confirming what Zanne would do while at the archives. We agreed Zanne would not come the next day as she needed to prepare for her week away… and I needed to at least have a look at what the new IT project required.

As I lay in bed tonight waiting for my eyelids to close, I felt torn. Part of me was keen to get stuck into the IT project as a way of taking a break from Granger research, but a larger part of me didn't want to know about the IT work. All that part of me was interested in was finding out more about this house and it occupants through the generations.

This will be a leisurely day, I told myself as I scrambled out of bed well past my usual time. I will print the IT project brief and take it outside to study it in the fresh air. As I made breakfast, thoughts of being out in the fresh air revisited me. These weren't connected with any IT project. They were about my current lifestyle. I had become a virtual hermit. Apart from the occasional visit to the Charlotte Cove General Store, and the odd trip to Zanne's Tern Cottage, I never left *Wellsprings*.

"This is not the way to assimilate into a community," I told the empty house, and then spent a few moments weighing up whether I really wanted to 'assimilate'. You don't know enough about Charlotte Cove to be able to make that decision, I told myself. You need to get out there to find out what it's like first. That was something to think about in quiet moments over the coming week.

About twenty minutes after I made myself comfortable at an outdoor table in the front yard, the wind came up. The leaden clouds rolling towards the Cove suggested a squall was on the way. Although it might not affect here for a while yet, the wind made it impossible to read the IT project document. Common sense kicked in. I relocated to my comfortable lounge chair inside. That's where I was when the storm vented its fury on the Cove.

The project brief didn't look too challenging. It was for an upgrade and some additional new work for an existing client for whom I created the original program. After scratching around on a scribble pad for several minutes, I had an accurate enough estimate of costs and the time required to complete the work. It would take about a week at my usual rate. I emailed the details to London. The speed of their acceptance of my quote surprised me.

If I'm honest, a week of working on a programming project probably was a good thing after many days of research. …And, with Zanne away all week, it's a good time to get stuck in and finished it before she returns. There's no time like the present to make a start, so I did. After a solid slog all day, the work had progressed well and was on schedule.

As dusk fell, I went outside and wandered around the grounds to take in some fresh air to clear my head. All that happened was my mind switched tracks. It left the programming work I'd done all day behind to return to the house and its former occupants. Although I'd known this house since childhood, and in spite of all our recent research, I still felt I knew nothing about the place.

I couldn't even explain it properly to myself, but somehow the not knowing gnawed at me. I tried to explain it to Zanne. She laughed and told me not to worry, as we would find out more about the place over time. To ease my frustration, she reminded me that what had gone before had happened over many decades, not overnight, but it wouldn't go away. The research we were doing was about history, history of place and people, and that history would remain long after we've gone. I knew what she was saying, and it made sense, but it didn't eradicate this thing that keeps gnawing at me.

Perhaps Zanne is right. It won't go away. It will still be there when we uncover it, regardless of how long that takes. Semi-convinced about the whole thing, I made my way to the back door and stepped inside. The doorway leading to the conservatory was on my right and dragged my eyes over to what lay beyond. I stood in the corridor, but couldn't bring myself to enter the conservatory. What am I going to do?

The place can't stay as it is now but, while I believe there is a possibility Gwendolyn's final resting place might be under that floor, I won't be able to go into that area. I found myself wondering whether Aunt Eddie knew about pouring the floor the morning after Gwendolyn disappeared. If she did, how did she cope with the uncertainty? It's clear she enjoyed the conservatory and spent considerable time in it. So, what's wrong with me that I can't even bring myself to go in there? To avoid falling into a black hole of depression, I resolutely marched past the conservatory and into the kitchen.

After behaving myself all week and not going anywhere near our research, I weakened on Thursday afternoon. I knew it was because my mind slipped into neutral and allowed me too much time to think about things other than my programming project. It had been a heavy week, and I was starting to feel like a blimp from sitting at a computer all day. The idea of doing something more physical started to crystallise. On Thursday morning, before I even thought about breakfast, I drove to the beach. It was a glorious morning, and I set myself the challenge of jogging along the sand to the other end of the beach and back again.

A woman walking her poodle didn't glance in my direction as I jogged past. Further along the beach, an elderly couple walking their dog ignored my cheery greeting. I didn't know whether their stony faces reflected their feelings towards people using the beach for anything other than walking dogs, or their dislike of strangers in their village. It wasn't a glorious start to my new early morning regime, but I was determined to persist.

The problem with that jog along the beach was that it allowed my mind plenty of time to roam free – and yes, it was a slow jog and it took me ages to get back to the car. For some reason my mind dredged up Wilfred and the question of when he died. It wasn't too many years after Jessica's fall down the stairs that Thomas inherited *Wellsprings.* Jessica was still a young woman when she died. Despite their age difference, and based on when ownership of the house passed to Thomas, I calculated that Wilfred too was not old when he died.

By the time I returned home and was dealing with breakfast, I believed all thoughts of Wilfred were stowed safely in the back of my mind. Those thoughts popped out again while I was having lunch. I had to check my calculations. Perhaps Wilfred was older than I thought when he died. Rather than let it niggle me all afternoon, straight after lunch I brought up the online deaths index. Remembering lessons learned when I was searching for his marriage, I searched on Wilfred's full name. The search returned one hit. Wilfred died in February 1948 aged fifty-six.

My calculations were correct, but now I want to know what caused his death. I want to believe it was due to illness, but a part of me fears another tragic incident. A call from Zanne around mid-afternoon brought me back on track. She expected to be home about lunchtime on Friday. That gave me only a few more hours to complete the programming project and be rid of it before her return. If she had managed to collect police files from the archives, I wanted nothing to delay exploring those files.

A late night saw the project work finished, leaving just checking everything to complete on Friday morning. I hadn't long emailed the finished work to London when Zanne parked in my driveway.

Chapter 10

Laden with lunch and a box of paper, Zanne arrived around midday. I carried the paper into the house while she peered in the fridge. "Don't worry about making room in the fridge. We'll eat as soon as you're ready," I said. "After lunch, we'll attack that paper you brought back from the archives… or have you already looked at it?"

"No, I haven't read any of it. All I did as I skimmed each file was to skip over anything irrelevant or unnecessary. There is a massive number of files in that pile. We now have all police case files as well as all the coroner's files. Going through that lot should keep us out of mischief a while I should think."

Conversation over lunch was of no consequence. I enquired about her various meetings and events, and her replies suggested the trip was a success. "There is some talk of another trip sometime in the near future. They are talking about a circuit from here, through a lot of country to the south and west and then back to Charlotte Cove. I had a bit of a think about it on the way home and I reckon it will take at least ten days. However, there is nothing definite yet and, knowing my agent and publisher, it could take until next year to organise."

While I think we both tried to present a laid back and relaxed image, lunch and the clean up afterwards happened in double quick time. …And then it was into my office to look at the printouts. I cleared my office table of everything and began unpacking the box. It took some time to arrange the files in a neat line down the centre of the table. As I sorted and placed the files on the table, Zanne followed along behind me either clipping or stapling pages together to ensure there was no chance of any mix up.

"I really could do with a coffee," Zanne said once we sorted the files. "I haven't had one since breakfast and I'm really suffering caffeine withdrawal. I didn't want to waste time messing about with coffee at lunchtime. Are we allowed a coffee break now?"

Weariness cloaked Zanne from head to foot. It was etched into her face. "You look tired. I think you should take the rest of the afternoon off, go home, have a shower, and do nothing." She started to protest, citing all those files that needed attention. I was having none of it, and within ten minutes of having finished our coffee, I stood at the door waving Zanne off on her way home.

Is it okay for me to start looking at those files now that Zanne has gone, or would that be a bit rude of me? I am weak and succumbed to temptation but only to the extent of a quick flick through the odd file here and there 'just to familiarise myself with them', I told myself. Not only was there a mountain of paper but, from the bits I saw, there was a hell of a lot of reading ahead of us. I managed to drag myself away and sat at my computer. In the interim, an email had arrived from London regarding the material I sent this morning. It seems everyone is happy, and money would appear in my bank account sometime in the next few days.

Too late in the day to start anything new, I told myself. In an amazing show of self-control, I shut down my computer and left the office for the day. It's going to be a long night before we make a start on those files tomorrow.

My new morning regime provided a way of filling in time until Zanne arrived. I set off on my jog along the beach, greeting everyone I passed as I went. None bothered to acknowledge the greeting. On the way back to my car, I noticed the elderly couple with the Labrador-cross dog came to walk their dog again. This morning, he was off the leash but obediently stayed close to his owners. As I jogged past, the dog started to prance and showed signs of wanting to join me. The old fellow reached down and grabbed his collar, and I heard a few stern words directed at the dog as I jogged away from them.

As I drove home, I couldn't help but think how I could do this better. My house isn't so far from the beach, but the walk is just a bit longer than I would like. It would make sense to have a bike to ride to and from the beach every morning. Where do you buy a bike at Charlotte Cove? That's a question for Zanne, but maybe not for today. Today, I think there will be plenty of other questions, and none of them about getting fit or going to the beach.

I still was cleaning up after breakfast when Zanne arrived. "Am I too early? I thought, you're an early riser, and particularly today, you'd be rearing to make a start on those files."

"No, you're not early. I've been to the beach. It's part of the new me; my new first thing in the morning routine. You're right though, I'm ready to make a start on those files. Shall we go to my office?"

We sat on opposite sides of the table and, starting from the end closest to the wall, each selected alternate files to examine. That seemed straightforward, but I knew it would go awry before we progressed too far. Some documents were centimetres thick, while others were no more than half a dozen pages.

The first file I selected comprised a number of transcripts of interviews. All were from of people interviewed previously in some cases on several occasions. They were being re-interviewed. The first transcript was a record of the third interview with the nurse, Esme McGregor. I flipped to the end to check the number of pages involved, and was surprised to see a handwritten note below Esme's signature. It seemed worthwhile to read the note before returning to the first page and wading through it all.

After struggling to read the crawly handwriting, it didn't tell me much. Although I couldn't decipher the name and rank at the end of the note, as far as I could make out, it was written by one of the police officers involved in the investigation. He stated that this version of Esme McGregor's story did not deviate in any way from her previously versions.

That was good to know I suppose, but did the lady have anything exciting to say? I returned to the front page and began a painstaking read of Esme's story. It told me nothing we didn't know. This interview gave details of Gwendolyn's illness, most of which had appeared in newspapers. Gwendolyn's illness had persisted for some time. There was evidence of it long before the family moved to Charlotte Cove.

The nurse confirmed the sea air had not helped with Gwendolyn's condition. Her decline continued and became more rapid in the month or so before her disappearance. At the time she disappeared, her nurse, Esme, assessed her as completely infirm. Esme's statement reiterated the story of the picnic and Rupert's late arrival to collect them from the beach.

The thing that intrigued me most about her statement was that Esme blatantly refuted comments by community members about what happened on the occasions when she parked Gwendolyn out in the yard. Esme asserted that Gwendolyn was unable to get out of her chair and, therefore, could not wander about the yard. …And, as Gwendolyn had lost the power of speech some months previously, she could not utter the things people claimed.

"Who would have believed there were so many dishonest townsfolk?" I muttered.

"What…? What are you on about?" Zanne asked as she looked up in surprise.

"Well, the only interesting thing about Esme McGregor's statement is that she inferred the townsfolk were liars. The stories they told about what happened when Gwendolyn was out in the yard are lies according to the nurse."

"So there you have it; we suspected there was something dodgy about this community," Zanne commented. We allowed ourselves a giggle before returning to the files.

Next in the file was the transcript of Mrs Mary Donovan's first and only interview. She claimed she was 'let go' about two weeks before Mrs Granger disappeared. Given no reason for her dismissal, she kicked up a fuss. They then explained that, as Mrs Granger was now totally bedridden, the nurse and the nurse's assistant could easily manage the household between them. It was a hostile parting of the ways, but Mrs Donovan realised there was nothing she could do and left. She went to visit her daughter in Queensland. When the police conducted their initial interviews, Mrs Donovan was interstate. She was away from Charlotte Cove for about six weeks.

Mrs Donovan was not a fan of the nurse, Esme McGregor. She accused her of assuming authority above her station, and questioned her qualifications. It seems Mrs Donovan didn't believe the nurse's care of Gwendolyn was appropriate or acceptable. There was inference of something amounting to misconduct, but she stopped short of openly stating it.

Zanne frowned as I paraphrased Mary Donovan's interview for her. "Taken on face value, Mary Donovan's comments might amount to a severe case of sour grapes; a chance to hit back for her sudden dismissal. However, I have a feeling that is not the case, especially when you read those comments towards the end of her statement. Her comments about Gwendolyn show she was fond of the woman. Her concern for Gwendolyn's poor treatment seems genuine."

The nurse's assistant, Nancy Snell, interviewed for the third time, left little doubt she remained bitter about her dismissal. The morning after Gwendolyn disappeared, Nancy was told her services were no longer required. As there were now only Mr Granger and his two daughters to look after, the nurse could manage the household on her own. Zanne and I agreed the timing of Nancy's dismissal tended to indicate no one expected Gwendolyn to reappear. The timing of the 'culling' of household staff suggested everything was planned well in advance.

I yelped. Zanne jumped and demanded to know what happened. "The next transcript is of an interview with one Angus Sinclair, who it turns out was the hermit at the mine site. I don't know what it says. I haven't read it yet, but just finding it got me excited." Several minutes later, I again interrupted Zanne to share the hermit's interview with her.

"This appears to be the only interview they had with the hermit. The police visited his hut at the mine site. They asked if he saw anything strange in the area around the time Gwendolyn disappeared. He claimed he was not aware of anything unusual happening and had seen no strangers. If anyone came to the site, he would be aware, as he was the only prospector left in the area. The Police asked if he knew Gwendolyn. Angus, the hermit, denied knowing her, but admitted meeting her on a couple of occasions."

"He didn't know her, but met her a couple of times…? Sounds like a bit of a yarn," Zanne said. I continued with the hermit's statement.

"A stray dog arrived at his camp. He had nothing to feed it. As the dog had a collar and looked well-cared for, he guessed it belonged to someone living close by. He asked at the first house he came to after tramping through the scrub. The gardener told him who the dog belonged to and gave him directions to find its owner. Hermit and gardener got chatting and the gardener asked if Angus would be interested in a few days' work. That resulted in Angus helping the gardener and one other man build a shed in the backyard. He met the 'lady of the house' a couple of times when she came out into the yard, but they exchanged nothing more than a hello. When the shed was complete, he never went to the house again, and never saw the woman again. After pointing out various landmarks in the mine site area, the hermit told police that, like the other prospectors, he was preparing to move on as there was nothing to be had there."

"He sounds very polite and chatty for a hermit. Still, I don't know much about hermits," Zanne admitted. "I suppose there are all sorts of reasons they choose to live like they do. I wonder if the *lady of the house* he said hello to on occasions was Gwendolyn, or maybe it was the nurse. It's interesting that he doesn't talk about that woman being in a chair, or infirm, or demented. What are your thoughts on what he had to say?"

"His comment about the woman being out in the yard caught my attention as well. I guess that, after all this time, there is no way of knowing. That shed he helped build is probably the one that's still there. The handwritten note at the end of his transcript says the police returned to talk to him a week later, but he had moved on."

"This bloke has caught your interest in a big way. What is it about him that intrigues you? Do you suspect him of doing away with Gwendolyn or something?"

"No, it's not that. I don't know what it is about him, but ever since hearing there was a hermit out there, I've been curious about him. I know we won't find out any more, and I'm not going to look, but I wish I did know more about him. Enough about the hermit; what's in the file you're reading?"

"These are more interview transcripts. They seem from quite early in the investigation. The neighbours and others from around the village stuck to their stories about Gwendolyn wandering about the yard and yelling out. What is interesting though is that they say that, often when Gwendolyn was in the garden, there was no one at home. They wheeled her outside, and then the others left – and sometimes were 'gone for hours on end'."

"Maybe Mary Donovan's comments about Gwendolyn's poor treatment were not sour grapes. It's a shame the police didn't take more notice of her. Anything else worthy of note in that file?"

"No. The rest of the file contains nothing more than we learned from newspaper articles. The next file in our line-up along the table is only a few pages. I thought I might have a quick look at that one and then break for coffee."

The next one for me to read, with only two and a half typed pages, wasn't much of a challenge either. "This one is a transcript of the interview with the farmer who saw the wagon race past his place."

"Good; see if it says anything the newspapers neglected to tell us."

The file took no time. I saw Zanne reach the end of hers, so I told her about mine. "Not a lot of new information in this one. Most of it is what was in the newspaper. Foxes kept raiding the farmer's chook pen and he was out shooting them. Most nights he finished his patrol of the property by ten or eleven o'clock. On the night he saw the wagon, the foxes were worse than usual. He continued his crusade until nearly one o'clock. The loaded wagon flying past at around midnight surprised him. He recognised it as belonging to Rupert as, in previous times, Rupert often went past his property in it on his way to *Whylara.* Now, this is the interesting bit. The farmer thought it strange on two counts: that Rupert was out and about at that hour, and that Rupert used the wagon. It seems that, in 'recent times', Rupert bought one of those 'new-fangled Ford motor cars'. After that, he appeared to abandon horses in favour of his new vehicle, and often went past in his car."

"I can understand the farmer's surprise at Rupert's use of the wagon again. It also raises those same two questions for me. He could only be up to no good. …And we know that to be the case because that was the night the rest of them from this house 'disappeared'. What I don't understand is how they managed to pack whatever they took with them without anyone noticing. The police still crawled all over the place at that stage. The other thing is how they managed to get the two young girls to go along with everything without making a fuss."

Zanne's questions were the same ones that bothered me. I thought about Rupert's midnight flit several times since reading about it. The more I thought about it, the more convinced I became that his disappearing act was all part of a grand plan. A plan that also included Gwendolyn's disappearance. I suppose, deep down, I believe Rupert responsible for whatever happened to her. Nevertheless, well-orchestrated plan or not, such an effective disappearance of four people is remarkable.

As I turned this over in my mind, I looked across the table to find Zanne studying me intently. "It would be easier to understand how they did it if we knew where they went, and how they managed to slip under the radar and remain 'hidden' when Gwendolyn's disappearance was in all the newspapers of the day. That's all there is to report from my file. What about yours?" I asked.

"Nothing to report; the same as, or more of, what we read in the papers. Time for a break I think."

Over coffee, I told Zanne about finding Wilfred's death and my surprise that he died so young. It grabbed Zanne's attention. She sat up straight, and I could almost see her mind churning as she looked at me.

"Did you follow up on it? I mean, do we know the cause of death? I hope it wasn't another of those tragic incidents that are becoming the trademark of this family."

How incompetent of me, I thought, as I tried to put together an acceptable response. "I don't know any more than what the index gave me. I wasn't supposed to be researching while you were away. I had other work to do, but I weakened. I managed not to do any more than find his death and order his death certificate… and I should see if it has arrived." I scurried across to my computer to check.

Wilfred's certificate awaited me. I sent it to the printer. While it printed, I read it from the screen for Zanne. "Cause of death appears to be organ failure. What is that supposed to mean? I know what organ failure is, but what caused it and how long had he suffered from whatever was the problem?"

Zanne reached for printout. "Oh, I see he's buried on *Whylara.* I wonder if Jessica's buried there too?"

"I didn't expect that. Somehow, I gained the impression Wilfred spent little time at the property and wasn't interested in the place. Yet it appears that's where he chose to be buried. I suppose it could have been the family's decision to bury him there. I don't know about Jessica, but my gut instinct tells me that's not where she is."

"Speaking of Jessica; I checked with the archives about her police files. They confirmed they have the files but they're not processed. They will dig them out and let me know the volume of paper involved so we can work out what we want to do about copies. In the meantime, I think we should pay Trove a visit to see if there's anything about Wilfred's death."

A thought occurred me the moment Zanne mentioned searching for Wilfred's death on Trove. "I don't know how much there will be in the papers. Since Jessica's death severed Wilfred's connection with Sir Hugh, a plain old Wilfred Granger might not merit a mention."

"You might have a point. It's still worth a look." After a few moments, Zanne commented, "Only one hit; it's the usual two-line, one sentence death notice. I'll print it anyway, and then I'll see if the regional newspapers have anything more to offer."

I sat with my chair pushback from the desk and my hands in my lap. Not wanting to start anything in case Zanne turned up something fascinating, I filled in time by thinking about Wilfred and his family. Although I still didn't know much about Rupert and his mob, Wilfred's family seemed even more obscure. Maybe it's just early days in researching them, but they're not giving up their story easily. My interlude of introspection ended when Zanne yelled, "Bingo…!"

"What…?" I yelped as I came back to earth. "What did you find? Come on; share it. Don't keep me in suspense."

"The local paper had a lengthy article on the loss of one of the 'leading lights of the district'. It gives details of the funeral, and talks about the lengthy cortege that followed the hearse to the property for Wilfred's burial there. There's a lovely little comment about how the gods smiled down on the mourners. For the occasion, the gods withheld the rain that drenched the district the previous few days, before letting it resume the following day. How considerate of them. There's an image of the man."

"Oh, great…! Print it. It will be the first image of any of them we've found so far." I couldn't believe we could be so lucky. That's the difference between local papers and the major tabloids I suppose.

"It's not a great reproduction. It's grainy and not particularly clear. Still, as you say, it's more than we have for any of the others. I could hazard a guess at what he died from: over indulgence." Zanne slapped a copy of the article with its associated image in front of me.

She was right. The reproduction was terrible. Fine detail was lost, as were most of the finer facial features. It showed an overdressed rotund man. If I were less generous, I would describe him as overweight, and his outfit as outdated even for that era. It looks like he is wearing a morning suit and top hat. I can't image what sort of event required him to dress like that. He had a cane, a walking stick with a fancy metallic head, perhaps for show rather than to aid mobility. My assessment might be unfair given I have no knowledge of the circumstances surrounding the image.

When she felt I had studied the image long enough, "Little by little, Anthea," Zanne said. "Little by little, we are getting to know these people. However, I don't think we are going to dredge up much more on Wilfred."

"What about his sons? This article's account of Wilfred's funeral doesn't mention his sons. Even Jessica only got a passing nod. Who she was didn't impress the local paper. Their only mention of her was to say that, in 1920, Wilfred married the former Jessica Fitzmaurice. Sir Hugh, if he were still around, might not be well pleased with that. Oh, on the list of notable citizens at the funeral, Sir Hugh's name is conspicuous by its absence. Was Sir Hugh no longer with us, or was this indicative of the situation subsequent to Jessica's death?"

Zanne giggled. "Well, we've got everything and everyone nailed down. If you feel so inclined, we could have a look for Sir Hugh's death. It won't tell us if there was bad blood in the end, but it might tell us why he wasn't at the funeral. However, we won't chase him until we have answers to all the other questions we created for ourselves."

After spending another hour or so peering at the screen, I felt as though my eyes were hanging out. I longed for a break. "Let's get a coffee and take it outside for a while. I feel as though I'm in danger of crashing headlong into my keyboard if I don't get some fresh air and move about a bit."

We settled on the bench under my favourite tree and, for a brief period, sat in silence taking in the sights and sounds around us. Zanne shattered the silence when she remembered something she meant to tell me yesterday. "Did I mention I ran into Ray Hartley?"

"No you didn't, but it wouldn't have meant anything if you had. Who is Ray Hartley? And I hope you don't mean you literally ran into him."

Zanne giggled and drained the last of her coffee. "That's exactly what I mean. It was in that hotel I stayed at in Sydney. I was rushing for the elevator and he was heading for the reception desk. Neither of us looked where we were going, and we literally ran into one another in the middle of the lobby."

"So, should I know this Ray Hartley?"

"Maybe not, I've known him for years. I met him when we were at university together. He was studying archaeology. I had a chance meeting with him not long after I came back from England, and I've used his expertise a couple of times since to confirm facts in my manuscripts were accurate. He moved on from archaeologist, to geoarchaeologist. At least, I think that's what he is, or something like that. He added geology to his degree and now spends his time on dig sites assessing what lies underground. They use all sorts of technical equipment in what he does now. I don't have a clue how it all works or exactly what he does. He tried explaining it to me once. I didn't want to appear thick, so I just tried looking intelligent without understanding any of it."

"And you are mentioning Ray Hartley to me now because…? Is there something more about this bloke I should know?"

"What…? No. We are just friends. That's all we've ever been. The reason I mentioned him is that I think he might prove useful. In the course of our conversation, I gave him an overview of Gwendolyn's disappearance… a-n-d I might have just happened to mention your fixation about what's hiding under the conservatory floor." I started to object, but she cut me off and continued with her story.

"The outcome of all that is, he offered to come and scan the floor. One of the tools he uses is ground penetrating radar – or GPR. The equipment sends some sort of signal down into the ground. An image of what lies below comes back to a computer. Instead of digging holes all over the place in the hope of finding something, it helps archaeologists work out where to dig. They use it to identify anomalies that are likely to be graves, foundations or other structures."

"What's scanning the conservatory floor going to find? When is this likely to occur, and how expensive is it going to be?"

"The way he explained it was that his equipment would show up everything, including foundations, under the floor. He currently is on a dig not too far from here. When his part of the job is finished, he will be heading south, and offered to come via Charlotte Cove to scan the floor. It won't cost anything, so relax. All that can happen is, he will prove whether Gwendolyn is under that floor or not. I can't have you spending the rest of your life not going in there because of what you think might be there. He thought it might be two or three weeks before his job finished, and will ring me to arrange a time and date. Are you okay with this?"

"I'm okay with it, but I think it might be a bit of a long shot. I'm not sure his gear will penetrate that concrete floor. He might be wasting his time coming here."

"Oh pessimism, your name is Anthea. Okay, what's the worst that can happen? If his equipment can't penetrate the floor, we won't know any more, or any less than we do now. I don't think that will shake the world off its axis."

She was right, and I knew it. I think my reaction was about self-preservation. If possible, I want to avoid getting my hopes up, only to find nothing. It's probably not worth trying to explain that to Zanne. She tends not to see things as I do.

By the time we stirred ourselves from under the tree, most of the afternoon was gone. We returned to my office without enthusiasm. I decided to take the initiative. "It's late and I think my brain's become fog-bound. I move we adjourn until tomorrow.

"I second that. Same time, same place…?" She asked as she began gathering up her belongings. I checked the time as she drove off. It was after five o'clock. I knew my mind would dwell on today's finds well into the night. I abandoned myself to it, and it kept me awake until almost midnight.

Chapter 11

My jog along the beach this morning produced troubling thoughts about Wilfred's children. No mention of his sons at Wilfred's funeral niggled at me until I fell asleep last night. It didn't matter from which angle I considered it, something was not right. Come to think of it, there was no mention of his daughters either. Was it a given that family members were at the funeral and, therefore, weren't mentioned? That made sense, but somehow I couldn't convince myself it was true. That started me wondering why. Perhaps I was intent on finding mystery and dark secrets, and found it impossible to take things at face value.

For a few minutes, I sat on a rock to allow the perspiration from my jog to dry a little before I climbed into my car to drive home. I do think a bike would be a good idea. I must ask Zanne about the nearest place to buy one. Thoughts of Wilfred and Jessica's children dogged me all the way home. As I made breakfast, I realised they were going to keep annoying me until I found out a bit more about them… And that's what I'll try to do as soon as I hit my office this morning.

As I waited for my computer to boot up, I did some soul-searching yet again in a bid to find out why these people were so important. If I think back to the first generation I looked at, apart from Rupert, I didn't know much about William Granger's children. That trend continued into the next generation where, apart from Wilfred, I knew nothing much of the rest of Rupert's family. While I know they're not relevant to the history of this house, something keeps nudging me to find out more about them. This isn't about becoming addicted to family history research. It's about understanding those people perched in my tree.

"Okay, now what? Where to begin…?" I asked the universe as I sat staring at my computer's bright desktop. I suppose the first thing to work out is what I want to know – and therein lies the problem. I'm sure I don't want to know 'everything', but what do I want to know, as opposed to what I need to know. If I were a family historian hell bent on documenting every branch of my family tree, I would want to know that elusive 'everyone and everything', but that's not what I'm about. "Get real; start with the basics," I chided myself aloud. Then I had to remind myself that 'the basics' were details of births, deaths and marriages. Hooray! At last I have some direction and can put fingers to keyboard.

After checking my family tree chart and filling in any missing birth dates, I searched for marriages for all of Wilfred's children with the exception of Thomas, whom I already knew something about, and Bethany, who died soon after her birth. When nothing appeared in the marriages index for this state, I turned my attention to the online indexes for other states. Later when Zanne arrived, I had nothing to report. It appeared none of those Granger children ever married.

Zanne, who is an expert at being unhelpful when trying to be helpful, again displayed her prowess in this art. "Perhaps you can't find them because they weren't married in Australia. This Granger mob seems to have some sort of penchant for sending their offspring to England. It's possible they married somewhere overseas. Rupert did, so why wouldn't some of the others do the same?"

"It's true; this Granger mob seemed to have difficulty cutting the ties with the 'old country'. Regardless, we haven't come across anything in the newspapers about marriages, or about their return home with spouses in tow. Perhaps it's worth a look on Trove on the off chance you're right. I'll look on the deaths index for Randolph although I have no idea how old he might have been when he died. I might have a bit of a look for Clara while I'm about it. However, if she married, I might need her married name to find her.

For the next few minutes, the click of our keyboards was the only sound in the room as we pursued our individual searches. Frustration was building. I searched every possible deaths index for Randolph and came up with nothing. I slammed back in my chair and folded my arms. If I can't find Randolph, how the hell am I going to find Clara, I asked myself. I looked over at Zanne. She looked at me with raised eyebrows. "Dare I ask what the problem is?" she asked quietly.

"There is no Randolph. I'm beginning to wonder if he ever existed. He didn't marry and he didn't die, so there must be an ancient bachelor tucked away somewhere laughing at my futile efforts to find him."

"If you said that a few minutes ago, I would have responded differently. My suggestion would be that he stayed in England; marrying, probably raising a family, and dying there. I won't…"

I was feeling testy enough to go on the attack. "What difference does it make when I mentioned Randolph's almost being a figment of my imagination? Are you suggesting you have a different answer for me now?"

"Whoa, hold on. I know you feeling frustrated, but don't take it out on me. After all, it's your mob that's being so uncooperative. Anyway, yes, I have something different to say now. I can tell you Randolph never married, he did die, and that he died young. While he didn't die in England, I expect his death will appear in English records somewhere."

After apologising for my outburst, I was my sweetest as I asked Zanne to tell me what she discovered. She tried hard to stifle the grin that twitched the corners of her mouth as she replied. "It appears Randolph had completed the first year of his engineering degree at university in England when he enlisted in 1939. He was assigned to one of the engineering corps and sent overseas. A few months later, towards the end of 1939, he was killed in action. I'm not sure if his body was repatriated to England, but it appears it wasn't brought back to Australia."

"Jesus…! That explains a lot of things. It explains why I couldn't find anything, apart from his birth, in any of the indexes. And, in terms of the history of this house, it explains why Thomas owned the place after Wilfred. At the risk of sounding crass, I'm happy to discover that information, but it is tragic to think of a lad of not much more than eighteen years old being cut down in that way."

It was a sad story, and a sombre air settled over my office in the wake of its discovery. After I updated the family tree chart, I had a nervous think about Clara. Perhaps my concern about not being able to find her because she changed her name by marriage was ill founded. Had she too died young, and worse still, in yet another set of tragic circumstances? I aired those concerns with Zanne.

"I was just about to type Clara's name into the search field to see what Trove might have to say about her. Hang on a minute; I'll see what it brings up." Only the click of Zanne's keyboard disturbed the silence. She leaned forward, and I saw what I interpreted as shock register on her face. I knew it was bad news.

"I know it is bad news, but I need to know what it is. What have you found? Come on, tell me. What happened to Clara?"

The printer whirred into life. Her actions confirmed everything I thought and felt. Zanne opted to print whatever was in the newspaper article rather than tell me about it. I raced over and snatched up the printout. While still standing at the printer, I scanned the page. I couldn't speak.

After flopping onto my chair, I closed my eyes and took a couple of deep breaths, before again slowly reading the printout. By the time I reached the bottom of the page, tears filled my eyes. I chanced a quick glance at Zanne. I'm not sure why I felt so emotional, but I was sure Zanne would not understand. She peered at her screen, steadfastly avoiding eye contact with me. I was relieved and grateful. Focused on regaining self-control, I blinked back the tears before she noticed.

"The search brought up quite a few hits," Zanne murmured, her voice almost lost in the sound of the printer doing its thing. "I think we may need a lot more files from the archives." I gave a half-hearted nod in response.

Stunned, I felt cold all over. Had I read it right? Maybe I didn't comprehend what I'd read. "Zanne, can we recap what I think happened here, please, so I'm sure I've got the story straight?"

"Good idea; grab the rest of those printouts and let's have a coffee. We can go through everything either in the kitchen or we can take it outside, whichever you prefer."

As I made coffee, Zanne arranged the printouts on the table. I opted to have coffee in the kitchen.

A long session teasing out the tragic story of Clara's death followed. It began with my interpretation of what happened. "The one indisputable fact about this whole thing is that Clara hanged herself from a tree in the scrub behind this house. I've worked out from the articles that this occurred early in 1941. If the information I have on the chart is correct, she wasn't yet seventeen years old. That period must've been devastating for the family. Jessica fell down the stairs in May 1940, then Clara hanged herself at the beginning of 1941, and now we know Randolph's death in action overseas was at the end of 1939. Do you agree so far?"

"Yeah, that just about nails it. I hadn't realised she was so young until you mentioned it. Do you feel up to exploring the circumstances leading up to her death? At this stage, we only have what's in newspapers, but that should provide us with a reasonable picture of what happened."

It took me a while to answer. It wasn't because I was uncertain about wanting to find out what happened. I was psyching myself up; preparing for what would follow. With the articles sorted into chronological order, we spent the best part of half an hour reading them. Then it was time to discuss what we gleaned from the small pile of paper containing Clara's tragic story. While I got my head around everything, Zanne made us fresh coffees. Then, after a tentative and stumbling start, I shared the story as I understood it from the information in the newspapers.

"It seems this became another of those Granger cases that involved a lengthy police investigation and coroner's inquest. The outcome of all that is Clara's death was found to be suicide and free from any suggestion of criminal involvement."

"That's a great way of saying she did it, and no one else was involved," Zanne commented, her disgust clear in her voice.

"Yeah, the comment seems unnecessary when it is deemed a suicide. Nevertheless, the circumstances leading to her death aren't well documented in these articles. In fact, it looks as though, to fill column inches, the reporters or whoever, resorted to speculation rather than facts."

"Perhaps it was being kept hush-hush. I don't know whether that was to prevent sullying Clara's reputation further, or if it were to protect Wilfred's image in the community. Regardless, to me, it smacks of some sort of cover up. Maybe it wasn't so much a cover-up as non-release of all the facts. What is your assessment of what's been written, apart from the speculation you already mentioned?"

I was looking at some of the comments by various people from the village. "People in the village report a change in Clara. While some claim the change occurred immediately after her mother's death, those a bit more discerning perhaps, claim they noticed the change a little while after Jessica's death. It seems she went from being a bright articulate young woman to someone who barely spoke and rarely laughed. There was some suggestion that some romantic upheaval might have been the cause. However, there is nothing in the police files to suggest there was any romance in her life. I can understand how upsetting the loss of a mother can be, particularly for someone close to their mother. If that is what triggered Clara's suicide, Jessica's death must have caused extreme depression. I wish I'd known previously what happened to Clara. There would have been opportunity to talk to Aunt Eddie about it."

"If there has been an attempted cover-up, Edwina might have refused to discuss it with you. Suicide might be more openly discussed these days. The stigma – and sin for some religions – associated with it back then would make it something to hide if possible. It might be that Wilfred used his influence to filter what was released to the newspapers. I haven't searched the regional newspapers archives to see what they have to say on the subject, but I suspect we won't learn much more. I'm afraid we have to go to the state archives if we want to know more about the investigations into both Jessica's and Clara's deaths."

"I've never researched at the state archives, so I don't know what's involved. However, I'm ready to go and learn, and to find out whatever there is to know, just as soon as you tell me when we're going. Whenever you're ready won't be soon enough for me."

"How about going the day after tomorrow? If I take care of a couple of things tomorrow, I will have no commitments for the rest of the week. Is that too soon… is it okay for you?"

Silly question, I thought. If it were up to me, I'd be happy to go now. After a search of the regional newspapers for anything more on Clara's suicide, we spent the remainder of the morning and the early part of the afternoon interrogating the state archives police files index, and making lists of potential files to examine.

It was an early start, as we aimed to be at the archives when they opened. At that time of day, traffic is light. Apart from one short stretch of roadworks that slowed us down, we had a glorious run, and arrived about twenty minutes before the archives opened. Zanne insisted on spending that time going over everything we planned to do, and on explaining to me the various procedures to follow.

When the doors finally opened, the queue outside numbered two, Zanne and I. Because I had never been there before, I didn't have a reader's ticket. The first ten minutes of our visit was taken up with getting me squared away and allowed to enter the search room. Then my initiation into a completely new world began. Zanne stayed with me while we ordered our first files. Zanne's arrived first. I blinked several times as the staff member placed it on the desk in front of Zanne. "What's that?" I hissed. "Is that what you ordered?"

Zanne grinned as she nodded. "Yes, it's the file I asked for. It's a microfilm. I'm going to take it into that room over there where all those machines are to read it. I'll be able to print copies of anything we want. Prints are by coin-in-the-slot, and can work out expensive if you are not discerning about what's important and what's not." As she finished speaking, a staff member placed a brown paper wrapped parcel on the desk in front of me. Tied with pink legal tape, the parcel was about 50 millimetres thick.

After giving me a string of instructions on what to do with it, Zanne went to read her film. "Untie and unwrap it carefully. Don't get the folders out of order and don't have more than one folder open at the same time. Don't get pages from one folder mixed up with those from another folder. If there are copies of documents required, fill out one of these forms – or come and get me to help you – and then slip it into the folder in front of the first page you want copied. When you're finished with the bundle, put everything back in the right order, loosely wrap the paper around it and take it to those shelves over there."

I tried looking confident, but that wasn't how I felt. However, once I made a start on the material, I felt transported to a most fascinating place and time. My files were from the police investigation into Jessica's death. It contained a few transcripts of interviews. As expected, there were interviews with everyone in the house on the night of the accident. There also was an interview with Mrs Elsie Nolan, the Grangers' housekeeper, who wasn't in the house that night. She lived in the village with her husband.

The police's questioning of Elsie focused not on the accident itself, but on Jessica's condition in the period leading up to the accident. What caught my attention was the police's interest in the state of the Grangers' marriage and other relationships within the household. I had to stifle a giggle as I read one part of her interview.

It was obvious she thought the police were suggesting she and Wilfred were involved, and that Jessica's accident might have been 'convenient'. Elsie was having none of it, and left the police in little doubt about her and Wilfred, and that she found such a suggestion insulting. After singing the praises of her husband, Ted Nolan, she assured them she would never lower herself to such a thing with someone as repulsive as Wilfred Granger. The police also interviewed Anne Matthews who worked for the Grangers as a day cleaner. She told the police she came in three days a week to clean and generally assist Mrs Nolan. Her comments about Wilfred echoed Elsie's sentiments.

My bundle of files was beginning to look like a porcupine; I had so many orders for printing protruding from it. I went in search of Zanne to inquire about the procedure for getting the stuff I had flagged printed. I found her immersed in something on the huge screen in front of her. The pile of paper at her elbow caught my attention. "I see you've been busy," I whispered, and nodded towards the paper.

"I'm pleased you're here. Would you mind going to the desk in the reception area?" She waved two empty small plastic bags at me. "I need more coins. You'll need cash or credit card to buy more. I think they have them bagged up in different amounts. See if you can buy two fifty-dollar bags. That should keep me going for a bit longer."

I turned to leave to go in search of the coins she wanted, but she called me back. "What's the time? Is it that late already? There is a food van comes every day. It goes around all the workplaces for workers to buy lunch or drinks and snacks. It calls here a bit early on its way to the industrial area. The front desk announces its arrival over the public address system. It's usually around 11.30, so keep your ears open. We will need to dash out to buy something for lunch."

When I returned with the two bags of coins as instructed, I managed to ask Zanne about what I did with all the files I marked for printing. She had reached the end of the film she was reading and set it to rewind. "Just give me a moment until this finishes, and I'll come with you." A couple of minutes later we were standing at the reference desk in the search room. I plonked my bundle on the desk in front of the archivist on duty.

"You want all of this material copied," she asked incredulously. "I suppose you'll want to take it with you when you leave…" I nodded. "Right; I'll have to get someone started on printing it." She recognised me as a rookie and explained the system. "When it's copied, everything is taken out to the front desk in reception. You will be able to pay for and collect it there." With that, she snatched up my bundle, turned on her heel and disappeared through to somewhere in the bowels of the building.

As we walked back to my desk, announcement of the arrival of the lunch van shattered the silence. A few minutes later, armed with sandwiches and bottles of iced coffee to sustain us through the afternoon, we sat in the small open-air dining area and discussed our morning's work. While my files related to Jessica's death, the film Zanne read was from the investigation into Clara's suicide. I couldn't help shuddering at the thought of so many trees sacrificed to produce the box of printouts we would be taking home with us. That thought became worse when I mentally added today's lot to the mountain of stuff on Gwendolyn's disappearance Zanne collected the last time she was here.

It was a relief when the public address system announced the search room would close in half an hour. During the afternoon,

I read an impressive stack of paper files, learned how to operate the microfilm readers and printers, bought more bags of coins, and contributed significantly to the sacrifice of more trees. My mind was a foggy turmoil as I carried the box of paper to the car.

Zanne seemed bright and chirpy, although she claimed her eyes were hanging out. Every item on our list of files to examine was ticked off. "That was a hell of an introduction to researching at the State archives for you," she commented as we fastened our seat belts. After a few moments of sitting in silence to relax and clear our minds, we were on our way to our motel. Neither of us felt much like conversation for the rest of the day. We dined in the motel's restaurant but, to a casual observer, it probably looked as though we'd rowed. Neither of us spoke much.

An early checkout, followed by a pleasant drive with the windows down so we could smell the blossoming trees and crops on the crisp morning air, had us back at Charlotte Cove a little before eleven o'clock. Zanne carried in the box of paper while I made coffee. She declined an invitation for lunch and left as soon as we finished our coffees. I luxuriated in being alone and idle for the first time in many hours. From my comfortable lounge chair, now reclined way back, I glanced across at the box of paper from the archives on the small hall table beside my office door.

A little voice kept urging me to go to that box, sort it out, and explore the wealth of information it contained. The flesh was weak – or was it my psyche? Whatever it was, something prevented me climbing out of my chair to do anything for the next couple of hours. I awoke with a start at three o'clock, decided it was too late for lunch and too early for dinner, and opted for a long walk along the beach instead in the hope it would clear my mind and reinvigorate me.

I found the beach deserted. My shoes in my hand, I walked along the water's edge with the incoming waves licking my feet as the gentle breeze lifted my hair and drifted it out behind me. The changing shades of blue and turquoise across the bay as the clouds scurried overhead had a cathartic effect. By the time I arrived back at my car, I felt both relaxed and refreshed. Although the afternoon slipped away, that box of printouts from the state archives called me to it the moment I came through the front door.

The large table I dragged out of the room when I set up my office remained abandoned near the staircase leading to the upper floor. It was just the place to unpack and sort out the printouts. What I thought would be a simple task not requiring too much time, turned into something else. It was after seven o'clock by the time I tore myself away from that table and went in search of food to appease my grumbling stomach.

After a quick stirfry dinner and an equally speedy clean up afterwards, I wandered back to the paper on the table. Part of me was desperate to uncover the secrets it might hold, but an even larger part of me – and in a much louder voice – told me tomorrow would be a good time to start. As I lay in bed after opting for an early night, the question occupying my mind was about where to start on those files.

Our investigation into Jessica's death was incomplete. It made sense to exhaust everything we had on that before looking at anything else. Nevertheless, Clara's suicide called to me. By the time I fell asleep, I knew I would not be able to resist exploring Clara's files. As I drifted off, I reconciled the situation in my mind by deciding that, if she came tomorrow, I would allocate Jessica's files to Zanne, while I kept Clara's files.

Chapter 12

This morning I was up early and feeling normal again. It was all I could do to stick to my new fitness regime and drag myself to the beach… and away from the paper spread out on that table. The fact that I am again itching to find out more suggests to me that I have recovered from the rigours of the archives visit. After my long stroll on the beach yesterday, I decided a short jog would do today.

Breakfast happened in a flash. Then I took a kitchen chair and myself over to the table and began work on the files. My first task was to sort the files so those relating to Jessica's death were at one end of the table and the others relating to Clara's suicide were at the opposite end. This wasn't an ideal place to work and I wasn't sure what would happen when Zanne arrived but, in the meantime, I am happy to work at the table.

Clara's files followed a similar pattern to those encountered previously. Much of it was transcripts of various people's interviews. There were a few reports by police officers, a doctor and the coroner. Although it was not the right place to begin, my eyes flew to the coronial inquest file. A quick flick through the file before I started reading it in earnest showed a long and wide-ranging list of people gave evidence at the hearing. As I worked through the transcripts of their testimony, I noted their names in a new notebook.

While the list included obvious people such as Wilfred, the medical examiner and police officers, Elsie Nolan, the housekeeper, and Anne Matthews, the cleaner, it also included many from the community. The latter group all claimed Clara changed after her mother's death. They said she went from being a happy, talkative young girl to being withdrawn and uncommunicative. Some went so far as to say she suffered deep depression following Jessica's accident and never recovered from it. As I looked through my new list of names, one thing stood out like a beacon in the night.

There were no young people on that list; no one who qualified as a sixteen-year old girl's best friend. No young friends appeared at the hearing. Even Clara's sister, Edwina, wasn't on the list. If they sought to interview people close to Clara who could speak about the state of her mind, surely Edwina would be the first they interviewed. I went through the file again. Edwina was not there.

Her name did not appear amongst interviewees from prior to the hearing either. It also seemed odd that Wilfred contributed nothing more to the hearing than three or four sentences. All he said after he identified himself was that Clara was his daughter, she had seemed troubled for some time, and that he was away at his pastoral property when she committed suicide.

"How convenient," I snarled... and nearly fell off my chair when my indignation caused a peel of raucous laughter. Engrossed in what I was doing, I hadn't heard Zanne arrive.

"Do you often have deep and meaningful conversations with yourself?" she asked, "And what did you find so convenient?"

"No, not me; Wilfred... I looked at what he said at the coronial hearing into Clara's death. Well, it's more a case of what he didn't say. It was convenient for him that he wasn't here when it happened."

"Did you find anything else interesting?"

"Interesting and curious; this is the first file I've looked at, but it has a list of all the interviewees. They didn't interview any young people. I would expect her friends to know more about her state of mind than the old busybodies around town."

"There might be a simple explanation. Maybe she didn't have any friends as such, or maybe no one in the household knew of any friends."

We took our positions at opposite ends of the table, and Zanne began work on files relating to Jessica's death while I continued with those relating to Clara's suicide. Work progressed in silence for some while until I shattered it. "Aha, that's interesting. How come that's not mentioned at the hearing?"

"Do tell; I could do with something interesting to relieve the tedium."

"I decided to leave the hearing stuff, and go back to the beginning of the investigation and the transcripts of the early interviews. That of Esme Nolan, the housekeeper, happened to fall open. She claims Clara was sweet on a local lad, although she didn't know whether it had reached the stage of being a genuine romance or not. Hang on a minute. There is a handwritten comment on the bottom that says… it's hard to read … something about re-interviewing her."

"See if there is a transcript of a second interview. Was there a young lad amongst those who gave evidence at the hearing?"

"No, there was nothing to suggest anyone was a young lad, or that any of them were romantically involved with Clara. I'll see what else Esme had to say the second time."

I found mention of the young lad almost at the start of Esme's first interview, so invested a few minutes in absorbing what else she said. Although there was nothing specific, I sensed a strong emotional undercurrent throughout her interview. My second reading of the transcript left me feeling it wasn't what she said that mattered so much as the inferences in her comments. The transcript left me feeling frustrated. What was she trying hard not to say? I rifled through the rest of the transcripts until I found the transcript of her second interview.

By the time of her second interview, she appeared less inhibited and spoke her mind more freely. It was clear she had no time or respect for Wilfred. She claimed that, following his wife's death, Wilfred forced his eldest daughter, Clara, to take over her mother's role of supervising the running of the household. Again, her responses seem to contain a code – a form of shorthand perhaps – that I didn't understand. However, they again had me believe she hinted at something she felt unable to state more clearly.

The police officer questioned her about the supposed romantic interest Esme mentioned in her previous interview. It seems her initial response was to be defensive and to play down the comment. However, persistent questioning brought a different, more detailed, response. It seems a young lad in the village caught Clara's eye, and Esme believed the interest was reciprocal. Nevertheless, Esme was uncertain whether a romance had blossomed.

Esme reiterated her previous comment that Jessica's death hit Clara hard, but no more than expected. In Esme's opinion, Clara coped with the grief and put the loss behind her. The slow but progressive change in the young girl's outlook on life began sometime after that, and it was Esme's opinion that something other than Jessica's death triggered it. Again, I felt Esme pointed the police towards something she couldn't say.

I sat back and looked at the key points from Esme's transcripts noted on my pad. There were two key issues: something to do with Wilfred's behaviour, and something to do with Clara's interest in the young lad. None of this came out at the hearing. I returned to the hearing file to check Esme's comments on that occasion.

Few questions were put to her during her time on the stand. Her answers were economical, mostly 'yes, no' responses. While not a hostile witness, she was not expansive. She volunteered no extra information. This left me wondering whether the questioning of the housekeeper at the coroner's hearing was orchestrated to elicit the responses it received.

After reading her second interview again, I was sure there was more to the story than Esme was willing or able to impart. Damn! My frustration level is just about through the ceiling and there's nothing I can do about it. If people weren't open and honest, I'll never know the truth. I slapped my hand on the table and snarled, "Dammit, talk to me. Tell me what happened."

Startled by my outburst, Zanne jerked herself upright, and then burst out laughing. "That's telling them. I'm sure they will tell you what you want to know now."

I felt foolish, and that added to my frustration. After a quick apology for my outburst, I returned to ploughing through the transcripts of interviews. As with the transcript of the hearing, the preliminary investigation interviews did not include one with a young lad from the village. I began to think this lad would remain a ghost. That depressed me further. This was not going well and I'm sure it wasn't doing my blood pressure any good. I turned to another part of the case file in the hope of finding something significant.

It took me a few moments to realise the file I opened was the doctor's report on his post-mortem examination of Clara. I almost put it aside, but I steeled myself and read on. The first part of the file listed technical details: how and where the body was found, the marks and injuries to the body and an estimated time of death based on technical information. I turned the page and gasped. “She was pregnant,” I exclaimed.

“Eh…? What’s it say?” Zanne said, as she put aside the file she was reading.

“This is the doctor’s autopsy report. After what I imagine are routine comments about the body being well nourished and exhibiting no signs of any illness, he drops the bombshell. When did Jessica die?”

“…May 1940. Why? How is that relevant? What’s this bombshell you’re talking about?”

“Clara died early in 1941. She was almost six months pregnant. Is that what drove her to commit suicide? In 1941, a pregnancy outside of marriage was scandalous. I wonder if Wilfred knew of the pregnancy before the suicide, or whether it came as a shock to learn of it later.” I searched the file for the doctor’s name, and then returned to a list of those who gave evidence at the coronial inquest.

The doctor’s name appeared on the list, so I searched the file for his evidence. His statements included the time, date and place he was called to retrieve the body. He described the scene when he arrived, the marks and injuries he found on the body in the course of the post-mortem examination, and his conclusion that the young woman’s death was consistent with suicide by hanging. “There is no mention of the pregnancy at the coronial inquest.”

“From what you’ve told me so far, there was no mention of some lad from the village in whom Clara developed an interest, and there is no mention of her pregnancy. That doesn’t make any sense. Once they found she was pregnant, surely the young lad would have been squarely in the frame for the situation. Maybe they did talk to him and somehow eliminated him from the equation.”

Although what Zanne suggested was feasible, I didn’t buy it. I didn’t know whether that was gut instinct telling me her suggestion was wide of the mark, or if it were my psyche refusing to accept the possibility. As I pondered the situation, a rogue thought slipped in from left field, elbowing every other thought out of the way. “Here’s another scenario to think about,” I said. “Maybe Wilfred applied his considerable influence to sanitise the situation. Maybe the whole hearing was engineered to avoid any mention of Clara’s pregnancy and, therefore, it eliminated any need to mention a potential romantic interest.”

“Let me think about that for a while. I’ve finished with Jessica’s files. There wasn’t much in them, but I’ve extracted a few comments. Something smells a bit off with this coroner’s inquest too. I’m wondering if there isn’t a bad smell about the whole of the investigation.”

After checking all the transcripts of interviews that occurred before the hearing were in the correct chronological order, I looked for anything that occurred after the doctor conducted the autopsy. There were transcripts of two more interviews. First, they interviewed Wilfred almost as soon as the doctor released his findings. The police confined their questioning to whether Wilfred knew of Clara’s pregnancy before her suicide. Wilfred denied any knowledge of it, claimed to be shocked, and struggling to come to terms with it.

A couple of days later, the police’s other interview was with Esme Nolan. While the transcript of Wilfred’s interview took less than half a page, Esme’s was multipage. If she had so much to say, it must be of some consequence. With that thought in mind, I read every word of the transcript with care. After a second reading of Esme’s interview, I sat back and stared at the wall. I tried to process what she said and what I thought she inferred. Zanne noticed and wanted to know what I had discovered.

“I’m not sure. In his interview, Wilfred gave the classic I-know-nothing performance. Esme’s interview is more intriguing. The police talked about having searched Clara’s bedroom at the outset of the investigation, and they asked Esme why Clara’s room was not on the upper floor where all the other bedrooms were located. They asked about the area where Clara had her room.”

“If they had already searched her bedroom, why was this important to them now? Does Esme clarify anything?”

“Yeah, she does a bit. I think Clara’s bedroom was the room that later became Edwina’s room. Anyway, Esme told them the area 'downstairs' was known as the servants' quarters. There was no longer live-in household staff, so the quarters were not occupied. Soon after her mother's death, Clara moved in down there and made what had been the staff sitting room into her bedroom. Esme thought at the time that it might have been a show of rebellion by Clara. She thought Clara's thinking was that, if she were to be treated like a servant, she would live like one. It's interesting that Esme commented that she believed Clara never again ventured onto the upper floor."

"Hmm … It does not appear things were going well for Clara, and that things might have been strained between Clara and Wilfred. Does Esme shed any light on what was happening in the house at that time?"

"The police moved their questioning on to Clara's social life. They wanted to know if she went out at night, how often she left the house, where she went and if she went alone. Esme's replies seem a little curt at first, but it appears she warmed to the task as it progressed. She was emphatic that Clara never went out at night except on the three or four occasions when she had to accompany Wilfred to official functions. According to Esme, Clara rarely left the house except to go to the post office, the store or the market garden. Pressed for more details about such outings, Esme claimed Clara sometimes went to the post office alone if Wilfred was away from Charlotte Cove. Whenever she went to the store, Esme usually went with her, and when the vegetable garden was not at its best, Clara and Esme went to the market garden to buy fresh produce."

"There's something missing from all that. If her room were down in the servants' quarters, perhaps she did slip out at night without anyone knowing. Let's face it, she was pregnant, so there had to be opportunity for that to happen."

"You're not the only one who thought about that. The police made much the same observation. Esme's response was that she believed the house was locked at night, although she admitted Clara would know where the key was if she wanted to let herself out. However, Esme thought it unlikely, as Clara was terrified of snakes, goannas and other wildlife that roamed the grounds at night. It's as though Esme was determined to quash any suggestion – any possibility – there was opportunity, either day or night, for Clara to have assignations that led to her condition. I don't think it was out of loyalty to Clara that Esme adopted this stance. She was so dogmatic, there had to be more to it."

"Is there anything else to suggest how it was possible, or when? What are you frowning about…? What have you found?"

"N-o-o, nothing; I was trying to work something out. Jessica died in the May of the previous year, and Clara committed suicide at the end of January 1941. It was only about eight months after Jessica's death and by then, Clara was already nearly six months pregnant. Even my tired brain can work out that it happened between two and three months after Jessica's death. However, Esme was adamant Clara had dealt with Jessica's death and moved on from grief before that."

"Okay, that's interesting, but is it important in our overall understanding of the situation?"

"I don't know – yet. Something tells me it is. I don't know why. There is something odd about this final interview with Esme; a couple of phrases she uses throughout the interview. To me, it seems they're used in a pointed way, and not just as a figure of speech. The one that also appears in her previous interviews is that Clara 'had to take over from her mother'. It's used in reference to overseeing the household staff. The other phrase she uses several times in this final interview is a bit different. Esme says, 'Clara had to replace her mother'. I suppose the comment is innocuous in itself, but it's the way and frequency of its use that makes it stand out. It suggests Esme is trying to tell the police something important without actually saying what she wants them to know. Does it ring any bells for you?"

"As you say, the comments themselves don't say anything. I think the key to understanding their use is to take a lateral view of what Esme said. We already knew that responsibility for supervising the household staff fell to Clara following Jessica's death. Nothing intriguing in that information. It's not until we get to this part of the story and notice the phraseology changes that it starts to take on a more complex meaning. In its every possible context, what connotations can attach to the phrase 'replace her mother'?"

For a few moments, we played a game of semantics without achieving anything. Zanne, who had slid down in her chair earlier in the discussions, suddenly sprung upright. Her face reflected her excitement as she posed her hypothesis. "What if Esme was trying to tell the police that Clara had to replace her mother in *every possible sense of the word...?* That Wilfred wasn't just insisting his daughter took over her mother's role of supervising the household, but that she took over the whole of her mother's previous role? Does it mean…?"

"Christ, are you suggesting what I think you're saying? Perhaps Clara didn't have to escape from the house to become pregnant, because it happened at home. That no one followed up the story about the local lad Clara was sweet on because it was a non-issue…? Because the pregnancy had nothing to do with him?" I sat there stunned. I suspect my mouth hung open. This is my family were talking about. Initially, it was too difficult for me to believe but, in the silence that ensued, I accepted the possibility that Clara's unborn child might be her father's. I needed to take a break. To walk away from it for a while and let everything percolate through the deep dark recesses of my mind.

It was too late for a coffee break, so we opted for an early lunch instead. Lunch was a subdued affair with food and coffee consumed almost in silence. We both spent the time wrestling with our speculations and, in spite of trying to rationalise our thinking, the possibilities of what happened to Clara didn't get any better. As soon as we finished lunch, I rushed back to the table and the file I worked on this morning. The first thing I discovered was that there were discrepancies in the list of transcripts of interviews.

A careful check through the transcripts uncovered several names missing from the list of interviewees from the outset of the investigation. The list of those interviewed a second time contained no missing names. And the list of interviews conducted after the autopsy findings were released was missing one name. A check of the initial interviews showed the same name was one of those missing from that list. I'm not a great believer in coincidence, and this one seemed just a tad too convenient.

I opened both of that interviewee's transcripts on the table in front of me. A check of the name of the interviewee in both cases confirmed they were the same. "Right, Nick, let's see what you have to say for yourself," I told the transcripts. Zanne, who volunteered to clean up after lunch, was rattling crockery in the sink at the time. It's fortunate she didn't hear me, or it would result in more raucous laughter.

After reading both transcripts and then reading them again, I yelled for Zanne. "Drop everything and come and listen to this. I gave her an abridged version of the police's first interview with Nick. "Nick said he knew Clara from her visits to the market garden he and his family conducted just outside the village. Clara and the housekeeper came to buy fresh vegetables sometimes. Both women always said hello and spoke to Nick and his mother. He also saw Clara at the Post Office on a couple of occasions. They exchanged hellos. In response to the police's question, Nick said he liked Clara. She was a nice friendly person, but he denied he and Clara were lovers."

"Poor bloke; I can imagine what sort of hard time the police gave him, especially if their investigation wasn't going anywhere. What does he say in the other interview?"

"Ah yes, this one was really rough for the lad. The police accused him of being her lover, of being sexually intimate with the young girl, and of fathering her unborn child."

"Jesus, I haven't seen anything that supports that. What did he say?"

"He told them again that they were not lovers, and never had done that 'sort of thing'. Over and over again, he insisted it was impossible he was the father of her child; that he could not be responsible for Clara's pregnancy. The police asked Nick if he was accusing Clara of playing up with someone else behind his back. At that point, it seems he became quite agitated and less articulate in his response. He accused the police of blackening Clara's name by such a suggestion. Clara was a Christian and a good girl. They would have to look somewhere else for the person guilty of this terrible thing that happened to her. He told the police they should ask at her home for information, and suggested that 'maybe someone there has information about it'."

"O-o-h, that's a bit pointed. Do you think he knew the truth; shared our thoughts on what Wilfred was up to?"

"Argh, I dunno. The more we look into this, the more it starts to come together. When I think about some of Esme Nolan's responses, and now Nick's suggestions, I am convinced they were trying to show the police the way but, for some reason, neither was game to say anything straight out. I suppose it might have cost Esme her job, but would she want to continue to work for Wilfred when she had so little respect for him?"

"I suppose that might depend on her situation. Maybe she needed the job. There wouldn't be too many jobs available in Charlotte Cove I shouldn't think. Perhaps, now that Clara was gone, if she stayed in the job, she might be able to protect the young Edwina from a similar fate similar."

Zanne made sense, but my frame of mind wouldn't let me accept anything so intelligent. I wondered what happened to Esme Nolan and Nick. Esme was either a very old woman by now or, more likely, gone to meet her maker. As for Nick, no one with his surname remained in Charlotte Cove today. I might try some careful questioning of Frank Kane when next an opportunity presents.

I couldn't settle to do further research this afternoon. Although I kept telling myself we had nothing but speculation about what Wilfred might have done to his daughter, somehow I couldn't convince myself it wasn't the truth. It would explain why Nick kept insisting it wasn't possible for him to be the father of Clara's child. All we uncovered about the family so far crowded in on me. I couldn't go on. I needed a break and told Zanne. "I don't think I want to do anymore of this for the moment. A break of some sort would be best I think. Sorry, Zanne, would you mind if we called it a day?"

"Of course not; all this has come as a shock to me, so I can imagine how it must be for you. I have things to do at home anyway. An early afternoon will be good."

Zanne gathered up her gear and I walked her to her car. I felt guilty about sending her home so early, but not only didn't I want to look into this family anymore today, I also didn't want company. On our way to her car, Zanne remembered a couple of things she meant to share with me earlier in the day.

"I have something scheduled for some time during tomorrow morning. I don't know how long it will take. I'll give you a call when I'm free to see how you are going and if you're inclined to return to all that paper." I nodded but kept my thoughts to myself. I doubted I would ever want to return to Granger research. She brought me back from the dark place I'd wandered into when she remembered one last thing and lowered her window to tell me. "Ray called to say their job had finished. They would be packing up their gear tomorrow and they would call in here on their way through to Melbourne the following day."

"What…? Who is Ray and why is he coming here?"

"Ray Hartley… you know; the archaeologist who is going to scan your conservatory floor for what lies beneath. He thinks it might take a couple of hours. I don't know what time they will arrive, but I'll bring something for lunch so we can feed them before they head off after they finish here."

I didn't have a chance to object. As she finished speaking, she raised the window and drove off, leaving me stunned and alone on my driveway. I had forgotten about this friend of Zanne's and his technology. No, that's not right. Truth be told, I didn't think it would come to anything, and that he wasn't likely to be interested in what's under my floor. Still, Zanne had arranged it, and he would be here in a couple of days' time. I spent a few heartbeats soul-searching to see how I felt about that. In the end, I decided it couldn't hurt. Anyway, his gadgets probably wouldn't penetrate that solid concrete floor. In which case, we would be no wiser and I wouldn't have another unpleasant shock to deal with.

As I walked back into the house, it occurred to me that, if Ray was coming in a couple of days' time, he would need everything removed from the conservatory in order to carry out the scan. Now it was likely to become a reality, I wanted the scan to happen, but that meant facing my demons and going into the conservatory. After a few stern words with myself, I marched to the shed and fetched the wheelbarrow. Poised in the conservatory doorway with my barrow, I took a couple of deep breaths before striding across the threshold.

My philosophy was that, if I didn't allow myself time to think about where I was, and just got on with the job in hand, I'd probably be all right. I went at it like an out-of-control threshing machine. From a start near the doorway, I worked my way through the conservatory, picking up pots, emptying their contents into the wheelbarrow, and stacking the empty pots inside one another at one end of the barrow. When the barrow was full, I'd made little impression on the room. The next problem was what to do with what I had in the barrow.

The empty pots I stacked outside against one of the shed walls. The potting mix and dead plants from the pots, I tipped into a pile under one of the trees at the edge of the yard. I had some fanciful notion that I might turn the resultant pile into a compost heap. There were many more loads added to both the stack of pots and my intended compost heap before the conservatory was empty. That left only giving the place a good cleanout before I could escape from the area.

I noticed there were a series of drainage grates along the centre of the floor. This made cleaning the place out much easier. I dragged in the hose and, using the jet spray setting, gave the place a good hosing. The floor obviously had the right amount of slope. I watched the water flow into the grates, leaving little for me to remove with a broom. After stowing away the hose, I again paused for a moment outside the conservatory doorway. Somehow, the place looked less threatening now it was cleaned out. I felt no small degree of pride and satisfaction in what I achieved this afternoon… not only in terms of cleaning out the place, but at having entered the conservatory at all.

Back in the kitchen, I wondered how I might fill in the rest of the afternoon. There wasn't much of it left, but I needed to keep busy. The piles of case files on the table across the room caught my eye. I decided to test my intestinal fortitude again, and forced myself to go to the table. The once neat piles of printouts, so carefully arranged to begin with, now looked as though chooks had scratched around amongst them. I'm not OCD, but I couldn't leave them like that.

After tidying the files, I armed myself with a glass of white wine and took myself out to sit under my favourite tree. I wanted to sit for a while, to stare off into the distance and watch the world slowly drift by.

Chapter 13

So much turmoil, confusion, angst and disgust seethed within me. Meddling with the past is not a good thing to do. Perhaps the old adage about sleeping dogs should apply when it comes to family history. I had not sought to discover some previously unknown distinguished lineage. All I wanted to achieve was an understanding of my Granger line associated for more than a century with this house I've inherited. To date, research has uncovered nothing but one tragic event after another.

How long I sat under my tree is unclear, but it must've been a couple of hours. Over that time, in a slow and a nonintrusive way, the solitude worked its magic on my state of mind. The whirlpool of emotion within me calmed and eventually receded. I felt chilled; it brought me back to reality. Sometime during my soul-searching, twilight began to settle over Charlotte Cove. The Murraya hedge, a mass of white flowers since the last storm, and the jasmine in the garden bed behind me filled the heavy evening air with their perfume. Although the sun had set, the reflection of its dying rays pushed their way through the scrub behind the house to anoint the rear of the building with a fading golden glow.

I looked over at the dark silhouette of that stark pile of masonry that is *Wellsprings.* This house has been a part of my life since before I was born. It was my mother's home before that. As the last of the sun disappeared, the house became an even darker shape dominating all the surrounding shadows and shapes. The place was huge, but not beautiful; a huge box-like structure. It seemed built with practicality in mind rather than aesthetics. That thought caused a double take. From what I know about it, why do I think practicality was involved in its design.

Over my thirty-plus years, I've spent so much time here, but I know so little of the house. Although my mother and I always had bedrooms on the upper floor, all we did was sleep up there. I don't remember ever exploring that floor beyond my bedroom. We even used the downstairs bathroom. I have no idea what there is in those boarded-up sections of the house. The timber partition to the rear of the staircase that defines the boundary of my current domain has been in place ever since I can remember. Who installed it? Why and when remains a mystery. I never heard its existence discussed.

The underlying question must be, do I need such a huge rambling place. My needs require no more area than the minuscule portion of the building I presently occupy. What would I do with more space? Since my arrival, I hadn't thought to investigate what maintenance the building might require. I've never even seen a plan of the house, so it's hard to imagine the potential of the place.

All that adds up to one significant question: do I want to live here at Charlotte Cove in this house? From the outset, I was told it was an unsuitable house – especially so for a woman alone. Should I sell and find a more suitable home, either at Charlotte Cove or somewhere else? No messenger from the gods arrived with the answer. I knew it was something I'd struggle to decide. I told myself there was no hurry. I need to think it through, consider the situation from all aspects, and in the light of increased knowledge.

Night replaced twilight. Darkness surrounded me, and the dark void above twinkled with a myriad of stars. I shivered. The night air chilled me to the bone. Continuing to sit out here made no sense. I snatched up my empty coffee mug and tramped across the dewy grass to the front door. A flick of the switch and my tiny world filled with light. It was time I was fixing something for dinner, but I didn't feel hungry… and I didn't feel inclined to culinary ventures. As I stood with my back against the sink, I surveyed my living area. It was inevitable my eyes would go to that ugly timber partition behind the staircase to the upper floor.

In my current mindset, it would be pointless trying to read a book, but the sight of that partition suggested another way of filling in my evening. This was as good a time as any to begin a familiarisation exercise; a good time to get to know my house. Something Zanne said a couple of days ago took me to the back door as a starting point for my survey of the place.

When we were walking through to the kitchen after coming in the back door, as we walked past the entrance to the conservatory, we both darted a quick glance in there but kept walking. Then Zanne halted abruptly, causing me to crash into her. After we untangled ourselves, she tapped on the left-hand wall of the hallway – the wall opposite the conservatory – and asked, "Why is this wall so long? This part of the house doesn't make any sense." My response was to shrug and shake my head. I didn't know. It never occurred to me there was anything strange about it.

I went down the short flight of stairs into the servants' quarters and walked along the short hallway, past Aunt Eddie's bedroom and another small bedroom before coming to an abrupt halt at a timber partition. I knocked on various parts of the partition. It sounded hollow. Okay, so some sort of cavity exists beyond the rough-looking timber barricade blocking the hallway. "Well, that's just begging to be investigated," I announced.

It was too late to do anything about it. I contented myself with making a list of the tools I might need, and promised myself I would fetch them from the shed first thing in the morning. As there was nothing more to learn from that partition tonight, I returned to the back door and headed for the kitchen. On my way along the hall, I knocked at various places on the wall that attracted Zanne's attention a couple of days ago.

This wall was different. It didn't sound hollow like the partition in the servants' quarters. Everywhere I tapped sounded solid. I wasn't convinced this was a partition. It was probably an original wall. Apart from the sound it made, it differed from the other partition in other ways. This area was well finished and painted to match the rest of the hallway. No nails or screw heads were obvious. For its entire length, it presented a smooth unblemished surface.

Back in the kitchen, I decided I was a bit peckish after all and took some time out from exploring to heat up some leftovers. Once I had eaten, I went to my office and cleared an area of my desk. On a large sheet of cartridge paper, I started to sketch the layout of the house. It didn't take long and only occupied a small area of the paper. I didn't know much yet, but the intention was to add to the sketch as I discovered areas of the house.

Then the power, which flickered a few times, went off and seemed set to stay off. I surrendered to the inevitable, showered by candlelight and went to bed for an early night.

At some time during the night, the power came back on and, having neglected to switch off one light before I went to bed, I came into the kitchen this morning to find it ablaze with light. The temptation was to abandon my morning excursion to the beach in favour of retrieving the necessary tools from the shed to attack that partition in the servants' quarters. In the end, I dragged myself off to the beach for a much shortened session.

No time wasted dispatching breakfast and then, dressed in clothes I didn't mind sacrificing in the event of mishaps, I took myself to the shed to sort out the requisite tools. Everything went into a wheelbarrow for transport to my worksite. Then there was a return trip to the shed to fetch a ladder. A quick check I had everything I needed and work began.

It was a bit of a struggle, but I managed to insert the end of the pinch bar between the edge of one of the bottom sheets of ply and the wall. More firmly attached than I thought, I worked up quite a sweat partially prising it loose. After about half an hour and a goodly dose or two of colourful language, I had removed one sheet. That allowed me to assess my challenge. Installed across the hallway was a timber frame, a bit like a wall frame, with four sheets of ply attached to it. An assessment of the structure confirmed my planned approach: remove the sheets of ply and then demolish the supporting frame.

By lunchtime, I had removed the sheets of ply, taken them out to the shed and stacked them in the space I cleared along the end wall. On my way back to the kitchen for lunch, I detoured into the servants' quarters for another look at that frame. Constructed from sturdy timber and securely fastened, removing the frame wouldn't be easy. A bigger hammer might prove useful. I went back to the shed in search of an appropriate tool. I was almost ready to abandon my search when I found a small sledgehammer under a pile of old rubbish. On my way back to the kitchen once more, I added the sledgehammer to the collection of tools in the wheelbarrow.

While dawdling over my lunchtime sandwich, I realised I hadn't heard from Zanne this morning. I couldn't work out whether that was a good or not, and if I should worry about it. Worrying about it seemed pointless. My morning of physical exertion seemed to improve my outlook on life. If Zanne comes, she won't want to demolish partitions. She will want to continue Granger research. I am not ready to return to that yet, and I'm uncertain when my interest in the family's history might return.

Dismantling and removing the frame across the hallway occupied the afternoon. The tools and frame timber went to the shed. Stacked neatly in there, the pile of timber that was once the partition took up significant space. If I ever get around to removing the huge petition near the staircase, I will need somewhere else to stack it as the shed has no free space. That is a problem for another day. I am not about to attack that living room partition any time soon.

It was just before four o'clock when Zanne called. Her day became complicated and made it impossible for her to leave home. She reminded me Ray Hartley and his offsider, Thin Tim, were to scan the conservatory floor tomorrow. "He confirmed it with me about half an hour ago. They expect to arrive at *Wellsprings* sometime between nine and ten o'clock."

"Who is 'Thin Tim', and what's with that name?"

"He is Ray's assistant and helps handle all the technical gear. When you meet him, you will understand why the name. Built like a pencil, he is just short of two metres tall. I'll be at your place by nine o'clock tomorrow, and will bring something from the bakery for morning tea. After their early morning start, the blokes might like a cup of coffee before beginning work."

Although it was late, I was keen to explore the hallway in the servants' quarters uncovered today. Another motivating factor was Zanne's impending arrival tomorrow. Somehow, it seemed imperative I explore and understand the area before sharing it with anyone else. From my time in that hallway after removing the partition, I knew the area was dark. I didn't know about the lighting and if it still worked. I went in search of my torch and replaced the batteries.

On my way to the servants' quarters, I tried to anticipate what I might find. That led me to think about what it was like for a servant living in this house. From reading the documents from the archives, I knew there were no live-in servants during the latter part of Jessica's time as mistress of this house. Regardless of when there was live-in staff, I doubted they had much time to themselves; little 'off duty' time. However, nothing prepared me for what I discovered.

This area, known as the servants' quarters, was a long narrow addition resembling a giant skillion attached to the rear wall of the house. Its entrance was a short distance along the wall from the back door. On a slightly lower level than the rest of the house, access was via flight of four steps leading down to a long narrow hallway running the length of the quarters. The first room, immediately across from the stairs, I knew well. It was Aunt Eddie's bedroom, and had been for at least the duration of my lifetime.

I stood outside the door to Aunt Eddie's room and felt around for a light switch. A pale yellow glow flooded the room. Nothing had changed. The same furniture, the same soft furnishings, the same wallpaper; it remained the same as it was from my earliest memory it. There is no point standing here looking at this room, I told myself. That's not why you are here. Get on with exploring the rest of the place. I found the light switch for the hallway. Some lights along it stirred into life, but an equal number refused to respond. Thank goodness I remembered a torch.

Already, the place looked depressing. It wasn't just to the lack of lighting. As I stood looking along the hallway, the wall on my right was the original rear wall of the house. It remained unadorned by even a coat of paint. A series of doors opened off at regular intervals along the left-hand side of the hallway. The bare concrete floor made something of a statement about the relationship in this house between master and servant.

As I moved along the hall, going from room to room and turning on lights as I went, I found myself becoming more depressed. These rooms were intended as bedrooms for individual staff members. There were seven rooms, each no bigger than a cell. No money wasted making these rooms pleasant or even liveable. They were bare and drab. Each contained a single narrow cot and one small cupboard. The accumulation of decades of dust and fluff did nothing to enhance their appearance.

Beyond the last bedroom, a room stretched right across the hallway, effectively foreshortening its length. This housed the staff amenities. The whole area made my skin crawl, and I almost gagged at the state of the toilet. 'Primitive' would be a generous description. I was in and out of the area in seconds. Even such a short time in the 'facilities' had me feeling desperately in need of a shower.

I knew this area hadn't been occupied for decades, and that I should view it in the light of the times in which it was in use. That didn't work. The whole area, with maybe the exception of Aunt Eddie's bedroom, disgusted me; maybe even horrified me. It wasn't just the appearance of the place. It was the evidence of a total lack of care and respect for the staff. The only bright spot in these quarters is Aunt Eddie's room. Slightly larger than the combined space of two of the other rooms, Esme Nolan's interview stated it had been the staff sitting-room. Nevertheless, the more I know of my Granger ancestors, the less I like them. The way they treated their staff does nothing to enhance their standing in my opinion.

While still stunned by what I discovered in the quarters, I made my way back towards the stairs. I did not want Zanne down here. I did not want anyone down here any time soon. I need to get my head around this, need to adjust to what I've found, before even discussing it with anyone. That gave me pause for thought. Tomorrow, not only Zanne would be here, but her friend Ray and his assistant as well. As I climbed the stairs back to the main level of the house, I dragged the door to the servants' quarters closed behind me. It was stiff and creaked as I heaved it closed. I doubt it's been closed during the last half century, but I am determined it will stay closed until I'm ready for others to venture down there.

Tonight's expedition of discovery was unsettling. I expected it might intrude on the rest of my night, and it did. Sleep eluded me as my memory replayed images from those quarters. Thoughts of servants being treated poorly dogged the rest of my night.

When I went to bed last night, I knew I would feel sub-par this morning. I was right. Apart from anything else, I felt as though I hadn't slept at all. Although I woke early, I decided to abandon my morning ritual of a jog along the beach in favour of a long lazy breakfast. Today, two cups of coffee were required to coax my system to change up a gear before anyone arrived and I had to appear enthusiastic about everything that was to happen today.

Zanne arrived a few minutes before nine o'clock and babbled on excitedly about what the scan of the conservatory floor might produce. She noticed my responses were less than enthusiastic. "What's wrong with you this morning? What are you so grumpy about? Are you concerned about what might be under that floor? Look, neither of us knows what's under there, and we won't until after the scan. Let's not get ahead of ourselves by imagining all sorts of horrors hiding beneath it. Try being a little more positive, at least until after the scan. After all, Ray is doing this as a favour to me. You might try to appear a bit grateful."

She had a point. I knew my attitude was lousy, and I knew it had nothing to do with the impending scan of the conservatory floor. I took a few moments to find the right words for an apology. "I'm sorry, Zanne. I didn't mean to be a pain in the arse. It's got nothing to do with the scan. I am curious about what they might find under that floor. I think all this Granger stuff is starting to overwhelm me. So far, there is nothing good in what we've learned. I guess I'm just a bit tired and depressed."

"Yeah, okay. I hope today's efforts cheer you up a bit and don't plunge you further into the depression that seems to be taking over. I think I heard a vehicle arrive."

A white van towing a trailer was parked at the end of the driveway. While someone on the other side of the trailer appeared to be unloading things, a bloke strode up to the front door to meet us. A hunk, who looked like he knew his way around a gym, threw out his hand and announced, "Hi, I'm Ray. You must be Anthea. Her, I already know," he added with a flick of his thumb in Zanne's direction. His grin revealed perfect white teeth that stood out in stark contrast against his deep tan. "If you lead the way, we will bring our gear through."

"Oh no, don't do that. Don't unload it here. Drive around the house to the back door and unload it there. You will be working just inside the back door."

"Hey, Tim, put it back in the trailer. Come and say hello, and then drive the van around the house to the back door."

The young bloke who emerged from behind the trailer justified his nickname. The long lanky guy seemed to have lots of moving parts as he ambled over to where we congregated near the front door. "This is Tim, my offsider," Ray said by way of introduction. "He usually answers to 'Thin Tim', so feel free to call him that." Ray's fiendish chuckle as he finished speaking left me in no doubt Ray was having a laugh at Tim's expense. I chose to ignore the comment. As I walked to the van with Tim, I gave him directions on how to navigate to the back door.

While Tim drove around the house and unloaded the gear, I took Ray through to the conservatory. Zanne and I left the men to get set up while we made coffee for everyone. Our coffee break stretched on longer than expected. Ray and Zanne revisited their shared anecdotes from the past as we drank coffee and demolished the strawberries and cream filled sponge Zanne provided. However, like all good things, it came to an end. We left the men to get on with their job while Zanne and I cleared away after coffee.

By the time we ventured out to see how work was progressing in the conservatory, Tim was pushing some strange looking piece of gear on its second lap along the length of the floor. When he reached the other end, he turned the machine around and started back towards us. After only a short distance he stopped. Ray walked down to meet him.

"Looks like they have a problem," I whispered to Zanne, as we watched the two men peering at a computer screen.

"Maybe not… they don't seem agitated about anything. Perhaps they're just checking that everything is okay before proceeding."

"Nah, it's more likely something about this concrete floor is a problem."

After a few moments, Ray started back towards us. As soon as he was close enough I had to ask. "What's the problem? Isn't it working?"

"Eh…? No, everything's fine. Do you understand what we're doing here?" He looked directly at me as he spoke. I shook my head. "Okay, we're using ground penetrating radar. That means we're sending a signal down through the floor and into the ground. It bounces back to the computer, and we see it on the screen as an image of what lies below. When we start a job, especially when we don't know too much about the surface, we do a couple of test runs to see how things look. Sometimes we have to adjust the machine and start again. There were no problems with the test run we did here. We received good clear images back, and now Tim will continue scanning the rest of the floor. You're welcome to stay and watch if you want to, but I would suggest you fetch chairs to make yourselves comfortable. It could take an hour or so to complete the job."

After exchanging glances, Zanne and I took ourselves off to the kitchen. As much as we are anxious to see the results, watching someone walk up and down the conservatory was akin to watching paint dry. We decided our time would be better utilised in preparing for lunch. Once a salad was made and the chicken pieces and quiche were in the oven, we returned to check on progress. Tim was almost finished. Ray estimated it would require only another fifteen minutes. We could stand for that long without needing to fetch chairs.

While Tim rolled up leads and loaded equipment into the van and trailer, Ray brought his computer to show us the results. It was going to be much easier to understand if we could see a printout, so the three of us traipsed through to my office and connected his computer to my printer. Moments later we were peering at a page full of squiggly lines that meant absolutely nothing to Zanne or me. Ray said everything had gone well, and he was pleased with the results… which he set about explaining.

"See these wriggles in the lines over here and all around there, they are the conservatory foundations. These wriggles here," he said, pointing to a line of wriggles running down the centre of the image for about three quarters of the length of the room. "That's the underfloor drainage system that's connected to those grates in the floor." After pointing out several other features on the image, Ray stepped back and looked at me. "When we first talked about this, Zanne mentioned that a woman had disappeared a long time ago when the conservatory was being built, and that there was speculation she might have ended up under that floor. Is that correct?"

I stammered out an answer. "Yes, that's … Uhmm … What I mean is, there was speculation at the time that she met with foul play and that she might have ended up under the floor. They poured the floor the day after the night she disappeared. It all seemed a bit too convenient. I hoped that scanning the floor would prove or disprove the speculation."

"Okay, you may rest easy. As I showed you on that image, and as I can assure you without any reservation, there is no one buried under that floor. In fact, there is nothing that shouldn't be under that floor, and we did find everything that should be there."

My face must have reflected my relief. Zanne and Ray, who watched me intently as Ray explained everything, were both almost rolling on the floor with laughter by the time he finished reassuring me. After Ray settled the issue of what was under the conservatory floor, we adjourned for lunch, just in time to save the chicken and quiche from ruin. Once again, lunch stretched on longer than expected as Zanne and Ray regaled us with tales of things they were a part of in the past.

At last, it was time for the men to head off. We stood on the driveway and waved until they disappeared from sight. Then, it was back inside to clean up the kitchen. There was little conversation until we were part way through the washing up, when Zanne asked quietly, "What is it about our research that's got the better of you? Whatever it was, it sent you into an ever-decreasing downward spiral. I was concerned about you last night."

"Thanks for the concern, but you had no need to worry. There has been so much to take in, and most of what we discovered is both tragic and depressing. I suppose the other thing on my mind at the moment is deciding the future of this place."

"Deciding the future of the place…? Are you thinking of leaving Charlotte Cove? What's brought this on?"

"No, no; I don't know what I'm thinking. Perhaps it's more a case of wondering whether I want to rattle around by myself in a place this big. Oh, I don't know how to explain it. I suppose that, after everything that happened, I found myself moved-in here without having given much, if any, thought to the future. You know me. I like things to be orderly; a bit more planned and structured than here is right now. Anyway, what about you; you were waiting for a call or something yesterday, and you seemed a bit concerned about it. Is everything all right?"

"It was a call from my agent. I knew a promotional tour discussed with various people some time ago might happen sometime soon. It seems I'm heading off next week on a tour of some of the rural areas of the state. I'll leave on Sunday afternoon and probably won't return until the following Sunday or Monday. I'll be exhausted by the end of it. I think my schedule has me appearing in a bookstore in a different town every day. To add to the joy of it all, my agent, and maybe my publisher, want to slot in a meeting as well. I was worried because I wasn't going to be here for you if you were in a bad way and needed support."

"Go and enjoy your trip. Smile at lots of people and sign lots of books. I'll try to think of you occasionally, but I will be fine without you."

Zanne laughed at me, but then turned serious. "Don't do anything rash about the house while I'm away. I have some ideas that might inform your thinking. I'll talk to you about them when I return from my trip.

The remaining couple of days before Zanne left on her epic road trip were lazy days. We saw each other for a couple of hours each day either for coffee of lunch, but we did no research. The

IT firm I'm contracted to had a couple of small jobs they wanted done in a hurry. I was pleased to oblige, and to take my mind off other things. They helped fill in the time until Zanne left and, when a third job arrived, work kept me occupied until late on Tuesday.

Tuesday night, as I sat with my feet up and sipping an after dinner glass of red wine, I wondered how I might spend the next few days. By the time I went to bed, I knew I wasn't going to do any research. I would be exploring more of this house.

Chapter 14

After a rigorous jog along the beach and a long slow breakfast, I eased into Wednesday, luxuriating in the knowledge that my time was my own today, and for the next few days. As with all good things, sitting around doing nothing had to end. I donned the now freshly laundered sacrificial outfit again. A rip in these clothes from snagging them on a nail or the like, was no great sacrifice. Then, after checking the batteries in my torch were okay, I strode to the servants' quarters.

The door I closed a few days before required all my weight against it before being persuaded to open again. My first task was to walk the length of the corridor, turning on every light switch I could find as I went. I'm sure a few more lights have 'died' since I was last here. Those that worked were less than effective. They had no shades, and were nothing more than bare bulbs on the end of a lead dangling from the ceiling.

On my way back along the corridor towards the stairs, I noticed a door set in the stonework of what was originally the rear wall of the house. None of the lights worked in that section of the corridor. Buried in deep shadow, I missed it on my first visit to the area. The door looked substantial and a bit daunting. But it's a door, I told myself, and a door needs opening if you want to find out what's on the other side.

I gave it a tentative push. Nothing happened. A more determined push produced the same result. The question of whether or not it was locked disappeared when I realised there was nowhere to insert a key. This door was never meant to be locked. "Okay, that makes life a bit easier," I reassured myself. I tested the large door handle. It seemed solid enough and unlikely to come off in my hands. With a firm grip on the handle and my shoulder against the door, I tried lifting the door as I pushed against it with all my strength. That worked – sort of. It moved about two centimetres.

After two encores of the same performance, it had opened about fifteen centimetres. My recent jogging along the beach had reduced most of the excess weight I gained in recent times, but I hadn't lost enough to fit through that opening. One more try, I told myself. Maybe that will widen it enough for me to slip through. I adopted the familiar stance and pushed with all my might. The door came free of whatever was binding it and banged open against the wall. I went along for the ride, and finished with my face mashed up against the door and a tender shoulder. As I scraped myself off the door and straighten up, I announced, "This door stays open from here on. God help anyone who closes it."

Then it was time to take stock of where I was. Surprise, surprise…; I was in a corridor. It was short, and intersected yet another corridor at a T-junction. For a moment, I wondered whether this was an example of a 'black hole' such as currently occupies astronomers. Maybe I would find it contained dark matter from the universe. The dense blackness pervading the area seemed to absorb the light from my torch. Some distance along the short corridor and high up on the wall, I found a light switch. Although not bright, the pale yellow light was better than nothing.

At the T-junction of the corridors, a decision was required. Should I go right or left? I shone my torch along the corridor to my right. The corridor seemed to go only a short distance before ending at a wall. To my left, the corridor stretched on beyond the range of my torch. Okay, it's to the right; let's see what lies between here and that wall.

The corridor was wide and took me past two separate rooms. Both were small. I didn't stop to inspect them, heading straight to the end of the corridor instead. This wall looked as though it was part of the original construction. The double door in the centre that opened almost the full width of the corridor intrigued me. It wasn't locked. I tried the right-hand door and it opened inwards towards me. That brought the next surprise.

There was nothing beyond the door and the wall it was set into except another wall. I open the other half of the door and shone my torch all over this second wall now blocking my way. My suspicion when I first saw that wall was confirmed. It seemed comprised of unpainted sheets of ply attached to the outside of the wall containing the double doors. Was this second wall yet another example of a partition blocking entry to this area? Although I examined as much as I could of the false wall, I found nothing to change my thinking about it.

With nothing more to interest me at that end of the corridor, I started back towards the T-junction, but took my time to explore everything as I went. I came to the first of the two little rooms I'd noticed. It contained a small desk, built-in cupboards lined the walls, and a nice coat stand stood in the corner. Like doors, cupboards need to be opened if you want to know what's in them, so I tried my luck – or my lack thereof as it turns out.

The cupboards lining the wall opposite the desk were locked. The first two cupboards I tried along the wall to one side of the desk gave me the same result. Feeling a bit dispirited by the whole exercise, I ignored the final cupboard along that wall, and flopped down on the rickety chair behind the desk. A cloud of dust rose up to envelop me. The desk looked interesting, and now that was I was sitting behind it, it begged to be investigated.

Three drawers on either side of the dark stained timber desk were too much temptation to ignore. I tested the drawers on the right-hand side; all locked. That's in keeping with how my luck is running today, I thought, and turned my attention to the drawers on the left-hand side. The top drawer was unlocked. As with their counterparts on the other side of the desk, the second and third drawers on the left-hand side also were locked. That allowed me only one desk drawer to explore. I wasn't going to ignore it.

It almost disappointed. There was little in it: four pencils, what I assumed was an ancient pencil sharpener, a wooden ruler, and a pair of not very sharp scissors. Everything was contained in a shallow cardboard box that looked a like the lid from a chocolate box. I lifted it out for a closer look, and something slid forward from the back of the drawer. It was a matchbox… and it rattled. The rattle was a small key; a small key that looked as though it might fit the locks on this desk. I thanked the gods for the find, saving me having to trek to the shed for something to bust open the desk's drawers.

So much for getting excited about finding the key… The top drawer on the right side of the desk seemed a good place to start. Although the key fitted, there was some resistance when I tried to turn it. After some wriggling and jiggling, it decided to co-operate. Disappointment is not a great emotion. I received my first dose of it for the morning. The top right hand drawer is where most people keep things they use often unless they are left-handed. This drawer contained white gloves, a bottle opener, a silver cigarette lighter, and a neatly folded apron. Essential butler's equipment, but not exciting from my point of view.

The other two drawers on the right side contained ledgers and account books associated with running the household. I chose to leave them where they were and congratulated myself on my self-control. These could provide me with much insight into the household in the past. I will retrieve them at some future time to study them in depth. With all the drawers on the right side investigated, it was time to look at the remaining two drawers on the left side.

That brought my second disappointment of the day. The middle drawer on the left was empty. I took a deep breath and inserted the key in the last locked drawer. This bottom drawer bound on its runners and required a fair amount of effort. Again, there was a cardboard box. It looked as though it might be the bottom half of the lid in the top drawer. There was nothing to excite me here either. The box held a couple of bottles of ink – one red and one blue– a collection of pens and nibs, a few pencil stubs, and one of those rocker type blotter gadgets. Remembering what happened with the top drawer, without upsetting the ink bottles, I removed the cardboard box.

A large piece of blotting paper lined the drawer. I stopped myself as I was about to reef it out. Wiser to check if anything else is in the drawer, than risk damaging something because I was too lazy to look. I slid my hand in and swiped it around a bit in a perfunctory search for hidden objects. When I found nothing, I pulled out the blotting paper… and something slid down from the back along with the paper.

It was a small wooden box with intricate carvings on the lid and all four sides, and an ornate tiny brass lock on the front. I tested the lid. It opened. I felt like a kid on Christmas day. This is one of the best presents I ever received. The box contained a number of keys. They looked more like cupboard keys than doors keys. In this room alone, there were a number of cupboards I wanted to unlock, so it seemed a good place to start testing the keys.

I selected a key. Starting at the cupboard nearest the door, I worked my way along the first wall. The key fitted in every lock but unlocked none. I turned the corner and started on the cupboards along the side wall. That produced the same result until I reached the final cupboard, the one I hadn't bothered to try opening before. The key belonged to this cupboard. Within moments, it was wide open.

There wasn't much on the narrow shelves; a notebook that looked like some sort of key register, an ancient looking torch with its metal casing corroded by its battery, and a tatty pair of leather gloves. However, the cupboard door was a veritable treasure trove. It explained the narrow shelves. The inside of the cupboard door was studded with row upon row of cup hooks, most of which held keys.

After studying the key rack for a few moments, I worked out that the keys on the hooks were spares. The rows of hooks stopped some distance from the bottom of the door. On the last hook of the last row, was a large bunch of keys. That bunch of keys captured my attention. Both the keys and the key ring showed signs of wear from frequent use. These were the keys a butler might carry around with him. I spent some time comparing the keys on the ring with those hanging on the hooks, and confirmed my assumption that those on the hooks were the original keys, while those on the ring were copies.

The cupboard held no further secrets or surprises, so I placed the key to that cupboard on the desk and selected another key from the box. It took some time, but I worked my way through the keys until I identified each key's respective cupboard. At the end of the exercise, each of the keys lay on the desk opposite its cupboard. I left them on the desk in that order until I tag them. The wooden box I also left on the desk. My intention was to relocate later it to my office so I could admire it from time to time.

On my way out of the room, I paused in the doorway to cast an eye over that tiny room. This was a butler's office, I felt sure.

Everything in it suggested that was the case. The cupboards lining the walls contained mainly silverware, not the sort of pieces that might be on display in other parts of the house where visitors could see and admire them. These were functional pieces that would be trotted out for use on special occasions. They included candelabra, individual candlesticks, condiment sets, and several sets of serving implements. Some pieces of crystal occupied one of the cupboards, but again, those pieces looked functional rather than to impress.

As the butler's office had nothing more to offer for now, I moved on to the next room along the corridor. It didn't take me long to work out that this shoebox of a room was the butler's pantry. The wine racks behind locked glass cupboard doors and the array of various paraphernalia associated with drinking were a dead giveaway. Perhaps in some ways, this room was another disappointment. No overlooked bottle remained in any cupboard. It would make my day to find some ancient bottle of red wine covered in dust and lying forgotten in one of the wine racks, but it wasn't to be.

With nothing of interest to waste my time in the butler's pantry, I moved along the corridor to the T-junction. Time had run away from me, and it was getting late. I hesitated at the junction of the corridors. Should I quit my tour of exploration, or continue for a bit longer? Never happy to leave a question unanswered, I elected to push on. I strode across the junction and along to the entrance of the first room beyond it.

All the walls were lined with shelves. Rails hanging down from the ceiling on chains had hooks of various sizes hooked over them. Against one wall where the bottom shelf was removed, a large chest like box caught my attention. Utilitarian in appearance, it seemed completely unadorned. A lid with a substantial handle formed most of the top of the box.

I could see a hook set in the wall behind it, and assumed that when opened, the handle could be slipped onto that hook to hold it open. I tried lifting the lid. It was heavy. Once the lid was hooked back, I examined the box, for that's what it was, a box. About 900 millimetres square, all sides of the box, including the lid, were at least 100 millimetres thick, and the interior face of all sides was metal sheeted. The box was empty, but a drainage hole in a back corner of the base suggested it was an icebox. This was the last thing I needed to convince me this was the larder.

Okay, I had identified the butler's domain, and now having identified what I believe to be the larder, excitement began to build. Somewhere along this corridor, surely there will be a kitchen. No point standing here wondering about it, I told myself. Keep moving along the corridor. I continued past quite a long wall before coming to the next doorway. This was close to two metres wide and had a strange door arrangement. It effectively required three doors to close the entrance. One full-length heavy timber door closed half of the entrance, while the other half sported a Dutch or stable type door that allowed one half of the door to be open or closed at any time.

Not wanting to scramble under the top half of the door or, alternatively to open both halves at that door, I chose to heave open the single door instead. Apart from being huge, there was something odd about the room. It took me a few moments to work out what that was.

It was lighter in here than anywhere else in this part of the building. Then I realised this room had the first windows I'd seen since entering the servants' quarters. That's not to suggest it was a bright, airy place. High up on the wall opposite the door were two small windows. Now covered in grime and cobwebs, they allowed a little light to penetrate. I found a bank of light switches that added their dim light to that of my torch and the windows.

I had found *Wellsprings'* own Aladdin's cave. This was the kitchen; the original kitchen. The most amazing place; it left me breathless. How long has passed since as much as a cup of tea was made in this kitchen? Everything is still here: huge wooden tables scrubbed bare, the stone hearth with a rotisserie, copper pots of every imaginable design and size – many dangling from rails hanging from the ceiling – and two huge brick ovens.

Two old-fashioned looking sinks occupied an area along one wall, and three trolleys of different designs appeared randomly abandoned around the room. No Formica or stainless steel here; unpainted timber predominated. All of it scrubbed to a shade much paler than its original colour. On one end of one of the table were two monstrous looking rolling pins. The size of them and their weight must have required two people to use them. I couldn't picture some little old woman, who was the cook, having the strength to use one on her own. Everywhere were cleavers, knives and choppers of every descript, and there were lots of them. Spoons in both metal and wood, some of them enormous, proliferated. Leaning against the wall beside one of the ovens were two wooden paddles of the type used to introduce loaves into an oven.

The sight of so much beautiful stuff – so much history – was overwhelming. I could linger so much longer in the kitchen, but I noticed the light, such as it was, from the windows was fading. The afternoon was slipping away, and I still had more to explore. With some reluctance, I left the kitchen and moved along the corridor to the next room.

This one was small, not much bigger than the butler's office. Again, shelves lined the walls leaving a narrow walkway through the centre of the room. An ancient hatbox remained on a top shelf, and a small travelling trunk was tucked in under the bottom shelf. For want of any other idea, I decided this was a box room. Although I was tempted to haul the trunk out to see if it contained anything, I was running out of time. From the doorway, one last quick look around the room, and I moved on.

I was almost at the end of the corridor when I came to the entrance to the last room. This was the laundry. There were washtubs, buckets and pails of all sizes, two mangles, several scrubbing boards, and airing racks – or maybe they were drying racks.

Most impressive were the two bricked-in, wood-fired coppers for boiling the washing. The 'pans' that held the water and washing were about a metre and a half in diameter and nearly 900 millimetres deep. They would take ages to come to the boil. Leaning against the wall near the coppers were the long stout poles used to lift washing out of the coppers and into the laundry trolleys. A shelf above what I assumed to be the 'ironing table' held an array of irons. The history of the house was displayed through the various models of irons on that shelf. To my untrained eye, each one looked more sinister than its successor.

Although I was at the end of the corridor, there was one more door I hadn't opened. I pushed it open, expecting it to reveal yet another room. What I saw made me gasp. The door opened into an external courtyard of sorts. Quite small, from the outside, its surrounding brick wall made it look as though this space was part of the building and not an outside area. The whole space was festooned with clothes lines strung from one side to the other, and all held aloft by sturdy bush-timber props.

With the sun having left the sky, twilight was settling in. Back in the corridor, I secured the external door before starting my trek out of the place. As I drew level with the box room, I noticed a set of stairs climbing upwards from the other side of the corridor. I shone my torch up it. As far as my torch let me see, there appeared to be two sections to the stairs. There was some sort of landing at about the half way point from which the second section continued on almost to roof level.

An expedition to explore those stairs was something for another day. My focus at that time was on getting back to the servants' quarters before darkness set in. I hurried along the corridor switching off lights as I went and, by the time I emerged from the servants' quarters, the world outside was bathed in night. I needed my torch to find the nearest light switch as the house too was now in darkness.

As soon as I switched lights on, I came back to that wall opposite the conservatory. This was the wall that Zanne thought wrong because it was so long and incongruous with the rest of the house. Again, close examination of the wall, including tapping all over it, found nothing untoward. However, having just explored what I now considered the 'domestic chores' area of the house, I thought this wall was a partition blocking entry to that domestic area of the house. My theory needed testing at some time but, if it proved correct, should the partition remain in situ or should I remove it?

I was hungry, but I felt filthy from the crud of ages collected on my expedition of discovery. My stomach would have to continue to rumble and complain until after I showered and felt human again. My mind was back in that domestic chores area as I stood there, the shower's needle-like spray stinging my skin. This afternoon I gained a bit more information to add to my sketch of the layout of this house, but more than that, I had given myself more questions without answers.

In spite of my best intentions not to indulge in any further research this week, I weakened. After dinner, I went to my office and ferreted out the copy of the local newspaper article about Wilfred's death that had the poor quality image of him. Something about the article nagged me, but I couldn't work out what it was. I read the article again, noting salient points as I did. Then, I sat back and studied my list of points. Still nothing jumped out at me.

I put aside the article and my notes, and let my mind roam free for a while. It all seemed straightforward. What was bothering me? Mentally, I revisited each of the facts I extracted from the article. At the end of the article, it said Wilfred's cortege moved to *Whylara* for his burial. From nowhere, a new question came to me… Did Wilfred bury Jessica at *Whylara* too? Was his intention that they be buried together at some favourite spot on the property? The sceptic in me had some doubts about that. As my mind explored the question of Jessica's burial, it came up with another question. Where did they bury Clara?

In the early 1940s, what was the church's position on suicide burials? Had they moved away from the view that no suicide could be buried in consecrated ground? Did that only ever apply to churchyard cemeteries? All these mental gymnastics proved was how little I knew about such matters. "I'll bet Zanne is an expert on them," I told my office. I didn't even know if Charlotte Cove had a cemetery… or a church for that matter. There is a building that looks like it was a church. These days, it's a shop with a residence above. I don't remember seeing any headstones in the surrounding grounds. I asked myself, is it really important; does it matter where they're buried? Yes, it is. I had to know.

Our research to date focused on charging forward towards the current era. Was this the right approach? I wanted to know those stories, but I wanted to know all there was to know. In spite of the time, effort and paper involved so far, I didn't feel I knew these people; couldn't tell you anything about them apart from when they were born married, and died – and how a couple of them died. What I didn't have were details of their lives. There was that question again: does it matter?

Rather than depress myself further, I abandoned my office, found a film dating from about four decades ago on TV, and tried to switch off all thoughts of the Granger family by sipping wine while watching TV.

Should have stuck with TV and given the wine a miss last night. As I jogged along the beach, I felt as though my thick head might fall off. My favourite dog and his elderly owners were on the beach again this morning. However, contrary to the usual practice, the dog was off his leash and roaming free. The trio arrived when I was about halfway back to my car. While not moving too far away, the dog distanced himself from his owners. He pranced and dashed backwards and forwards along the edge of the water, while this owners ambled along on the hard dry sand higher up the beach.

I caught up to and jogged past the dog, passing between him and his owners. He didn't see me, so intent was he on investigating a small crab. When he noticed me, I already was a little way ahead of him. He pounded along the sand after me, and then trotted along with me all the way to my car. I was ready to go home. He wanted to play. I felt sorry for him. We chased one another around on the sand. He is fitter than I am. I called it quits and went to my car. The moment I opened the door, he tried to dart around me and into the car.

Is this a disobedient dog in need of training, or could it be deaf? I'm not sure which explanation I prefer, but either way, his owners' strident calls and commands met with no response. While retaining a firm grip on his collar, I tried convincing him he wasn't coming home with me. He didn't seem interested in what I wanted, and was determined to achieve what he wanted. We were still negotiating when the angry elderly man, leash in hand, stormed up to the car and belted the dog one across the snout. That brought my dark side to the fore in a rush.

"That's no way to treat the dog. No wonder he wants to get away from you. Why do you have a dog when you clearly don't want to care for it, or train it?" Elevated blood pressure was making my already thick head thump. My hackles were up and, although I knew I would not make any friends, I would not back down. To my surprise, the old man seemed to crumple. He sagged against my car's mudguard.

"Do you want him?" he rasped. I could see he had trouble speaking, and offered him a drink of water, which he gulped down. Then he tried again. "I'm sorry. What I meant to say is, would you like to have him? He really is too much for us to look after, but he was hoisted on us. We don't want him, but we couldn't bring ourselves to put him down."

"Christ, thank God you didn't do that. He's a beautiful dog, but I understand how he might be a bit much for you." I found myself in a quandary. I like the dog and he seemed to like me, but did I want a dog? A pet wasn't on my radar at the moment. This was not a decision to make while standing on the beach with a thumping headache. I was saved from having to respond when the man started speaking again.

"He belonged to our grandson who was killed a few months ago in a car accident. The lad was only fifteen. He was a good student and sportsman. His mother was driving him home from basketball training that night. She ran off the road and crashed into some trees. Although high on drugs at the time, she was unhurt. She is an ice addict, and somehow when the dust settled after the accident, we found ourselves with the dog to look after. We'd be happy to see him go to a good home. Apart from the fact that he's a bit much for us to care for, he is a reminder of our grandson. My wife finds it hard to cope."

Okay, now I feel suitably chastised for my outburst. I begged time to think about it, but struck a deal for the meantime. Every morning, on my way to the beach, I would collect the dog and take him for a run before dropping him back home again. I could see it fell short of what he hoped for, but we shook hands on the deal. I scrambled into my car and reversed out of the parking lot while the man attached the leash to the dog's collar and dragged him back onto the beach. Jesus, Zanne, where are you when I need you? There's too much going on in my head to be able to decide about the dog without talking it through with somebody. Still, it would be handy to have a dog. That way, if I was caught talking to myself, I could say I was talking to the dog.

I had enough to think about right now. There would be no decision about the dog for a while but, before doing anything, I will run it past Zanne when she gets back.

Chapter 15

After Thursday as a day of contemplation and list making, Friday brought renewed energy and enthusiasm for exploring the house. It didn't bring sufficient energy to contemplate tearing down any more partitions. However, I still had that mysterious set of stairs in the domestic chores area to investigate, and to explore the top floor. The decision was easier than expected. The top floor won out over tearing up and down flights of stairs.

I stood at the foot of the grand sweeping staircase that might be straight out of Gone with the Wind except there is no Scarlett O'Hara on the stairs and I'm no Rhett Butler. The staircase, a mass of polished timber and well-worn carpet, sweeps upwards in a graceful flare to the small landing above. Almost as an afterthought before beginning the climb, I fetched my torch. As is the case with much of the rest of the house, probably not many lights still work up there.

The landing overlooked the entrance area of the house below. It was more like an oversized balcony than a landing; a bit like a Juliet balcony on steroids. Two doors led off the balcony, one located centrally and one about halfway along the right hand side. I knew the central doorway well although, in my memories, this door was always open. It could wait. The second door, to the right and further along the balcony, I never saw open whenever Mum and I visited here. That had to merit first look.

"That's not what I expected," I exclaimed when I discovered the door locked. I giggled. This was one of those occasions when having a dog around would save my dignity if anyone overheard me talking to myself. Focus on the job in hand, I told myself, and went back to the main door. I wondered how long ago anyone last closed this door. Some time had elapsed since my mother visited *Wellsprings*. Once I was no longer around, she would be the only person using a bedroom on this floor. Why had Aunt Eddie seen the need to close it after it remained open for decades? I suspected that question would remain another of life's mysteries.

It took a bit of pushing and shoving to convince the stiff hinges to co-operate and allow the door to open fully. There it was, just as I remembered it. In front of me, a wide central hallway dividing the top floor stretched to the opposite wall. From both sides of the hallway, doors opened into what I assumed were bedrooms. I found the switch for the hall lights. Some came on, some didn't. The result made little improvement to the lighting along the hallway. I strode to the first door on the left side of the hall.

This door led to the rooms that were our bedrooms when mum and I visited. There were two rooms joined by an interconnecting door. The hall door opened into a good-sized room, while access to the second smaller room was via a door from within the main room. Mum always took the large room. Nothing had changed in either room. In the main room, the same furniture remained; plain dark-stained solid timber furniture, possibly Jacobean in style.

The main room contained a large bed, two bedside cabinets, a dressing table and large wardrobe-type cupboard. The only items incongruous with the rest of the furniture were a desk against the wall under the window, and an ornate looking chair pulled up to the dressing table. Both items were a more recent vintage than the other furniture. The drapes pulled closed across the single narrow window were the ones I remembered. Now dingy with their accumulation of dust, to my mind, they were ancient. These drapes had always been in this room. I reached out to open them to let in more light. The fabric disintegrated in my hand. The drapes and other soft furnishings weren't the only things in the room that hadn't changed. Although now curling off in places, the bayadere-patterned wallpaper featuring a regular floral stripe on a yellow background remained unchanged. The only thing to exhibit any noticeable change was the dressing table mirror. Its silvering, always blemished in places, for much of the mirror now was damaged.

My small bedroom had the same wallpaper. It would not be my choice for such a small room. Although the style of furniture echoed that of the main room, there was little of it; a single bed and a small cupboard. No bedside tables or dressing table occupied precious space in this room.

As I stood in the larger room, a deeper understanding of these two rooms came to me. In previous times, this was the nursery. One room was for the nanny or nursery maid, while the other was for the child. It was a convenient set-up. The child tucked away in the attached small room was close to the nanny when it needed attention. There was something depressing about standing here in these dusty and forlorn looking rooms. I returned to the equally cheerless corridor and moved on to the next door along this side.

At the door, I stopped and scanned the corridor. I could make-out six doors on this side of the corridor, but it seemed the configuration of rooms on the opposite side differed. The corridor was dull and uninviting, partly due to the number of lights that weren't working, but the dust and neglect of decades contributed to an overall feeling of abandonment. I tried wiping the dust from a small area of wall near the door. Some came off but most didn't. I spat on my finger and used it to clean a small area. The paint it revealed, about one shade lighter than the colour of mustard, never lightened or brightened this thoroughfare.

I inspected each of the bedrooms as I made my way along the corridor. They all looked much the same. All looked as though their occupants went out one day many years ago and forgot to come home. The furniture in each room was basic, sturdy, wooden and unadorned. Each room contained only a narrow bed and a cupboard. I didn't dare touch the drapes.

After exploring five bedrooms along this side of the corridor, what lay behind the sixth door was both a shock and an unpleasant experience. Although from the corridor, it seemed the sixth door opened into an extra-large room. In reality, it provided access to two small rooms. I had found the upper floor facilities. From the door, a narrow passageway went past the toilet and opened into a bathroom complete with cast-iron claw-footed bathtub. We had never used these facilities during our visits, always using the bathroom downstairs. Although installed decades ago, the ground floor facilities were positively modern by comparison.

My time in this area was brief. Everything was filthy, and I don't mean just dusty. The thought of touching anything so horrified me, I kept my hands in my pockets for most of the time, except for when I pulled back the plastic shower curtain and opened the toilet door. The rough shower arrangement over the bathtub was the only nod to modern living. In the bathtub, the plughole and surrounding area supported a thick black accretion. A scum of some sort coated the rest of the interior of the tub and would require chemical attack rather than elbow grease to remove it. The hand basin was a primitive arrangement. There was no built-in cupboard to hide its plumbing and, as there was only one tap, I guessed there was no hot water to the basin.

If I found the bathroom unpleasant, the state of the toilet was appalling. The room was tiny, almost requiring anyone wishing to use the toilet to back in, as there was little enough room to turn around. A big old-fashioned pedestal had a polished timber seat and lid sporting stains I didn't want to know about. Without giving too much thought to it, I lifted the lid… and almost gagged. "That was not a good move," I croaked as I dropped the lid, the sound reverberating through the place.

I hurriedly closed the door and stood outside dragging in a few deep breaths before setting out to investigate the rooms along the opposite side of the corridor. Again I started from the landing and made my way to the first door on the right side. Yet another passageway…! I stepped through the door into a narrow passageway running off in both directions and parallel to the main central hallway. I turned right and, a short distance later, entered a sitting room.

The locked door on the far side of the room unlocked from the inside. I opened it and stepped through to find myself on the landing at the top of the staircase. This was the locked door I discovered earlier. Under dust covers were three overstuffed lounge chairs upholstered in well-worn vaguely patterned dark brown velvet. I lifted a cushion and looked at its underside. Here the fabric was less worn and the pattern more distinct. The fabric sported a Paisley pattern in shades of browns and beige, and with a splash of orange here and there. It took a few moments for the dust cloud I created to settle. A couple of side tables and a threadbare carpet square in the middle of the floor completed the furnishings in this room.

Leaving the dust mites to settle at their leisure, I went to the other end of the passage. It opened into a good-sized bedroom containing a huge bed, two bedside cabinets, fancy writing desk, a utilitarian-looking dressing table, and another ancient looking lounge chair accompanied by a side table and standard lamp. Everything about this room and the sitting room at the other end of the passage screamed 'male'. Set off to the side of the passage, another small room was sandwiched between the sitting room and bedroom. This room's fittings included hanging space and shelving, and a hatstand graced one corner. Access to the suite of three rooms was via one door from the central corridor. I was confident this was Wilfred's domain, and possible Rupert's before him. There was nothing feminine in any of these three rooms.

With nothing more to see in those rooms, I moved along to hallway to the next door opening off it. I discovered a similar suite of three rooms. However, there was a marked difference. These rooms exhibited a distinct feminine influence. From the chintz covered sitting room chairs to the lace doyleys and crystal duchess set on the dressing table, these were a woman's rooms. Even the fittings in the dressing room between the bedroom and sitting room reflected the different needs of a female occupant.

The third door along this side of the corridor opened into another set of facilities. Although smaller and in slightly better state than the other bathroom, I took one quick look around and shut the door again. That brought my tour of the neglected upper floor to an end. Something about the way it appeared to be waiting for its inhabitants to return reminded me of the *Mary Celeste*. I found it almost impossible to comprehend how, after such a long time, the whole floor remained exactly as it was when its last occupants abandoned it.

Yet again depressed by what I found, I stood on the balcony at the top of the stairs and took a few moments to imagine what it was like when this top floor was in use every day. It didn't work. My mind held fast to the dusty forlorn abandoned place it is now. Something drew me off the balcony and back inside. As I entered the central hallway again, I realised I hadn't examined the hall itself.

As I strolled along flashing my torch in every direction, I wondered what a corridor could tell me. The grime covered walls were still there. However, this time, I noticed the 'hall runner' carpet snaking along the centre. About a metre and a half wide and well worn, its colour was indistinguishable. A closer look revealed a patterned border along its length. It was about 200 millimetres wide and ran down both sides of the carpet strip. Although the pattern featured lighter colours, I make out the pattern.

I turned my attention to the lighting, and shone my torch along both walls. For the first time, I noticed a small wall sconce positioned high up on the wall near each door. None was working. The bulbs probably burnt out long ago. However, it's possible they are not working because I haven't found the switch for them yet. That focused my attention on the overhead lights. Nothing fancy here, just 'ladies' skirts' type shades mounted directly on the ceiling in a neat row above the centre of the hallway. About half were not working.

Cobwebs, hanging like forgotten Christmas decorations, festooned the entire length of the corridor. The dust and fluff accumulated over time gave them added substance; more like Halloween decorations now. With my neck craned upwards, I strolled the length of the corridor checking the lights and the cobwebs as I went. The area outside the bathrooms at the far end of the corridor was the darkest. Here the cobwebs were thickest. What began as thin threads attached to the ceiling, over the years grew into thin ropes that wove themselves into lacy patterns and connected with their colleagues to form spectacular constructions. Those industrious creatures created a thick lacy curtain stretching across the corridor.

It was while I stood gazing in admiration of such creativity that something else caught my attention. An area of the ceiling looked somehow different. I thought I could make out marks but wasn't sure what they were. The ceiling was too high, but I thought I detected the fine line outline of a square with other marks surrounding it.

My pulse quickened. Could I be looking at a manhole cover in the ceiling? Why would a manhole cover excite me? I needed a closer look, but that was one high ceiling. It would take the longest ladder I had to reach it. Well, standing here thinking about it isn't going to get you up there, and it won't fetch the ladder, I told myself. On my way to the shed, I thought about those cobwebs. Best I take a broom up with me to shift them for a clear look at everything.

Lugging the tallest stepladder I had up those stairs was no mean feat. By the time I had the ladder in place and the broom at the ready, I felt exhausted. I decided on a break for lunch before exploring further. That required restraint. No sooner was I in the kitchen than I was itching to be up the ladder investigating that ceiling. As a result, I wasted no time over lunch. How long does it take to eat a piece of fruit? I laughed when I checked the time as I climbed the staircase. It wasn't yet eleven o'clock, and I'd had lunch. It was time for a closer look at the ceiling.

I was right. It was a manhole cover, and the marks around it were scratch marks. "Should I be worrying about what's in the roof cavity when I don't know what's in most of the house?" I wondered aloud. There was no reply, so I allowed my curiosity to dictate what to do next. I placed both hands firmly on the manhole cover and pushed. Nothing happened. For my next attempt, I tried giving it all I had – with the same result. Pounding all over it with a clenched fist proved futile as well.

Never one to let a challenge go unanswered, I climbed a couple of rungs higher on the ladder. From my new height, I could no longer stand upright. I was so close to the ceiling, I had to bend my knees. Determined not to let a poxy manhole cover defeat me, I straightened up enough to place my shoulders, neck and the back of my head against the cover. Then, using my hands to balance me, I pushed on the cover by straightening my legs. They didn't straighten too far as the cover didn't budge. One more attempt to loosen it by thumping all over it with a clenched fist and I was ready to try another shoulder charge.

This time there was some movement. I checked my handiwork. The cover had moved upwards about two or three centimetres. That's encouraging. After delivering it another good thumping, I adopted my shoulder charge position, and jerked myself upwards with all my might...and almost fell off the ladder when the cover came free. I climbed down one rung and with both hands balancing the cover, slid it across to one side of the manhole.

After taking a moment to steady myself again, I stood on top of the ladder, ready for the big moment. I had an idle thought about where the nearest physiotherapist had their practice. My neck and shoulders might need professional help after today. As I straightened my legs – gently this time – my head and upper torso rose up through the manhole and into the black void beyond. Although I allowed my eyes a few seconds to adjust to the darkness, I still couldn't see anything. "Nothing ventured, nothing gained," I said aloud, more to reassure myself than anything else. The area surrounding the manhole seemed solid. I hoped it was solid enough to cope with what I was about to do.

With my hands firmly planted on an area beside the manhole, I bounced upwards, twisted, and plonked my backside down. I was sitting inside the roof cavity with my legs dangling out through the opening. From my new perch, my torch seemed to make little impact on the impenetrable blackness of the space. For safety sake, I shuffled a short distance on my backside away from the opening before standing up. There was plenty of space above my head. I trained my torch on the floor beneath my feet as I took a few tentative steps into the black abyss.

It only required three or four short steps before I started making out lumpy shapes through the gloom. After another couple of steps, I could see enough to know where I was. I was in another *Wellsprings'* version of Aladdin's cave. Although the roof cavity wasn't designed as an attic, sometime during the house's history, the space became one. The first step in that conversion was the installation of solid ply flooring – for which I was ever so grateful.

Although the blackness seemed to absorb the light from my torch, I could make out pieces of furniture, several shipping trunks of various sizes, and a myriad of boxes and baskets all overflowing with whatever contents they held. I stood transfixed by the scene, and unable to decide what to do next. Rather than logical thought, instinct intervened to drive me forward. I moved to the nearest objects, and began picking my way through the horde of material piled haphazardly in roughly the centre of the space.

As I stepped around what looked like an antique writing desk, I almost fell over a stash of toys. A couple of fruit boxes contained a collection of boys' toys; wooden boats and bi-wing planes, miniature rifle and swords, and various bits of a train set. As I ran my hand over the toys, I wondered which of the Granger boys owned them, and did more than one generation play with them.

Tucked behind the box of boy's toys were three more fruit boxes of toys and a doll's pram. These were girl's toys. The boxes held a menagerie of stuffed animals, including a koala missing one of its arms and a Paddington bear minus its eyes. The pram held dolls, one of which had a stuffed fabric body and ceramic head, arms and lower legs.

I began to choke as I lifted each doll out of the pram to examine it. It was a poignant few moments. From the makes and ages of the dolls in that pram, it was possible to gain an insight into the daughters who lived in this house over the generations. I put aside the last doll, and peered into the pram to see if there were other treasures. The tears welled up. In the bottom of the pram were echoes of my own long gone childhood.

Here was a child's small beaded purse containing a miniature fake lipstick and comb, a small container holding a number of fancy hairclips, several pieces of a pink ceramic tea set with vivid blue painted flowers decoration, a tiny metal teapot now badly dented, and a wind-up toy in the form of an Edwardian lady. Although mine were different, as a child I had similar things. I put everything back in the pram and spent a few moments reliving my own childhood.

When I managed to drag myself away from the toys, I moved on to boxes further back in the horde. Amongst the boxes was a small shipping trunk. Its contents propped its lid ajar. A quick riffle through the contents established they were all paper: files, a couple of books, and some old magazines. The files contained invoices, shipping documentation, and other business letters. While it would be interesting to examine these, they could wait until some future date. One trunk towards the back contained old clothes; all women's and from more than one fashion era. Again, these could wait until another day.

A picnic hamper, complete with cutlery and crockery, was interesting but not particularly enlightening. I moved on. There were three large shipping trunks. All were wooden sided with metal reinforcing bands and locks. None was locked. They contained various papers and books. One contained a number of journals. I couldn't resist the temptation to flick through some. They were account books. The first one appeared to document household accounts, while the next couple appeared to be business ledgers. Although I was sure they would prove fascinating, they too could wait.

I found a small writing desk – one I think called a secretaire. Over the years, junk of every description found a resting place on it. As I was about to remove some of the material for a better look at it, I caught sight of wooden box off to one side. It resembled a toolbox or small footlocker. On closer inspection, I found it had a bigger companion hiding under an old rug carelessly thrown over it. The larger box was not locked and gave me a surprise.

Stacked neatly inside in separate trays and compartments were medical instruments. Some looked more like instruments of torture and made me wonder about their use. The smaller box was locked but the lock was rusted and corroded. I figured it wouldn't take much to bust it open, but I'll keep that surprise for some other time.

A shout startled me. I stood amongst the stuff wondering what to look at next when the sound floated up from somewhere below. As I carefully picked my way towards the manhole, a head bobbed up through the opening. "What are you doing, and what have you found up here? I tried ringing you a couple of times. When you didn't answer, I became worried. Why didn't you answer your phone?

Were you planning on staying up here all night? If that's your intention, I hope you brought a packet of sandwiches or something."

"Zanne, what are you doing home already? I wasn't expecting you for another couple of days. And I didn't answer my phone because it's downstairs somewhere. Climb down the ladder again and I'll follow you."

It was already dark outside. My stomach rumbled loudly as Zanne and I descended the staircase to my kitchen. "See if you can find something cold to drink while I have a quick shower to remove some of this grime," I told Zanne as I hurried to the bathroom. She had two glasses of white wine poured when I returned. "It seems like ages since I had lunch, and I'm starving. How about we get started on some chops and salad for dinner? The chops can grill while we drink our wine."

Zanne wanted to know about my sortie into the roof cavity. I wanted to hear about her trip. I managed to duck her initial questions about my activities, while steering her around to explaining why she returned so early.

"It was a combination of two things. My agent and publisher had a meeting at a place close to where I made one of my appearances. They decided that, since they were so close, they would drive across to meet with me in the town where I was to do my second last appearance. That took care of the meeting we were to have this weekend after my tour ended. Then, the thing that really made a difference, involved the place where my last book signing was scheduled. The night before I was due to arrive, that area was inundated by heavy storm rains that caused flash flooding. I received a call cancelling the next day's event. That allowed me to arrive home today."

She confirmed the tour had been a success with good attendances, and that she had nothing scheduled now until the next time her agent arranged something. The conversation swung round to what I did while she was away. I explained my demolition of the partition in the servants' quarters. She wanted to see what I discovered, but it was late and with such poor lighting throughout that area, I suggested we leave her guided tour until tomorrow.

I noticed she looked weary. Not surprising, given her long drive today. It wasn't hard to persuade her to go home, but I knew she would arrive on my doorstep early tomorrow, eager and ready to explore all I'd discovered. By the time I saw her off and cleaned up the kitchen, my neck and shoulders were telling me they'd had a hard and brutal day. I did the best I could at rubbing analgesic into the affected parts, and then climbed into bed. Sleep came easily. No bad dreams bothered me.

Chapter 16

True to my new routine, I headed to the beach this morning. Again, there was no elderly couple on the beach and no dog. I'm not sure what is happening about the proposed arrangement with the dog. The man was to discuss it with his wife before I started taking the dog to the beach every morning. Since discussing the matter, they hadn't appeared at the beach. I couldn't go to collect the dog until the elderly couple agreed the arrangement.

After jogging my usual circuit, I strolled to the opposite end of the beach in the hope Frank Kane might be doing a bit of early morning fishing. There was no sign of Frank either. Having drawn a blank all round, I drove home feeling a bit dejected. Although Zanne might arrive early today, as I drove home, I thought about what to do until she arrived. I discounted returning to the roof cavity. I wanted to explore that area on my own before sharing it with Zanne.

Straight after breakfast, I intended to return to Aunt Eddie's bedroom. I didn't know why, but a little voice kept insisting I should. On my way to the servants' quarters, the conservatory waylaid me. From the doorway, I stood surveying the space. I tried imagining how I wanted it to look. I don't know how long I spent at there but, by the time I moved on, I had a vision for the conservatory. First, I needed to assess existing furniture for its suitability for inclusion in my design.

I continued on to the servants' quarters. The comfortable chair in Aunt Eddie's bedroom would fit well with my ideas for the conservatory. Nothing else in this area excited me. In the absence of other suitable furniture, the conservatory might remain an empty space for a while. My sparse living area didn't have too much to offer. However, the long table, presently buried under the paper from the state archives, would fit in well with my design. I ran up the staircase and in through the first door on the right side. The sitting room in that suite contained a couple of small side tables. The lounge chairs left me cold. I wasn't going to lug them downstairs. I picked up one of the side tables. It was heavier than I expected, but I managed to carry it down the stairs without dropping it. Unsure where its final place in the room would be, I plonked it in the centre of the conservatory.

As I considered bringing up the chair from Aunt Eddie's room, Zanne arrived full of apologies for being held up by a long call from her agent. She didn't waste any time on polite conversation. "Let's have coffee and then you can show me what you discovered in my absence. What's this little table doing in the middle of the conservatory?" I was shepherded out to the kitchen, and finally got a word in when we sat down with our coffees.

I explained my vision for the conservatory and the few pieces of suitable furniture I identified. Then, I shared with her my recent conversation with the elderly man about the dog. Although I was almost decided I would take ownership of the dog if and when the opportunity arose, I wanted her thoughts on the matter. Her initial comments urged caution but, after some discussion and further thought, she agreed owning a dog would be good for me. That was reassuring. That's when I told her of not seeing the trio since the dog was discussed.

As we rinsed our coffee mugs before taking her on a tour of the places I discovered, her final words on the subject of the dog surprised me. "Just go to the house on your way to the beach one morning – tomorrow would be good – and announce you have come to take the dog for a run on the beach. They will either rush to hand you the dog's leash, or tell you to bugger off, as they have changed their minds." For some strange reason neither of those outcomes appealed to me. I sent her off to retrieve a torch from her car before we went to the servants' quarters.

Our tour of the newly revealed servants' quarters went well. However, Zanne only made occasional comment as we worked our way from room to room along the corridor. I shouldn't have expected much more. They were depressing at best. Then I walked her back to the door leading to the domestic chores area. At the T-junction in the passageways, I turned right and took Zanne past the butler's pantry and office to the wide door at the end. I opened the door to show her the barricade attached to the other side of this end wall. "I think the barricade that blocks use of this door is that long wall that caught your attention recently. I'm still undecided about whether to leave as is, or to demolish it and restore the place to its original state."

"I'm not sure what I think about that. My first thought was to remove the barricade. Now I think I should reserve my opinion until I see what removing the barricade might open up. What's along here might be better left hidden." I understood her hesitancy. It mirrors what I'm suffering

Our exploration of the butler's area took some time. Zanne's interest extended to everything in every cupboard and drawer. However, the kitchen halted our progress. My exploration of the kitchen had been superficial at best. We augmented the poor overhead lighting with our torches and spent the next hour examining every fitting, fixture, pot, pan, and utensil.

"Do we know when this kitchen went out of use?" Zanne asked. "There is nothing modern in here; nothing electrical. I find it hard to reconcile this kitchen with, say, the 1940s. We have established that Edwina owned the place since the end of the 1940s, and that she most likely is responsible for installing that kitchen you use now. That tends to suggest that, until installation of the present kitchen, this was 'food preparation central'."

I hadn't thought about it in those terms, but Zanne was right. Nothing in this kitchen reflected what was around in the 1940s. How difficult must it have been for household staff toiling away in this mediaeval place? "I don't know who was responsible for that kitchen I use now, but it has been there for as long as I can remember. I agree it is likely Edwina installed it. If that is the case, did she also install the various partitions in the house?" I wondered.

The tour of the domestic chores area moved on to the laundry and promptly stalled again. "I think this is worse than the kitchen," Zanne said. "Can you imagine having to work in these primitive conditions? By the late 1940s, synthetic fabrics were around. How would you deal with them in this primitive set-up?"

"I suppose some of the equipment, like the mangles for instance, had long gone out of use, but was left in situ rather than being removed. However, I agree that this part of the house doesn't seem updated since its construction. If this laundry were still in use in the 1940s, I would expect to find at least some sort of washing machine in here. There is no evidence of any sort of washing machine ever being used."

After giving Zanne a quick look at the courtyard with its array of clotheslines, we returned to the more modern kitchen and raided my modern fridge for something for lunch. Over lunch, I mentioned the local newspaper article about Wilfred's death and its statement that Wilfred's burial was somewhere on *Whylara.* "I wondered who owned the property then, and their reaction to being asked to allow the burial on their land. Can we find out who the current owner is?" I asked Zanne.

"I hadn't thought about Wilfred's burial, but I suppose it's not surprising he would want it there. Why do you suppose Wilfred wasn't still the owner of *Whylara* when he died? The thought that he wasn't never occurred to me."

"I don't know why I think that. I suppose it was only an assumption that the place was sold at some time along the way. It's a bit like that wharf complex that Rupert built. Who owns that now? Who disposed of it and when?"

"Hmm…all good questions; anything else I hadn't noted along the way?"

"Well, since you're asking, where are Jessica and Clara buried? Did they plan to be buried at *Whylara,* or was it up to those left behind to decide their burial place? …And how do we go about finding out who now owns the wharf complex and the grazing property?"

"I suppose I left myself open to that barrage. I think we should start with the death certificates for Jessica and Clara. They should indicate place of burial. Finding out about the wharf complex and the property is a different matter. I think we should attempt to obtain a copy of the wills of everyone from Jessica through to Edwina. It might be worth seeing if Rupert's will came into play when Wilfred inherited. The inventories attached to those wills should show what was handed down through the generations. Do you have a copy of Edwina's will?"

"No. I didn't bother with a copy of mum's either. Is that a problem?"

"Copies of the earlier ones should be available from the state archives, but the more recent ones might not be at the archives yet."

"I'll talk to the solicitors. They have been the family's legal firm forever. Edwina used the father of mum's solicitor and, as I understand it, he was the son of the one Wilfred used."

"All the copies we want might be available from that legal firm. However, you need to prepare for a disappointment. It is possible Jessica didn't make a will, and it's unlikely Clara, being so young, thought to make one. Nevertheless, go ahead and talk to the legal firm, while I order us some death certificates."

Lunch had stretched on, but there was still an hour or two in which to achieve a bit more today. "There's something in that domestic chores area we didn't look at this morning. I wouldn't mind exploring it before we call it a day." Zanne didn't argue, I showed her the staircase opposite the boxroom. "I haven't investigated it, but I want to know why it's here and where it goes."

Armed with fresh batteries in our torches, we climbed the first set of stairs to the strange landing arrangement. A door confronted us at the landing. While Zanne moaned about how steep the stairs were, I tried the door. Nothing happened. It was either locked or so firmly stuck, I couldn't shift it.

"If it is locked, are we likely to find a key?" Zanne asked as she tried the door.

"Not really, but I can think of somewhere to look." I led the way down to the butler's office. "A key rack is inside this cupboard door," I told Zanne. "Some of the keys are labelled. Maybe one will indicate it fits that door."

We drew a blank. None of the labels suggested they were for the door. The ones without labels remained a mystery. Zanne's phone rang while I was checking the keys. It was a brief call, but she wasn't too pleased about it.

"Bugger, that call was my agent. He has emailed me a document he wants signed and returned today. I'll leave you to search for a key while I go and deal with whatever it is. I'll see you tomorrow."

I walked her to her car and was surprised to see it was already dark outside. It was later than I thought, but in part, the darkness was due to another gathering storm. The first heavy drops of rain arrived as I finished closing windows and doors. The storm created an amazing lightning display. As I stood in the conservatory admiring nature's light show, I remembered other keys. That bunch of keys belonging to the butler might be worth a look. I thought they were keys the butler carried with him at all times. I couldn't picture the stereotypical butler racing up and down those stairs too often. However, you never know your luck unless you test it. By then, it was too late, too dark and I didn't have my torch with me. Checking those keys would have to wait until tomorrow.

This morning, I chose to ignore Zanne's advice about the dog and went to the beach as usual. A part of me hoped the couple and the dog would be at the beach today and I would learn of their decision. Disappointment is not a great way to start the day, but that's how things went today. By the time I arrived home again, I almost had persuaded myself to give up on the dog, and to leave it to the gods to decide.

While I prepared breakfast, Zanne called to say she didn't know what time she would arrive, but it would be nearer lunch than breakfast. That allowed me to do a few things beforehand. My office hadn't seen much of me lately. As soon as breakfast was over, I booted up my computer to attend to those boring but necessary administrative tasks. After paying a few bills, I logged onto my emails.

The IT firm I work for offered another contract job. A quick look at the brief suggested the work might take no more than two or three days. I decided to ignore it until I finished exploring those stairs in the domestic chores area. Of more interest was an email from the legal firm regarding my requests for copies of wills. They were happy to oblige, warned it would take a few days to produce them, and asked that I call them to clarify some aspects of my request. That last part caused a nervous reaction. I was sure they were going to point out all sorts of obstacles to providing the copies.

It was a civilised hour to call a legal firm, so I did… and was pleasantly surprised. There were no problems. They wanted to confirm that I required the whole of each file. Of course I did. Who knows what gems I might discover. It wasn't until later that something occurred to me. There was no suggestion that they had no will for any of the people in my request. I could accept that Jessica might have made a will, but I was surprised they didn't query Clara. Now comes the hard part; waiting for the copies.

I figured it still was too early for Zanne to arrive. So, I decided to continue my quest to open that door off the landing. I snatched up the butler's keys and my torch from the table where I left them, and had started towards the servants' quarters when I heard a car arrive. "The anticipated delay ended earlier than expected," Zanne announced as she strode in. "So, now I'm here, what are we doing today? Are we heading up those stairs again? I will be slim and fit If I go up and down them a few more times."

She had a point. They stairs are steep. My legs reminded me of the fact when I went for my jog along the beach this morning. And they complained when we set off for the landing again. However, climbing the stairs turned out to be the easy part of the exercise. With Zanne looking over my shoulder, I worked my way through all the likely looking keys in the bundle. A few fitted but didn't unlock the door. As is often the case, it was the second last key I tried that did the trick… but the door still wouldn't open.

It seemed determination might be critical to opening this door. Although I put all my weight against it, nothing happened. I tried throwing my shoulder against it. Definitely need that physiotherapist if I persist with this nonsense. After a couple of attempts, common sense prevailed and I enlisted Zanne's help. "Instead of being a spectator, how about coming over here and adding some weight to the exercise? Position yourself against the door and get ready to push when I try lifting it and throwing my weight against it."

Our first attempted joint effort moved the door only about a centimetre, but that was encouraging. We tried again, and again, and managed an opening of about a four centimetres. The next attempt resulted in an opening about eight centimetres wide. Neither of us was ever going to fit through that gap. "One more time…," I told Zanne, before counting down from three and yelling, "Push…!"

Success; the bottom edge of the door came free of whatever it was binding on and swung wide open. At the end of its travel, it slammed against the wall. Zanne, with all her weight against it, travelled with the door, and received a face plant against the door when it hit the wall. For a few moments, we both stood there massaging our affected parts. Zanne rubbed the side of her face, while I tried to ease my shoulder with a poor attempt at massage. In spite of the hard work required, we had the door open and were inside. Inside where, was the question.

It appeared we were in some sort of storage space; long and narrow, with wide shelves attached along both side walls. The space was dark and musty. I felt around the usual places for a light switch, but found none. We flicked our torches around the shelves. A few lumpy objects appeared. At last, I found a light switch. I half expected it wouldn't work, but the light – such as it was – came on. So dim, it made little difference. However, combined with our torches, it was enough to recognise the lumpy objects on the shelves.

We were in a linen storage area. I recognised a couple of neatly folded bath towels. Further along and on the shelf below was a pile of stiff, thick white sheets with a couple of pillowcases beside them. Everything bore a good coating of dust and, within seconds, the space swirled with dust particles. I reached up for a large lump on the top shelf ... shouldn't have done that. The 'lump' was an old kapok pillow folded in half. Its fabric casing disintegrated at my touch, covering me in a shower of kapok and adding kapok dust to the fug already fouling the air.

A door, centrally located at the end of the space, offered the chance of finding out where we were. For a change from what we've encountered so far, this one opened without resistance. I stepped through to find myself in the central hallway of the top floor. How can this be? I explored every inch of this floor and found no linen cupboard. "Zanne, pull the door closed please." Once that was done, it was easy to understand how I overlooked it earlier. With the door closed completely, any suggestion it was a cupboard disappeared. The door now looked like a join in the wall panels.

Leaving open the doors at both ends of the linen storage space, Zanne and I returned to the kitchen via the main staircase to regroup over coffee. Coffee seemed to take longer than normal this morning. We were both willing our legs to face up to the task ahead. I shared my thoughts on our next 'journey of exploration' with Zanne.

"If those stairs we climbed this morning stop at the upper floor, I'm wondering if the second staircase leads to the roof cavity. I don't doubt our second challenge will be opening the door at the top of those stairs. Our first challenge will be to climb those two flights of stairs."

Zanne groaned. "I can't get over how steep they are. I suppose they had to be like that, so they fitted in the available space without creating a problem. As I said, I will be fit – or drop dead from exhaustion – by the end of the day." I tried telling her there was no pressure on her to accompany me, but she would have none of it. I knew it was a waste of time before I tried. Her curiosity was as compelling as mine.

As we rinsed our mugs, an idea came to me. That main staircase offered a lazy way of reaching the landing outside the top floor. We hurried up the main staircase and soon stood on the landing outside the linen cupboard again. Viewed from either ground level or the landing, the second set of stairs appeared to reach almost to the roof. Inspection of the landing suggested that, at some time after the first set of stairs was installed, the landing was extended to accommodate the installation of the second set of stairs.

After checking the batteries in our torches and tucking a bottle of water in our back pockets, we set off on our next marathon climb. My legs screamed in protest as I set off up the stairs. I felt my thighs wanting to cramp as I negotiated the last few steps. However, we both made it to the top, and spent moments leaning against the top landing's railings to allow our legs to recover. This top landing was large; as long as but wider than its counterpart below. "Okay, that's our first challenge met and conquered," I announced. "Now, let's see if we have the requisite magic key to unlock this door… or if our second challenge defeats us."

We again went through the ritual of trying every likely looking key. None unlocked the door. "…So, we are beaten. The door has won and we must humbly accept defeat," Zanne said.

"So, it seems… unless we manage to find another key somewhere."

Back on the ground floor, I headed straight for the butler's office. "What are we looking for? I know we are looking for a key, but I thought we checked all the ones in here," Zanne said as we entered the office.

"I don't know the key is here, but we'll check everywhere again, including that key rack. I'm almost convinced that door opens into the attic space, so check the key rack for any labels like that."

As a last resort, I went through the tedious process of comparing the unlabelled keys on the rack with the keys on the butler's keyring. Most of the keys matched. Only two keys on the rack did not have a duplicate in the bundle. One looked like it was the key to a cupboard. I disregarded that one. It was obvious the other one was a door key. I slipped it into my pocket.

"It makes sense if this turns out to be the right key for that door," I told Zanne. "There would be no need for anyone to visit that attic on a regular basis, so why would a butler carry around an unnecessary key. It would be taken from the rack only when something was to be moved into storage up there." I was trying to convince myself as much as Zanne that my thinking was rational and logical.

"Hmm… I almost accept your reasoning, but shall we have lunch before we test your theory?"

Unlike our morning coffee break, lunch was over in little more than a blink. However, as we cleaned up after lunch, we both admitted to no inclination to climb those stairs again. After some debate, we agreed a different strategy. We would go up to the top floor and use the ladder still positioned under the open manhole to enter the attic. Somehow, the main staircase and the ladder, although requiring expending some energy, did not seem nearly as tortuous as those other stairs.

"Should we take a pack of sandwiches in case we find ourselves trapped up there?" Zanne asked tongue in cheek.

"I don't think that will be necessary, but I am inclined to replace the batteries in my torch before we head up. It's a black hole up there and we will be relying on our torches the whole time."

With our water bottles topped up and fresh batteries in our torches, we were soon perched with our legs dangling through the manhole opening.

"Right, lead on. What's our next move, and what are we going to do now that we are up here?"

"Everything and anything that looks interesting …. But first of all, I want to see if there is a door in that far wall." I pulled my legs up through the manhole and attempted to boost myself to my feet. My thighs felt like jelly. I quickly placed my hands on the top of my thighs to help lever myself upright. Then, taking great care not to trip over anything, I picked my way towards the wall where I thought I might find a door.

Chapter 17

Through the gloom, I thought I could distinguish the outline of a door. My foot contacted something hard and immovable. I almost pitched forward onto my hands and knees. Zanne, trailing along behind me, as she caught and steadied me, said, “It’s a rolled up carpet.” Wiser for my experience, after that I kept my torch trained on where I put my feet.

About a metre from what I now knew was a door, I shrieked as something brushed my neck and shoulder, and continued down to tickle my upper arm. Startled by my performance, Zanne swung her torch around and tried to shine it on me. I was frantic, and flapped about trying to brush the ‘thing’ off me. In the process, something brushed across my hand. I let out another yelp. Then, in a show of bravery, I grabbed at the ‘thing’, and caught the end of a thin cord. While maintaining a hold on the cord, I stepped out from under it. Zanne shone her torch on the cord and followed it up towards the ceiling. I had been attacked by the cord from an old-fashioned pull-cord light switch.

Although I expected nothing to happen, I yanked the cord. My expectation was almost correct. A couple of lights obliged with a dull yellow glow, while a few of their mates chose to ignore the invitation. Nevertheless, the meagre additional light augmenting our torches made exploring the space easier. As I attempted to regain my bearings, something near the door caught my eye. Hanging on a nail beside the door was a key. “I’ll bet that’s the key to this door,” Zanne said as she too focused her torch on the key.

“Ye-e-s, it might be, but why would you leave the key inside a locked room?”

“…Unless you didn’t want anyone to enter that locked room,” Zanne suggested.

She had a point. It was one way of making sure nobody came poking around in this roof cavity, but that only begged the question of why someone would be so desperate to ensure no one came in here. As with everything else we discovered so far, it came back to that same basic question: who did it and why. "Let's leave the questions aside until we know whether this key unlocks this door. Zanne, shine your torch on the lock so I can see what I'm doing."

The key slid into the lock easily enough, but the mechanism was stiff and I was concerned about snapping the key off in the lock. After a bit of wriggling and jiggling, and a few persuasive words, I felt the lock release. Again, it needed the two of us to lift and pull the door open. I stepped out onto the top landing. "For the moment, we'll leave this door open too. Anyone sneaking in via the backdoor would be a masochist to be bothered climbing up here." However, I did make a point of keeping the backdoor closed for a while after that.

Then, it was time to explore this treasure trove. My previous superficial fossick through the material lacked strategy or structure. While I was pleased Zanne was there with me, and there are no secrets between us, I wanted this to be my journey of discovery. I didn't want her nosing about in anything before I had a chance to look at it. I devised an approach that I thought would meet my needs without offending her. "There's so much stuff up here, we need to create a rough catalogue of everything for future reference." I produced a notebook and pen from my shirt pocket and handed them to Zanne. "Would you mind following me around and noting what we find as we come to it?" Zanne seemed happy enough with that, so we made a start on what would be a mammoth task.

After working out a rough grid pattern across all the material, we started from the corner closest to the door. I ignored the rolled up carpet I almost fell over earlier and picked my way carefully across the floor to the first item of any significance. It was one of the large shipping trunks. Unlocked, the lid creaked ominously as I opened it, but the hinges remained intact and, once the lid was fully open, it stayed there while I sifted through the contents.

It contained women's clothing and other fripperies that generated quite a debate between us regarding the age of the material. My initial guess was that these were Jessica's belongings, packed and stored up here after her death. Zanne insisted they were from an earlier era. After scrutinising dresses and other bits of clothing and discussing style and fabric, I had to admit I was wrong. If these contents were from an era earlier than Jessica, was it safe to assume contents of this trunk were Gwendolyn's?

"Rupert and Gwendolyn were well off, but how vast would her wardrobe have been?" Zanne asked. "There is a lot of material in this trunk, enough to make you wonder if anything went with her when she disappeared."

"I suppose that rather depends on the manner in which she 'disappeared'. If general consensus was correct, she might not have needed anything where she was going. Even if she only ran away, as opposed to being dispatched to meet her maker, I don't suppose she would be able to take much with her." By the time we went through the trunk's contents, we agreed things we expected to find in the trunk weren't there.

We allowed that, although her daughters might have commandeered some things, we had enough evidence to conclude that some things either had been disposed of, or 'disappeared' along with Gwendolyn. In spite of everything, Zanne retained some scepticism. She remained unconvinced that someone wouldn't notice some of Gwendolyn's belongings were missing and, on the strength of that, would take pains to quash any suggestion that she had met with foul play.

After returning everything to the trunk, we moved on to the next container. This was a smaller trunk, about half the size of the first. I assumed any material in close proximity probably came up to the attic at around the same time and would be from the same era. This second trunk disproved my thinking. It contained business papers from *Whylara* for a period extending to late-1939. While this might provide interesting reading at some future time, it generated little interest now. I left the trunk as I found it and moved on.

Our next target was the smaller of two wooden boxes. Its larger counterpart I opened when I first discovered this storage area. Although I hadn't spent too much time on it, I knew it contained medical instruments. Instruments I assumed belonged to Rupert, which were stored up here after he returned from England and never practiced again. My other assumption was that the small wooden box I was about to open also would contain Rupert's belongings. I was to learn I was wrong again.

This small box contained personal items; a monogrammed toiletry set, a small trinket box containing several sets of cufflinks and tie pins, silver monogrammed hip flask and cigarette lighter, pocket watch and wrist watch, a leather bound writing case including an expensive looking fountain pen, and a desk set that looked alabaster and contained red and blue ink containers and one of those 'rocker' style blotter things. All these items were wrapped individually either in calico or stiff brown paper. Below these items was a layer of men's accessories including silk ties and cravats, handkerchiefs, a couple of leather belts with monogrammed buckles, and an empty leather wallet. There was little doubt all this belonged to a Granger male... but which one?

Papers and books languished below everything else. A large envelope contained photographs and unused souvenir-type postcards from various European places. The books, mainly medical texts, also included a prayer book, a hymn book and a bible. An impressive leather bound book at the bottom turned out to be a daily journal. A checked of the books and photographs provided no clue to the owner's identity. We both examined the monograms on the various items. They were so elaborate that the actual letters became lost in all the swirls and curlicues. "Did you check all the textbooks?" Zanne asked. I noticed her eyes glued to two books off to one side on the floor.

"I thought I had, but maybe I missed those two." The first one told me nothing. The second one caused a 'Eureka' moment. "Bingo," I yelped. "This one is inscribed as belonging to Michael Prendergast Granger."

"When I saw they were medical texts, I thought they were Rupert's."

"I suppose I did too. Maybe some, or all, of them were Rupert's and were passed down to Michael. Who knows? There is nothing in those other books to indicate ownership."

"Okay… well, now we know Michael followed in his father's footsteps and studied medicine. Are we agreed on that?" Zanne asked. I nodded.

"I want to take the photographs and books downstairs. I'll put everything else back in the box, but keep your eyes open for a container we can empty to use to carry these and anything else downstairs."

As I replaced the rest of the material in the box, Zanne said, "Right, let's move on then. Is this the next thing to look at?" She pointed to a large open box overflowing with journals and files. I moved to the box and started removing the contents item by item. After a minute or so, I stopped and reviewed the pile of journals on the floor.

"So far, those on the floor are files, cashbooks, journals and ledgers from *Whylara,* but this one in my hand is from the wharf complex. I'll start a separate pile in case there are more from there." While I spoke, Zanne scratched around amongst stuff a little way off.

She came back with what looked like an old baby's carry basket. "I think it might be the basket part of a bassinette, but I can't see the stand for it anywhere. So long as you don't load it up too much, we could use this to carry stuff downstairs. By the way, as a matter of interest, if you take some of this downstairs, where do you intend to put it? We are just about up to the back teeth with paper already down there."

"Yeah, I know and I've been giving it some thought. As an interim measure, I think I might store it in those empty cupboards in the butler's office or on the shelves in the larder. I want to have it downstairs so it is easy to access if I want to look up something or to fill in some spare time."

About half an hour later, Zanne exclaimed. "God, look at the time. It's almost six o'clock. No wonder I feel as though I haven't eaten in a week. How much longer are you going to dig around up here tonight?"

"That probably explains why my stomach is grumbling. We could spend a week up here and still not be finished. I'll finish this box and that will be it for today." The box in question only required another five minutes. Then it was time to go. I stood up slowly and stretched. Every part of me seemed stiff after bending over or scrambling around on my knees all afternoon. "Come on, let's go downstairs and have us a drink."

"Are we taking any of the stuff you've sorted out down with us tonight?"

"If we don't, there will be a hell of a lot to take down by the time we are finished; better to remove it as we go along."

"Ri-i-ght... do we take it down those stairs or down the ladder?"

The ladder seemed the easier option, although perhaps a bit more risky. However, once we had everything down the ladder, it still had to be carried down the main staircase to the ground floor. After weighing up the options, I settled for taking it down the ladder. Zanne breathed a sigh of relief. "I was praying you weren't going to say we had to carry it down those other stairs. The thought of the number of times we would have to climb them to move all this stuff was more than I wanted to think about."

There were four fruit boxes and the baby's basket to deal with. The boxes I thought wouldn't pose too many problems, but the basket was another matter. Although I kept its load light, its size and shape would make it difficult to carry safely down the ladder.

I positioned myself a couple of rungs down from the top of the ladder. Zanne placed the first box on top of the ladder. Although a bit heavy and cumbersome, it wasn't difficult to manage. After placing it on the floor, I climbed back up for the next load and repeated the process. When I climbed back up to ready myself for the third time, Zanne insisted we swap roles, and she would carry the next two boxes down the ladder. While she descended with her first box, I had a quick scout around for something to replace the baby's basket. I found what looked like a small cane laundry basket. While Zanne took her second box down the ladder, I transferred every from the baby's basket to the laundry basket.

As she reached the bottom of the ladder, I yelled down to her. "Don't come back up. I'll join you down there when I bring this last one down." Not quite as easy to manage as the boxes, the laundry basket didn't cause too much concern, and I and my load made it safely onto the upper floor.

"Have you thought about storing this stuff in one of the rooms up here? It would avoid cluttering up your downstairs area any more than it is now." Zanne suggested.

"God, no; everything is so dirty and dusty up here. I know the domestic chores area isn't much better, but it doesn't have all the soft furnishings loaded with dust and whatever else as there are up here." Did I hear a barely audible groan as I finished speaking? However, as I didn't receive any direct complaint from Zanne, we each picked up a box, took it down the main staircase to my living area, dumping them on the floor along the wall outside my office. We repeated the process until all the boxes and the basket were downstairs.

"There's leftover lasagne in the fridge we could heat up for dinner, and maybe put a salad with it. How does that suit you?" I asked.

"Sounds great; you deal with the lasagne while I pour us a drink, and then we can relax for a while."

By the time we drank our wine, made a salad and set the table, the lasagne was ready to eat. Although we were ravenous and wasted no time dispatching the food, we lingered at the table discussing what today had uncovered. It was getting late and I was sure Zanne must be as weary as I was, so I suggested she take herself off home.

"I would if I thought you were finished for the day, but you're not, are you?"

"I won't do much more. I'm only going to unpack that stuff we brought down from the attic so we can use the containers again the next we go up there."

"Okay, let's wash these dishes and then do that."

We sat on the floor, unpacked everything and stacked it against the wall without examining any of it. As soon as we finished, I stacked the empty boxes and basket out of the way at the foot of the staircase. It was just after ten o'clock when I walked Zanne to her car and waved her off.

There was no jogging along the beach this morning, contenting myself with a sedate stroll along the sand instead. I thought my legs might collapse under me if I tried anything more strenuous. Twice during the night cramps in my legs woke me. In spite of a burning desire to explore more of that attic, there would be no climbing of ladders or stairs today.

Slow motion seemed to apply to everything I did this morning. My usual breakfast routine involved dashing about the kitchen making coffee, preparing food and setting the table, before wasting no time eating and cleaning up afterwards. Today, I seemed to be stumbling about, dropping things and spilling stuff. It's not serious; just the result of doing something physical when so unfit. Nevertheless, today would involve nothing more physical than looking through documents and books. When Zanne arrived, I was still at the table with half a mug of cold coffee.

"Good to see you are no more energetic than I am today," she quipped as she joined me at the table. "Do you think we both might perk up a bit if we had another coffee?"

Coffee seemed like a good idea as it delayed having to do anything else for a bit longer. As I drained my mug, Zanne asked, "What are our plans for today? I'm expecting a call from my agent after lunch, so I'll be here only until lunchtime."

We made ourselves comfortable cross-legged on the floor in front of the stuff we stacked against the wall last night. "I think our first step is to sort it into specific piles for *Whylara,* the wharf complex, this place and each individual Granger family member. I suppose we should look through everything as we go, so we know exactly what we have and can make an assessment of its relevance." That's how we occupied ourselves until about eleven o'clock, when we stopped work for yet another coffee. This time the coffee break was quick. I wanted to return to the last few things to be sorted. Zanne said she could stay until one o'clock, so we returned to our positions on the floor and continued.

There wasn't much to do, and soon there remained only the three books – hymn, prayer and Bible – that were amongst what I believed were Michael Granger's belongings. The hymn and prayer books had nothing to offer; no inscription on their fly leaves or anything else to confirm their ownership. Neither looked worn, suggesting they had not seen much use in their day. I turned my attention to the Bible. Children often received these as gifts to mark the occasion of their baptism, and they came with an appropriate inscription to commemorate the event.

That was not the case with this Bible. There was no inscription or anything else, and it too had seen little use along the way. As I fanned the pages, it slipped from my hands and landed tent-like on the floor. I picked it up by its two covers, leaving the pages to hang downwards. Something fell out and floated down onto the floor. I laid the book aside and snatched up what fell out. It was yellowed with age and folded up neatly.

I checked the back pages of the Bible as that is where I thought it fell from. A tell-tale mark between the last page of the Bible and its flyleaf showed a clear impression of where the document rested for so long. Then I turned my attention to what fell out. Folded around a photograph was a single small sheet of unlined paper from a fancy notepad. I felt my pulse rate step up a few notches as my excitement skyrocketed. Zanne was busy with something else and hadn't seen what happened. I didn't want to share this with her until I knew more.

The photo was of two people, a man and a woman, dressed in heavy winter clothing and standing in front of an unfamiliar-looking background as they smiled at the camera. I didn't recognise the people. How could I? They could be Rupert and Gwendolyn for all I knew … or Michael Granger and his girlfriend … or anyone else for that matter. Staring at the photo was getting me nowhere. I slipped it back into the Bible and turned my attention to the note… and caught my breath.

"Oh God; oh God, I don't believe this," I whispered. It wasn't loud enough for Zanne to understand what I said, but she heard me say something. She spun around to face me, and her concern for me went into overdrive.

"What has happened? What have you found? You look as though you've seen a ghost… no, something worse than that. Talk to me, Anthea."

I nodded and swallowed hard to convince my vocal chords to work. My first attempt came out as a croak. I swallowed twice more and tried again. This time, although my voice broke with emotion, I managed to tell Zanne what I found. "Look at this photo that fell out of the Bible."

"Hmm… it's old, and they look cold. Who are they?"

"Listen to what's in the brief note that was with the photo." I cleared my throat again and started reading. *My Precious Son t*he note began, and I saw Zanne's eyebrows shoot up her forehead. I continued reading.

This is a difficult note for me to write, for it is the last I will write you. I hope you come to realise and understand sometime in the future, why it has to be this way. Know that I have always cherished you beyond all else and always will until my dying day. As you know only too well, life has not been easy for some of us in this family. We must take every opportunity to make what we can of what the Good Lord sees fit to give us.

Follow your dreams, achieve whatever you wish from life but, above all else, strive for happiness. It is not always easy to find, but well worth whatever it took when you find it. I continue to pray your life will be blessed with contentment and happiness, as mine is now.

Although everything that was between us has changed and what we had now must be no more, know that I will never forget you and will always love you.

Goodbye my darling son.

After I finished reading, I didn't trust myself to look at Zanne as I struggled to fight back the tears that welled up. Silence hung heavy for quite a few moments before I dared to look at her. Tears rolled down her cheeks. She swiped her face on her sleeve and attempted to clear her throat before speaking.

"I assume there is no signature." I nodded. "Are we to assume the 'precious son' it addresses is Michael Granger." I nodded again.

"I feel sure this is a letter to Michael from his mother; her last letter, as she intimates."

"If it is from his mother, it's Gwendolyn who wrote it. Is there a date or anything to indicate when she wrote it?"

"Nothing on the note, but there might be something on the photograph." It was a longshot. Cameras back then didn't date stamp photographs. We both took a moment again to look at the couple in the photo. "Look at that," I yelped. "See there in the background…"

"What…? The background is not exactly plastered with familiar landmarks."

"No, but look there near the bloke's elbow; does that look like a crofter's cottage to you?"

"Eh...? O-o-h, you are right. I remember seeing crofters' cottages just like that in the Orkneys. Are you suggesting what I think you are suggesting?"

"Don't know what you think I'm suggesting but, if that is a crofter's cottage, it suggests this photo was taken somewhere in Scotland… and who with Scottish connections have we come across recently?"

"The hermit…! What was his name?"

"Angus Sinclair… and I think he was from somewhere around the Orkneys." As we mulled over that possibility, I idly turned the photo over and studied the back of it. Something like tiny ants crawling along the edge in one corner caught my eye. I angled the photo up to the light to see what it was. Written in a soft pencil was a date. "Jesus…! We are right. This photo was taken after Gwendolyn disappeared. When did the hermit disappear from Tremaine's Bluff?"

Neither of us could remember when the police went a second time to speak to the hermit, Angus Sinclair, and found him gone. I scrambled up from the floor and rushed to my office for the notes I made from transcripts of interviews regarding Gwendolyn's disappearance. "Yeah, here it is," I called to Zanne as she joined me in the office. "There are two dates in my notes: the date they interviewed him while they were searching the area, and the date they went back to talk to him again and found him gone. As you would expect, both those dates are after Gwendolyn's disappearance… but the second date, when he was gone from Tremaine's Bluff, was about three months before that photo was taken."

"So, let me check. We now believe the note and photo were from Gwendolyn to her son, Michael, to let him know she was okay, but that she had run away and was now in hiding with this Angus bloke in the Orkneys."

"Correct... and that poses another question. Did Gwendolyn send other carefully worded messages to any other members of the family and, if she did, to whom?"

"Is that a possibility?"

"It's possible, but somehow I don't think she did. I can't say why, but that note gives me the impression Michael was 'special' somehow, and I'm almost certain he kept her secret safe. If others had known, I'm sure Rupert would have found out and his midnight flit would not be necessary."

"I suppose our list of challenges now includes searching for any other similar notes. I have to go and wait for the call I'm expecting but, if you find anything else like this, call me."

After Zanne left, I resumed my place on the floor and again went through everything we brought down from the attic. I knew it was pointless, but I had to do it. I was looking through a household ledger from the 1930s when my phone rang. I scrambled onto my knees and reached it down from the table. It was Zanne.

"I'll be spending the weekend in the city. That call was about appearing at a writers' festival being held at the university. There was a tentative booking ages ago. The publisher confirmed the booking with my agent about six weeks ago, but my agent forgot to tell me. I suppose, as he was on an overseas holiday at the time, it slipped his mind. Anyway, the reason I called is that I'll be in the city by Friday afternoon. If your solicitor's mob has the copies of those wills ready, I could collect them. I'll leave it with you to give them a call to see what you can organise."

The copies were almost ready and they thought they would be mailing them in the next day or two. I had no problem organising for Zanne to collect them on Friday afternoon, and rang her back to let her know and give her the details of where to go. She said she might not make it to my place the next day as she thought she would need most of Thursday to prepare for the presentation she was to deliver at the writers' festival.

In a funny way, that was a relief. It meant I would have from Thursday through to maybe Monday to myself. It would give me time to come to terms in my own way with everything we had discovered to date… and I had a gut feeling I would be visiting that attic again.

Chapter 18

Still no sign of the elderly couple with the dog this morning. I am about to give up on the idea, and wonder if it ever made sense. However, there was something positive this morning. As I sat on the rocks near my car to dry off and cool down a little before driving home, Frank Kane wandered along the beach. Tackle box slung over his shoulder and fishing rod in hand, he looked ready to spend some time on the beach. I sauntered down to join him. Now that I'd caught up with Frank, I couldn't remember what I wanted to ask him.

He saved me the embarrassment of wondering what to ask. "I'm pleased I've caught up with you," he announced. "After lunch the other day, I kept thinking about your family. We talked about Edwina Granger and I told you how she never married. The more I thought about it, the more unsure I became about that. She was a few years older than me you see, so I didn't have anything to do with her; never kept up with what was going on in her life. I do remember there was a child, a little girl I think, who lived with Edwina. I don't know what became of the child when she grew up. She didn't stay around here. Anyway, my point is that I might have been wrong about Edwina not marrying. Perhaps she did marry and had a child. If she wasn't married and had a child, knowing this community, it would be the talk of the town. I don't remember any such stories. Doesn't mean there weren't any, just that I don't recall any."

"Thanks, Frank. I'm sorry it occupied your mind for so long. That's the one bit of the Granger family history I do know. The child was my mother. Edwina was her aunt, and she brought her up. I don't know how that situation came about. It was never mentioned, but I think whatever happened occurred when my mother was so young as not to remember."

We chatted about nothing in particular for a while, and then something he might know about occurred to me. "Frank, you and your father had a fair bit to do with that wharf complex over the years. I don't know whether I'm right or not, but I believe Rupert Granger started that enterprise." Frank nodded so I continued. "I'm curious about what happened to it, whether it was handed down through the family or was sold. Do you know who owns it now?"

Frank looked taken aback and took a moment to answer. "I've never given it any thought, not since I left the fishing industry. I don't know who the current owner is. I would assume it still belongs to the Grangers. It's a while since I left the industry though. Anything could have happened since then."

I could see that my asking Frank something about his community that he couldn't answer upset him. Perhaps I should have been more sensitive, but I hadn't realised that, with all his knowledge about the community, not knowing something would have significant impact. I was tempted to ask about the elderly couple with the dog and if he knew why they'd stopped coming to the beach. After upsetting him once already, I decided to leave the matter alone. Citing plenty to do and a busy day ahead, I left him to get on with his fishing and drove home.

With no clear plan for what I would do today, after breakfast I wandered into my office to check my emails. It was a couple of days since I'd last checked and quite a few had arrived in the interim. My IT firm bosses came through again with the detailed brief of the work they wanted done. The work wouldn't take long to do and, with Zanne away for a few days, I could get it done and out of the way before she returned. After printing off the brief, I started work on the job.

By the time I took a break for a late lunch, I estimated I was about halfway through the job. I dawdled over lunch, and along the way managed to convince myself I could complete the rest of the IT job either tonight or first thing tomorrow morning. They allowed me plenty of time to do it, but I'm nothing if not big on procrastination. While I'm still interested in working for the IT firm on occasions, my priority area of interest remains elsewhere. I felt I needed to do something physical this afternoon, so I took the empty fruit boxes and the laundry basket up to the top floor, climbed the ladder and shoved them up through the open manhole. That's when I decided to really punish myself, and headed for the domestic chores area and those two steep sets of stairs to the attic.

Maybe I'm getting used to the climb; it didn't seem quite so exhausting today. Once I was in the attic, I had to stop myself wandering around to search through things. I forced myself to stick to the grid pattern we established, and worked on from where we previously left off. The next few things I came to were pieces of old furniture, and I was about to dismiss them as rubbish and move on when something caught my eye.

After removing other junk from the top of the pile, I had indeed found myself a gem. Although in need of a clean, I had found a gorgeous small round wrought iron table with a glass top, and two matching wrought iron chairs with padded seats. "These will be brilliant in the conservatory," I told the attic. However, getting them down to the conservatory was another matter. All three pieces were heavy. I wasn't inclined to carry them down all those stairs. I lifted them out from the remaining junk and moved them over to the manhole. They would have to remain there until Zanne returned to help me. It would be tricky, but I think carrying them down the ladder is a better alternative to carting them all the way down those stairs.

The rest of the afternoon I used to explore a few more squares of my grid pattern. By five o'clock, I'd had enough of dirt, dust and cobwebs and called it quits for the day. Apart from the table and two chairs parked near the manhole, I also filled two fruit boxes with journals and other bits and pieces to take downstairs. Again, carrying them down the stairs didn't appeal to me either, so I also parked them at the edge of the manhole. Then, empty-handed I descended the steep stairs, came around to the main staircase and used the ladder to bring down from the attic the two fruit boxes I'd filled.

A fine mist of rain blanketed the Cove this morning and showed promise of something more as the day wore on. It took only one look outside to convince me I wasn't going to the beach today. Perhaps it was just as well, as I slept way past my normal time. My slow start to the day persisted until after breakfast. Not being able to think of anything I wanted to do, I gave in and went to my office to complete the IT job I started yesterday.

For a few more moments of procrastination before beginning work, I checked my emails. The IT firm featured in my inbox again. The client my current job was for had asked for a few further refinements to be added to the original job. I swore, printed out the details, and logged out of my emails. “There is no point sitting here sulking about it, get on and finish the job,” I told myself and anyone else in the universe who cared to listen.

At lunchtime, the temptation was to stop work on the IT job and leave the last little bit until tomorrow to finish, but that would mean stuffing up another day. Why leave it? Get it finished. By mid-afternoon I had finished the work, except for one final check. I opted to follow my usual practice of leaving the work for a few hours before giving it that final check. I put it aside until after dinner tonight.

With a few hours of daylight remaining, I found myself wondering how to fill in the rest of Friday. The wrought iron table and chairs in the attic came to mind. I was soon up the ladder and testing the weight of one of the chairs. It was heavy but I thought I could carry it down safely. Once I worked out how to hold it, carrying it down the ladder proved easier than expected. About twenty minutes later, both chairs were in the conservatory. Although I thought the table would have to wait until Zanne was available, after removing the glass top from its drop-in recess, I discovered it wasn’t too heavy or too difficult to carry. I stopped short of trying to move the glass top by myself.

In the conservatory, I dragged the wooden side table over to the wrought iron chairs and placed my coffee on it. Then, sitting on one of the chairs and with my feet up on the other, I drank my coffee while watching the rain now bucketing down outside. There is only so long you can make a mug of coffee last. As the conservatory had captured my interest again, I thought about the big comfortable chair in Aunt Eddie’s bedroom that I identified earlier as a good candidate for the conservatory. “Let’s give it a go,” I said as I marched down to Aunt Eddie’s room.

The chair remained every bit as heavy as when I tested a few days ago. It seemed logical to minimise carrying the thing as much as possible. With this in mind, I dragged and pushed it from where it sat for years, out of the bedroom, and across to the bottom of the short flight of stairs leading out of the servants' quarters. I went back into the bedroom to check again if anything else might be suitable for the conservatory. While sitting on the side of the bed to recovered my strength before attempting to move that chair up those stairs, I revisited memories of Aunt Eddie in this room. The bed was high and I sat well back on it. My feet didn't touch the floor. After a few moments, as I sat looking around the room with my mind in neutral, I started swinging my feet.

My left foot hit something hard under the bed. "Oh no, I don't believe it," I said as visions of a chamber pot hiding under there danced through my mind. I climbed off the bed and gingerly lifted the edge of the covers. No chamber pot; I breathed a sigh of relief. Hidden under the bed was some sort of metal box. I dragged it out. It was rectangular, metal, grey in colour, and looked like a cashbox on steroids. And, it was locked. There were no keys in the dressing table drawers, and none hiding in the wardrobe or cupboard. That left the drawers in the two bedside cabinets to check before going to the butler's office again for that bundle of keys.

In spite of my hefty yank, the drawers in the cabinet on the same side of the bed as the box, refused to budge. All three drawers were either stiff or stuck. My problem was that, when I yanked on the drawer handles, the whole cabinet slid forward across the floor. I felt around for somewhere on the top or just over the back of the cabinet where I could hold it firm while I pulled on the drawers. There was nothing to grab hold of, but I did find something. As I felt around on the back of the cabinet, my fingers brushed across something paper. I suspected it was a maker's label or a delivery slip.

With the cabinet away from the wall, I turned it a little to one side to see behind it. For a moment, my hands froze in mid-air. My mind couldn't compute what I saw. There, held fast to the back of the cabinet with several strips of sticking plaster, was a small brown envelope. I ran my fingers over the envelope. There was something inside it; something hard and key-shaped. The envelope and its sticking plaster came off the unpainted back board with a loud ripping sound.

It took a couple of heartbeats to rip open the envelope and tip out the key. A deep breath first, and the key was in the lock. It was stubborn but yielded after only minimal persuasion. My hands trembled as I tried to grip the lid of the box. What did Aunt Eddie have that she needed to go to such lengths to hide and protect? Maybe there was more to her life than I realised. Was Frank's half-hearted suggestion that my mother might be Edwina's illegitimate daughter correct? "Don't be bloody ridiculous. Open the box," I told me and Aunt Eddie's ghost in no uncertain tone.

I snapped open the lid, and peered down on yet more paper. The immediate view was of books and documents, with a few photographs sprinkled throughout. Later, towards the bottom of the box, I found four pieces of jewellery. Good quality expensive pieces I guessed from the look of them. Although only about 100 millimetres deep and with plenty in it, the box wasn't crammed full. As I lifted each item out of the box, I placed it on the bed. There were three bundles of letters: two bound with narrow black ribbon, while the other sported blue satin ribbon.

Under the bundles of letters was that same trio of holy books: hymn book, prayer book and Bible. I put the Bible to one side while I checked the other two books. There was no inscriptions in either. As was the case with Michael's neither looked well-used, and nothing fell out when I upended and shook them. Could I strike it lucky a second time with the Bible?

I picked up the Bible and ran my hands all over the cover. This book did look as though it had been used, but not much. It was pointless hoping there would be family information inscribed on the flyleaf, but I checked anyway. There wasn't. Likewise, there wasn't a name or anything else to indicate whose book it was. Although deep down I knew there wouldn't be anything, finding nothing still disappointed. With Michael's Bible still fresh in my mind, I turned this one upside down and gave it a gentle shake. Nothing fell out. I closed the Bible and held it in my hands for a moment as I tried to accept my disappointment. I brushed my hand over the front cover in something of a final dismissal before laying it beside its companions.

The cover felt 'lumpy'. It wasn't flat and smooth as expected, but seemed to have a contour to it. Maybe there was something secreted in the book that hadn't dislodged. I opened the cover and attempted to fan through the pages. It didn't work. They stuck together. I tried again. This time the pages started to fan, but stopped after only a few pages. The next few pages crumpled together as I tried to fan them. I put the book down open on the bed so I could untangle the pages and flatten them out. I caught my breath.

All the centre of the book had been carved out, leaving only a few millimetres of intact pages at the start and end of the book. The rectangular niche created held another small book. This was a pocket diary. For a few moments, I could do nothing more than sit looking at it lying there in its secret place. Then, in slow motion, I picked up the Bible and turned it over to allow the diary to fall out into my hand. Someone went to a lot of trouble to keep this diary from prying eyes. I felt about to violate someone's privacy as I stared at the small book in my hand. Whoever owned this diary is now gone, I told myself. No harm can come from looking at it now.

Written in a neat hand – female I guessed – the first few pages told me only about the weather and buying fabric for a new dress. Such 'nothingness' reassured me I was violating nothing private or secret by reading this book. Rather than wading through pages of more comments about the weather, I searched for the last entries. I expected them to be at or near the end of the book. They weren't. The last entries were about three quarters of the way through the thick little book. As I read the last entry, I caught my breath and almost dropped the book.

I turned back through the pages until I found what looked like the start of a heart-wrenching story. There no longer was any doubt about whose diary this was. I marvelled at Edwina's efforts to keep her sister's diary hidden for so long after Clara's death. Clara's diary documented the sad story of those last months of her life. It recorded the heartbreak and devastation that drove her to take her life. As evening closed in, it became too dark to read anymore.

It seemed almost sacrilege to remove the book from this sanctuary just to read it more easily. Aunt Eddie had the good sense to install decent lights in her room. I switched them on and returned to reading the diary. An hour later, I had read most of the book, including the entire final story that began soon after her mother's death. After a quick trip to the kitchen to fetch a glass of wine, I returned determined to read the diary from start to finish.

I read only three pages before realising my original assessment of the early writings as rubbish was incorrect. It took Clara a couple of pages of entries to get the hang of keeping a journal and, by the third page, she was recording daily happenings in the household – trivial though some of them were. One thing that became clear from early in the book was the close bond between Clara and her mother. A major issue that runs through the early part of the diary is Clara's yearning to be granted the same opportunities as her brothers. She resented not being sent to complete her education in England, not having the opportunity to develop a career, being denied access to the social life away from Charlotte Cove enjoyed by her brothers, and having only the occasional visit to the city to ease the monotony of life here.

Sprinkled throughout her writing, are Clara's comments about her mother. While they only reflect Clara's view of things, I suspect she was astute enough for her comments to provide a reasonable picture of the situation. The overarching message was that Jessica's marriage to Wilfred was not a happy one. Although Clara applied a certain degree of circumspection in her writing, it is clear her parents' marriage had broken down years earlier. It seems they shared little. Jessica only accompanied Wilfred to important functions when a wife's presence was required. There are veiled comments written in Clara's own brand of shorthand that I interpret as suggesting Wilfred's interest was in other females' company – and services.

There is the initial mention of a young lad who first catches Clara's attention when she accompanies the housekeeper to the local market garden to buy fresh vegetables. Although the entry isn't specific, it is clear the lad made quite an impression. Soon after, Clara mentions him to her mother, who counsels her not to mention him to anyone else, and warns her not to try to develop her interest in the lad. Is this the Nick who is interviewed after Clara' suicide, I wonder. It seems likely to me it is.

It's then that the story takes a dark turn. Jessica becomes ill with some form of influenza or fever that keeps her delirious and bedridden for more than a fortnight. Clara criticises her father for not hiring a nurse to care for Jessica. Her daughters, and various household staff, whenever time permitted, take on the responsibility of caring for her. Jessica recovers, is left weak, and it takes more than a week before she is strong enough to leave her bed even for a few minutes. It is hard for me to imagine how difficult that time must have been for the daughters. Jessica's daughters, Clara and Edwina, were sixteen and thirteen at the time; by today's standards, not old enough to shoulder the load of caring for their critically ill mother.

Then the defining event happens. Jessica, supposedly on her way to the kitchen for a glass of water, dies when she falls down the stairs. The daughters are not allowed to attend the funeral, but have to endure the police investigation that follows their mother's death. Clara's graphic entries that follow paint a clear picture of her grief and sense of loss. …And then, Clara is pushed into taking on her mother's role of running the household. She writes warmly of the assistance and support provided by the housekeeper, Elsie Nolan, and it becomes clear that they become close over the next few months.

If Zanne and I harboured any doubts about what 'taking over her mother's role' meant, they were dispelled as I continued reading the diary. She was careful not to be too precise, but it didn't take much to work out what was happening. The unthinkable seems to have started on the night Clara had to accompany her father to some awards presentation night in the city.

She makes it clear she didn't want to go, and she felt the gown he chose and insisted she wear was more suited to an older woman. The night was long and boring, and she resented being ogled by ancient lecherous males all night. On returning to their hotel, and in the apparent absence of any other female, Wilfred forced himself on Clara after insisting it was her responsibility as part of fulfilling her mother's role. The shock of it all is clear as she describes being sick all night afterwards and 'shedding buckets of tears'. As there was no live-in staff by then, Wilfred insisted Clara move into a bedroom in the servants' quarters. I suppose there was less chance of Edwina discovering the truth about what was happening while she slept upstairs and Clara was in the servants' quarters.

"The rotten bastard…" I exclaimed. "How dare he… how could he…?" There was no way I couldn't read any further, not right now anyway. I marked the page, turned off the lights and left Aunt Eddie's room. At the foot of the stairs, I roughly shoved the lounge chair I parked there out of the way and stomped up the stairs and through to the kitchen. I thought about another glass of wine, but opted for something stronger. With two fingers of single malt scotch in a glass, I took myself out into the night for a stroll around the grounds in the dark. We already suspected Wilfred was guilty of incest, so why was having it confirmed so disturbing? Perhaps it was seeing it with such clarity in Clara's own hand that was so confronting.

Everything was damp; whether from the earlier rain or dew was unclear. Dead leaves and grass clippings clung to my feet and ankles as I wandered about. My stroll arrived at my favourite bench seat under the iron bark tree. It was wet. I brushed it off with my free hand and flopped down on its cold wet concrete. For a long time, I sat there trying to rid my mind of what that poor teenager went through. My glass was empty. I shivered. A cool breeze had sprung up. Wet clothes didn't help. I was aware of feeling chilled. Time to go inside, I told myself and, a few minutes later, I managed to drag myself to my feet and head into the house.

Although a bit hungry, I didn't feel like cooking, so settled for avocado on toast before forcing myself to read the rest of that diary. I think my philosophy was along the lines of getting all the shock and horror out of the way on the one day, so tomorrow I might start coming to terms with it. In spite of willing myself to get on with it, I sat there holding the closed diary for several moments before forcing myself to start reading it again.

I suppose the worst shock was over. Although the remainder of the diary told a sad and disturbing story leading up to the tragedy that ended Clara's life, somehow it didn't affect me as deeply as that first revelation. Her relationship with the young lad, whom she now identified as Nick, developed in spite of everything else. Theirs was a covert romance with nothing more than exchanged glances and smiles at first. Later, they engineered to run into one another at the post office, the store, or at his family's market garden, so they could exchange a few words without arousing suspicions.

In spite of their careful management of the situation, Wilfred grew suspicious. Her opportunities to leave the house were curtailed, and he refused to countenance any contact between his daughter and the lad – any lad. It seems the housekeeper was aware and tried to assist, but there was little she could do to help facilitate meetings between the young lovers. Clara recorded telling Elsie Nolan that there was no hope Wilfred would come to accept the situation. She wrote that Wilfred 'would never see past the colour of Nick's skin'. However, whenever Wilfred was away on one of his trips, the young couple continued to meet after dark in the bushland behind *Wellsprings*.

So no one else could be implicated in their actions, Clara would wait until Edwina was asleep before slipping out of the house to meet Nick. As I continued to read, I discovered that Edwina was aware of the romance and, at some point, found out about the clandestine meetings, but not about what Wilfred was up to. However, the bond between sisters was strong. Clara and Nick's secret was safe with Edwina. I didn't have to read too much further before the next awful truth was revealed. Clara was pregnant.

She confided in Elsie Nolan who, having had six children of her own, knew enough about being pregnant to confirm Clara's fears. Elsie suggested, the next time Wilfred was out of town for a few days, she would take Clara to a doctor in the next town. Clara knew there was no way they could do that without Wilfred finding out. It would cost Elsie her job, and Clara would lose her closest confidant and only support. Apart from that, Clara was terrified of what Wilfred might do to her.

The next few diary entries contain Clara's concern for what Nick will think and do when he learns the truth about her condition. She didn't have to worry about Nick for too much longer. Without notice or explanation, Nick's father lost his job at the wharf complex. That left the family with only the income from their market garden, but the townsfolk seemed not to need fresh fruit or vegetables after that. There appeared to be some unspoken boycott of the market garden. The family were forced to leave town. With no buyer forthcoming to purchase their property before they left, the family were facing dire financial times.

Clara was heartbroken. Not only had she lost the love of her life, but she knew all that happened to that family was down to Wilfred's exercising his power and influence in the community. Her growing desperation is clear in the entries leading up to the end. She didn't want her unborn child… couldn't have the child… but had limited options to do anything about it. It is in the second last entry in the diary that she names Wilfred as the father of her child: *If I have this child, they will all blame Nick. Poor Nick. Little do they know it could never be his. He was a gentleman with old-fashioned gentleman's values. We agreed to wait until I was 21 and we were married before we shared anything more intimate that a kiss. I wish to God there was some way to tell the town – tell the whole world – what this big man, Wilfred Granger, has done to his daughter. I know there is no way I can do that but I will not have his child.*

Her last entry almost tore my heart out. Clara says she is calm and at peace now; no longer concerned, no longer frightened. It sounds as though she was that way when she wrote it. She says everything is in place now. She had given Elsie a letter addressed to Nick should she ever see him again or find out where he is. Elsie has promised never to open it, and has promised to look out for Edwina if Clara is not here. 'She must not let the same things happen to my little sister, and must go to the police if she even suspects it. If needs be, she can tell them what she knows about me if it helps to protect Edwina'. Clara's final words are almost impossible to read: *It is all done, everything I need to do for other people. Now is the time for me. I have decided the place. It is a sacred place to me, sacred to the happiest times of my life; somewhere so precious for the time I spent there with Nick. I know it will shock and upset people important to me, but they will move on from their grief. I believe this will be easiest for all of us in the long run. Goodbye my loved one, try not to think too badly of me.*

I sobbed and tears rolled down my cheeks. Although I had closed the diary, I could not put it down. It took me a few minutes before I brought the sobbing under control, and sniffled away the tears. I felt devastated and heartbroken over what happened to that young girl more than seventy years ago. It was all too much for me to handle. Maybe there is some truth after all in that old adage about ignorance being bliss. I had to get out of Aunt Eddie's room. I needed to shut to door and rush away from there.

After putting everything back into the box as I found it, and sliding the box back under the bed, that's what I did. I shut the door on my way out – I'd never seen it shut before – and bolted up the stairs and into the kitchen. I don't remember much about the rest of the night, except that my sleep was haunted by dreams of a fat, ugly man chasing a young girl – and sometimes me – through bushland. The dreams woke me in a lather of sweat several times during the night. I remember thinking how wonderful it would be to see morning arrive.

Chapter 19

Sunday morning found me lacking a decent night's sleep and still battling the blue funk resulting from reading Clara's diary. At the beach, I jogged my usual circuit and then walked to the far end of the beach, past the wharf complex and the few cottages further along. As I ambled back to my car, I became aware of how deserted the beach was today. That probably is a good thing. In my present state of mind, being sociable was not on my agenda. I drove home and extended my usual breakfast routine by an extra cup of coffee. Either the coffee had lost its potency or I was beyond help, but I lacked interest in doing anything.

When all else fails, attend to domestic chores is my motto, so that's what I did. There was laundry to do and dust to chase. I drew the line at trying to unpack any more of my belongings. Why do that when there is nowhere to put anything? However, by the time I finished the floors, the place – or that part I inhabited – was spotless and I was so hot and sweaty, I needed a shower. Then, feeling cleaner and a bit brighter, I took a sandwich to eat out into the garden under my favourite tree.

The air was still and heavy. What are we doing to the climate of this planet? We are in the middle of spring and should be enjoying balmy days. That's what we get some days, but of late, every other day already seems hell bent on launching into summer. Today is shaping up to be one of the latter. Humidity is high, and yet again I see storm clouds building over the bay. We could be in for another decent storm this afternoon. With nothing better to do than sit and wait, my mind roamed free across a myriad of topics of its own choosing.

"Invisible women," I said aloud, frightening a couple of birds from the tree above me. My mind had drifted to the women who once lived in this house. As a general rule, women were invisible except for those few who left their mark on the historical record through their occasional mention in the major newspapers' social pages; mentions merited through their connection to husbands or fathers. What did their immediate communities know about them? That was another future question for Frank Kane. He had provided precious little information about my Granger women. As a life-long member of the Charlotte Cove community, what did he know of Jessica and Clara, who lived here during his lifetime? I mean, what did he know about what their lives were like, how they filled in their time, or what the community thought of them?

My mind wound back to my earliest days at university, when I thought to study social science. Whatever possessed me to choose that course? I'll never know, but it didn't take me more than one term to work out that it wasn't for me. I switched to IT. While much of what we studied during that term slipped by without note, the realisation of the extent of the invisibility of women in history left its mark. One could be led to believe that, in the settlement and colonisation of much of Australia, only men were involved. Yet, the records of the day show plenty of births occurred. The cemeteries bear testimony to the high level of infant mortality prevalent along with the frequency of women's death in childbirth. Surely, based on that evidence, there can be no denying women were here – even here in Charlotte Cove. However, the challenge lies in trying to find out something about them. They were so inconsequential as to warrant no mention in most records; so inconsequential as to be invisible in history.

Their husbands, sons, fathers and brothers probably rated mention, if not because they were amongst the leading lights of the community of the day, then because they fell afoul of the law on occasion. The names of these men appear in newspapers, in legal documents, in the records of various clubs and enterprises, and on servicemen's honour boards and monuments. Where are the women? Unless their marriage was a society event, they broke the law, got themselves hanged, or created some other scandal, they don't exist in the annals of history for today's researchers to find them.

Those Granger women who met such tragic ends were no different. For most of their lives they were invisible. It is only through the infamy which attached to their tragic ends that they appear in records of the day, while it appears their husbands' almost every move is recorded for posterity. The Granger men were well-to-do, owned extensive property, served on various boards, patronised various clubs, and chaired and supported various charities and other philanthropic organisations. They were visible, highly visible, both within their own community and the wider one.

My maudlin thoughts of invisible women and their unjust treatment by history were rudely interrupted by the sound of a car's horn as it pulled up in the driveway. Zanne had returned earlier than expected. The next few minutes involved transferring stuff from her car into the house before settling for a coffee break.

"Earth to Anthea...," Zanne chirped from the kitchen table as I fussed with the coffee machine. "What's gone wrong? It's obvious something is bothering you. Have you found out something upsetting while I was away?"

"No, it's nothing like that," I lied. I wasn't ready yet to revisit or share the contents of Clara's diary. "I suppose, if anything, while you were away, I've had time to think about a few things."

"Ah hah, that's probably not a good thing, given the way our research has been going. I know you found some of it hard to accept, and some of it has been depressing. Too much time to think when you already are in that state of mind is bound to do no good at all."

"You're probably right about too much time to think not being a good thing, but what's upsetting me probably is not what you think. In fact, I don't know that 'upsetting' is the right word to describe what I'm feeling. Some of it is about making decisions. Decisions I think I'd rather avoid, but know I can't. However, there are a couple of things I want to run past you."

"Okay, so roll them out, these things that are bothering you, and let's attack them."

"There are two things, this house and invisible women."

"Invisible women...? Have you lost it all together? Christ, are we now starting to talk about ghosts?"

"What...? No. Who said anything about ghosts? I'm talking about how women are invisible in history. It's obvious there were herds of women around getting on with their lives, and perhaps the lives of their men and their families depended on how well they did that. However, it's hard to find out anything about those women. In the case of the Granger wives, if they had not been connected to prominent men, they would never have appeared in the social pages. It is only through their deaths – or disappearance, before you remind me – that they finally have some exposure in their own right, and end up as entries in historical records."

"Yes, I agree. Even now, things haven't improved all that much. It's only those few women who make it to the highest echelons of the business world or politics who become well-known outside their own families. However, I'm not sure I see why that should suddenly trouble you so much. That was the way it was back in the days of those women. The way it is today reflects whatever changes might have occurred since then."

"I suppose exploring the house made me wonder what the lives of those women were like. What was it like living in this house in the different eras? I suspect they had little interaction with the local community, and probably lived their lives like hermits in this house, except on occasions to accompany their husbands on his trips to the city."

"Yeah, probably much like you are now; living your life like a hermit in this house, I mean."

The discussion was becoming awkward. To end it, I suggested we take another look at the domestic chores area. I convinced Zanne I wanted to see where I might store the ledgers and journals that came down from the attic. That didn't take too long. On our way back to the kitchen, we detoured into the conservatory. I showed her what bits I had added and told her about the glass top for the wrought iron table still to come down from the attic. We swapped ideas on setting the room up and the types of plants that would add to its ambiance.

I thought Zanne looked tired. She agreed she was feeling a bit weary after the long drive back to Charlotte Cove and suggested another coffee would revive her enough for the drive back to her own place. She wouldn't hear of letting me drive her home, so I fired up the coffee machine and we had another coffee. Conversation was light and spasmodic. I guessed Zanne was more tired than she looked. She had trouble focusing on any one topic for any length of time. There was brief discussion of the history that lived on in those kitchen and laundry areas of the domestic chores part of the house, before Zanne brought up my 'invisible women' again.

"Don't go getting yourself tied in a knot over the invisible women who lived in this house, or any other women history has elected to keep invisible. Sometime in the future, you and I will have joined the ranks of those invisible women. Our lives will be every bit as invisible to future generations as your ancestors' lives, and those of other women from down through the ages, are to us now."

As I walked Zanne to her car, my mind mulled over her final comment on my 'invisible women' issue. She probably was right on a couple of counts. I should not get worked up about invisible women when I have so much other stuff about my family to digest. The second point she made that struck a chord with me was the fact that the future will find me also consigned to the ranks of those invisible women. However, in her case, she was wrong. As a bestselling author with so many novels out there in the market place, she will be visible to future generations through her legacy. Somehow, those thoughts did not improve my outlook on life.

Once Zanne went, for want of something better to do, I took myself off to the domestic chores area and wiped down some shelves in the old larder. For the next hour, I transferred and stacked the journals and ledgers brought down from the attic on those shelves. With them in discrete stacks according to their specific enterprise or whatever, it was easier to appreciate the knowledge I was accumulating about this house, the family and its business interests. That brought a sense of achievement and satisfaction, and lifted my mood no end.

On my way out of the domestic chores area, as I passed the closed door to Aunt Eddie's room, I remembered I had left the bedside cabinet askew. It seemed important to fix that, so I diverted into the bedroom and walked around the bed to the cabinet. I grabbed the cabinet, leant over it and went to push it back against the wall. Something a little odd caught my attention.

About two hundred millimetres up from the floor, the outline of a brick was visible. Wallpaper and plaster rendered the other bricks in this wall invisible. Instead of pushing the cabinet back against the wall, I shoved it off to one side so I could take a look at that brick. It was as though someone had sliced all around it. I could see it wasn't a replacement brick inserted in the wall in a more recent time. The surface of the brick was covered with the same wallpaper as the rest of the wall. Down on my haunches in front of it, I ran my hand over the brick. It wobbled a bit. This brick is loose.

Why in the vast expanse of this wall would there be one loose brick, one loose brick hidden behind a bedside cabinet? Scrambling to my feet again, I went in search of any other loose or obvious bricks in any other wall. There was none. This one was unique. That alone was enough to ensure I had to investigate further. I tried easing the brick out with my fingers. It fitted too tightly into the wall to come out easily, and there wasn't anywhere for me to get a good grip on it. After a quick trip to the shed for a large screwdriver, I was ready to attack the brick again.

By inserting the blade of the screwdriver in the narrow gap on one side of the brick, I managed to lever it forward a millimetre or two. After repeating this procedure twice on all four sides of the brick, it protruded far enough for me to get a reasonable grip on it. After a bit of wriggling and jiggling, and sacrificing a bit of skin off a couple of fingers, the brick came free and I placed it on the floor. I saw a fair sized cavity behind the now gaping hole in the wall. No point sitting here staring at it, I told myself. Nothing is going to come out to meet you.

With more than a little trepidation, I eased my fingers in to explore the cavity. Inserted only up to the first knuckle, they came in contact with something. It seemed loose and removable. With nothing more than a precarious fingertip grip on the object, I worked it forward until it appeared at the edge of the opening. "Argh, bloody hell, it's another book," I cursed, as I carefully freed it from its hiding place.

Christ, it's another diary. I dread to think who this one belongs to and what revelations it contains. It must hold something significant, or why go to the trouble of creating a safe hiding place? As I sat cross-legged holding the book in my lap, I hesitated. Now I had found it, I knew I had to read it, but I wasn't sure I wanted to. When in doubt, procrastinate; that seemed a reasonable approach. I put the diary on the bed, left everything else as it was and exited the room.

If I were going to read that diary, I was going to do it in comfort and not in that bedroom. Why was that important, I wondered? It didn't matter why it was important. I knew what I was going to do and got on with it. I marched up to the lounge chair I parked near the stairs, took hold of both armrests and lifted it. After struggling it onto the first step, I managed to work it up the remaining stairs and onto the main floor level. Then, it was a simple matter of pushing it across the floor and into the conservatory. Without too much thought to positioning it, I dragged a small table over beside it. A quick check that there was nothing else required, and I turned on my heel and returned to Aunt Eddie's bedroom to collect the diary.

When I settled myself in the lounge chair, the sun had started to dip below the scrub. I didn't know what the lighting was like in this room, but I suspected it was no better than in most of the rest of the house. Maybe I should see if I can find a lamp before I start. I thought I remembered one in a bedroom upstairs, and set off in search of it. At the door of the conservatory, I decided to try the switch to see if the lights even worked. So unprepared for what resulted, I was almost blinded by the brightness. It seems the conservatory was a favourite place for Aunt Eddie, and she upgraded the lighting to facilitate her use of the room.

After fetching a glass of wine, I reclined the chair, put my feet up, took a couple of deep breaths, and picked up the book from the side table. I didn't have to go beyond the first page to realise it was Aunt Eddie's diary. Her first entries were from around the time when her mother, Jessica, first became ill. In a young girl's way, she chronicles the period of her mother's illness. It's obvious from her writing, she found this period stressful and frightening. She often comments on the way her sister Clara has shouldered the task of looking after their mother, and of how supportive Clara is of her little sister.

I turned the page and scanned the first entry. It made me catch my breath. "Jesus, here we go again," I exclaimed. After taking a moment or two to brace myself, I took my time reading that next page of the diary. "Poor bloody kid…! I wonder if she shared the information with Clara." I returned to the top of the page and re-read the shocking entry that dealt with the night her mother died.

Edwina woke from a bad dream and heard someone moving about in her mother's bedroom. Fearing her mother might have taken a turn for the worst, Edwina crept to her bedroom door and peered out into the central hallway. She was in time to see her mother hobble out of her bedroom and towards the main staircase. Edwina was about to rush after her mother to help her when she heard the sound of another door opening. Her father, Wilfred, came out into the hall. Assuming Wilfred was going to help his wife, Edwina remained in her room, but kept an eye on what was happening side.

"Jesus Christ, she saw the whole bloody thing." After reading what Edwina wrote, I struggled to take it in. Edwina watched her father rush to Jessica's side and appear to be going to help his wife down the stairs. Then, when they were on the top step, he gave his wife an almighty shove that sent her hurtling down the staircase. Once he had seen her on her way, Wilfred rushed back along the hallway and into his own room. It seems what followed was close to an Oscar winning performance.

Wilfred came out of his room and made a show of going to Jessica's room to check on her. A moment later, he rushed back into the corridor and went to the top of the staircase. There he seems to give the performance of his life as a distraught husband. At first, his yelling and wailing frightened Edwina and she dived into bed and hid under the covers. However, she realised that would look strange, and she should respond in a more natural way to commotion going on outside her room. Putting on a show of just having woken up, she wandered out and along to the staircase. She took up a position against the banister on one side of the staircase, leaving a wide gap between herself and her father. When she looked down at the scene below, Clara was already kneeling beside her mother's body. She didn't need to ask how her mother was, Clara's wailing told her all she needed to know.

It seems until sometime after Clara's death, Edwina shared her knowledge of what happened that night with nobody other than her diary. The diary records Edwina's thoughts on the investigation into Jessica's death, the investigation that Edwina refers to as a farce. About a month after the coroner's inquest was held, Wilfred called Edwina into his office and told her she was to take over running the house now that both her mother and Clara were gone. Edwina protested her lack of experience and knowledge in such matters. Wilfred brought Elsie Nolan to his office and instructed her to train Edwina in the intricacies of running a household.

About two weeks later, while Wilfred was on a trip to the city, Elsie Nolan took a rare day off and went to the neighbouring town. At the close of the coroner's inquest, Elsie had chatted to one of the young detectives involved in the investigation. She managed to elicit details of Nick's current whereabouts. On her day off, she went to the stock & station agent in Rolleston where Nick worked and handed him Clara's letter. As Elsie later told Edwina, she gave Nick the letter with only a brief explanation of how she came to have it, said she had no idea what was in it, told him how much Clara loved him, and then left so Nick could read the letter in private. Edwina noted that Nick never contacted them after that event.

Edwina's life must have been terrible. Such a young girl kept a virtual prisoner in her own home. She was not allowed out at all, not even to accompany Elsie Nolan to the store. In frustration, she asked her father if she might visit her mother's parents, Sir Hugh and Lady Fitzmaurice, who then resided permanently in England. Her hope was that, if he let her visit them, she would refuse to return; would stay in England and resume her education to develop a career as her brothers had done. Wilfred's angry dismissal told her that was never going to happen.

Time dragged on in a monotonous routine until about three months after the coroner's inquest into Clara's death. On his return from a few days in the city, Wilfred suggested Edwina should move into Clara's former room in the servants' quarters. Edwina demanded to know why and, when no satisfactory answer was forthcoming, she refused. It appears that's when things turned nasty. She recorded that Wilfred told her it didn't matter where she slept. She hadn't been fulfilling her duties properly and it was time she did so. He had needs that required taking care of, and she would start fulfilling that part of her role forthwith. Tonight, would be a good time, he told her … and she recorded it in her diary.

Soon after Clara's death, Elsie had told her that, if ever such a situation occurred, Edwina must tell Elsie at once. Elsie was at the store and running a few other household errands when Wilfred's demand was delivered. Cornered and with few options open to her, Edwina blurted out that she knew what he had done. She saw him push her mother down the stairs. Wilfred laughed at her. Edwina told her father that, unlike Clara, she wouldn't consider committing suicide and she wouldn't take care of his 'needs'. Then she delivered her trump card: she hadn't kept his actions secret. There were safety measures in place and, should anything happen to her … anything at all against her will … those safety measures would come into play and he could expect the police to come.

I stopped reading at that point. Filled with admiration for Edwina's courage, I needed a moment to collect myself before continuing. When I resumed reading, I felt reassured; almost relieved in some way. It seems Wilfred took Edwina at her word and chose to leave her alone rather than risk the consequences. However, it appears their relationship remained strained until Wilfred died. They avoided one another when they were both in the house, and fortunately that doesn't seem to have been too often. Edwina's diary entries suggest her father spent increasing time away from home, either in the city or attending to some of his other business interests.

She must have welcomed his absences with great relief. It was only on such occasions she could escape this house. Elsie Nolan appears a willing conspirator in her escape by allowing Edwina to take care of errands for her. This allowed Edwina to at least visit the village, and on occasion she accompanied Elsie to Rolleston. From the entries in the diary, it seems little of import occurred at *Wellsprings* until Edwina's surviving older brother, Thomas, came home from England at the end of 1944.

Wilfred seems to spend even more time away from home after Thomas' return. Then, only a few months later in mid-1945, Thomas married Catherine Bonham-Stewart. There is no mention of the young couple for a while after they married. The next mention is about six weeks after the wedding when Thomas brings his new wife back to live at *Wellsprings.* I couldn't help but think that must have been an interesting experience for the young woman. I don't know about her background but, with a hyphenated name, I suspect she was more upper-crust than peasant, and probably used to living somewhere a little more 'well appointed' than this archaic place. That's not to mention living in the same house as a father-in-law with dubious morals.

Edwina seems to have developed a sound friendship with Catherine and there was great excitement when Catherine became pregnant. However, that was nothing compared to the celebrations when Thomas and Catherine brought home the next generation of Grangers. It was obvious from Edwina's comments that Esther was the centre of her parents' universe, and that Edwina adored her niece. That brought a tear to my eyes. These were my grandparents and the birth of my mother Edwina was writing about.

Diary entries after that mainly recorded Esther's developmental milestones and funny antics. Little else worth recording seemed to happen until Wilfred became ill. There were a few terse comments during the short illness that led to his death. There was no grief, or even a hint of sadness, in Edwina's recording of his death. Although, she stopped short of an outright 'good riddance', the inference was clear. There is no doubt in my mind, Edwina was pleased to see that part of her life ended.

There were only a couple of entries in the diary after Wilfred's death. The first of those mentions his funeral, which Edwina attended, more for appearances' sake than out of respect. However, she refused to attend Wilfred's burial. The last entry Edwina made two days after Wilfred's funeral speaks volumes.

She claimed that 'the house feels as though every door and window has been opened to let in fresh air and sunlight'.

I closed the diary and let it lie in my lap. If only Aunt Eddie had continued with this diary, maybe I would know more of my grandparents, and of my mother's early life. Nevertheless, I tried being positive about the information Aunt Eddie did provide and, since reading her diary, how enlightened I am about this family of which I am now the last generation.

That 'last generation' thought haunted me over dinner. There was something depressing and final about it. However, given all I learnt about my mob, perhaps the end of the Granger line might not be a bad thing. I found myself wishing I did know more about my grandfather, Thomas Prendergast Granger. Was he a mongrel of the same ilk as his predecessors? I might never know the answer to that.

I suspect there is a good chance Wilfred will haunt my dreams again tonight.

Chapter 20

An early morning downpour and the threat of more to come was all the excuse I needed not to go to the beach this morning. The only downside to that was it gave me extra time to occupy. Over breakfast, I remembered I hadn't finished and sent off that last IT work I received days ago. That took care of filling in my extra time.

When I opened the work I had done, I realised only a final check was needed before I sent if off. By nine o'clock, I had dispatched the work accompanied by my abject apologies for my tardiness. As I sat at my desk luxuriating in the feeling of having achieved something today, my thoughts turned to the likely imminent arrival of Zanne. So much for my smug glow; guilt replaced it as I thought about all I had discovered and not shared with her over the last few days. That needed to change today, I told myself as I mentally braced for revisiting some of the most horrendous stuff I've ever read.

When all else fails, make a list. I made a list of everything I needed to share with Zanne, and was adding an afterthought to it when she arrived. It might be a bit early for coffee, but it might be easier to discuss some of the events over coffee. I don't think it was. As I anticipated, she wanted to read the diaries herself.

I felt lousy about doing it, but I refused. Those diaries were back in their long-time hiding places. Regardless of Zanne's being my best friend and the closest thing I had to a family member, sharing those intimate records with someone who was still an outsider seemed a violation of Clara and Edwina's privacy. Although I think my stance caused some hurt in the first instance, Zanne rose above it and later said she understood and appreciated my decision.

We moved on to the question of what we might tackle today. I was adamant I wanted to take a break from research for a while. After some discussion of the options open to us, we decided our first task was to bring down from the attic the glass top for the wrought iron table. Then, we would drive to Rolleston to visit the nursery to look at potential plants for the conservatory. With the two of us on the job, the glass tabletop posed no problems and, about ten minutes later, we were installing it in its table.

Although it was close to lunchtime, we headed for Rolleston with the intention of shouting ourselves lunch in the best eatery the place had to offer. There weren't a lot of choices. We settled for a counter lunch at the Rolleston Hotel. The food was typical pub fare, but was good. As there were few patrons in the place at the time, we sat at a table in relative peace and quiet in the hotel's beer garden. Following lunch, we got on with the serious business we came to do.

As I drove, Zanne gave directions to the nursery. The place, a sprawling complex larger than I expected on the western outskirts of town, had an overwhelming array of plants, potting mixes, fertilisers, gardening tools, and weird and wonderful garden ornaments. "I didn't plan to buy anything today. I only wanted to see what might be available," I reminded Zanne.

"Okay, you can continue browsing if you wish, or you could select one or two things – or more – that you like to the point of 'must have', and we could take them home with us today."

"I suppose that would make the space more inviting. It is quite stark at the moment."

The potential 'one or two plants' increased to have us loading eight pots of various sizes into the luggage compartment of my SUV. Of course, we couldn't have the plants remain in those black plastic nursery pots, so 'suitable' decorative faux stone pots had to go into the car as well. I discovered buying plants could be a lengthy business that surreptitiously consumed large amounts of time – and money. As we drove along the Rolleston main street, Zanne spotted the golden arches of a McDonalds up ahead. "We could have a coffee before we leave town," she suggested, "And they often have nice cakes."

As we sat indulging in cake and coffee made by someone else, I remembered my interest some time ago in buying a trike to ride to the beach, and maybe a stand-up paddle board. At the time, Zanne mentioned there was a sports store here in Rolleston.

"Seeing as we are in town, perhaps we might see what that sports store has to offer," I suggested.

"Eh… sports store… What do you want with a sports store?"

"If you think back, you'll remember I was interested in a trike and a paddle board."

"Oh, I thought you managed to get over that idea by now… but okay, we can have a look while we are here."

Once more she guided me through town to a huge sports warehouse type building on the opposite side of town to the nursery. "I don't know if they have trikes in stock, but I'm sure you will find something in here to suit your new fitness campaign," she whispered as we entered through the automatic doors.

I scanned the vast open area display in front of me before responding. "You're right. There probably is something in here I can use. I'm just not sure I'll be able to find it in amongst all this stuff before they close for the day."

"Aah, I see some nice gaudy coloured active wear over there. I might wander over for a closer look."

Although I wasn't in the market for knock-your-eyes-out active wear, I followed Zanne over to the 'active wear' area. There were plenty of brightly coloured bits and pieces, but there were just as many that suited boring conservatives like me. As I fingered through the racks, I found myself thinking, I probably could do with another one or two of those. In a display of absolutely no self-control, I bought a couple of pairs of cropped leggings and tops to match. Then, it was down to the serious business that brought me here.

"They do have trikes… look over there," Zanne squeaked. "What colour do you fancy?"

"Oh God, I hadn't expected they would be so brightly coloured. I don't know if I like any of them."

"For goodness sake, Anthea, liven yourself up a bit. Besides, if you are going to be riding it out on the road, other road users need to be able to see you. You need it to be bright."

While we stood arguing about the limited range of colours available and my lack of taste when it came to colour, a young salesman arrived. I assured him I was 'just looking' at this stage, but he insisted on waxing lyrical about the trikes. In a bid to stop the flow of sales pitch, I asked if the store stocked paddle boards, as I was more interested in one of those. That set him off again.

"Yes, the paddle boards are in that section over there behind the fitness machines. If you're thinking of getting a board, there's something you should know about these trikes." He snatched a brochure from a stand nearby and shoved it under my nose. "See… you can carry your board to the beach on your trike."

Sceptical to say the least, I peered at the image on the brochure for a moment. In that time the salesman grabbed a package from a display stand and thrust it into my hands. He flipped the brochure over to the back page to show me an image of a trike with a board mounted along one side of it. "This is how you carry a board on your trike," he said, jabbing a finger at the image on the brochure. "And these are the brackets that attach to the trike to hold the board."

"What a great idea…," Zanne chirped. "That would solve all your problems. You should get the yellow trike. Yellow is a safe colour on the road."

"I'm going to look at boards. Anyway, Zanne, how am I supposed to get one home? It won't fit in my car, even if I didn't have the plants and other stuff."

"Did madam wish to assemble it herself? It comes in two largish boxes that would fit in your car."

"Oh, it's one of those 'some assembly required' situations which, when you open the box, you're confronted with a million parts that only require a month at least to assemble. No, I don't think 'Madam' is interested."

"That's understandable; if madam doesn't want to assemble it herself, there is the fully-assembled option for just a small addition to the purchase price."

"I have even less chance of getting an assembled unit into my car. Come on, Zanne, let's look at boards." I started to drag Zanne in the direction the salesman indicated I'd find the boards when I heard the salesman chuckle. I turned and gave him a how-dare-you look.

"I beg your pardon, Madam. You wouldn't have to get the assembled version into your car; we deliver, right across the surrounding area. It would arrive and be dropped off at your door, fully assembled and ready to go."

Although I was starting to warm to the idea, I decided it was safer to look at boards. I told the young bloke I would think about it, grabbed Zanne by the arm and dragged her across the store. It felt like I was doing really well. I don't know where it all went wrong. By the time we left the store, I was the proud owner of a blue trike complete with board brackets, and a paddleboard along with the free paddle thrown in as part of some current 'special' deal.

As we drove out of the parking lot, I announced, "That's the last time I go shopping with you. I'm pleased they weren't selling the Taj Mahal. I'd probably be still there trying to work out how to get that into this car."

"No you wouldn't. They deliver. They would have to work out how to get it to your house." We both ended up laughing. As we were exiting the Rolleston outskirts on our way back to Charlotte Cove, Zanne became serious again.

"Yesterday you said there were two things you wanted to talk to me about. I think we dealt with your 'invisible women' concerns. What was the other thing you mentioned?"

"The house … *Wellsprings* … I wanted to talk to you about my house." She looked enquiringly at me and held her hands out, palms up. I didn't know how to begin the discussion but made a start. "I don't know what to do with the house. It seems ridiculous for me to rattle around on my own in a place that size when I've demonstrated I can live comfortably in less than a quarter of the place. It needs a family with at least six kids to fill it and utilise the space."

"You plan on having six kids sometime soon? Do I know with whom?"

"What…? Don't be daft. What I'm saying is that maybe I should look at selling the place."

"At the bottom of this, is it about missing the bright lights of the city? Who would want to buy the place anyway? It's cursed, remember."

"No, I'm not missing the city and yes, I know it needs a lot of work to drag it –probably kicking and screaming – in the twenty-first century. The question is, should I live in it, or would it be better to sell it and try to find a small place, something like your Tern Cottage?"

"There are not a lot of those available in Charlotte Cove, so are you trying to tell me you are thinking of leaving the Cove? I hope you're not."

"No-o-o… Oh, I don't know what I'm thinking, other than it is ridiculous for me to live alone a place that size. If I don't sell, what else can I do?"

"I'll leave that question for the moment. You say you are living in less than a quarter of the house. You're not. What you're doing is camping in a tiny part of it; 'roughing it' would be a good description. Edwina lived in the place alone for more than sixty years… and, yes, I admit that probably is why she blocked off so much of the house. That reminds me. We need to have a lot of barbeques in the future."

"Where did this barbeque stuff come from?"

"Well, we are going to have a lot of wood to contend with when we remove all those partitions. You've already used up all the free space in the shed with the timber out of that one small partition. I assume you still want to remove the partitions."

"Yes, of course I do. I want to explore the place; to know what the house is really like."

"Right… and you're not planning on getting married any time soon?"

"What…? No. Why would I want to do that? What would be my chances anyway? There isn't exactly a herd of eligible bachelors hanging about in Charlotte Cove just waiting for me to choose one of them."

"…But you have been checking out the possibilities?"

"No, I have not. I am not sure who or what lives in Charlotte Cove. Not that it matters. I am not in the market for a husband. Come to think of it, I can't even manage to get myself a dog."

"We'll come back to the dog another time. If I may be serious for a moment, I think your real question is whether you want to stay in Charlotte Cove. If that is the case, then I have some ideas about how to deal with your problem about the size of the house. Now, are we done with fussing about the house?"

"Yes… well, no. Maybe the locals are right. Maybe the place is cursed. Maybe it isn't safe for me to live there; that is me as a Granger. The house hasn't done the Grangers much good since it was built, particularly the Granger women."

"That's a whole different can of worms, and we've come to the end of the road. Let's unload these plants and then resume this conversation."

I drove around to the rear of the house and we unloaded the stuff for the conservatory near the backdoor. As we walked into the house, Zanne said, "I know it's a bit early, but the sun will be over the yard arm somewhere in the world. Let's get something to drink and then pick up that conversation again."

We carried our iced teas out into the yard and took a moment to relax – or so I thought – before allowing conversation to intrude. However, I think that while I was relaxing, Zanne was mentally rehearsing phase two of my enlightenment.

"I'll agree; everything our research has dug up does not paint a great picture of the Granger family or of this house. If you think about it, it is what happened to the women that led to the house getting the 'cursed' tag. Neither of us believes that 'cursed' rubbish. Those women, with the exception of one, were not Grangers. They were women who married into the Granger family. If you want to lay blame anywhere, it was the Granger men who were responsible for the myth about the place. Yes, I know Clara was a Granger, but her situation was different. A Granger male was the cause of it all, but she had the strength not to let him or this house's reputation give her a life she didn't want. The only true Granger women who lived in this house were women who were born Grangers; Edwina, your mother Esther. They managed to live to grand old ages."

Although I knew what she was saying made sense, there was another aspect of the story. "Yes, I agree with that. But they never married. There were never husbands to do them harm or get rid of them in some other way."

"For God's sake, Anthea, they would be safe if they had married. Their husbands would not be Grangers, and it is the

Granger men who created havoc throughout the life of this house. Also, if they married, they would no longer be Grangers, and there no longer would be Grangers living in this house. You are the third generation to own this place and not meet with some tragic mishap. If you still harbour some nervousness about the Granger name, get married and change your name. If this is what is impacting on your thinking about selling the place, then get over it. This is some kind of excuse you are creating for yourself in order to avoid having to make logical and realistic decisions. When you decide what to do with the house and whether you're going to stay in Charlotte Cove, let me know. That's when I'll share my ideas about what you could do with the place."

By the end of the conversation, I was feeling a bit bruised and I think Zanne realised that. She stopped talking. We sat in silence for a minute or two. Zanne was right. The argument I put forward was rubbish. I don't know how much of it was true, how much of it was me kidding myself, or how much of it was simply reaction to all the tragic stories I'd uncovered in the last few days. I broke our silence.

"I hear what you're saying … everything you're saying … and I don't have an argument. However, I will try to give this whole issue about the house some logical thought. If for no other reason than hearing your ideas about what I can do with it. I don't know how long that might take but, if it looks like it's taking too long, get on my case again. In the meantime, can we think about demolishing those partitions, and where to start?"

We went back inside and examined the huge partition immediately behind the main staircase. Although finely finished, it remained unpainted. If Aunt Eddie installed it, I'm surprised she lived with it in such a prominent position for all those years without painting it. All of a sudden, I felt excitement stirring. Excitement about what we might find behind that partition. An idle thought drifted through my mind. Might whatever is beyond that partition influence Zanne's ideas about what I might do with this place? My curiosity about her ideas almost rivalled my curiosity about what lay beyond the partition.

Although, I didn't know what it would be, I invited Zanne to stay for dinner. She declined, saying she had emails and some phone calls to attend to, and wasn't sure what time she might arrive tomorrow. After waving her off, I poured myself a glass of wine, sat outside and let the night close in around me. I'm not sure how long I sat there lost in my own thoughts, but I was stiff and cold when I got up to go inside.

As I wasn't sure what time Zanne would arrive today, straight after breakfast, my first task was to transfer my new plants into the new pots and move them into the conservatory. In my ignorance, I thought it would only take a few minutes. By the time I had them in place and was standing back admiring my handiwork, it was coffee time. In the doorway to the conservatory, I stopped and took another look at what I'd achieved. Those few plants made a world of difference, and I could see myself spending plenty of time in there in future. I was on my way to the kitchen when I heard Zanne arrive. Before I had the coffee organised, the van towing a trailer pulled up next to Zanne's car.

My trike and paddleboard had arrived. We invested a few minutes in watching everything being unloaded and then admiring my latest acquisitions. If nothing else, I was now committed to doing things at the beach on a regular basis. A thought about what might happen regarding the dog momentarily occupied my mind, but I dismissed it as something that would have to resolve itself.

This morning, coffee wasn't a long drawn out affair. As soon as we drained our mugs, Zanne was eager to get started. "I assume you still want to remove the partition, and haven't changed your mind overnight."

It was a silly question that didn't deserve an answer. I gave her a look that said so as I led the way out to the shed. We were soon on our way back to the house with a barrow full of every conceivable tool we might use and a ladder. "What is in that building over there?" Zanne asked.

"Nothing as far as I know; well, maybe junk and old stuff, but it's not used for anything today. I think it's what's called the mews. In the good old days, it was the stables. It had a tack room and accommodation upstairs for grooms and drivers, and up this end was where the carriages were housed. The newer looking bit on the end was added when cars were discovered by the Grangers and started the death knell sounding for the horse and carriage at *Wellsprings*. For some transition period, both horses and carriages and early model cars were used. As there was no room in the mews for the cars, the new bit was added to the building. I use that bit as the garage for my car and my trike will go in there as well. The mews building is never open. I 'borrowed' the key once when I was about ten or eleven, and nosed around in there for a while before I was discovered. It got me into all sorts of trouble; borrowing the key, I mean, not for going into the building. Why do you ask?"

"No reason; as I have never seen it open, I was wondering if it were used for anything and, if it is not in use, might it have some future use."

After some discussion about where to start our attack, we launched into demolition mode with enthusiasm. I found this partition better constructed than the one in the servants' quarters. Nevertheless, with plenty of effort and some swearing, by lunch time, we had removed two of the lower level sheets of ply. It proved disappointing. The area beyond the partition was so dark, it was impossible even to make out shapes.

So keen were we to explore what was behind the partition, lunch happened in record time. We were back on the job after less than half an hour. There wasn't another break until around four o'clock, by which time we were nearing exhaustion. There is so little room in my living area, each sheet of ply removed, had to be taken outside to allow us enough room to continue working. We stacked the ply outside against the end wall of the shed. When we stopped work for the day, all lower level sheeting was removed. Tomorrow would be even more taxing. After a day of up and down ladders as we remove the ply from higher up.

Zanne yelled over her shoulder as she rushed out the front door. "I'll be back in a minute. make us coffee. while I'm gone."

"Yes, Ma'am, coffee coming up," I mumbled. A few moments later, she was back and came in brandishing her torch.

"Before you make the coffee, get your torch. Let's see if shining two torches into the space behind the partition helps us see what's there."

They didn't. All we established was that the tiled floor of my living area continued on the other side of the partition. I thought I could make out a few lumpy shapes in the distance. What a frustrating note on which to end the day. I was so excited about being so close to discovering what the rest of the house was like. In addition to that, my growing curiosity about all the paperwork Zanne brought back from the solicitors was creating a tug-of-war between wanting to demolish the partition and resuming our research.

When we finally sat down with our coffees, Zanne's phone rang. I heard her tell the caller she would call them back in about ten minutes. "I have to go home to make the call. I'll see you first thing in the morning, and we will get on with removing the rest of that sheeting. I didn't get a chance to answer. She was out the door and jogging to her car. Although I didn't know why, that call and Zanne's response to it gave me an uneasy feeling. Telling myself I was jumping at shadows didn't help. I needed to do something to take my mind off it, or the feeling would niggle me all night. There was still an hour or two of daylight left. I could make a start on removing that next lot of sheeting.

It was gone seven o'clock when I slid the second sheet of ply to the floor and scrambled down from the ladder for the last time today. By the time I removed the first sheet, it already was dark outside. Instead of taking the sheets I removed after Zanne left to the shed, I took them outside and leant them again the wall near the backdoor. I hoped it wouldn't rain. There was about half a forest of good timber stacked out in the open.

I don't know whether it was the physical activity involved in removing the sheeting or the ache in my legs from going up and down that ladder, but my earlier concern about Zanne's phone call disappeared. All I had in mind was a hot soak in a tub of bubble bath followed by an early night.

Chapter 21

No point in delaying the inevitable, this trike has to go to the beach sometime. I was ready a little earlier than usual this morning when I remembered my new trike. No need for these brackets today. I'm not taking the board with me. I patted the board as I walked past it. "Don't fret; your turn is coming, but you will have to wait until I get the rest of my life in order," I told it.

It was a beautiful morning, there was no one around as I pedalled my trike along the main street, and the beach was deserted. What more could I ask for? Well, I could ask for legs that weren't quite so stiff from climbing that ladder yesterday. Any excuse will do I suppose, but a short jog that was more like a brisk stroll, and then I was pedalling my way home again.

Although breakfast was long finished, I was still at the table and deep in thought when Zanne arrived. "Is everything all right? I get worried when I see you sitting around thinking. Either something has gone wrong, or it's about to. Which is it today?"

"No, nothing has gone wrong, and nothing is about to. In fact, everything is great."

"Hmm … maybe you had better tell me about that. I feel as though I'm waiting for the other shoe to drop."

"Okay, that's easy. I've made a decision." I watched Zanne grimace in expectation. "I'm not going anywhere. I love Charlotte Cove, and I think I love this house… or I'm at least coming around to it. I'm not moving and I'm not selling. I can't sell. I would be doing so many people a disservice, not least of whom would be Aunt Eddie and my mother. This was their home. They saw fit it should come to me, and I owe it to them to make a bloody effort to settle into the place… and maybe put all those ghosts and curses to bed while I'm about it. So, my friend, I'll be needing those ideas of yours about what to do with the place. In the meantime, let's get the rest of that partition removed so we can see what we have to work with."

When I finished speaking and looked across at her, Zanne was grinning wide enough to split her face in two. "Thank God the dark clouds have rolled on. Let's get stuck into that partition and then, do you think we might go through that box of wills I brought back from the solicitors?"

By working straight through until lunchtime, all of partition was removed except for a few bits of timber from the frame. With an amazing display of self-control, we left exploring the newly accessible area until after lunch. How long does it take to make and eat tomato and cheese sandwiches? Today, it took about fifteen minutes.

Then, armed with our torches, we crossed the mark on the floor from where the partition stood for decades. Although a little more light filtered into the space now, it was still too dark to see anything clearly. Our first priority was to find light switches. Some lights worked, at least for a little while, but most didn't. "I think a good electrician to check out the wiring and install a few new lights might be handy," Zanne quipped as I tried yet another light switch and nothing happened.

"In the meantime, do you think opening those drapes might help the situation?" I asked, tongue in cheek. Opening them wasn't difficult. They fell apart in our hands. We discovered the windows were in a series of rooms running along the front side of the house. By leaving any doors to those rooms open, a little more light came into what looked like a grand ballroom running through the centre of the space. More rooms opened off the other side of the 'ballroom'. There were no windows in those rooms as they shared their back wall with the domestic chores area.

For the next hour or so we were lunatics criss-crossing the ballroom as we rushed from room to room. Some of the rooms we identified immediately. There was the formal dining room. It had an enormous table with twenty chairs drawn up to it. More chairs were pushed back against the wall. Identifying the library was a no-brainer. It was the room fully lined with bookcases, and all of them still packed with books. Other rooms were not so easy to identify. We would need to rely on furniture and other artefacts in each room to help identify their use. That process would take time. Before we embark on any of that, I want to add the layout of this part of the house to my sketch.

It was time to regroup. We headed back to the kitchen and sat in silence for a few moments. Then the floodgates opened and we were both talking at once as we discussed and tried to make sense of our discoveries. After a while, normalcy returned, along with deep thought and speculation about how to utilise the space in the future.

"I'm thinking about that library," Zanne said. "It makes you wonder what Edwina's state of mind was when she installed that partition… if it was Edwina's doing. To do that without first removing the books, suggests she was driven by some strong emotional reaction to something that happened. I wonder what that was and when it happened. Maybe it was a latent emotion simmering for years until ownership passed to her and she could do what she wanted to the place."

"Possibly… I used to think it was a case of rationalising running the place. If you are not going to use most of it, close it off. That way, you don't have to clean it or worry about it in any other way. However, now that I see how everything was left when partitions were installed, I'm inclined to agree a significant motivating force was at play."

"It's a shame Edwina didn't keep that diary of hers going a bit longer. I suppose you did look for any late entries or after-thoughts. It would be good to know how she came to inherit the house and why she brought up your mother."

"Yeah…," I murmured. That's all I could manage, as I hadn't checked through to the end of the diary. I stopped reading when I encountered consecutive blank pages. Zanne had a point. I will go back to the diary and check to its end… but I will do it when I'm alone. For now, adding the layout of that new area to my sketch is the priority.

As Zanne watched, she commented, "I can picture a debutante ball or some other gala event happening in that great hall. We shouldn't call it a ballroom. I'm sure it wasn't, but I think major functions were held there. Did you notice that chandelier? I bet it looked magical when lit."

"Has seeing that new space given you any further ideas about what I might do with this place? I suppose, if I'm going to stay here, I should start getting my head around it and making plans accordingly."

"It has, but so have a couple of other things. Give me a couple of days to firm up my thoughts, and then we will sit down to discuss the possibilities. However, what you can do now is show me the mews. You said you only saw inside it once years ago, so let's see what it's like inside." Strange request, I thought, but worthwhile doing. In case the building was locked, I collected the butler's bundle of keys.

While the newer garage end of the building was unlocked when I arrived, I found the older stable end of it locked. A key that unlocked all the doors in that part of the building was in the bundle. I pulled open the first door – the one I had snuck in through all those years ago. An overwhelming aroma of mould, leather, dust and God knows what else flowed out to meet me. We opened all the external doors to allow the place to air a bit before venturing inside.

The building didn't seem much changed from how I remembered it. There were four small bedrooms and another primitive bathroom upstairs. Carriages still occupied the ground floor. A large tack room, complete with harnesses, saddles and other strange equipment, was at one end of the ground floor. This was another area of the property left intact and undisturbed for decades. Aunt Eddie, or someone before her, cleaned out the garage area and used it, but the only things missing from the original mews were the horses and a couple of carriages. I remembered there were four carriages before. Now only two remained. It struck me as strange that, at some point over the last twenty years, Edwina had seen fit to get rid of two carriages, but nothing else.

Zanne was deep in thought as we walked back to the house after touring the mews. If nothing else, I had learnt to leave her alone with her thoughts at such times. Conversation remained scarce as we sat at the kitchen table with our coffees. "Perhaps we should utilise that dining room in future," I said by way of livening things up a bit. “I can just about picture us sitting at opposite ends of that huge table.”

“If there were to be any conversation, we would need out mobile phones. I don’t think there would be much conversation if we had to yell at each down the length of that table.”

As we washed up, Zanne became excited. “If you haven’t got anything else to do, how about we start having a look at those wills I brought back from the solicitors?”

“I hadn’t forgotten them. How could I when they are sitting there looking at me all the time. As we don’t seem to have any other spare tables, we’ll have to read them at the kitchen table.” I thought we would select one each to read. Zanne had other ideas.

“We should read each will together. Otherwise neither of us will end up know the whole story of the continuity of bequests.” That’s what we did, and the first will out of the box was Rupert’s. It answered another question. After a period of time, Wilfred made application for Rupert to be declared dead. It took a little while to happen, but that’s how Wilfred came to inherit when he did.

“Well, as the thing that prompted us to get these wills was the question of what happened to the grazing property and the wharf complex, maybe we should start by reading the inventory pages,” Zanne said.

There was the usual long list of everything, including things I would think too trivial to include. I was still running my eye down the page when Zanne yelped. “Bingo! Here they are. The two enterprises are here. The will treats everything listed in the inventory as a package deal. So, when the will says everything goes to Wilfred, *everything* goes to him.”

“Okay, but we knew Rupert still owned those properties at the time of his midnight flit. It’s what happened to them after that I want to know about.”

“Right… here is Wilfred’s will. Let’s see what he had to bequeath to anyone.” I watched as Zanne opened out the will and turned to the inventory pages.

Much the same long list of possessions greeted us. Towards the bottom of the second page we found the listing of the two enterprises. “What’s the date on this will?” Zanne asked, as she flicked back through the pages to find a date. "Ah, it was made not long before his death. That means it probably is safe to assume what's listed here is what he still owned when he died. It seems everything went to his son, Thomas."

We followed the same procedure for Thomas' and then Edwina's wills and, in both instances, found *Whylara* and the wharf complex listed in the inventory. That made me think for a moment before voicing a tentative thought. I picked up Edwina's will and shook it at Zanne. "This means Edwina still owned those two enterprises when she died. How can that be?"

"That's easy; it means Edwina inherited them from Thomas and didn't sell them."

"But her will bequeaths everything, including those properties, to my mother. My mother didn't sell them. When Aunt Eddie died – and my mother inherited everything – my mother didn't even know what day it was, let alone that Aunt Eddie had died. She was comatose and had only days to live."

After weighing up my comments for a few moments, Zanne asked, "What's the date on Edwina's will? Maybe it was made sometime before her death, and things were disposed of in the intervening period before her death."

I searched my memory for the exact date of Edwina's death and then checked the date of the will. "This will was made a few months before she died. Shortly after that, she went into fulltime care until her death. She wasn't in a fit state to authorise the sale of anything during those months."

Zanne took Edwina's will and examined it for a few moments before murmuring, "So, what did your mother do with them?"

"What … what do you mean by that? My mother didn't do anything with them. She was busy dying at the time," I replied a touch too sharply.

"Okay, so they should be listed in your mother's inventory. The question then is, what did you do with them? Were they included in the inventory?"

How to look stupid without even trying? Just watch me, I'm good at it, I thought as I shook my head. "I don't know. I haven't looked beyond the first couple of pages. And, yes, before you say it, I know I am the executor, so how can I not know. That's a good question, and one I prefer you didn't ask."

There they were, listed in the inventory of mum's possessions… along with other properties I didn't know anything about. "Jesus, does this mean I now own all this stuff?"

"It looks that way. Maybe you should have a long chat with your solicitor mates."

"Tomorrow…," was the only response I could manage.

When a day starts out well, you can't help but wonder if it's lulling you into a false sense of security before everything goes pear-shaped. I was about to pedal home on my trusty chariot when I noticed the elderly couple and the dog. Yelling for me to wait, the man rushed towards me. They had a death in the family and had been away for a couple of weeks. He said his wife still wasn't quite sure about giving away the dog. She was concerned the dog wouldn't take to me and might pine for his old keepers. However, they agreed it would be good if I brought the dog to the beach with me whenever I came. That way, they could see how things went between me and the dog, and might encourage them to give him up later.

I noted their address and said I would collect the dog the following day. All the way home, I question whether I had done the right thing, and whether I really wanted a dog. By the time I finished breakfast, I had decided everything was good for now and, if the dog came to live with me in the future, it would be good too. I made a mental note to ask if the dog had a name, because I hadn't heard one used.

As soon as a civilised hour arrived, I rang the legal firm in Sydney. The receptionist asked which solicitor I wanted. I decided, although the son handled mum's will, I should talk to the father who handled earlier family probates. He hadn't arrived for the day, but she would ask him to call me back. I groaned as the call ended. I'd be lucky if he called by the end of the month. Maybe I should have spoken to the son instead. About ten minutes later, the man I wanted rang me. I made him a mental apology for my doubts.

After I stumbled through the explanation for my call, the solicitor sounded relieved that I contacted him. "I have been waiting to hear from you. I knew it would take time for you to come to terms with things and that it was best to wait until you were ready to talk about everything else." That 'everything else' made my stomach tighten a bit. How much else could there be for me to come to terms with?

He was happy to explain things over the phone, but wanted a meeting with me the next time I came to Sydney … allow plenty of time, he suggested. Then he got down to business answering my questions and explaining matters I knew nothing about. In the course of our conversation, he confirmed I owned the grazing property and the wharf complex, as well as three other properties in the centre of Sydney, another property in an industrial precinct on the outskirts of the city, and a huge market garden area, as well as the properties that were mum's. It was all too much to comprehend. After a few moments, I managed to ask how they were continuing to operate. I didn't know about *Whylara,* but the wharf complex was still operating.

"Edwina, as she grew older, found everything too much for her to manage. About five years before she died, she asked me to take over management of all her properties. We agreed, and set up discrete property management to do that. There were existing managers for the grazing property and the wharf operations. We did a full audit of all properties and, within six months, replaced both those managers with our own recruits, who have proved more honest. Those men are still running your enterprises. The income from all the properties goes into a number of trust accounts. Their balances were quite high when Edwina died, so we included some drawdown of funds in our probate work. Those funds were included in some of the cash you inherited – via your mother, of course. Those balances again are at extreme levels. We would recommend further withdrawals be made."

"I remember during that time when everything was a blur around me, you sent me out with a property manager to look at Aunt Eddie's Sydney properties. At the time, I thought it a ploy to get me out of the hospital for a while and give me a break from sitting with my mother. Am I right in thinking there was more to it than that?"

He murmured confirmation of my assumption, and I continued. "When I came back to your office, you asked my opinion of the properties and what I would do with them if they were mine. I recall saying two of the properties in the city were old, not in the best areas anymore and, if I owned them, I would try to sell. The other central property I thought a good investment, as were the industrial property and the market garden. You were trying to establish what I might do *when* they were mine."

"You are correct and, at your earliest convenience, I would ask you to revisit those properties and provide us with some indication of your intentions regarding them. There is a bit for you to do and see. I would recommend allowing at least three days for your visit. When you have indicative dates, please call my secretary to arrange the times. We will arrange for the relevant property managers to accompany you on visits to your properties, to introduce you and bring you up to speed on everything… Oh, and please make it soon." His closing comment made me a little nervous, but I shouldn't be surprised they want me to pick up my responsibilities.

A few minutes after the call ended, Zanne arrived. Some time was spent sharing the solicitor's information with her, and telling her about the developments with the elderly couple and the dog. While talking to her, I decided to drive to Sydney on Sunday to meet with the solicitor on Monday and then spend as many days as required sorting out things. I left Zanne in charge of the coffee machine while I went to make the necessary arrangements. By the time I returned, coffee was on the table and she had decided she wanted to come with me, not to visit the solicitor with me, but to take care of business of her own.

As we rinsed our mugs, Zanne said, "Do you realise that, in spite of all our research on the Granger family, we still don't know much about your grandparents?"

That had loitered in the back of my mind for some time but, with so much happening, there wasn't time to follow up on them. Zanne was all for doing something about that oversight now, and suggested a number of research options to get us started. I couldn't muster any enthusiasm for research. Perhaps my mind was busy digesting everything I'd heard this morning. Not wanting to upset Zanne, I tried to sound interested. I was saved by the bell; by the clanging bell ringtone on Zanne's phone. It was a short call but, from the little I heard, it sounded urgent. As soon as the call ended, she admitted she forgot a Skype call scheduled for this morning. The call was to remind her, and tell her it had been rescheduled to occur in half an hour. In less than a minute, she was on her way home.

That left me wondering what to do next. Zanne's comments yesterday about Edwina's diary came back to me. Now on my own again, it seemed a good time to break out that diary to see if there were any later entries. Almost convinced there wasn't anything in the diary I hadn't already read, I elected not to take the book out of the bedroom, but sat on the bed to go through it.

At first, things were much as I expected. There were quite a few blank pages, but I forced myself and looked at each one to make sure I missed nothing. "Shit, there is more." I came to a lengthy entry, and a quick fan through subsequent pages showed there was quite a bit more. That first entry told of Thomas and Catherine's trip to England to attend the wedding of Catherine's cousin. Their decision to leave their two-year-old daughter at home meant Edwina would have Esther all to herself for a month while the parents were away.

The next few entries indicate how much Edwina revelled in that situation and how, as time drew near for the young couple to return, she was dreading having to hand Esther back to her parents. All the entries from that time seemed to be light and chatty until the one that documented details of the young couple's departure for Australia. They were to leave Heathrow on an early morning flight, but a news broadcast told Edwina blizzard-like conditions blanketed much of England and Europe. As a consequence, airports in England were closed for more than twenty-four hours, causing major flight disruptions. Indications were that things had improved and flights were returning to normal.

Somehow, I knew that recording such information suggested something terrible was to follow. My instincts were right.

Edwina's next entry tells of receiving the news that the flight on which Thomas and Catherine were returning to Australia had crashed somewhere over the Alps. There were no survivors. Through the next few entries, I learned that the crash was so horrific that bodies could not be repatriated. In the aftermath of the crash, as executor of Thomas' will, Edwina records struggling to manage the task while dealing with her own grief. She wondered if Thomas had some premonition that something terrible might happen. A few days before the couple left for England, Thomas made a new will leaving everything to his sister, Edwina, and appointing Edwina guardian of his two-year-old daughter, Esther.

Now I knew it all. I understood why the succession of ownership in this house happened as it did. In some cases, such as with Wilfred, I knew more than I wanted to about the people and what happened. Perhaps the only questions that remain relate to Rupert and maybe Gwendolyn. I feel certain that photograph we found amongst Michael's possessions tells of Gwendolyn's escape with her Scottish hermit to live in the Orkneys. If I accept that, then the only remaining unknown is what became of Rupert, his housekeeper, and two young daughters.

It was several months later when we found a hint that helped solve that mystery as well. Zanne browsed a Melbourne newspaper dated a few months after Rupert and his crew embarked on their midnight flit. Following a series of articles over a few days, and employing a bit of reading between the lines, we gathered first-hand information from an embittered former *Sydney Morning Herald* reporter. The reporter's feature articles often appeared in the Sydney paper, but his regular column was coverage of social events, including shipping passengers' comings and goings.

About a week after Rupert disappeared, the reporter claimed to see a man who he identified as Rupert Granger boarding a ship destined for overseas. The man he saw was accompanied by a woman and two young girls. By calling in a favour, he got a look at the passenger list. No Rupert Granger appeared on the list, but there was a group travelling together that fitted the bill. However, they were travelling under different names… and as Mr and Mrs and two daughters. He managed to snap a photo of the group, and a single one of the man having a nervous look around before making his way onto the ship. A comparison of his photographs with earlier ones of Rupert convinced the reporter he was right, and this was Rupert Granger boarding a ship for overseas.

The reporter put together an exposé piece, complete with photographs. His editor threw it out. He took it higher but it was rejected again. This time it came with the warning not to pursue such 'nonsense'. Tension ran high, words were said, and the reported was sacked. He claimed he was blackballed in Sydney so, sometime later and still without work, the reporter moved to Melbourne and found work with a paper perhaps less fastidious than his previous employer. They jumped at the chance and ran the story. However, it seems influence stretches a long way.

A few days later, the paper ran a retraction, claiming a case of mistaken identity. Then, a few weeks later, the same newspaper carried a brief mention of that unfortunate reporter's suicide. "The bastard," Zanne exclaimed. "He knew the police had him in their sights and he shot through overseas. You don't have to think too hard to work out the woman was more than a housekeeper."

"A housekeeper with optional extras perhaps…," I added. "I wonder how long that had gone on."

"Are we going to accept that Rupert buggered off overseas with his entourage, or do we dismiss the story?"

"I think that maybe we should accept it, if only to stop us wondering about it. However, I would like to see the original material, especially the photographs. Regardless, I think we put Rupert to bed along with the rest of this disgusting family. Anyway, if he did dash overseas, we would never be able to confirm it. …Best to accept the story and forget about it." While I believed what I said, I remained only half convinced. Not knowing would haunt me for a long time to come.

Chapter 22

Life settled in to a steady routine over the next few months. We slowly uncovered more of the house's secrets, an electrician rewired the house, and the conservatory was becoming my favourite place to spend time. The addition of more plants, a small water feature and several new pieces of furniture changed the whole space.

On a couple of days, I collected the dog and he ran beside me as I pedalled my way to the beach. Then, he either trotted beside me as I jogged my usual circuit, or he frolicked in the shallows before joining me as I headed back to the trike. I learnt his name was Chief. It wasn't a name I would choose, but it suited him, and changing it would only confuse the poor animal. When I returned him at the end of our second morning together, he wanted to come with me when I left, and put on a terrible performance that upset everyone. Unsure about my possible reception the following morning, I was relieved to find the elderly man waiting for me to arrive. After watching the dog's performance the previous day, his wife had no doubts Chief wanted to be with me… and did I still want to take him?

Yes, I did, but I needed to prepare first, my trip to Sydney would see me away from Charlotte Cove for a few days. I asked if I could leave collecting him until the end of next week. After I reassured them that this was a rare event and that I wouldn't be spending time away and neglecting the dog in the future, they agreed. Before I left for Sydney, I visited the pet store in Rolleston and purchased, food and water containers, brushes, a bed and rug, bags of dried food, chewy things that were supposed to be good for his teeth, and a couple of squeaky toys. Once Chief became mine, my next dog expense would be for the vet to check him out.

That left only two other matters still occupying my mind: my trip to Sydney, and what to do with all the space in this house. The Sydney matters are about to be dealt with, I told myself as

I drove to the city. Zanne spent most of the trip scribbling in a notebook. After breakfast, we parted company for the day. Zanne went off to talk to people associated with the literary world, and I kept my appointment with the solicitor. It was a long, intense day, and I was brain dead at the end of it, having gone over endless legal documents and volumes of figures.

At least my second day saw me out and about. I was taken around all the Sydney properties once more. My opinion regarding the two inner city properties still held. They should be sold. The third one appeared still a sound investment. I wanted to keep it. Then it was off to an industrial precinct on what were once the outskirts of the city. Urban sprawl extended right up to the fence line, where zoning regulations halted it. My part of the precinct involved a huge property comprising a number of large warehouse type buildings. A different enterprise operated out of each building, and all seemed to be doing as nicely as the last time I was here.

Then the ever attentive property manager assigned to show me around today drove us to the market garden complex that backed onto the industrial complex. It seemed to cover vast hectares. Here too, the urban sprawl had crept as close as zoning laws allowed. I was introduced to Dominic, the second of three generations of the same family working the garden. By my estimation, he was in his late-sixties or early seventies. The property manager left me to talk to Dom while he went off to talk to Dom's son, Mick. As Dom and I sat under a pergola attached to his office, an elderly gentleman came out of a packing shed and marched towards us. I didn't realise how old he was until he was quite close and I could see his age etched into his face.

"When are the pickers bringing the next truckload?" he demanded of Dom.

"Soon, Papa, but come and meet our guest. This is …."

"No...no … It can't be. It's not possible." I feared the old man was about to have a heart attack as he stared at me. His face lost colour and he brought his hands up to his mouth as if to stop himself from screaming.

"I'm sorry if I have upset you. There's nothing to be concerned about. I'm Anthea Granger, the new owner, and I've come to see what you do here. Are you all right? You don't look so good. Here, take my chair and sit down."

"You are Granger?" he asked in a shaky voice. "It's me who should apologise. You looked like someone… argh, it's nothing. It was all a long time ago." He pulled my chair over and sat down. Dom ducked into the office and came out with another chair for me. I was still recovering from the shock the old man gave me when a women came rushing around the corner of the building.

"Nick, have you seen Dom? I've been looking everywhere for him. There's a phone call for him over in the shed."

"I'm here," Dom said. "I just went into the office. What's the problem?"

"Phone call …for you … over in the shed," the woman said economically. They rushed off to the shed together. Based on the term of endearment Dom used when he spoke to the woman, I assumed she was his wife. That left me with the old man. He spoke first.

"So, you are the new owner. I suppose you have come to talk about our lease. I think you will find everything is okay. We have been here a long time now, and we work hard. We have never had any trouble with the previous owner." Again, I explained visit was nothing more than a familiarisation tour. In a bid to ease his anxiety, I changed the subject.

"You gave me quite a start before. I thought you might be about to have a heart attack. I seemed to shock you. You said I looked like someone… I think you meant someone from your past. Can you tell me what that was about?"

"It was nothing; just a silly old man and his memories. You say your name is Granger. I knew Edwina Granger who owned this place before. She was very good to me and my family; always renewed our lease. She was a special lady."

"She was, and she was my mother's aunt. We always called her Aunt Eddie." The old man – Nick – eyed me cautiously.

"So, now you own this place, what will you do with it? I always hoped someday I would be able to own property to leave to Dom and his son when I die. I hoped for a long time to buy this place, but it wasn't to be and I am too old now to do anything about it." As Nick spoke, a powerful thought struck me.

"Tell me, Nick, did I remind you of Clara? Do I look like her?" I heard him catch his breath and saw the colour drain from his face again.

"You know? I didn't think she would ever betray me or Clara."

"Do you mean Edwina?" he nodded. "She didn't betray anyone. Edwina had Clara's diary. She kept it hidden until her death. I found it. I've been trying to understand my Granger family. I haven't found anything in any of the men to be proud of, but Clara and Edwina have nothing but my admiration."

"You know what he did to her?" My turn to nod. "He tried to put the blame on me. I didn't know until a while afterwards. The housekeeper gave me a letter from Clara. It broke my heart that I hadn't done anything to help her."

"I've read her diary. She loved you very much. The only thing that worried her at the end was what you might think of her. That's why she wrote the letter. She hoped it would help you understand that tragic thing she did."

"My family was forced to leave Charlotte Cove or we would starve. Her father did that. I wanted to keep in touch; to write to her via the housekeeper. My father forbade it. When I challenged him about it, he told me her father threatened bad things would happen to Clara and my sister if I ever contacted Clara again. I would do anything to keep Clara safe."

"Do I look like Clara?"

"Like looking in the mirror; of course, she would be old now like me, and not as I still remember her. It makes an old man happy to see the Granger women have defeated those men. They have taken over and triumphed. It was Edwina who came to me and offered to lease this place to me."

"You and your family have a wonderful business here. I'm pleased Edwina did that, but I don't think that makes up for everything that happened. You don't happened to have some spare cash lying around, do you? …Say, maybe five thousand dollars."

"Who has spare cash? We have done well and we are not short of money, but why do you ask?"

"I want to sell you this place. I can't give it to you because that might be contested by anyone who might be interested in the land, but I can sell it to you, and I think that is a fair price under the circumstances. Are you interested?"

"I must call Dom to deal with this."

"I'm not selling to Dom. I'm selling to you. What you do with it in your will is up to you. Do we have a deal?" Before Nick could answer, my trusty property manager came back.

"What deal? What do you think you are doing? You can't go around making deals. It's up to me as the property manager to make any deals that are to be made."

I stood up and pulled myself up as tall as I could. "You forget your place, I think. You are an employee who acts on my behalf. I own this property and I make my own deals. Your job now is to draw up any paperwork necessary for the sale."

"I will not do that. I think it's you who doesn't know how the system works."

"Don't go away," I said as I stepped into the office. I pulled out my phone and hit speed dial for my solicitor. The call only lasted a couple of minutes and, when it ended, I went back outside in time to hear the property manager making veiled threats to Nick.

"Stop that," I bellowed. "Sir, your services have been terminated as of about five minutes ago."

"Sure, you can think that but I will be talking to the solicitor managing this property. We'll see what happens then."

"Perhaps, if you hadn't been so intent on shouting at Nick, you might have heard your phone. I think you have been sacked… by the solicitor you thought was going to save you. And, you are to hand over the keys to the vehicle and find your own way back. And just so you are aware, I have insisted on a full detailed audit of the management of all my properties you managed." He threw the keys on the ground and stormed off.

"You are a true Granger woman. You have the courage and determination like my Clara. If you are sure about selling me this property, I will call Dom to arrange the money for you."

"There's no hurry. All the paperwork needs to be done before any money needs to change hands. I should be on my way to start that process happening." I extended the old man my hand. "Nick, it is not much compensation after all these years, but this is for Clara and the life you might have made together. I'd like to keep in touch if I may." I saw the tears welled up in his eyes as he came and threw his arms around me.

As I picked my way back to the solicitor's office in an unfamiliar car and a city I wasn't familiar with any more, I thought about the hand life sometimes deals you. In spite of a few ups and downs along the way, I had been dealt one of the best and, although the last of my family were now gone, in their passing I had received an incredible prize. With that came the realisation that I needed to do the best I could with what I'd been given. I have been lucky, I have a precious friend in Zanne, and I live in a beautiful part of the world… and it would appear I am not going to be short of cash any time soon. Added to all that, the one small thing I could do for Nick – and for Clara – gave me the most wonderful feeling I ever experienced in my entire life. I don't know that it was a debt paid in full, but maybe it went some way to righting a wrong.

When I made it back to the hotel, Zanne was already waiting with a bottle of white wine on ice. "You are positively glowing. I'm almost not game to ask what you got up to today. Whatever it was, it agrees with you and the look suits you."

I didn't enlighten her but, after catching up on what each other had done during the day and pouring a second glass of wine, I did have something I wanted to share with her. "As soon as we are finished in Sydney, I want to start hearing your ideas about what to do with *Wellsprings*. I have come to realise how much I enjoy living at Charlotte Cove and how much I love my house. I'm about ready to move me and the house – and Chief – into a new era. Want to come along for the ride?"

My third day in Sydney turned out to be only a morning session spent back at the legal firm's offices with my solicitor. I confirmed I wanted to sell the two properties in the centre of the city and that I had an agreement with Nick to sell him the market garden property. The price I set for the latter raised the solicitor's eyebrows, but he thought better of arguing with me. He said he would take care of the paperwork for the sale. Before I left his office at about one o'clock, one of the firm's external auditors called in to update us on the audit they had started after my phone call yesterday. Audit staff worked until quite late last night and began again this morning. They already had uncovered significant discrepancies in the trust fund. A joint charge between the auditor's firm and the legal firm would be filed against the property manager. Yes, I did feel my pleasure on hearing that was a bit vindictive, but I also felt justified and triumphant.

We arrive home as dusk began closing in. I dropped Zanne at Tern Cottage before driving to the beach. Until the blackness of night and the chill off the bay got the better of me, I sat on the rocks and bid farewell to a few personal demons developed over recent weeks. Then I went home and, after a hot shower, slept deep and untroubled all night.

This morning was the last time I collected Chief from the elderly couple. They put his food dish and a couple of battered toys in the basket of the trike and said their goodbyes to the dog. At the end of today's morning constitutional along the beach, Chief would come home to *Wellsprings* with me and we would start adapting to sharing the house.

Zanne is not expected today. She has something resulting from her Sydney visit she wants to take care of first thing, and then she feels compelled to indulge in some domestic chores. Like me, she puts off doing domestic chores until the point where they can be ignored no longer. I wouldn't have told her not to come today, but I'm please she isn't planning to do so. It allows me to spend the day getting to know Chief and helping him familiarise himself with his new home.

When I gathered all the gear for bringing a dog into my life, I asked the lady at the pet shop about books on dog training. She grabbed one from the shelf behind the counter and handed it to me, while explaining in the most apologetic way *it is pretty basic and really for absolute beginners, but it's the only one we have.* Whatever it had to offer is more than I know now, so I added the book to my list of purchases. I tried reading the book, but decided it might make more sense if I had a dog to practise on as I went through it. Somehow, I think Chief knows more about how dogs behave and what they should and shouldn't do than

I'll ever know. I suspect this dog training exercise will be about Chief training me.

The day went without a hitch. Chief seemed to settle in without fuss. He explored the grounds but showed no interest in straying outside the boundary. A couple of times during the day, he took to his new bed for a nap and seemed content with his new life.

Twice during that first night, I awoke with a start as something moved in my bedroom. Chief had come in to check on me. He wasn't intent on disturbing me; just put his head over the edge of the bed and sniffed a couple of times. I scratched his muzzle to let him know I was there and okay. I heard his tail thumping the bed as it wagged in response. Then, reassured, he wandered back out to his own bed.

Chief and I spent longer at the beach than usual this morning before returning home to refine our breakfast arrangements. We hadn't long finished breakfast when Zanne arrived. This could be interesting, I thought, and hung back to see what Chief did. As Zanne started towards the front door, Chief trotted out to meet her. He was wary but not aggressive. She held her hand down to him. After a couple of sniffs, his tail started wagging. He looked back at me as if to say, 'this one is okay'. Then he fell into a trot beside Zanne and escorted her into the kitchen.

His acceptance of Zanne was important, as I would rely on her to keep an eye on him if I went out of town for any reason. I soon discovered Zanne was besotted with the dog. Then my concern became that he would be overfed and spoiled rotten.

Life settled into a comfortable routine. Zanne and I were working our way through everything in the attic. Chief soon learnt that, if he climbed those two sets of steep stairs he could join us in the roof cavity. He usually curled up and went to sleep as soon as he got there. I could understand that. Those stairs are exhausting.

On my third day back from Sydney, I visited the wharf complex and introduced myself to the manager. My arrival seemed to cause him some concern, so I went to some pains to reassure him his job was safe, and that I intended everything should remain as is for now. The only difference is, he would report to me directly now and not to a property manager. He was personable enough and seemed to have a sound understanding of the operation. We agreed I would spend time at the complex over the next few weeks learning about its operation.

Later that day, the papers arrived for the sale to Nick of the four parcels of land that comprised the market garden complex. After they were signed and witnessed, I mailed them back the same day. Over our afternoon coffee, I told Zanne I was going to try to arrange a visit to *Whylara* for some time next week. "Are you interested in seeing the place? I might have to leave you to your own devices a bit if the manager wants to discuss facts and figures. I'm only going to introduce myself and inform him of the new reporting arrangements."

"Yeah, I'm up for a visit. Are we taking Chief?"

"Hmm… I hadn't thought that far ahead, but yes, he can come too. After all, a dog on a grazing property shouldn't be a problem."

"Let's see what havoc he creates," Zanne said.

"Okay, now let's put everything else aside for the rest of the afternoon. I want to hear your ideas on what I might do with this house."

Zanne leaped up and headed for the door, calling over her shoulder as she went, "Wait a bit; I'll be back in a minute." She returned with a grey box file tucked under her arm.

"Right, here are my ideas," she said as she resumed her seat at the table. "I'll talk you through it as I feed you the relevant bits of paper."

I hadn't expected anything quite so structured and well-prepared, but it gave me a good feeling about where this conversation might be headed.

"I see this place being utilised a writers' retreat. Quite a few big houses and estates in the UK and parts of Europe offer writers such a facility. The writers get peace and quiet to work, solitude if they want it, somewhere quiet and inspiring to stroll and arouse their creative juices, and they pay for the privilege. I see that mews building – not the garage part – being turned into accommodation for up to six writers at any one time. Here's a sketch of what I think can be done to achieve this. Length of stay could be for a weekend, a long weekend, or a week at a time. I have the scale of fees being charged at various places in the UK. They are converted to Aussie dollars at the current conversion rate. It's quite a lucrative business over there, but we might have to lower those prices here to suit the Aussie market."

"Is there a market? Are writers likely to be interested?"

"It was a constant topic of networking conversation at a writers' festival I went to several weeks ago, and it got quite a bit of airing at that festival at the university I went to. That one even had a paper by a writer who had shouted herself such a retreat while on a trip to the UK. She waxed lyrical about the experience and the benefits that accrued. Aussie writers want this opportunity too. There already are bursaries and grants out there for writers who want to go and sit under a tree somewhere and get on with their writing."

"It sounds good until you think about the cleaning and cooking, and all the other hospitality stuff involved. I don't want to spend my time skivvying after writers."

"No, you don't do that. That's why they utilise a discrete building on an estate or wherever, and don't involve the owner's residence. The accommodation has a group share kitchen and other facilities, so the retreat is fully self-contained in a separate building. The writers do for themselves. There are two approaches to dealing with the providoring side of things. Some places provide all the food and let the writers do what they will with it. Other places leave it to the writers to organise their own food. Fees for the retreat reflect which approach is in place. However, you would need cleaners to come in after each group's departure, to clean the place and leave it ready for the next lot of writers."

"So, I would have to find cleaners who are happy to work on an ad hoc basis."

"I think you'll find you have no problem engaging all the cleaners you want from among local women. The fact that it isn't set hours every day will suit households looking for an occasional bit of additional income."

"Ye-e-s, I'm starting to see how it might work. But turning the mews into a writers' retreat doesn't solve the problem of what to do with all the space in this house."

"Ah, yes, but I have a plan for that too. It will require a bit of thought and planning on your part before the idea takes definite shape. There are lots of groups and organisations, even business enterprises, who want to run workshops for select groups of people from time to time. This is an ideal place for small workshops that require accommodation for participants. They could stay in the mews, and maybe the servants' quarters could be done up to provide additional accommodation. Those two areas would provide twelve rooms, complete with shared facilities."

"Twelve participants would be a small workshop indeed, and so few rooms would hardly have suitable venue appeal for festival organisers."

"Well, yes … but other moves afoot will eliminate that argument." Zanne tapped the side of her nose and gave me a knowing nod.

"You might have to tell me about those if you want to convince me."

"The Education Department is looking to relieve itself of the long defunct Charlotte Cove primary school. I have entered into a contract to purchase it. The deal includes the land and all of the buildings on it; plenty of scope for accommodation and enough rooms for workshops."

"I hope you aren't buying it just so I can do something with this place."

"No, we signed the contract about eight weeks ago. The hold-up is with rezoning of the land. I'm not paying until the rezoning is through. My initial thought was to turn it into tourist accommodation, and I could still utilise it that way when it wasn't booked for workshops or festivals. So, what do you think?"

"I think I'm stunned … and that it will take me some time to get my head around everything."

"Good; while you are about it, you might think about what parts of the house you want to retain as private spaces, and any that you might consider turning into paid accommodation."

Silence hung heavy over the kitchen as we both sat there digesting all that had been proposed. After a few moments, I shattered the silence by announcing I would ring the manager of *Whylara* to arrange a visit. The call took no more than five minutes, and I suspect he already had heard of the change. He was a bit stiff and reticent when I spoke to him. I guessed it would require some reassurance regarding the future to put him at ease.

"How does Tuesday suit you for a trip to *Whylara?"* I asked as I returned to the kitchen.

"Perfect…,"

"Good; we'll leave early, drive out, have a bit of a look around, and drive home again. There will be lunch with the manager at the homestead. It will be a long day, but it will tick off one more thing on my list."

"Seeing as how we are going to the property, maybe we could ask to see where Wilfred is buried. Oh, and maybe before we go, we should check if any of the other family members are buried out there."

"It's too late to start anything now, but we will do that first thing tomorrow. In the meantime, I think we should drink to new ventures before we put the day to bed." Chief came with us as we carried our drinks out into the garden.

As I climbed into bed, I wondered how often Chief would disturb my sleep tonight. Somehow, I don't think he will feel the need. Already, he doesn't seem too bothered if I am out of sight for a while. That was a happy thought on which to fall asleep.

Chapter 23

It was three months since I brought Chief home to live with me. Everything was serene until about a month ago when our lives became absolute chaos. Things were wearing a bit thin for me, and poor Chief constantly looked confused.

After a couple of months of discussing and planning, it was happening. The mews were being turned into a writers' retreat. For the last month, all manner of tradesmen invaded our lives. Vehicles came and went all day. I thought once they had the plans, the work would just happen, but it wasn't that simple. I am constantly be called to come and look at things, and asked to make decisions I couldn't care less about. I really don't care what taps and spouts go in the bathroom and kitchen, so long as they work and are relatively maintenance free. I suppose I shouldn't complain too much. There is worse to come.

Present indications are that about midway through next week, Chief and I will relocate to the refurbished mews while renovations happen in the house itself. They started in the house at the end of last week, but that work was confined to the servants' quarters, so we remained here. Apart from making sure everything was removed from Aunt Eddie's bedroom and safely hidden elsewhere, and the door to the domestic chores area was fitted with a lock, only the noise from the work bothered us. However, next week they will turn off the water to the house while they refurbish the facilities in the servants' quarters. When that is finished, they will start on the bathrooms on the upper floor.

No one appears prepared to commit to a likely completion date for the scheduled work. There also has been the problem that once a job is started, other work is identified as required. Again, no one is prepared to say how long the unscheduled work will delay the completion of the project, but it is having some impact. A part of me is excited about what the house will be like when the work is completed, but a part of me feels guilty about changing things that remained static for so long.

The upside to all this is the two real benefits that accrue from all the work being undertaken. All the timber acquired from the removal of the partitions has been reused in the refurbishment of the mews and, when the work in the hose is finished, I will have a large bright, freshly painted office. And it will be nice to have a library, a den, and a sitting room available to use without needing breathing apparatus to avoid some lung condition from all the dust and mould.

While we waited for work to begin, Zanne and I discussed possible launch dates for our new ventures. We decided an interval of six months after work began should see everything ready to go. Now I'm not so sure. The work here seems to be taking longer than expected, and then there will be the work Zanne wants done at the former school. She was hoping to have the accommodation part of her venture up and running in time for the Christmas holiday period. We can only hope.

Apart from trying to survive the construction work going on around me, the IT firm I contract for seems to be finding an endless stream of jobs for me. I've often resorted to working on them at night after the tradesmen leave and the place becomes quiet enough to allow me to think.

Zanne says that, within the next month or so, we need to think about the staff required to service the venues. We will need to either place advertisements for staff, or investigate hiring contract services. On top of all this, I am still trying to pick up overall management of the wharf complex and *Whylara.* There are nights when I lie awake wondering about the wisdom of what I have done, and whether I really need it in my life.

On Monday, I started moving essentials across to the mews prior to vacating the house by Wednesday morning. Much of the weekend was spent moving all of the documents and files we accumulated in the course of my family history research into storage in the larder in the domestic chores area. The bed from Aunt Eddie's room went across to a room in the mews when clearing out the servants' quarters. After much cleaning and disinfecting, I will use it rather than moving my own bed over. After the tradesmen left on Monday evening, I dismantled my computer set-up, loaded it onto a trolley and moved it across to the mews. A couple more trips with the trolley and I had moved everything I would need for the foreseeable future.

I switched on the new fridge in the mews' kitchen ready for when I emptied my fridge in the house. Clothes and other personal stuff I'd move after the workmen left on Tuesday.

It was while I was cleaning out the fridge on Tuesday morning that Zanne arrived looking excited and pleased with herself. "We have our first booking for a week long writers' retreat in mid-January. Two writers, husband and wife; he writes thrillers and she writes children's books."

"Will we be ready in time?"

"Jesus, I bloody hope so. I can't see why we won't be, but it does give us a target date. We need to have everything in place at least a week beforehand. It would be nice if we could launch it with a full house, but even one or two more guests would make for a good opening."

"All we have to do now is hope for a few Christmas holiday-makers for your venture… and that we have the staff in place to deal with them."

"Oh, I haven't told you. I've had four inquiries and sent out brochures and info on fees and stuff. I sent all that out yesterday, so I imagine it will take a while for any response."

Now feeling so settled and 'at home' in the mews, I was tempted to make that my permanent home and let the guests have the run of the big house. Work had finished. The tradesmen were cleaning up and packing their gear ready to depart for the last time. Zanne and I hovered, ready to thank them and wave them off.

The list of 'unscheduled' work had increased. A standalone small shed was refurbished to provide a new garage for my car and trike. This left the garage attached to the mews available for conversions to a seminar space seating up to twenty people. My interim bedroom became a small sitting room, and my previous kitchen was now a casual dining room. The partition opposite the conservatory went and the butler's office and pantry were sacrificed to a new kitchen accessed through the original wide doors. A new partition at the junction of the hallways in the domestic chores area prevented unauthorised intrusion into the remainder of that historic area.

If I utilised all the single bedrooms on the left hand side of the hallway on the upper floor, the place could accommodate up to twenty people. The huge dining room and that grand ballroom could be ideal conference spaces allowing, in conjunction with the old school, major events to be held at Charlotte Cove.

Firms had been contracted for laundry services and grounds maintenance at the former school, and kitchen and wait staff interviewed. A wedding was booked for the week before Christmas and the guests had booked out all accommodation at the school. Zanne was beside herself with excitement. After the wedding guests left, a further ten guests were booked to spend the Christmas-New Year break at *The Cove Resort.* It appears Zanne's venture is off and running. She is busy dealing with inquiries for January and Easter.

In three weeks' time, Wellsprings would welcome its first guests. There were five confirmed bookings, with a sixth writer still to confirm. I contracted the same firm as Zanne for laundry services. A couple of local women accepted casual contracts to take care of the cleaning. The end of January would see another week-long retreat. So far, there were three definite bookings for that.

In between everything, I was settling back into the big house. At the end of a long day of moving furniture around, Zanne and I took our glasses of wine out into the grounds. With Chief curled up at our feet, we saluted the year that was drawing to a close and drank a toast to our new ventures.

"We are going to need office staff," Zanne admitted as we watched evening fall. "I thought we would manage it ourselves, but maybe that was a pipedream. It's already become so time consuming, there isn't time for anything else."

I murmured my agreement. It was my contention from the outset that we would not be able to manage it on our own. I for one didn't want to be tied down to that life. "Let's leave it until the New Year before assessing what staff we might need… and where to locate them."

"Unless you want someone at *Wellsprings* to look after your side of things, there is office space at my resort. Staff to look after both places could be located there."

There wasn't much else to discuss. Everything was ready. Our new lives were about to begin in earnest. That thought was both exciting and scary. We drank another toast to the New Year and our new lives. Then Zanne dropped her bombshell.

"I've spoken to my agent and publisher and they are wrapped in the proposal. They want me to write the Granger story. You now have to make a final decision about whether you want that to proceed and, if you do, whether it should be the truth or fiction. No pressure; you have until the end of January to decide. That's when I would start work on the manuscript if you decide to go ahead."

Something tells me life in Charlotte Cove, not only for me, but a few other locals as well, will be quite different from the start of next year… and that's a good thing. For the first time in a long while, I'm excited and looking forward to the future. There is a new Granger in residence at Wellsprings. A new era has begun, and life in this *unsuitable house* is about to become very different.

The End.

ALSO BY THE AUTHOR

Revenge is not Enough
Harbour Plaza: built on dreams
On the Way to Istanbul

ABOUT THE AUTHOR

KAYLA DANOLI spent her early years traipsing around Australia and then Europe with her parents, and then completed her tertiary education in England before returning to Australia. There were a variety of jobs in various parts of Queensland before eventually making her way towards the coast. She now lives in a small coastal town on the Queensland coast where she works part-time on a charter vessel.

In the early days after settling in that small town, to fill in her spare time, both when at home and while on cruises, she started scribbling down her ideas for stories. These days, she writes whenever time permits. Her *Harbour Plaza* series, previously released in 2015 as monthly eBook episodes, was updated and extended and released in 2016 as the compilation *Harbour Plaza: built on dreams. Revenge is not Enough,* also released in 2016, was her first full-length novel.

Discover more about Kayla and her work by visiting

www.kayladanoli.com

or contact her at

contact@kayladanoli.com

www.ingramcontent.com/pod-product-compliance
Lightning Source LLC
Chambersburg PA
CBHW031231120726
47905CB00002B/549
9780995353350